MEXICAN HEAT

(Nick Woods, No. 2)

By Stan R. Mitchell

FOREWORD

To James and Sheila Michel. Two wonderful friends who helped me through one of the darkest periods of my life.

And to Capt. Eaton, United States Marine Corps, and Sgt. Major Hill, United States Marine Corps; two men who epitomized leadership and strength, and who made an unforgettable impression on me.

PROLOGUE

Nick Woods was minding his own business at a gas station beside the interstate when trouble came to find him.

He had pulled off the interstate and he was pretty well whipped, sore from sitting too long and pretty dad-gone hungry. It was time to pull off the road. Had probably been time more than an hour ago, but he had kept on, his deep and natural stubbornness pushing him on even when he didn't will it.

Nick stopped at a large gas station that sat just off the exit. He was making good time, working his way through the backwoods of South Carolina, but he needed gas, he needed to piss, and he needed a Diet Coke and a Snickers.

He parked his '97 Jeep Grand Cherokee by a pump and closed the door gently. The SUV had nearly 200,000 miles on the odometer, but it still ran well and he treated it like a queen. Frequent maintenance and plenty of love had kept it in top shape, just like the old Colt 1911 .45 automatic pistol stashed under his seat.

The Colt .45 was more than thirty years old. It had been hidden in a cave and carried under some tough conditions, when a lot of bad men were hunting him just a couple of years earlier. It had killed many of those men, as well as one woman. Following such excellent and trusty service, Nick had decided to keep it for sentimental value.

But unlike the old 1911 under the seat, the newer pistol on his hip, a Kimber 1911 .45, carried no sentimental value. It was kept for use. Instant use.

The Kimber was also customized and upgraded in almost every way: green Tritium 3-dot night sight, adjusted trigger pull, and higher quality springs to reduce recoil, allowing him to get back on target faster. Of course, like any good gunman, Nick had loaded a round in the chamber prior to loading the seven-round mag into the pistol, so he toted eight rounds of .45 caliber ammo instead of seven.

Under his blue-jean jacket, he also had two more magazines of seven rounds for the gun. Twenty-two rounds total, plus an emergency .38 pistol strapped to the inside of his left ankle and a one-hand opening knife clipped to the right pocket of his jeans.

Nick had been accused of being paranoid and he knew it to be true, but he viewed it as being prepared. And given that he had needed every weapon on him – and more – several times in his life, he didn't mind being labeled paranoid. And he didn't mind toting a bunch of firepower around with him whether he was on foot or in a vehicle.

Nick stood by the door of his red Grand Cherokee, pausing a moment before walking away. The vehicle provided cover and held a number of better weapons than what he could carry with him concealed. Like his M14. And his 12-gauge pump loaded with double-ought buck. And, of course, his trusty, bolt gun. A scoped M40 rifle in .308/7.62. It was the weapon favored by snipers; older snipers, at least. And Nick was a sniper. An "older" sniper, if he were honest.

He was a lot of things, but at his core, he was a sniper. Still one of the best ones alive, even if he did have some mileage on his forty-seven-year-old legs. Oh, he definitely had some mileage, he thought, feeling a knee that creaked from sitting too long in the SUV.

But he stayed by the Grand Cherokee just a moment longer. Maybe it was the sniper in him. Maybe it was the paranoid Marine, who'd been betrayed by his country. Twice.

He didn't want to leave the safety of the vehicle. Besides the weapons, the Grand Cherokee was his best chance of getting away if things suddenly got hairy. And Nick never walked away from escape possibilities lightly. He shuddered at the memory of hundreds of Soviet troops hunting him in the mountains of Afghanistan a couple of decades earlier.

Nick shook his head to erase the terrifying thoughts and, breathing deeply, set to burying the pains of so many old war wounds. He looked about and refocused on the present. He scanned the gas pumps nearest him, looking quickly in a 360 around him as unobtrusively as possible. He gave the thick woods opposite the gas station a once over and finally took a long look at the customers in the gas station.

Some of them waited in line. Others picked junk food off the aisles. No one looked frightened or frozen in fear, as if a hold-up was underway. So far, so good.

Taking another deep breath, Nick adjusted the holstered Kimber .45 on his hip and walked toward the door. He dreaded the people he'd have to interact with, having spent the better part of two years in solitude up in the mountains of Montana.

There, he had expected the government to double-cross him again. The deal they made was very similar to one they made many years ago. Essentially, it was, "You go away. You keep your mouth shut. We'll leave you alone."

That hadn't worked out so well for Nick the first time. He'd done his part of the bargain, but a rogue element of the government had come after him after his story was published by a hard-nosed reporter. And after agreeing to the second deal, Nick had fully expected the government to come after him again in Montana.

But a damn strange thing happened this time: they never came. He'd been prepared, waiting for them with an almost eager, expectant intensity. But the dawns and dusks passed with him hidden behind his guns, no one in sight.

He'd grown tired of waiting and realized he probably needed to be around people again. He was mentally losing it, becoming crazier and lonelier by the day, and thus a big reason for this cross-country trip was to tear down his paranoia and get him comfortable being around people again.

Anne would be proud, Nick thought, to see him making such progress.

I'm trying, baby. I really am.

He smiled at her memory and wished she hadn't been taken so soon. Gunned down by an incompetent, pencil-pushing FBI agent, who didn't get into the field much.

Nick pushed the thought of Anne from his mind, just as he'd pushed the screams from Afghanistan out of his mind moments earlier.

Nick started for the gas station. But he hadn't made it ten steps toward the double doors of the gas station when motion off to his flank caught his attention. A gray, unmarked police cruiser pulled into the gas station, slow and unthreatening. But Nick still paused, unsure. And suddenly he was aware that he had stopped mid-stride and stood transfixed on the cruiser.

The driver seemed to be watching him from behind the tinted window. Nick stood frozen, watching the car. Unmoving. He looked guilty as hell and he knew it.

No question, he *was* guilty as hell. He had no concealed carry permit and he had two loaded weapons on him, not to mention the locked and loaded long guns in the Jeep. And once they found his rucksack with the thousands of rounds, he'd be completely toast.

Not that they'd ever get him in cuffs. Nope. No siree.

Nick considered drawing and rushing forward to hold the man at gunpoint. Nick couldn't let him get on his radio, so if the man made one move toward the radio in the console, Nick would have to act. He was only twelve feet away and Nick couldn't let him call in the cavalry.

But then the man did the damnedest thing. He eased the car into a parking space and motioned Nick over. Nick couldn't believe it.

But he also knew he was screwed. The officer would notice the gun on his hip. The man would want to see his concealed carry permit. The man might even draw on Nick before he asked the question.

Nick couldn't take chances. He yanked the pistol from his hip so fast that it was a blur. A motion practiced so many thousand times that it would take a slow-motion video to pinpoint each individual movement.

But now the man's head was centered in Nick's sights and a woman was screaming. Folks scurried and hid and frantically dialed cell phones. Nick saw this movement around him, but kept his focus on the man in the cruiser. He could feel all the eyes on him and his mind raced, wondering how fast the 911 calls happening around him would get the local boys on the scene.

He'd want his M14 and pack before they arrived and he'd take his chances in the woods. He'd have a better chance on foot than in his vehicle. In his vehicle, they'd just pit-maneuver him on the interstate with their powerful pursuit cars.

As Nick considered his moves, he noticed the man was saying something behind the tinted window, both hands up in surrender. He strained to hear and realized the man was saying his name.

"Nick Woods, it's okay. It's okay. Don't shoot. Please don't shoot."

Nick leaned forward a bit and saw fear and pleading in the guy's face. Just at the edges of his senses, he heard the words again, clearer this time, "Nick Woods, it's okay. It's okay. Don't shoot. Please don't shoot."

Nick advanced toward the car – fast and agile for a man who looked too country to be a runner. But a runner Nick was. And he was damn near a ninja, as well. A martial arts addict, he could jump and roll and strike and kick with the best of them.

And now he stood at the window, his pistol six inches from the glass and the man's head. The man looked beyond frantic now.

"Don't shoot," he screamed. "Don't shoot. I need to talk to you. Just talk. Please lower the weapon."

Nick grabbed the door handle with his left hand while keeping the pistol directed toward the man's face. He ripped the door open, moving his pistol out of its arc, before stepping in closer and pressing the pistol against the man's forehead.

"You squirm one inch," Nick said, "and I'll blow a hole out the back of your head. What do you want? How did you know my name? Why were you looking at me?"

"Nick," the man said. "Just relax. I've just come to talk with you."

"Talk," Nick said, his pistol unmoved.

"My name doesn't matter, but I volunteered to make contact with you. Nick, we need your help."

"Who is we?" Nick asked.

"The government," the man said.

"Last time you all needed my help," Nick said, "you sold my partner and I out five hundred miles inside Afghanistan.

Forgive me if I'm a little hesitant to sign up again."

"That was a rogue operation run by a dishonorable man. You have to trust us on that."

"I'll decide who I trust," Nick said, remembering the shredded body of his spotter. And then flashing to the sight of his wife lying dead in the grass, her white gown ruined by blood and mud. Yeah, he'd been fooled too many times to go trusting the government again, even if they hadn't come after him in the mountains of Montana.

"Nick, let me up and I'll call the police off before they get here. Whether you accept our offer or not, you don't need to be on the run again. And I don't want you gunned down in some ugly gunfight with the cops."

Nick needed to act. And fast. The clock was ticking, and the cops were certainly racing on their way to the gas station. Too many 911 calls had been made for that not to happen.

"Get out and don't try anything stupid," Nick said, making a decision. He'd take the man with him. As a hostage, you might say. The man exited the police cruiser awkwardly, both men aware of the loaded gun and the danger each posed to the other.

They stood now, the man with his hands up.

"Everyone, calm down," the man in the suit said, looking toward those around him. "This is simply a training exercise. An anti-terrorism drill. There is no need to panic. My friend here is playing the part of a quote terrorist."

He looked back at Nick and said, "Let me get my phone out of my jacket pocket and I'll get the cops called off."

"Do it slowly," Nick growled.

The man, who looked about thirty, reached inside the jacket and slowly pulled out a cell phone. He dialed three numbers, which Nick assumed was 911.

"Yes, ma'am. I am a member of Federal Task Force Apache. Code Number 894673-736492."

He paused, then said, "Yes, ma'am. Please call Gen. Compton to confirm and then please call off the responding units before we have any blue-on-blue accidents."

The suited man closed his phone, pointed to his inside coat pocket, and asked, "May I?"

Nick said, "Slowly. Damn slowly."

The man replaced the phone and said, "If you'll let me lock the car, we'll take a ride in your vehicle and talk."

"Car doesn't need to be locked. It's a police cruiser. Nobody's going to touch it."

Nick waved the pistol toward his Grand Cherokee.

"Let's go, Hoss. And you better pray nobody comes after me."

"Nobody will," the man said.

They walked to Nick's red SUV and the man opened the passenger door, slowly climbing in and sitting down. Nick followed and stayed behind him, about four feet away. Just enough distance to make sure the man didn't get cute and try something stupid.

"You got any weapons on you?" Nick asked.

"Hell, no," the guy said. "We were afraid that would set you off. I left my service pistol back at the office."

Nick could tell he was telling the truth, but better safe than sorry.

"Lift your jacket and both legs of your pants," Nick said. "I want to make sure you're not trying anything cute."

"I'm not that stupid," the man said, buckling his seatbelt.

"You better not be," Nick said.

He slammed the passenger door and smiled at the stunned crowd.

"Nothing to see folks," Nick said. "He's just a good actor and this gun isn't even real. It's rubber, even though it does look real. Y'all have a good day."

They drove a short distance and Nick pulled into a Motel 6.

"We'll talk in a room," Nick said. "I'm not talking to you in any restaurant with lots of windows and doors. That's too risky for me. And if anyone's dumb enough to try to come rescue you in this room, there will be a stack of bodies."

"No one's coming," the man said. "I'll wait in the vehicle or come in with you while you rent the room. Whichever you prefer."

"Come with me, hoss," Nick said. "I'm not letting you out of my sight until I figure out what's up."

Ten minutes later, the two were in a room. Nick asked the man to sit in the chair and not move. Once the man was seated, Nick stepped out to the Grand Cherokee and made a quick trip into the room with some extra firepower.

"Slide that chair over by the window," Nick said.

Once the agent had done that, Nick said, "Now slide that dresser in front of the door. We don't want any surprise guests busting down the door. I'd like to relax a bit while we talk, if you know what I mean."

The agent grunted and groaned as he dragged a dresser in front of the door, barring it from opening inward.

While he did that, Nick placed his M14, shotgun, and pack on the bed. The pack itself was crammed with M14 magazines, shotgun shells, and other necessary gear. Nick removed his Kimber .45, as well, laying it on the bed. He was sick of it digging in his side. Plus, with Nick by the bed, almost twenty feet away, he wasn't worried about the agent trying anything.

"You wanted to talk," Nick said, "let's talk."

"It'd be an honor to," the man said.

To Nick, the man appeared genuinely sincere. But it irked him. It also made him suspicious as hell.

"Listen up, Hoss," Nick said. "This isn't a game. I'm going to ask you some questions and you're going to answer them. If you delay answering them, or if I sense you're lying, you're not going to like what I do. How'd you know my name?"

The man, a baby-faced guy who nonetheless looked fit and squared away in his suit, said, "I've read and memorized your file. I was the only one who would volunteer to approach you."

"Why were the others afraid?"

The man looked incredulous, glancing at the weapons on the bed and then over at the dresser in front of the door. He looked as if he was trying to find a way to soften his answer. Nick didn't want softened answers.

"Just say it," Nick said.

"Everyone thinks you're crazy."

"And you don't?"

The agent wondered if he'd miscalculated. This guy, well, he was crazy. But the agent controlled his answer, lying as best he could. Although maybe deep down he wanted to believe the words he said.

"No," the agent said. "I don't think you're crazy. I think you've reacted exactly as I would have, given everything you've been through."

"And you still believe that?"

"I'm trying to remain optimistic," the agent said. "But this has gotten a little more serious than I expected." After a moment, the agent added, "I may have been wrong."

Nick cursed. Wow. What a mess he had on his hands. The loneliness of Montana didn't seem so bad compared to this.

"Earlier," Nick said, " you stated 'approach' me. Why were you to approach me?"

"We need your help."

"Who's we?" Nick asked. "I don't want to hear any more vague, gray language."

"The CIA, of course."

"Spit it out," Nick said angrily. "Why do you need my help? Want to send me overseas? Get me to do some dirty work? Then sell my ass out again?"

"No, sir. We need your skill set in Mexico."

"Mexico?" Nick asked, letting the word sink in.

"Yes, Mexico," the agent said. "Their government is about to collapse, their President is about to flee the country, and we think that you're the only man that can prevent this."

CHAPTER 1

The country of Mexico, 2014

Mexico's president knew the fate of the entire country rested on how he handled the upcoming meeting.

No pressure, he thought.

Yeah, right. Was he exaggerating? Could Mexico really fall? Its entire government? He wondered at that, as his limo jerked into a sharp turn out of the presidential compound.

President Roberto Rivera saw loads of SUVs in front of him. He knew how many troops were in front of them, as well, even if he couldn't see the vehicles and guns that protected him.

It made him sick, but Mexico was basically in a state of war against a single, ruthless cartel. And the country was in such a state of siege, such a state of war, that it took a ton of work to get him anywhere. It was embarrassing to admit, but Mexico's Army and Police forces had to work hard to keep President Rivera alive.

No pressure, Rivera thought again.

But he had to arrive safely first. He knew at this very moment, as soon as his limo had left the protection of the presidential compound, he was in serious danger. And that's why he was protected by twelve armored Humvees, twenty-four armored-up SUVs (crammed with Mexican troops in full battle gear), and six police helicopters with snipers stationed with them. Plus, there were another two hundred police officers stationed along the route.

President Rivera shook his head in disgust. Why did he have to travel in a convoy that was more suited for a war zone than the busy traffic of Mexico City? How had it gotten to this point? And why were six of the armored Humvees packing fifty-caliber heavy machine guns? And the other six packing

7.62 medium machine guns?

Was the threat to his life that serious?

He knew the answer. It was. It truly was.

And it was about to get a lot worse.

Juan Soto, Mexico's richest businessman, was about to leave the country.

That's what Rivera's sources were saying. It couldn't be true, but if it were? Rivera had to stop him. He had to. Somehow.

His senior advisers and top-level economists were saying that if President Rivera failed in this meeting, it would be over for Mexico.

If multi-billionaire Juan Soto had decided to leave, then Mexico was a lost cause. Rivera had to stop Soto from leaving.

And he had only one tool to do so: friendship. Friendship and a healthy dose of guilt. Two weapons that Rivera would have to expertly yield.

President Rivera rubbed his temples and shuddered at the thought that Soto might leave the country. Soto's exit would mean he would sell off his numerous companies and Rivera knew who the buyer would be. Hernan Flores, a fellow billionaire.

But Flores and Soto were two completely different people.

Juan Soto was a great businessman: honest, ethical, and legit. A supporter of the Mexican government. A man who had the country's best interest at heart.

Hernan Flores was a cartel leader: dishonest, evil, and dirty. An enemy of the Mexican government. A man whose greed for money and power knew no bounds.

I've just got to get Juan Soto to stay somehow, Rivera thought. I've got to. Or I better consider leaving with my family, too.

The thought made him sick to his stomach.

You can do this, he thought. You're a salesman. He's your friend. Just make the sale. Make the sale or. Or what? Or maybe Rivera would be running, too.

Thirty minutes after departing the Presidential Palace,

the massive, armed convoy of President Rivera arrived at the headquarters of Juan Soto. The building was an eight-story building in the heart of the city. The presidential convoy stopped at the front of the building and a hundred armed men in full battle uniforms leaped from the two dozen SUVs. They spread out with full-size rifles and secured the area, aiming at buildings and windows throughout the area.

Worried onlookers hustled into buildings. In Mexico, you never knew if the presence of troops meant a multi-hour firefight or the prevention of something worse.

Rivera's presidential convoy looked more like an assault than a routine visit. Closer to his vehicle, a phalanx of hyper-alert men circled around the limo. They carried Uzi's on slings and they looked ready to use them.

One of the suited men opened the limo door for Rivera. Rumors of another serious assassination attempt had been growing and Rivera rushed behind the mass group of men toward the safety of the building.

Juan Soto met President Rivera in the atrium of the building and the two said little as they walked to the elevators and ascended to the top floor. Rivera shook some hands and nodded to some employees and senior executives that he knew as they worked their way to Soto's inner sanctum, but he was too distracted by the importance of this meeting to be his usual confident self.

Once inside a conference room on the eighth floor, President Rivera dismissed his closest security personnel.

"You guys can secure the top floor," he said, "or the whole building, or whatever you want. But you're not staying in the conference room with me."

A senior protective man nodded with great reluctance and began issuing orders to the other men in suits.

Finally alone, inside a massive conference room with Juan Soto, Rivera took a deep breath.

It was just him and his best friend, he told himself.

It was just him and the future of Mexico. Everything was on the line.

The blinds were already closed and Rivera knew the windows were designed to block electronic intrusion. Juan Soto's security was almost as good as Rivera's. It had to be.

The two men smiled for a second time – this time deeply; this time it wasn't just a front for others to see. They hugged and Soto asked Rivera to have a seat.

Rivera thought that Juan Soto looked as thin and sharp as ever. The man took discipline and ambition to levels that even Rivera could not reach, which was saying something. Most political observers saw Rivera as the most ambitious, most disciplined president that Mexico had ever had. Rivera wanted to not just be a successful president, but to transform the entire country into something great. Not just a country seen by many as having a major crime problem – if not war – raging inside its borders.

"My good friend," Soto said. "Why did you not call? I would have gladly come to you."

"I wanted to honor and respect you by coming to your office," Rivera said.

"We only received word ten minutes ago. Otherwise, we would have prepared a better welcome."

"We've increased my security measures with the latest threats of assassination," Rivera said. "Even our top police did not know my destination until we arrived."

"But how did you know I'd be here?"

Rivera smiled. "I believe you have a hastily-scheduled meeting with our finance minister in twenty minutes?"

Juan Soto grinned as he realized his old friend had shown his sense of cunning once again – something Soto had been following since the man began his political career.

Changing topics, Rivera studied the modern interior.

"Your conference room has been updated," Rivera said.

"Twice, maybe three times since you were here."

Rivera looked down. He *had* been too busy and been away for too long.

"I haven't been here since I was governor," Rivera said softly, genuine regret in his voice. "But, we must skip the small talk, I'm afraid."

"Yes, of course. I think I know why you're here."

"Then, it's true?" Rivera asked. "You're leaving?"

Soto looked away. He could not stand to disappoint his friend.

"It is, isn't it?" Rivera asked.

"Yes, my friend. I'm very sorry, but I decided yesterday. My executives are already making it happen."

"You can't, Juan. I need you!"

"You'll be fine," Soto said.

Rivera grabbed Soto's forearm.

"Your country needs you."

Soto yanked his arm away, with a coldness that shook Rivera.

"My country has failed me," he said, angrier than he meant.

Rivera averted his gaze. Said nothing. He walked over to the bar and poured himself a glass of brandy. It was beyond early, but he couldn't allow his impatience for success to screw up this meeting. It was more than just his political reputation on the line. It was Mexico's fate.

Rivera sipped the drink, savoring the taste and feeling the warmth. He scanned the landscape of Mexico City, the capital and densely populated metropolis of nine million people. He couldn't fail these people in this city he loved. Nor could he fail the 125 million in his country. He would never surrender to the filthy Hernan Flores and his Godesto Cartel. Rivera took a deep breath and turned back to Soto.

"I am so sorry about what happened to Gabriella," Rivera said, referring to a recent kidnapping attempt of Juan's daughter. That attempt had been stopped – barely – but three of her bodyguards had died in the shootout, which involved more than nine attackers; all members of the Godesto Cartel, of course.

"It's not just about Gabby," Soto said. "Did you hear about my shift supervisor yesterday? Or my chief financial officer a month ago? Or any of the other twenty-plus employees who have been killed in the past two months?"

"Twenty?" Rivera asked. "You've lost twenty people in the past two months?"

"Hernan Flores is trying to destroy everything of mine. He

is trying to break me because he knows if he succeeds, it ends for you."

Rivera looked down at his brandy. "I did not realize it had gotten that bad for you, my friend. You should have called me. I am truly sorry."

Soto nodded, then dropped his eyes.

Rivera saw that Soto no longer appeared angry and that the normally energetic and unstoppable billionaire businessman now looked tired. Defeated. And he appeared to have made up his mind.

Was Rivera too late?

Rivera took another drink of his brandy. This one larger. He walked toward Soto and sat in a chair next to his friend. He swirled his drink in his hand as he thought of honest friends he knew who had gambled their lives by joining his government and trying to take back their country from the Godesto Cartel. So many of them had died. So many others lived in terrifying fear.

"Juan, could you give me six months? Just six months to fix it?"

"I'm sorry, Roberto, but not even you, with all your energy and intellect, could fix the country in six months. You haven't been able to in five years. What makes you think you could in six months?"

"We've done much in those five years," Rivera said. "Made important police appointments and purged many dirty officials. And," Rivera paused and swallowed. "I'll finally get help from the Americans. Like you've suggested before. I'll tell them we're in desperate need." Rivera was talking fast now. "We'll get American Special Forces down here and we'll go after that bastard Hernan Flores and the Godesto Cartel. I know he's behind it all. You know he's behind it all."

Soto smiled.

"Now, Roberto," he said, "are you forgetting that even your appointed attorney general admitted in a news conference that there is no real evidence against Flores?"

It was true. They couldn't find any evidence of Flores being tied to the Godesto Cartel and its crimes. Everyone sort of knew it, but the evidence was scarce. He was too sly. And no one would testify against him. Several times, he had *nearly* been charged, but the moment it nearly all came together, people started dying or running for their lives. Cops. Prosecutors. Judges.

No one would take the man on, which allowed the devious bastard to pretend in public to be a legitimate businessman. A modern-day Al Capone who gave millions to charity and loved Mexico as much as any man in the country. It was all a lie, but the public mostly bought it.

"We'll make up some crimes," Rivera said quietly, surprising even himself as he said that. "That way we can finally arrest him."

Rivera's own words stunned him. He had never done even the slightest thing wrong or illegal since becoming an elected official. He had climbed his way to president of the country based upon his rigid ethics and strong morals. But the country was at stake, right? Hadn't that been what his advisors and several prominent economists told him earlier today?

Was it okay to bend the law to save an entire country? That was a serious moral question.

Maybe so, Rivera thought. He felt himself leaning toward framing the leader of Mexico's international drug empire.

"Flores keeps killing and silencing people," Rivera said, "so to hell with the law. If you're on the verge of leaving, then we'll have to fight fire with fire. This is for Mexico's own sake."

Juan reached across the table and laid his hand on the top of Rivera's forearm. "My friend. Do not soil your soul. It is your integrity that sets you apart from all the others. It is your integrity and faith that inspires millions of Mexicans. Do not become dirty and soiled like a filthy bar towel. Do not become like Flores. Or like all those politicians before you."

Rivera sat back, realizing the horror of what he'd considered. He sat there, a deep shame bearing down on him.

"Forget I said that," Rivera said, now looking his friend in the eyes. How had he suddenly been so tempted to sell out the very reputation that he had spent decades building up?

"We all have our moments of weakness, my friend," Soto said, "but you have your strength and you still believe. I, however, no longer do. My decision has been made."

Rivera grabbed Juan's hand and enclosed it in both of his. "Please don't say that, Juan. Please, give me just six months. That's all I'm asking for. I beg of you. If not for your country, for me. And for my family. You know we will not survive without your support."

Juan looked at Rivera and felt the man's desperate grip. He knew he could say "no" to him in the darkness of night and with a greater distance between them, but he simply could not abandon the man when he had to look him in the eyes. Not without giving him one final chance. He stood and pulled Rivera to him.

"I'll give you six months, my friend, though I must tell you that I doubt you will be successful. Privately, I will continue planning my departure and liquidation of all my assets in the country. However, I will appear optimistic in all public appearances to my employees and friends. Truthfully, I say in all honesty that *if* it can be done, it is you who will achieve it."

Rivera released Juan's hand, stood, and grabbed his friend in a hard hug.

"Thank you, my dear friend. Thank you. I will not let you down."

Soto held the embrace of his friend and president. Releasing each other, Soto straightened Rivera's jacket and said, "Now compose yourself, my friend. Our country is depending on your strength and nerve."

Rivera stood straighter and pulled his jacket down.

"Don't look at properties elsewhere," Rivera said. "It will be a waste of time and energy. I will have you convinced to stay within five months."

"Now that's the president I'm used to seeing," Juan Soto said. "Call me if I can be of assistance."

They hugged again and Rivera left the eight-story building feeling as if he were on top of the world. But Rivera would not have felt this way had he been able to see the future. Because had he been able to see the future? He might have left the country that very day. And he might have begged Juan Soto to abandon his billions immediately and flee the country, as well.

CHAPTER 2

President Roberto Rivera wasted no time following his meeting with billionaire Juan Soto. Rivera used his cell phone to call the American Ambassador once he climbed into the limo. Rivera told the Ambassador that he needed to meet. Immediately.

President Rivera's Chief of Staff passed along the change of plans and the new destination to the head of Rivera's security and, after some protesting from the head of police about unplanned schedules and complications, the massive convoy circled around and headed for the American Embassy. Traffic snarled around Mexico City and drivers cursed as the police cordon maneuvered the twelve armored Humvees and twenty-four SUVs through red lights and intersections of the downtown district. Rivera ignored the screaming sirens and ear-shattering roar of helicopters around him as he rehearsed what he would say to the American Ambassador.

He wasn't the only one scrambling. Inside his own protected fortress, the Ambassador hastily cleared his schedule and canceled several meetings. He also called Washington, D.C., and alerted his boss, the Secretary of State, about the emergency meeting.

In his three years as Ambassador to Mexico, the U.S. Ambassador to Mexico had never been called to an emergency meeting with President Rivera.

The Secretary of State ended the call and immediately called the CIA. Most of the internal communication inside Mexico's government was monitored by the National Security Agency, who sent weekly – and at times, daily – reports to the CIA. The CIA compiled that info and the head CIA man, who oversaw the Mexican Bureau, confirmed to the Secretary of

State that neither the NSA nor the CIA had a clue as to what the emergency meeting was about.

"You better start looking harder," the Secretary of State said. "Something is happening down there and the CIA doesn't need another black eye from missing some big event happening."

The Secretary of State hung up the phone and sighed, a sense of fear growing. He decided he'd better alert the Department of Defense, just in case. It seemed there was a chance a coup d'état was about to take place in Mexico. And, he decided he'd better alert the President of the United States, as well. Or, at least the President's Chief of Staff.

Something big was happening in Mexico. Something no one in the United States seemed to know about. That meant that whatever it was, it certainly wasn't good.

Inside the walled compound of the American Embassy, President Rivera's hundred-plus hand-picked soldiers deployed, escorting the president and his aides toward the Ambassador's residence. As Juan Soto had done at his own building earlier that day, the American Ambassador met Rivera at the door. And as the American aides greeted their Mexican counterparts, the two walked off in haste toward the inner sanctum.

Minutes later, inside the Ambassador's highly-secure meeting room, guarded outside by two hulking Marines, Rivera summarized the situation from a high-level standpoint. Then he explained exactly what would happen if events unfolded as expected.

"Mr. Ambassador," Rivera said, "if Juan Soto sells his assets, you need to understand what that means. We're talking dozens of major corporations, thousands of employees, and miles and miles of property and real estate that will be sold at a deep discount. Soto will sell all of this under duress and it will be cartel leaders such as Hernan Flores who scoop it up. And these companies and properties will almost certainly stop paying even half of the taxes they owe. Not to mention how they'll be used to launder money, as well as traffic more drugs to your country."

Rivera noticed a flash of panic cross the Ambassador's face.

"It gets worse," Rivera said. "The news will eventually come out that Soto is exiting Mexico. And other investors, equity companies, American companies, and pretty much anyone with half a brain will flee the country. Mexico's very economic future is on the line."

"Is it possible," the Ambassador asked, "that Soto was exaggerating? Six months is very little time. Would he seriously consider abandoning his empire at a loss?"

"Juan is not bluffing," Rivera said. "I have known him for a long time and he did not even inform me of this situation. I learned of it from rumors as his top executives began looking for buyers for his companies and properties."

"I believe Mr. Soto is one of your closest supporters? A major donor and advisor. Even a family friend."

"He is all of those things," Rivera said. "I'm assuming he did not tell me because he feared disappointing me. Or he was ashamed."

"Do you think he still wants to leave?" the Ambassador asked.

"I do," Rivera said. "His daughter was nearly kidnapped recently in an attempt that killed three of her bodyguards. And just today, Juan told me that he has lost twenty-plus employees in the past two months. Because he supports me, as well as the rule of law, his entire business empire is under assault by the Godesto Cartel."

Rivera looked away, feeling overwhelmed and helpless. He wondered what the Ambassador thought of him at that moment. Did he see a broken man? A defeated man? A weak man?

Rivera sat up straighter and composed himself. He lifted his head and spoke deeper and surer.

"Juan Soto gave me six months and I take him at his word. Now, what can America do to help me save this country and prevent its collapse? I presume you really don't want a toppled government, which is controlled by the Godesto Cartel, just across from your border?"

The Ambassador smiled and said, "No, I imagine that would be quite unpleasant. The president in the past has made it clear that he will offer whatever assistance he can in your efforts against the Godesto. I will inform him of this news immediately."

President Rivera stood and stepped closer to the Ambassador, who had stood, as well. He gripped the man's hand as hard as he could and said, "We will need more than words, weapons, and communication intercepts. We need your best troops here. *Immediately.*"

Rivera stated the last word so firm that it came across as an order. And he supposed it was.

"Mr. President," the Ambassador said, "I will see if I can get some support for you in a week or so."

"Not good enough," Rivera said, not releasing the hand; not backing up even an inch. "In fact, not even close to being good enough. We need either your Special Forces or Navy SEALs here within the next few days. Period. This is non-negotiable."

The Ambassador laughed.

"Come now, Mr. President. That's nearly impossible. We have active units operating all over the world. And the ones that aren't active are on leave or in training. We can't just bring troops down here on some ill-advised adventure. What would be their mission?"

Rivera released the Ambassador's hand and stepped back. But he raised his finger, pointing it directly at the Ambassador's face.

"The troops better be here within three days or my family and I will be on a plane with Juan Soto and his family. We will flee Mexico and will seek asylum either in your country or the UK."

The Ambassador looked floored and Rivera continued.

"I am not bluffing. We have six months and we need a team down here, operating in just a few days, if we're going to start making a dent in Flores's operations. If you think you have problems now, wait until our government collapses and Flores puts in one of his puppets as president. They'll have the Mexican military flying drugs across your border. You think it's bad now? Wait and see how bad it is then."

The Ambassador said nothing.

"Now, call your Secretary of State and President immediately and tell them to get some of your finest men down here. I don't care if you have to redeploy them from elsewhere and I don't want to hear any excuses on this one. They're here in three days or we're packing up and leaving. I'll hand you the keys to the place before we leave."

The Ambassador had collected himself by now and said with stunned, but practiced, formality, "Mr. President, I will relay your words to my government and we will move as quickly as we can."

The Ambassador was a diplomat and he needed to control his emotions. And especially his words.

"Our country is proud of our long history with the Mexican people and your government," the Ambassador continued, "and I am confident we will support your efforts against the Godesto Cartel as you –"

"Save the speech," Rivera said, cutting him off. " I don't even want to hear it. This isn't the time for words. We have troops here within three days or my family and I are gone."

The Ambassador went to say something, but Rivera raised his hand.

"No more words. We need action. And I will see myself out."

And with that, Rivera walked out of the room and toward his convoy waiting inside the walled Embassy compound.

CHAPTER 3

The United States deployed one of its elite counter-terror teams from SEAL Team Six to Mexico. Led by Lieutenant Commander Steve Todd and Master Chief David Adair, they arrived one day prior to President Rivera's three-day deadline. The SEAL Team and its support staff quickly set up on a military compound just outside Mexico City, prepared for operations.

"This is going to be some good shit," Adair said, walking across the tarmac with his commander.

"Are the men ready to go?" Todd asked.

"They're pumped as hell," Adair said. "All of them have seen the desert or mountains about four times too many."

"Iraq and Afghanistan are definitely hell holes," Todd said. "We just need to keep a low profile while we're down here."

"Keeping a low profile is what SEALs do best," Adair replied.

But the men were wrong about this.

Hernan Flores and the Godesto Cartel had learned of the SEAL Team deployment before the troops even loaded planes in the United States. His millions in payouts to officials throughout both governments proved their worth. And while it was surprising at how fast he learned it, both Mexico and the United States knew he would learn of it quickly.

You didn't run the most powerful drug cartel in North America without having an intelligence network powerful enough to make the CIA blush.

Hernan Flores laughed at President Rivera.

Flores had learned the full situation by this point – both the threat by Juan Soto to sell his companies and leave the country, and Rivera's desperate pleas for help from America.

He laughed harder at the thought that Rivera had threatened to seek asylum. That fool thinks he can flee and spare his family, Flores thought. No way. Rivera had killed and jailed men close to Flores and he would pay for his actions with his life. Even if he fled to America.

It hadn't needed to be this way. Had Rivera cooperated with Flores and the Godesto, the country could have been much better off. Rivera could have gotten enormously rich. There would have been limited bloodshed. Tourism would have increased. And the Godesto could have kept its power and reach out of public view.

But no, Rivera had to be the honorable president. The man who thought he could save the country. Fat chance, Flores thought, laughing.

Flores spewed out half-chewed Funyuns, nearly choking with laughter. He leaned back further at his desk and his chair groaned beneath his voluminous weight. His feet lay propped across the top of his twenty-thousand-dollar mahogany desk and he held in his lap a big bag of Funyuns chips.

After wolfing down three more Funyuns, Flores flicked the spewed crumbs from his sprawling stomach. Since he no longer wore suits, he didn't worry about getting grease on his clothes. He looked down at the front of his button-down, short-sleeve shirt and saw the dark shirt showed no greasy stains.

He shook his head in wonder that he used to wear suits – even three-piece suits complete with vests at one time. He used to dress to impress, with confining custom-fitted suits. Now, he preferred the comfort of a loose Hawaiian shirt. Untucked, of course.

Short-sleeve shirts were all he ever wore these days – he liked not having to tuck the shirts in – and the short sleeves helped keep him from sweating too badly. That was one of the downsides to being big, or really big, quite frankly: You sweat like a whore working overtime. And you smelled like one, too.

Well, it didn't matter if you were rich like Flores. So many women wanted him that he rarely had to actually pay for any women. But he did sometimes. But usually, these women thought he was the greatest thing ever. And they certainly never called him fat. Or complained of his smell.

Women only cared about money, he thought. They'd date an angry, stinking grizzly bear if the damned thing had enough money.

Hernan Flores wiped his hairy forearm across his sweaty forehead and grabbed some more chips. Christ, he was hot. His office thermostat was set to sixty-six degrees and it still wasn't enough. I've got to start exercising at some point, he thought.

He was a big man and he knew these chips wouldn't help the cause, but he dug deep in the bag and grabbed two more. Just two more, he said. After all, he was celebrating. Juan Soto was on the verge of leaving. President Rivera had messed his drawers and called in actual combat troops from the Americans, not just advisers.

Flores laughed again at the thought.

The proud Mexican people would be outraged at Rivera's decision to bring in American troops. Flores chuckled as he stuffed more Funyuns down. (He had now gone past the final two he was supposed to stop at, but who cared?)

Flores imagined his plan to take down Rivera coming to completion. Now, he just hoped the cocky SEAL Team from America took the bait.

Americans were arrogant. They'd think they could do anything. But the Godesto Cartel, and the proud Mexican people, would show them.

Flores started laughing again, reaching his hand into his bag of Funyuns for one final time. Or maybe not, but who was counting?

Flores imagined the death of so many SEALs. And the departure of Rivera and Soto. He could taste victory; even over the taste of the Funyuns.

CHAPTER 4

The Navy SEAL Team struck its first blow against the Godesto Cartel four days after arriving in Mexico. They struck at 3 a.m., in the dead of night.

Four helicopters tore across the massive metropolis of Mexico City, racing toward an old, decrepit warehouse. At the target site, two guards – caught by surprise on the roof – scrambled for cover and brought their AK-74s to bear against the helicopters, foolishly thinking they could shoot down the helicopters.

All the men did was sign their death warrants. Two SEAL Sniper teams were already on station, observing the target site. They had moved into their positions a full day prior to the mission, wearing civilian clothes and dressed as repairmen carrying HVAC equipment. The snipers had been watching the men since the two Godesto men began their shift two hours ago.

The guards lifted their guns, went to aim, and then deflated like balloons as bullets ripped through them both.

"Roofs are cleared," the sniper team leader said.

"Bring 'em in," Lieutenant Commander Steve Todd said. He loved this part of life. There were no thoughts about worrying about his daughter at UNLV, worrying about his wife, who was caring for her father in the man's last weeks of life, trying to keep him out of an assisted living facility.

"Let's look sharp," Master Chief David Adair growled into his radio. The bearded, tattooed man had spent twenty-plus years hunting men on almost every continent in the world. He lived for the adrenaline rushes, having watched two marriages crash and burn. He was a workaholic, living and breathing SEAL life, but even when he was off, he was skydiving, pushing stacks of weights, or burning up his own money on ammunition he fired on civilian ranges. He was easily in the top 1 percent of Special Forces troops in the world. There weren't many who could outshoot him or who had a higher kill count.

The helicopters screamed across the sky, pushing a hundred miles per hour, then flared above the warehouse. Crew chiefs kicked out lines and SEALs fast-roped onto the roof.

The SEALs assembled quickly, weapons covering danger areas. They sprinted to a steel door, blew it off its hinges inward, and rushed down the stairwell into a dark warehouse.

Outside the building, a convoy of almost a hundred Mexican Special Forces troops raced toward the target in Humvees. They encircled the target and covered both the warehouse and the routes leading up to it. The goal was for no reinforcements to arrive and for no Godesto men to escape.

Inside, the SEALs cleared the warehouse and easily killed seven barely-trained men, who foolishly attempted to stop them with light weapons ranging from AKs to pistols. But these cartel men were used to unskillful fighting against other cartels and gang members; not Navy SEALs who fired thousands of rounds a week.

Once the building was secure, Mexican Police arrived and and took over the operation from the Mexican Special Forces. By the time this had happened, The SEALs had collected loads of additional intel and departed the scene on the helicopters that had dropped them off.

"A good first operation," the SEAL Team Leader Steve Todd said hours after the raid had hit the news.

"Yes," said the liaison from the Mexican military, who was sitting on an ammo can next to the mountain of a man named Master Chief David Adair. The news showed Mexican police standing around crates of assault rifles and sea bags crammed full of heroin. The Navy SEALs were *not* mentioned, as was the plan. Give all the credit to the Mexican Army and Police, as well as President Rivera. That was the plan.

"That shit was fun," Adair said, working an oily rag on his SIG Sauer pistol.

"We won't know the tally for a few hours," Todd said, "but

I figure that seizure was worth several million dollars."

"Did you see how many bags of cocaine there was?" Adair asked. "Dias here says he thinks we nabbed more than ten million in drugs alone."

"Plus the cash," Dias added. "Your men moved quickly on the roof and throughout the building.'

"We were a little slow," Adair said. "About ten seconds slower than I would have liked."

"They never stood a chance," said the liaison from the Mexican military, who was still in awe at the precision and smoothness of the operation.

The SEAL Team Leader smiled.

"That's how we like it," Todd replied.

Just a short distance away, with news anchors still almost breathlessly reporting the raid, President Roberto Rivera called Juan Soto.

"It has begun," Rivera said with satisfaction.

"It began many years ago," Soto said, "when you were elected with lofty promises."

Rivera ignored the remark and quickly briefed Soto on the dead guards and seized weapons and heroin.

"Not bad, but that's barely a dent in Hernan Flores's empire," Soto said.

"You promised to be optimistic until the six months ended."

"No, I promised to be publicly optimistic. That does not mean I'm buying into this plan of yours. I'm sorry, Roberto, but my men continue to plan our departure."

"You didn't see the Navy SEALs in action," Rivera said. "I watched them on a drone video. They're really something else."

Soto sighed.

"No, what's something is Hernan Flores and the Godesto. They have an army of thousands. Foot soldiers, informers, corrupt police officers. Do not think your gleeful report from a single night's operation will change my mind."

Rivera kept his spirits up. "You'll see, my friend. Last night was just the beginning. We will talk again soon."

Later that night, Hernan Flores was doing one of the things he did best: entertaining others. He stood among several distinguished guests at a fundraiser gala, laughing and smiling. One of his best skills was his ability to charm anyone, whether it was the man picking up the garbage or an Ivy League-educated candidate running for governor.

Hernan Flores lacked a college degree, but he made up for it with his salesman-like skills and his street-hardened cunning. And he was generous to a fault, donating to various causes with mind-boggling ferocity. Some thought him a saint. Those who knew he wasn't still happily accepted his checks.

Flores excused himself from the crowd when one of his bodyguards stepped forward and reached out his phone.

"Boss, you got a call," the bodyguard said.

"I'll be right there," Flores said. And with that, he bade farewell to his guests and exited the event. He wondered which site the SEALs would hit next. Flores had left intel on various locations to several government informers.

He was tracking which raid sites lined up with which source that he had leaked to.

It might take a while for him to pull off his plan, and he might lose quite a few men and resources in the process, but Flores was a patient man. And while he hated to lose the men and the guns and drugs, he knew there was a long-term benefit to that, as well.

The men would take their training more seriously and stay more alert in the future. And if they didn't, then he would replace them with men who would. In a country as poor as Mexico, you could always hire new men.

A new stage in this war against President Rivera had arrived, and Flores and the Godesto Cartel would take down the SEALs first. And then they would make their final moves against Juan Soto, President Rivera, and his government.

CHAPTER 5

Things were going well for President Rivera. It seemed the tide had turned against the Godesto.

Out of the public eye, the SEALs under Lieutenant Commander Steve Todd and Master Chief David Adair continued to land blows against the Godesto Cartel, raiding warehouses and other drug caches. These strikes made the typically ineffective Mexican military look effective. President Rivera rode the wave of good news, making a number of speeches and public announcements of his government's renewed efforts against the Godesto Cartel.

"We will drive them out of the country for good," he said, his approval ratings at their highest totals to date.

Flores accepted the necessary losses and laughed at Rivera (in private). In public, he continued to praise President Rivera and his efforts. And he said the government needed to do more to crush the Godesto Cartel, which was feeding on Flores's legitimate businesses as well. It was quite the act and the public bought Rivera's and Flores's words.

Privately, Flores could feel that the time to spring his grand trap was rapidly approaching. Flores needed his enemies to implicitly trust the tips coming to them and the best way to make that happen was for the tips to be accurate and noteworthy. And noteworthy they were, as the millions and millions in losses for the Godesto Cartel stacked higher and higher. The number of men he lost piled higher, too.

The SEALs *were* good, but they hadn't tasted the power of the Godesto Cartel yet. So far, they had been hitting the Godesto; the Godesto on the ropes, just taking the punches. Soon, the Godesto would stop taking hits and would punch back. And when they did? It would be felt from Mexico City all the way to Washington, D.C.

Hernan Flores never flinched. He'd battled many competing cartels for years. In his younger days, as a nobody seller, he'd fought men for the control of a single street corner. He had made his name, starting from the very bottom, and he was now an experienced gangster. He just dressed nice and held fundraisers and galas; and he killed men these days with orders and phone calls, not with a pistol or shotgun. But he was still a gangster. Still a killer.

Soon, the people of Mexico would know their government could not stand up against his Godesto Cartel.

The night of the catastrophe, the night everything changed, it was just after 3 a.m. and the SEALs were getting used to the nightly raid schedule. Their four Blackhawk helicopters raced toward their target, their engines screaming as the pilots pushed the machines to their limit, flying low at less than two hundred feet and racing across the skyline of Mexico City at more than one hundred miles per hour.

Master Chief David Adair had a bad feeling about the mission, but he kept that to himself. He didn't get bad feelings often, but what could he do? He was the second in command. He was the crazy, bearded, ink-covered man who had a reputation for showing no fear. No, he couldn't say a word, so he boarded the birds as if nothing was wrong.

At the target – yet another warehouse – a group of guards stood ready and alert tonight. They hadn't been warned of any impending dangers by their leadership, so it was business as usual for the guards. Except for the fact that tonight they were hyper alert. Word had gotten out that the Americans struck at roughly 3 a.m. and the guards had adjusted on their own, coming to full attention at all of Flores's facilities in the early morning hours.

The men guarded rows of stacked drugs intended to be moved across the border into Arizona the following day, as well as something else – the contents of which they weren't aware. A special delivery had been brought in the day prior and laborers had hauled in crate after crate and positioned them throughout the warehouse. The guards thought the placement random and strange, but were ordered not to move the items or touch them at all. Worse, if any man handled them, sat on them, or opened them to inspect their contents, they could face the wrath of Hernan Flores himself.

Given how many cameras were in the warehouse and given the ruthlessness that Flores had exhibited hundreds of times against soldiers of the Godesto who did not obey orders, it was safe to say that the crates weren't going to be touched.

And as the SEALs under Lieutenant Commander Steve Todd and Master Chief David Adair hit the rooftop, the boxes lay precisely where they had been placed. They hadn't been moved, opened, or even bumped.

Outside the warehouse, at ground level on the street several blocks away, two teams of Hernan Flores's men waited. The guards on the roof had no idea about these men. Neither did the SEAL sniper teams, who had infiltrated in prior to the mission; same as they always did.

These outside teams were beyond the perimeter of the SEAL snipers and they held shoulder-launched anti-air missiles, alert and ready. These weren't Mexican locals. Instead, Flores had hired some A-list talent: Russian mercenaries, who had been trained by the Soviet Army, and flown in purely for this single mission. Flores had learned the hard way two years earlier how complicated the anti-air missiles were. He had attempted to train some of his own men to use them, but it had proved too expensive and time consuming. And ultimately, his men had missed their shots.

But these experienced Russians near the warehouse with the missiles weren't the only surprise in store. Flores had also placed Godesto Cartel members near the Presidential Palace. In a five-story apartment complex that overlooked the Presidential Palace, four men knocked on the door of a fifth-floor residence. When the door was answered, the male occupant – a man in his thirties – was shoved into the room

STAN R MITCHELL

and promptly executed with a silenced 9mm pistol. Then the four men walked back into the hallway to carry in four heavy duffle bags.

Outside the apartment complex – seven blocks away in a small park that was empty in the dead of night – several trucks waited. The trucks had their tailgates covered with tarps, and nearby, had you been an observant passerby, you would have seen vans idling nearby, as well.

All were waiting on the command to strike. All were about to take part in the largest attack by the Godesto Cartel in its history.

Back at the target warehouse, Flores had positioned additional forces besides the two teams of Russians with the shoulder-launched, anti-air missiles. Lookouts dressed as civilians were posted miles away from the warehouse, watching likely routes into the target.

These lookouts, ranging from teenagers to older business owners, watched the major roads that lead toward the warehouse. Once the lookouts discovered the entry route in for the Mexican ground forces, Hernan Flores would position more than two dozen of his men to ambush them. These men carried assault weapons, RPGs, medium machine guns, and Claymore directional mines, which were difficult and dangerous to get. But for tonight's move, Flores had spared no expense.

State-of-the-art Soviet anti-air missiles, which he had purchased from Egypt. Claymore mines, which he had bought from a cartel in South America. The cartel had purchased them from military units in Colombia, which the United States had provided for the drug war happening near the Amazon.

American weapons killing pro-American forces, loyal to the government of Mexico? How delicious. It had been costly to get the weapons, but it was going to be worth every penny, Flores thought.

After tonight, President Rivera would either be powerless or forced to resign. And Juan Soto? He'd race out of the country like a complete coward. And if he didn't, then Flores would make him wish he had.

Back at the warehouse, the Blackhawks neared their target. The crew chiefs signaled the SEALs on board to make ready and the men slid across the metal floor of the choppers to the doors.

The SEAL Leader Steve Todd ordered the sniper surveillance teams watching the building to take their shots. The snipers fired, dropping the guards on the roof that were firing at the black shapes in the sky.

Unfortunately for them, neither the leader or sniper teams knew of the anti-air teams just another thousand meters outside the target zone.

The helicopters closed the final distance, flaring up and coming to an instant, bone-jarring stop.

So far, so good.

Crew chiefs shoved ropes out and the SEALs descended as black shapes in the pitch-black night. They fast-roped down, rushed by the dead guards, and secured the roof.

Six seconds later, the breacher had secured the charges on the steel door and they blew it inward, running behind the explosion into the bowels of the building. A gunfight erupted with the guards below, who were ready for an attack on this night. Not that they had been warned by Flores – that would have led to them acting differently and might've tipped off the SEAL snipers watching the building.

Instead, they just knew really bad people came in the middle of the night. Rumor had it that they were special forces from America.

These men of the Godesto wanted to be ready and they had game planned among themselves what they would do if their warehouse was targeted. Shooting from hidden locations in darkened corners, the mostly untrained men did fairly well.

As the bullets flew across the warehouse, two SEALs took nasty hits. But the SEALs recovered well, Master Chief David Adair taking the lead on some nasty fighting. No damn way would any men die under his command. He, with no family and a lot of years under his belt, didn't care if he died. But no damn way would he let these cartel thugs kill one of his men.

He gunned down a Godesto shooter in the corner, flash-banged a room and killed two men in it, and single-handedly encouraged his men to pull off a well-executed assault, despite their casualties.

Rehearsed drills, precision shots, and speedy movements drove the enemy to a basement area, confining a few men down below.

"Top floors secure," Lieutenant Commander Steve Todd reported. "Get us a medical evac here, immediately. I've got two shooters hit."

"Understood," a man from command stated. "We'll get an evac on the way."

Just a few miles away, a convoy of Mexican Army Humvees gunned their motors as they raced around corners to reach the warehouse. It was tricky timing. They didn't want to arrive early or it would tip off the Godesto. But they also wanted to be able to reinforce the SEALs in case more Godesto responded to the raid.

The Mexican Humvees rushed as fast as they could to back up the SEALs. Things didn't sound as good tonight. Their radios reported wounded men and a force that had defended this warehouse to the last man. The Mexican commander worried more cartel reinforcements might be on their way – the target warehouse was in a very dangerous neighborhood – and he urged his drivers to speed up.

"We have to get there!" he said, slapping his hand on his driver's shoulder.

The driver pushed the pace even harder.

A call from a bored drug pusher nicknamed "Too High" tipped Hernan Flores to the route the Mexican forces were using.

Flores alerted his men – who happened to be nearby as it was the most obvious and anticipated route.

"The dumbass Army was overconfident, as usual," Flores

thought.

Flores was about to reinforce why Soto had planned to flee the country. And also why President Rivera had made so little headway against the Godesto in four-plus years. Flores was truly street smart and cunning, like a modern-day General, but without the stars or oath to the country.

While the Mexican forces proceeded to their nasty surprise, Godesto men deployed quickly following the tip from "Too High." They ran out onto the sidewalks, trailing wires behind them. They aimed the crescent-shaped Claymore mines purchased from South America up and down the road in some excellent, pre-selected positions.

The Humvees from the Mexican Army would enter an L-shaped ambush that no force could have dealt with.

The Mexican convoy forged ahead toward its target and its commander – a good man and an even stronger leader – tried to stay calm.

Men are dying, he thought, hearing gunfire over his radio from the SEALs who were calling in updates. But I need to stay calm. My men need to see me calm.

The Mexican commander really like the SEALs. He had met both Lieutenant Commander Steve Todd and Master Chief David Adair, the group sharing some beers and a few hands of poker; their go-to after missions were finished.

The Mexican commander of the Quick Reaction Force knew he wasn't supposed to be in the lead vehicle, but he led from the front regardless of the situation. He had learned this lesson from the Americans, in one of their training assignments where soldiers from foreign countries came to train in the United States. And he had heard stories over bottles of beer about how Adair liked to lead from the front when things got especially hot.

We'll be there soon, he thought, reaching for his handset in the Humvee. He needed to relay their position to the SEALs – they were just minutes away. But a strange sight stopped him mid-movement. Four men pushed and shoved an old car across the road ahead of them. Across from those men, more guys shoved another car toward it. Oh shit, he thought. Ambush.

"Stop!" he screamed to his driver, who had seen the threat, as well, and was already slamming the brakes for all they were worth.

The road was narrow through this stretch, both sides enclosed by small shops and diners. And now that the two junk cars had been shoved into each other – nose to nose, with a small crunch from the impact – the road was completely blocked.

The Mexican Commander yelled into the handset, "Back up!"

He glanced into the rear view mirror and saw his other vehicles were following too close. Why hadn't he told them to keep their distance?

That's right, because they were going above typical speed to get to the fight.

Above him, his turret gunner began firing his M240 medium machine gun at the men who had shoved the vehicle into the street from the right. The men had produced weapons.

The machine gun spewed out 7.62 mm rounds and caught one Godesto man in the lower leg, shattering the bones that supported his weight and dropping him as his leg broke outward at nearly ninety degrees. Another round from the gunner's weapon caught the man's buddy through the gut. The bullet sounded like a hand clapping down on wet ham when it found its target.

Below the gunner, the Mexican commander continued to scream into his radio, "Back up! It's an ambush." The entire convoy had squealed to a stop but hadn't begun reversing yet. He switched frequencies to call the SEAL Team commander and alert him to the ambush. There would almost certainly be a delay in their arrival. They would need to re-route.

"Blackbird Six. Blackbird Six," he said, waiting for a response from Lieutenant Commander Steve Todd. They were the last words he ever spoke.

One of the Godesto leaders on the ground saw the convoy of Humvees had halted and would advance no further into the kill zone. The junk cars blocking the road had served their purpose, but now it was time.

As the convoy's lead machine gunner fired at the men who had pushed the cars into the street, the ambush leader screamed into his radio for his men to stay down. None of the men in their hidden positions believed the Claymores would wound any of them with their backblast, but it was better safe than sorry. And there *were* a lot of Claymores out there.

The leader ducked his head below the window, checked to confirm his earplugs were in, and squeezed the clacker, from which all the Claymores were daisy-chained and linked together.

They would go off all at once, in a simultaneous explosion, and on the third squeeze, they did just that. A monstrous explosion erupted in the street. Windows up and down the road imploded and shattered from the concussion alone, while down in the tight street thousands of well-aimed ball bearings flew out and decimated everything in their path.

The mines had been positioned well, and the Mexican troops, riding in unarmored Humvees (American hand-me-downs from years before), took heavy casualties from the Claymores. Nearly the entire front half of the convoy was killed or wounded.

The dead looked as if they had been blown to pieces by heavy buckshot fired from a shotgun. Their skin had been more than just chopped up by the ball bearings; it had been ripped and torn and shredded. Mangled flesh hung from bones like strips of rotted cloth.

Those still alive at the front of the column sat wounded and stunned, their eardrums shattered, their limbs bleeding and numb. And though they knew that they must move in order to survive, their brains refused to act, racked instead with shock and indecision: the classic initial effects of severe concussions.

Even the men in the rear of the convoy were rocked by the shockwave that raced out from the killzone. These men, momentarily shook up, had to open and close their mouths to relieve the pressure in their heads and shake the cobwebs out. Unfortunately for them, they wouldn't get enough time to fully recover.

Godesto men emerged from behind windows along one side of the ambush line and at the very front, rushing up behind the stalled vehicles that blocked the path forward. It was a textbook "L-shaped ambush" and the men, blooded veterans, had been in many a fight.

These veterans, who had fought for years on street corners and dark alleys, opened up with AK-74s along the smoky, black-scarred street. Bullets snapped and whipped into the convoy.

Unaffected Humvees further back in the column tried to get unjammed. Their gunners returned fire but were quickly felled by hidden sharpshooters. Medium machine guns, firing from bipods, began lacing the street with a deadly crossfire that wouldn't stop. Their gunners were firing from the hoods of the two stalled vehicles, and the two men poured through their belts of ammo.

They wanted to keep up the shock and maintain fire superiority.

While the machine gunners bathed the killing zone with lead, designated marksmen and snipers assisted killed Mexican Army soldiers foolish enough to man the turrets.

This alone was probably enough, but Flores had prepared more surprises for this Mexican force.

Two Godesto men lifted up RPGs from a rooftop and launched them at vehicles still attempting to retreat near the rear of the column. Explosions boomed and one Humvee lost most of its front end, while the other lost a rear axle. Completely, with a couple of men dying in that explosion.

As the return fire from the Mexican Quick Reaction Force died down, Hernan Flores's men rose up behind the cars. They formed a line and moved down the street, weapons at the ready. To their left, their comrades in the windows continued to provide covering fire, suppressing those few Mexican soldiers who were still alive and fighting.

Methodically, the Godesto men in the street moved

through the kill zone. There would be no prisoners taken. The Godesto executed survivors and fired rounds into those who lay wounded, just to be sure.

More Godesto arrived. Three Godesto pickup trucks rolled into the now silent area. Through the burning vehicles and bleeding bodies, the new arrivals salvaged weapons, flak jackets, and radios from the Mexican Army.

Three of the Godesto had been wounded by the Mexican Quick Reaction Force and they were rushed to waiting doctors, who were paid handsomely for working from their homes and not reporting the wounded to the police.

With the casualties removed and the dead picked clean of their gear, the Godesto performed one final act: they spread gasoline on the vehicles that weren't already burning and lit them up.

It had been a complete and total massacre. A well-armed force of nearly fifty men, trained by the Americans and among the very best of the Mexican Army, had been slaughtered like schoolyard kids.

The worst part? Hernan Flores wasn't close to being done with his assault on this day. No, not even close.

Back at the warehouse, the SEALs had breached the basement and fought their way forward. They now moved toward the last part of the building. It was a lone office. They had no idea about the ambush on their Quick Reaction Force since its commander had died before he could get his warning out by radio.

A few SEALs had heard the man say, "Blackbird Six, Blackbird Six," but nothing else. Communication in cities on radios was often difficult and since they had heard nothing else, they assumed the old adage of, "No news is good news."

Presumably, the Mexican reinforcements would arrive on time as they had in every other previous mission.

All-in-all, the SEALs had come to see that the Mexican troops weren't that bad. Not as good as American ground troops, for sure, but not that bad.

In the warehouse, resistance had been stiffer than expected, but the end was in sight. Just this one final office. Soon, they'd be back at base drinking beers, cleaning their weapons, and having their two comrades stitched up at the hospital. The wounds were both relatively minor.

Six SEALs moved along the bay of the warehouse, led by Master Chief David Adair. They covered stacks of boxes and crates as they advanced the final feet toward the remaining office. Other SEAL Team members covered entrances and exits throughout the building, ensuring more of the enemy didn't enter the warehouse. Near the rooftop, two wounded SEALs waited for medevac.

It had been a bloody day for the SEALs, but they had once again persevered. That's what all the men were thinking.

At the final remaining office, a cartel thug edged his AK out and blasted a long burst toward the approaching SEALs.

Adair was on point, all the SEALs moving toward the office in a smooth, toe-to-heel fashion favored by special operators. Like silent ninjas. But these ninjas had MP-5s and M4s trained on their destination, not swords, and as the rounds flew toward them from the gunman, they did not panic like raw recruits. Instead, they returned fire – accurately, of course – to suppress the man. Their gunfire drove the man back inside the room and the SEALs kept moving forward.

Before the Godesto man could regain his nerve to engage the SEALs again, Adair stacked on the door, the SEAL behind him heaved a flashbang into the room, and a blast erupted. They rushed inward, seeing immediately that the explosion had blinded and rocked the thug, as well as his partner who was waiting behind him.

The Godesto men attempted to move their weapons toward the SEALs, but it was too late. Thee SEALs' weapons tore into the men.

The Godesto men jerked and shook as the rounds ripped through them. The cartel thugs fell hard, twitching and bleeding grotesquely. Blood spatters painted the walls and lines of blood streaked to the floor like slow-moving paint.

The SEALs checked the ceiling and cleared the final dead space behind a desk.

"All clear," one of them said into his mic.

Adair hit the transmit button on his radio.

"Blackbird Six, basement secure."

"Roger," Lieutenant Commander Steve Todd replied. "Collect any intel and bring your men back to the bottom level. We'll egress one the Quick Reaction Force arrives."

The Quick Reaction Force referred to their Mexican reinforcements.

"What's the ETA on the convoy?" Adair asked, referring to the Estimated Time of Arrival for the Quick Reaction Force.

"Should've already been here," Todd said. "I'll call them again. Comms seems pretty unreliable around here."

Adair heard Todd say, "Bison Herd Six, this is Blackbird Six. Come in, over."

The silence lingered, causing Todd to repeat the command two more times.

"Bison Herd Six, this is Blackbird Six. Come in, over."

"Bison Herd Six, this is Blackbird Six. Come in, over."

In the silence of no answer from the Mexican Quick Reaction Force, Master Chief David Adair felt that bad feeling he had sensed prior to the mission return.

"This shit doesn't feel good," he said to a SEAL near him.

"You've been bugged out about this mission since before we left," said the Petty Officer, a man named Rick Norris.

"It showed?" Adair asked.

"I've known you for three years," Norris replied. "Of course it showed."

"What's in all these crates?" Adair asked. "We've never come across crates like this in the previous warehouses."

And that's when Norris and Adair both saw the blinking red light buried in the depths of one of the crates that had its wood exterior damaged by the flashbang.

"Steve!" Adair screamed into his radio, breaking all military protocol. "The place is wired to blow!"

A single man watched the factory from a block away in the darkness. The helicopters had zoomed off. Not that he could see such a thing, but their sounds had raced away as quickly as they had arrived. Off in the distance, he could barely hear them circling. He dialed his prepaid cellphone and said, "Stage Two commencing. There's no more gunfire at the target site."

With that, he pocketed the phone, turned his back to the target, and put on a pair of hearing protection earmuffs. He ducked down behind a metal refrigerator and cringed as he pressed the detonator he held in his hand.

Inside the warehouse, the explosive concussion dropped the building with ease. It was like a boulder hitting water: The roof and walls collapsed and disappeared deep into the ground, while an outward cloud of dust and force expanded outward in a perfect circle.

Upon seeing the flash in the night sky, the Blackhawk pilots knew something terrible had happened.

"Was that our building?" asked one pilot. "Tell me that wasn't our target objective."

His navigator said, "That was ours, sir."

He said it with as little emotion as possible – air traffic was recorded and monitored by Command and you didn't want to sound like an idiot in some Congressional hearing some day – but that *had* been the target building. And it *had* just exploded and crumbled to the ground in a heap.

How many SEALs were back there? How many had they dropped off? Was it sixteen? It was sixteen, the navigator thought.

The helicopters rushed back to the scene and pulled up in horror as the smoke and dust rose into a column that their night vision devices could barely see through.

"No!" screamed one of the pilots, who knew three of the men in the building, including Lieutenant Commander Steve Todd and Master Chief David Adair. The two men had saved his life once when his helicopter had been shot out of the sky in Afghanistan. The pilot knew that Todd's wife was caring for her elderly father. And that Todd's daughter was in college. Somewhere out west. Oh, yeah, UNLV, he remembered. They'd both be devastated.

Then the pilot heard the beeping warning in his ears and

knew a bad night for the SEALs on the ground had just turned a whole lot worse for himself and his flight crew, as well.

He yanked the Blackhawk left, but a missile screeching toward him adjusted with his move and exploded into the tail of the helicopter, throwing it into a multi-G force tailspin. The Blackhawk sped to the ground like a wounded bird and slammed into a street, four hundred gallons of fuel mushrooming into a towering fireball.

The only American survivors watched the scene in sickening horror. The SEAL Team snipers stared in disbelief, too shocked to even react. No way did any of the SEALs survive the building falling in on them. And even if they did, rescue personnel would need to arrive immediately. And given that they were deep in land controlled by the Godesto Cartel and Hernan Flores, that wouldn't be happening.

Nor had anyone survived the two helo crashes.

The snipers knew they were in deep shit and it would take all of their collective wits to get out of this one alive, so despite feeling enraged and helpless, they knew there was nothing they could do. Not for their SEAL brethren inside the rubble, nor for the men in the blazing inferno of the two helicopter heaps still blazing.

So, the two sniper teams slipped off into the night, livid that they couldn't spill more blood and horrified at leaving so many of their comrades behind. But four men against possibly hundreds just wasn't good odds, even when you were four badass SEALs.

At the Mexican Presidential Palace, all was quiet. Neither news of the ambush on the Mexican forces or the catastrophe of the SEAL team had reached President Rivera. For the moment, all was still calm in the world.

But, Stage Three of Hernan Flores's elaborately planned operation commenced. This time, the pain would hit much closer to home for President Rivera. Much closer.

The command was given and the Godesto Cartel began their complex attack on the Presidential Palace. At the five-story apartment complex, where the four men had broken into an apartment and executed its owner with a silenced pistol, the four intruders began their role in the attack. The men unpacked the duffel bags they had carried into the apartment. In them were three RPGs and an AK. The man with the AK covered the door in the prone, watching their rear, his weapon aimed at it should anyone try to breach the door. They had deadbolted and chain locked it, but better safe than sorry.

The three men with the RPGs loaded their weapons and stacked additional rounds where they could quickly be accessed.

During this entire time, the room remained dark with no lights on anywhere. The men used their familiarity with the weapons to load and arm them, and other than the clicking of weapons locking rockets into place or the AK ratcheting a round into the chamber, they were quiet.

Seven blocks away from the RPG team, in the public park, more men sprang into action in the black of night. Men leaped out of trucks and vans, brandishing AK's and M-16's. The area was lit by a few scattered streetlights, but the men were mostly shadows. Not that anyone was awake and looking out at three o'clock in the morning.

The heavily armed men established a quick perimeter in the forested area of the park, while unarmed Godesto men yanked tarps off the trucks. They carried equipment toward an open area typically used by picnickers.

With expert precision, the men set up a pair of 81 mm mortars. Police had been paid to avoid the area, but the men on the perimeter would not hesitate to drop anyone stupid enough to show up with a badge.

The mortars were leveled and aimed while other men cracked open ammo crates and prepared for an all-out barrage against the Presidential Palace. A woman, walking home from a long night bartending, saw the men setting up with their weapons. She shrieked and fled. A Godesto man nearly shot her with an M-16, but decided to avoid the noise. Not until the attack began, he thought. And if any police decided to respond, they'd be quickly overpowered by the heavily-armed Godesto men.

One person who heard the shriek and saw the armed men shut her curtains in fear. Others ignored the sound and refused to look. Seeing bad people in the night in Mexico was a good way to get on the bad side of the cartel. Or to be bullied by police, who were desperate for leads against the cartels. It was, in short, a great way to end up dead.

The distance of the mortars being merely seven blocks away was so short that missing would be difficult, but a spotter with a cellphone watched the Presidential Palace from the shadows, ready to call in adjustments for the mortars. Best of all, numerous buildings stood between the mortars and their target.

The Presidential Palace would literally have no way to respond to the indirect fire, falling down from the sky.

And while it might seem improbable to most that Hernan Flores's men could get their hands on mortars and ammo, it hadn't been hard at all.

The mortars were borrowed from a Mexican Army captain who was being paid $30,000 for their use. The captain had also stockpiled the ammunition for the attack by underfiring the allotted rounds for numerous training exercises the past three months. And since the troops under the captain had no idea how many live rounds they were allotted for each session, no one was the wiser.

Bottom line: The rounds wouldn't be missed and if the police intercepted Flores's men after the attack and managed to get their hands on the mortars, the serial numbers would show them reported as stolen. The captain would still be in the clear as he'd been told to report them as stolen if he didn't have them back in his possession within two hours after they had been picked up.

And the captain was so nervous that he waited in his vehicle a mile from the front gate, desperate to get the mortars back into the armory as quickly as possible. Thirty thousand dollars was nice, but the stress it was causing him was about to kill him. He really hoped they were only being used against another cartel's outpost, as he'd been told, but the thought they could be used otherwise only brought more sweat to his forehead and more pain to his stomach. He was covered in sweat and on the verge of puking, but his family had been threatened and the money was good for a night's work...

Back at the mortar firing site, a man who was obviously in charge called out a final grid point, the mortars were adjusted the final, incremental amounts, and the first rounds were dropped into the mortar tubes. The tubes fired – thump, thump – two 81 mm mortars arcing high into the sky. They soared higher and higher, over the buildings in front of them and thousands of feet into the air.

And after what seemed like a minute but was more like thirty seconds, they slammed into the compound of the Presidential Palace. Both landed long, missing the palace completely. One shot struck near a Humvee on the perimeter, another outside the compound and into the side of a popular coffee shop, where it blasted out glass and flipped tables and chairs.

The spotter saw the impacts and said into a phone, on which the mortar commander waited, "Drop fifty meters. Fire for effect."

Inside the Presidential Palace, the explosions caused an immediate response. Guards rushed the sleeping quarters of President Roberto Rivera and practically dragged him out of the bed before he was even awake.

"We must get your family down into the basement for safety," one screamed.

Rivera, half-awake, grabbed his wife by the arm and the two rushed out of the room. They had started down the hall when Rivera stopped and ripped his forearm from the guard's hand.

"What about my kids?"

"We're getting them," the guard said. "Let's go! We don't have much time."

The mortar team commander received the adjustment from the spotter on his cellphone and dropped it in the pocket of his jeans. He instructed his men to drop fifty on their mortars and he spoke these words without haste or worry.

He felt certain no authorities would enter their area until well after they had fired their massive volley and departed.

Besides, his men fed off of his confidence and it was important they get this right. Hernan Flores and his Godesto Cartel had spent a fortune on this operation. Paying former Army soldiers to fire into the country's Presidential compound was not cheap. And in a few cases, the Godesto had been forced to threaten family members of the soldiers in order to secure their loyalty. But they needed solid mortarmen and you didn't find mortarmen on every street corner.

The men shifted the angle of the mortars to move the impact back fifty yards. With a slight final adjustment and double-check of the sights, the loaders began dropping the mortar rounds in as fast as possible. The gunners adjusted the tubes to the left or right with each shot – they didn't want each round landing in the same impact zone. The goal was to cover the entire compound of the Presidential Palace.

It was an immediate suppression drill – a simple one they all knew – and each tube had ten rounds. The men fired all twenty rounds in twenty-five seconds. Not bad, really. Almost U.S. Army standards.

The delay needed to call in the adjustment and more accurately aim the mortars gave the Palace security detail time to get the Rivera family in the Presidential Palace's basement, which doubled as a bunker. Guards slammed shut a safe-like steel door and looked up with obvious relief to now be under a reinforced roof.

Rivera's assistant head of security – the actual head of security was at home asleep – double-checked his headcount for the people in the room. After confirming that the President and his entire family were safe, "The President is secure. Get the react force on the wall and alert the reserve force. Have them scramble to our position."

Four platoons of men, dressed for war, rushed from

two large rooms above the basement inside the Presidential Palace. The soldiers wore flak jackets and helmets. And they carried full-sized battle rifles: M-16s. They poured out onto the grounds and reinforced the perimeter and the guard stations. Their numbers swelled the sixty already in place by an extra hundred men.

The reserve force waited on a base ten minutes from the Presidential Palace. A full battalion of additional soldiers – a thousand men – comprised the reserve force and upon getting the call, they began forming up and grabbing their gear, piling into tarp-covered heavy trucks and roaring toward the area.

Back in the bunker, the assistant head of security then used his radio to request a status report from each position on the perimeter. He still didn't know yet what had happened – whether it was a car bomb, a rocket attack, or a couple of grenades thrown across the wall.

Meanwhile, high in the sky, death approached slowly, as only a mortar barrage can. In a world of supersonic weapons, the high-flying and slow-falling mortars were hardly the sexiest of weapons.

But it was their high arc and nearly vertical descent that allowed them to clear walls and buildings between them and the target; the things that blocked direct fire weapons like machine guns and missiles proved no obstacle for their indirect fire. And it was this nearly vertical arc that caused such destruction.

Buildings have strong walls. Tanks, thick armor. Yet neither has reinforced ceilings or roofs. Hit them from the top and they crater and burst apart like an icing-covered cake. And on this night, the buildings and vehicles in the Presidential Palace proved no different.

Flores's men only had basic ammunition – High Explosive M374s, which had been given to the Mexican Army by the United States – but it didn't matter. The nine-pound shells exploded with such force that none of the structures stood a chance. Their blast radius was almost forty yards. Or, one hundred feet. Anything within that circle was likely wounded or killed.

These were proven, battle-tested heavy weapons that had been used by armies for hundreds of years.

The rounds fell in an almost continuous wave just seconds apart. Each round landed in a different area as the gunners moved their sights incrementally after each round left the tube.

Ten rounds per tube. Twenty rounds total. A crescendo of explosions that seemed to never end. Buildings blew apart. Windows shattered. The Presidential Palace ate three rounds that were direct hits. These shots tore through the roof of the Presidential Palace and exploded inside it like a pressure cooker blowing its lid. Even the Presidential limo – the real one, not the two decoys – took a hit to its trunk. Despite the thick armor along the sides, it blew the back end completely off. That car wouldn't be carrying the president for a long time; if ever.

But the mortars claimed more than just buildings and vehicles. Guards in bunkers, and those who had responded to investigate the first two shots, were caught in the open by the explosions. Many caught shrapnel in chunks varying from the size of a pocketknife to smaller bits the size of a dime, all of which cut through them like shotgun slugs.

The circular blasts left almost nothing untouched in the ten-acre compound of President Rivera. And while men in the perimeter lay curled up with their fingers in their ears, praying they might survive the next impact, the RPG team watching from the five-story apartment raised their rockets.

The guards and groundforce was suppressed and it was time to add the final, killing blows.

The three men targeted the Presidential Palace – not so much for the men they might kill, but more for the permanent scarring their rockets would cause. The government needed to look vulnerable. How better to make such an appearance than to wreck the very structure that personified the strength of the federal government to the people?

Each RPG gunner aimed at the walls between windows – what good would a round fired through a window cause in a

Presidential Palace that was mostly deserted at this time of night? They fired with alarming accuracy. At this distance – roughly four hundred meters – and with such wide gaps to hit between windows, none of them missed.

They blasted gaping holes into the walls with delight. In the fury of the mortar barrage, it wasn't until their final round was fired that they were noticed by the troops, who were ostensibly supposed to be protecting the compound.

A guard on the line saw the flash of their final shot and yelled out the position to a man near him. After alerting his fellow squad member, he swung his M240 medium machine gun at the spot.

He loosed a burst – more than ten feet off the mark, but, hey, it was his first burst. It was dark. And his adrenaline was out the roof. He had never been under a mortar barrage before.

The machine gunner reoriented his aim more accurately. Inside the room, the men had pulled back from the window and were packing up when the next set of bullets came flying into the room, finally on target.

Two of them took nasty hits before diving to the ground and crawling out.

On the wall, with the mortars no longer falling, other guards heard the friendly machine gun roaring in the night. And though they didn't know the target, they could see the tracer rounds tearing into the apartment building across from them.

There must be a threat of some kind firing from the building, they all assumed. First one, then others joined in to help suppress what must have been a serious threat. They had just sustained the most potent attack any of them had seen and then intended to punish the bastards who had done it. And while none of them could see targets, it was better to be safe than sorry and so they began spraying wider and wider into rooms throughout the building.

The four men who had started the carnage by firing the RPGs assisted their wounded brethren as they carried themselves out of the building, exiting the far side with their duffle bags and weapons. The bullets hitting the front of the building were inconsequential to them now, but a nice side effect of the plan by Hernan Flores. The government troops would kill and wound dozens of innocent civilians, most likely.

CHAPTER 6

It was early morning and Nick Woods was driving across the South, trying to re-enter society and his own sanity. He had no idea of what was going on in Mexico. He barely kept up with the news. And he had no idea a government agent would soon be assigned to approach him.

But the fight in Mexico was rushing his direction at a speed that would prove mind bending to most. Nick was one day closer to having his entire life thrown upside down. Again.

Eighteen hundred miles away, the Mexican government was scrambling to assess the damage it had sustained in the three separate devastating attacks in the night. The government was also working to prevent any further attacks from occurring; all units were at the highest state of alert. Even the Army Reserves were being called up. Everyone from cooks to candlestick makers was told to report to their Reserve units. Mexico was going into a state of war.

President Roberto Rivera sat in a bustling conference room, with more than a dozen advisors and cabinet secretaries. They all awaited news and a return of their courage. Two of the cabinet secretaries had sent their families to America. One of them had withdrawn their entire savings, minus some spending money, and wired it to an overseas account.

Even President Rivera was shaken. He wondered if his government could survive the terrible onslaught. News stations were already saying that most Mexican citizens planned not to go to school or work today.

The nation was in a crisis and its people were holding their breath while awaiting developments.

Rivera had changed from his pajamas into khakis and a polo. He'd shaved because if ever the country needed to see a solid, capable man, it was today.

Yeah, right, he thought. He was standing in a conference room and he had two suit-wearing Secret Service members standing to each side of him. They carried Uzi's slung across their chests and wore thick assault vests *outside* of their suits.

Hell, why stop there? Rivera wondered. Why didn't they just put on helmets and hook a couple of grenades to their gear?

Outside the room, twelve more men waited; these men didn't bother with the decency associated with wearing suits. Instead, they wore camouflage full battle gear, including helmets and full-size assault rifles. M-16s, for those taking notes, which Rivera knew the press would, if he showed up with the men around him.

On the outskirts of the Presidential Palace, more than two-thousand armed men had locked down a ten-mile area. Checkpoints, armored personnel carriers, razor wire across streets. Above, jets streaked across the sky, implementing a no-fly zone, and military helicopters whirled over buildings, watching windows with snipers positioned in firing stations.

Besides all the armed force, the entire Presidential Palace Compound was covered with firemen and EMTs, as well.

It was simply impossible to look in control when the place had been bombed out to the level of Sarajevo. Fires had burned for nearly a half hour before security allowed the firemen to fight them. And now Rivera was coming to grips with the fact that the attack on the Palace was just a small portion of the night's disaster.

A tired-looking advisor stood wobbly before him, unshaven and too shaken for Rivera's preference.

"Sir, we lost them all," he said, repeating an earlier report.

"Grab some coffee and explain," Rivera said.

"Sir, that's what I'm trying to say. There's nothing to explain. We've got police officers on the scene. The entire convoy was wiped out. All the troops are dead. Many of them executed. We've found one survivor, who crawled away and hid behind a trash can, but he's in shock and unable to explain much."

Rivera swallowed. He had hoped he had heard wrong the

first time.

"I understand," he said.

What was he supposed to say? He could scream. He could demand answers. But he was at a loss as to what would be most presidential, so he decided to remain in control. To remain calm.

A door opened and slammed shut off to his flank. Another suited man had barged into the conference room.

"Sir," the man said, "we must issue a statement. News agencies from across the world are demanding a statement. They're calling it a coup attempt. A few are saying you were killed. A few are even saying our government has fallen. Or been overthrown. The rumors are out of control."

Rivera looked over at a high-ranking American from the U.S. Embassy, who sat in the corner of the cramped room. Even the experienced diplomat appeared pale. And also worried, like everyone else in the room, that more mortars might fall at any moment.

"I'm alive," River said. "Look at me," he said holding his arms out. "Do I look dead? Or injured? Or like I'm fleeing the country? Deny those absurd lies in the strongest possible terms."

Rivera sighed, his anger on the verge of exploding.

"Forget a statement from me. Draft this into something that works: Tell them we've suffered a setback. We're evaluating what happened. We don't know how many casualties we have. We'll bring the killers to justice. You know the deal. Get the hell out of here and make it happen. I have too much to do to be worrying about issuing a statement. Do your job and say the things that need to be said."

The man turned and left, looking embarrassed. Another took his place.

"Mr. President," the man said. "The Police Chief of Mexico City wants to meet and discuss their findings."

"Not now," Rivera said. "Tell him to give you a summary and tell me the short of it in just a sentence or two. Now, everyone, get out. Everyone out. I want everyone out now."

The room – filled with aides, advisors, and military officers, far too many for Rivera's comfort – quickly emptied.

Mexican President Roberto Rivera wasn't the only elected leader trapped in a room filled with too many government types. Twenty-five hundred miles to his northeast, the president of the United States sat in a remarkably similar situation, but with far less fear.

"What the hell happened?" the President asked.

It was 8 a.m. and he had his CIA Director, the Joint Chiefs of Staff, the Secretary of State, and the National Security Advisor in a room, along with their deputy directors, aides, and intel analysts; nearly two dozen folks in all.

It was more than the President preferred to have in a room for a top-secret meeting, but the directors would all share the information with aides anyway – usually as soon as they left the room – so what did it matter?

Besides, half of the department heads didn't know the information they should have known, so the President had learned through experience to get the info straight from an analyst or aide who knew. That allowed him to learn stuff quickly and completely unfiltered.

Apparently in answer to his question of "What the hell happened," an Army major stood and clicked a handheld pointer that lit up a projector.

"Mr. President, the Defense Department worked with the CIA and the State Department to pull together this presentation for you. I've been asked to give you this summary briefing. As it currently stands, this presentation is our combined analysis of the situation in Mexico, but I must warn you that information is still pretty sketchy. It's coming together, but we're not there yet. Here's the gist of what we know at this time."

The major clicked a button and a picture of the smoking, battle-scarred Mexican Presidential Palace appeared on the wall.

"Sir, at approximately 3 a.m. this morning, the Mexican Presidential Palace came under a devastating attack. It began with a mortar barrage that included a significant RPG rocket attack, as well."

The major clicked again and an aerial view showed impact craters dotting the landscape of the presidential compound, which offered a better perspective of the damage from the widespread mortar attack. Vehicles were wrecked, buildings smoldered in the image, emergency crews blanketed the area.

"Jesus!" the President said. "How many rounds were fired?"

"We're not sure, Mr. President. But it was enough to suppress the entire defending force and we're estimating as many as fifty rounds right now."

"Was this the Gadestin guys?"

The major tried to not show anything on his face at the grossly inaccurate mispronunciation.

"Yes, sir. We believe it was the Godesto Cartel."

"How do you go shooting a bunch of mortars off in an attack like this?" the President asked, looking over at the Joint Chiefs of Staff.

The four-star general cleared his throat and said, "We're not sure of their firing location yet, sir, but we'll know soon enough. We're measuring the impacts and trying to determine the caliber, which would give us the range of the mortars. At this point, we think the assault force used 81 mm mortars. Once we've confirmed that, we'll find from where the mortars were fired. That should lead to some intel and hopefully some witnesses. But the short answer to your question is this: All you would need is a few men to secure a perimeter. And then about six or eight guys to fire the mortars. And obviously you'd need the mortars, but those wouldn't be too hard to get."

The general saw the President raise his eyebrows with alarm, so the general added, "At least not in Mexico."

"Mr. President," the major said, trying to get the briefing back on track. This briefing was *not* supposed to be about the attack on the Presidential compound. Hell, there were dead Americans to tell the President about. Plus, a ton of Mexican civilian casualties.

"The news gets a bit worse, unfortunately," the major said.

"Go on then," the President said, waving his hand.

"The man in charge of protecting the President managed to get him and his family to safety. That's the good news. But, eight guards were killed and at least forty were wounded in the barrage."

The President shook his head but seemed to show relief that the news wasn't worse.

The major saw this reaction and wondered how to bring up the next part. He didn't earn enough money to deal with this kind of stress when it should have been the Joint Chiefs of Staff briefing the President.

"Sir," the major said. "That wasn't the bad news. The bad news is the guards on the line spotted the RPG firing position and those guards engaged."

The major paused, uncertain, and the President leaned forward, waiting.

"Well, sir, other guards along the line joined in. They'd been getting pounded pretty badly by the mortars and had seen a lot of men go down or get cut in half. And, well, they fired a hell of a lot of rounds before they finally got under control. I figure they must have really been shaken. And we're talking thousands of rounds here."

The President seemed exasperated. "Just tell me, damn it."

"Sir, the RPG position was in a five-story apartment complex that overlooks the Presidential Palace. And Mexican forces killed at least fifty civilians in their return fire. Maybe as many as eighty. And at least a hundred more were wounded. These people were piled in pretty tight in this apartment complex, and the emergency services and hospitals were completely caught off guard by so many casualties. So, a lot of people died who shouldn't have. In fact, we're still not sure how many actually did die. They've enacted triage operations and have yet to even get a firm number on how many patients they're treating."

"Did they get the men who fired these RPGs or mortars?" the President bellowed, slamming his fist on the table.

The major didn't have it in him to answer and looked to his boss, the four-star general. The Joint Chief looked to the President and almost whispered, "No, sir, they didn't."

"They found some blood trails," the general added, "but the blood was mixed with those of the civilians, so we don't think the Mexican forces killed any of their targets."

"Ho-ly hell," the President said, slamming his palm against the conference table and jumping to his feet. "I thought we were training these men? Spending billions each year and sending them weapons? We're doing this year after year and apparently they can't even defend their Presidential Palace or hit what they're aiming at."

The Joint Chief said nothing and a couple of generals reached for coffee mugs, their eyes turned away.

"What are we going to do?" the President asked, sitting back down and sighing under the weight of the office. "I want good recommendations on how we respond."

"Sir?" The major said tentatively from where he stood. The President looked at him, clearly annoyed. The major would have rather been back in the mountains of Afghanistan dodging rounds than meet the President's stare. And he'd have rather been shot again than to say what he was about to say.

"Sir, there's more," he said, barely whispering the words.

"Go on, major. Spit it out! We don't have all day."

"Sir, at approximately the same time, Mexican forces were accompanying an American SEAL Team on a mission to take down a drug cartel warehouse. We're still not sure what happened, but we lost contact with the SEAL Team and we're pretty sure we lost them."

"Lost who?" the President asked, still annoyed. He wasn't overly concerned with how many more Mexicans were killed. He had a more pressing thought on his mind: How to handle the PR on this attack at the Presidential Palace.

"The SEAL Team Platoon," the major said.

"What do you mean we lost them? Don't they have GPS's and weapons? I seriously doubt the cartel took down a SEAL Team. Now you're just being pessimistic."

The President looked over to the Joint Chief, a man he considered too old and worn down to be running things. But the man averted his eyes down and cleared his throat. Suddenly, the President knew it was true.

"How do we lose a god-damn SEAL Team?" he said leaping to his feet and slamming both of his fists into the conference table. "These are the best men we have!"

"Sir," the major said, "we're still not sure yet, as the snipers we had on the target site have not been found yet. They'll know for sure, but aerial reports from helicopters we had in the air show that the entire building that the SEALs were assaulting exploded and collapsed on the SEAL Team once they were all inside."

"Are we digging them out? How many survivors are there? What are the chances some of them lived. I need to know percentages on survivors. How long they can live under rubble? How much construction equipment is digging them out of the rubble?"

"Sir," the major said, his eyes on the ground, unable to meet the President's. "Sir, we're not even on the location yet. A quick reaction force of Mexican troops sent to reinforce the SEAL Team raid was ambushed and completely wiped out. And these men were in Humvees with heavy weapons. This is enemy territory, completely controlled by the Godesto Cartel. Quite frankly, we're not sure how many Mexican soldiers were killed in that ambush, but it was probably another fifty. And we, ahem," the major paused, "also lost a helicopter, sir, to an anti-air missile. We're afraid to send more aircraft to the area at this time because of the threat of these missiles. We did not believe the Godesto had anti-air capabilities, so this is a new threat. One we weren't aware of. And it's severely hampering our ability to respond."

The President cursed, but no one else spoke at the table.

"This is why a hammer isn't always the best solution," the deputy Secretary of State said. He was an avid fan of peace and avoidance of all violence.

"Just shut up," the President said. "This isn't the time for that."

The man dropped back in his chair, a look of horror on his face.

The major wanted to say something, as well. He wanted to say that it would have been nice if the President had sent in more American forces, as recommended, but the President wanted a lean footprint. Well, he had a lean footprint. And now the United States was completely helpless on how to attempt a rescue of the SEAL detachment and aircrew. Assuming any were still alive.

After a moment, the major continued, "So we're not sure how many SEALs may be alive, whether the aircrew may be alive, or whether our snipers were able to escape the area. As I said, this area is under heavy Godesto control. It's riddled with informants, dishonest cops, and armed thugs."

The President returned to his seat and leaned back, stunned. He cursed himself for thinking about it, but his re-election effort was just kicking off. With a sudden certainty, he knew that more than likely, his campaign was over before it had even started. Over a decision that had been presented to him as a minor point of discussion during a long, drawn out meeting. American SEALs and Special Forces had been deploying to South America to help fight drug wars for decades. This was just a slightly more aggressive measure.

The President had approved it and added to keep it a light footprint. That had been all. And now? Maybe sixteen SEALs dead? A helicopter shot down? An aircrew likely dead. He could imagine the men, assuming any lived, ending up on camera. Or being dragged through the streets.

He sat there in complete shock. A SEAL Team Platoon? An entire SEAL Team Platoon? Dead? Plus an air crew? Maybe even four SEAL snipers? It just didn't seem possible and yet it had happened.

How? And why had he sent the SEALs in the first place? This would demand a response of some kind. No way would the public accept so many losses without vengeance.

"Does the media know about the SEALs or American helicopter yet?" the President asked.

"Not yet, sir," an aide responded.

So, he had some time. But for what?

CHAPTER 7

If Hernan Flores thought the largest anti-government attack in Mexican history might push Juan Soto from the country, he calculated wrong. Within two hours of catching the news of the assault, Hernan Flores's fellow billionaire Juan Soto was touring the devastation at the Presidential Palace.

Rubble and debris littered the ground and Juan stood by his friend President Roberto Rivera. More than fifty armed soldiers stood around them, alert and dangerous, while military helicopters criss-crossed overhead. News cameras watched Soto and Rivera closely – they were, after all, Mexico's two most powerful (non-cartel) men – and both stood tall and determined, like confident leaders. Men who were unshaken and full of resolve.

Rivera had changed to his finest suit and Soto looked his typical dapper self, including cufflinks, narrow cotton tie, and polished shoes.

Hernan Flores saw the footage live, as did nearly everyone else in Mexico who had access to a TV. This was a national tragedy reminiscent of America's 9/11 and all work had stopped as the country sat paralyzed in complete shock, wondering if more attacks were to come.

Flores watched the two men on a massive TV and he assumed Soto was there only because the President had begged him to be. Surely in the shock and ruin of the morning light, Rivera had needed his strongest supporter to come forward and reassure him. Surely Rivera had begged and pleaded his friend Soto to come.

But that wasn't the case at all. President Rivera hadn't even asked. Instead, Juan Soto had heard of the attack from an assistant, turned on the news, and texted his friend to tell him he was on his way. Now they stood, on full display, while millions of shocked and worried Mexicans watched their every move.

"You coming here means more than I could possibly say," Rivera said, his hand on Soto's arm.

"It is nothing," Soto said. "I saw the chaos and destruction and I felt my grandfather's eyes on me, God rest his soul. Any patriotic Mexican in my position would have done the same."

Soto stared at a still-smoldering, wrecked Humvee near them and he gritted his teeth. Some blood on the side of it had darkened from the heat of the fire but hadn't burned off completely. It added a sweet, sick smell to the chalky grittiness that resulted from the smell of cordite, dust, and blasted concrete.

Juan Soto glanced away from the blood, swallowed hard, and continued. "I think my grandfather, with his single fishing boat that he borrowed to the max to buy, would have stood up to the kind of men who would do this, as he once stood up to men who tried to gouge those who simply wanted to fish in the sea. He killed one of those men."

Rivera nodded. He had heard the story in the past, but never with such anger from Soto. Before, the story had been a distant tale of an old man in the early (and lawless) 1900's, who had started for scratch, literally fought for his fishing grounds, and handed off a fleet of twenty mid-sized boats to Soto's father, who had also built on that fortune. But with the near abduction of Soto's daughter, and with the attack on the Presidential Palace, the story from the past seemed a lot more relevant and real.

Soto turned to study the wrecked Presidential Palace – once a source of pride for all Mexicans – and the shot-up apartment complex across from it (once a high-end place for residents, now a bullet-riddled memorial). He returned his attention and eyes, now fierce and piercing, upon Rivera.

"Roberto, my friend, we have been friends for nearly ten years. I am pledging to you now, on my soul, and on the soul of my grandfather, that I will not leave this land. Not today. Not tomorrow. Not ever. They will have to carry my body out in pieces. I am sorry I ever even considered leaving."

Rivera saw the burning determination of Mexico's strongest businessman. A man whose fierce determination was typically hidden behind an easy-going manner. But that pleasantness was gone. The man that knew not defeat was staring at Rivera. The man that had risked it all several times, but always walked away a winner, he stood before Rivera and his cutting look inspired Rivera. It scared him a little, too.

This was a man who had no idea how to yield or concede. And while he didn't use his resources the way Flores did, he knew how to fight. He might not use gunmen, bribes, and blackmail on his enemies as Fores did, but he knew how to sue others into the ground. He knew how to drop prices and lose money by the millions to leave a competitor gasping for breath, dying on dry land like a stranded fish. Soto knew how to harden his heart and crush those that wanted to unionize or take his family fortune. He could be merciless when he needed to be and that's what Rivera saw in front of him.

Roberto Rivera, and certainly the government of Mexico, needed more folks like Juan Soto to stand up and say "enough." More men and women needed to stand up to the cartels. To report their activities. To scold them and shoot them and do whatever it took to retake their streets.

Perhaps this would be the start of a monumental shift in momentum. And with the knowledge that Soto wouldn't be leaving Mexico – taking away his money and support – Rivera felt renewed strength and faith, despite the unprecedented setback his government had just suffered.

While Juan Soto was squaring his shoulders for a fight, the government of the United States was doing the exact opposite. Even before the news had leaked that nearly an entire Navy SEAL Platoon had been lost, the President of the United States had decided to abandon his shaky neighbor to the south. No more troops. Reduced aid. And nothing that could stick to him with his re-election campaign around the corner.

Early public opinion polls indicated Americans opposed

intervening in Mexico. The country already faced enough carnage in Iraq and Afghanistan. The public wasn't looking for another quagmire to jump into.

Besides figuring out what he ought to do, the President had his own problems. He already faced demands for congressional hearings on why a Navy SEAL Platoon had been in Mexico in the first place, when the War on Terror was still in full swing. Weren't they supposed to be hunting Al Qaeda or ISIS? Families of the dead SEALs were already talking. The men had been training for an upcoming deployment to Afghanistan. Why the sudden change? Were the men even mentally prepared for an urban environment? Had they been honed to a razor's edge in their training for an urban environment?

These questions were being asked and with the election approaching, the President knew his opponents would work this angle as hard (and for as long) as they could. So, he made it very clear: he wanted to support Mexico, but it had to be in the shadows. It would have to be the CIA only. No more public involvement in Mexico that could be traced back to the U.S. government. No troops. No major financial aid packages. Nothing that could be directly tied to him. Period.

The CIA didn't want the task of trying to save Mexico from the Godesto Cartel. Already, the Agency was stretched to the max. Operatives from the CIA stalked and hunted terrorists and extremist groups literally across the globe. From the cities of Pakistan to the mountains of Afghanistan, from the deserts of Saudi Arabia to the prayer mats of mosques in Syria, from the shanties in Yemen to the very edges of north, south, and west Africa, the CIA was fighting an all-out, win-at-all-costs war of both offense and defense.

All that activity, however, meant the Agency was over-extended, exhausted, and under-manned. It lacked enough quality operatives, spies, and analysts to fully pursue the War on Terror, as it was still called. So, regardless of what the President wanted, or what the CIA Director wanted, or what Mexican President Roberto Rivera actually needed, shifting forces to take on a massive drug cartel in Mexico – one which had nearly taken down the entire government in a single strike, while also batting down a full platoon of SEALs as if it had been no challenge – was not something the CIA was looking forward to adding to their list of priorities.

Inside the CIA, an endless amount of meetings were held, from low-level strategists all the way up to the Director. They knew the President wanted something to happen – off the radar, of course – but none of them knew how to make it happen without undermining more crucial efforts elsewhere.

The overall opinion at the CIA was that little could be done in Mexico. And frankly, bigger battles needed to be fought across the globe. Battles against radicalism and terrorism were the true focus of the CIA, not some dangerous drug fight to America's south.

This was 2014. Not the '80's.

This was the era of Vince Flynn. Not Tom Clancy.

Plus, Mexico was corrupt through and through. Anyone sent there by the CIA would be dimed out by ten different Mexican officials before they even arrived, so why bother? Wasn't that what happened to the SEAL Team? How else could they have been ambushed so perfectly?

In addition to these facts, the drug cartels left America alone. So why go after them?

But besides this multitude of problems facing the CIA, there was one even larger one that they all knew. Even *if* you toppled the Godesto Cartel and Hernan Flores, and that was a damn big *if*, they would simply be replaced by a successor.

The drug war in Mexico was unceasing. Endless. And unwinnable.

Yet, the folks at the CIA also knew they had to follow orders. They had to do something. The President insisted he wanted options to support President Rivera. So, the Director continued to press for more meetings within the Agency until they had solutions – at this point, any kind of solution.

And in the palpable desperation of one of these follow-up meetings, a name was sarcastically spat out, as simply a joke. It was a joke that, under the stress of the circumstances, was funnier than hell. Without question, jokes and laughs were what the meetings had all turned to – after all, they had no solutions; none even in sight.

The only solution they had was literally a joke.

But the name that started out as a cruel joke began circulating after the meeting. A kind of snide remark. And the name kept getting brought up in future meetings. Initially, as a joke, of course. But every time it was brought up, the same pattern emerged: rip-roaring, hard laughs followed by slow consideration as the idea was chewed on.

And eventually, one of the braver people in the room – or one with the least to lose – would say something along the lines of, "He actually might be the perfect person." Or as one analyst said, "the only son of a bitch crazy – and paranoid – enough to pull it off."

And as meeting notes were shared, a consensus emerged. Nearly everyone agreed there was no other person better suited.

If it could be done, Nick Woods was the man. And if something needed to be done, who better to send than the man who had wrecked more Soviet Spetsnaz and CIA operatives than any other living man on the planet.

And on the flip side, if the mission failed as most felt it would, Nick Woods was no big loss. Not even a current employee. The CIA Director could legitimately tell the President they were sending their best man, the situation would remain in the background and off the books, and the President would either be re-elected or not.

But most importantly, the CIA would be maintaining its focus around the globe.

No way would the CIA endanger American lives at the whims of a President worried about his re-election effort. And so the decision was made: Nick Woods would be found. And he would be convinced to pick up his rifle again in service of his country.

All that was left was to decide who among them was ballsy enough (and crazy enough) to actually recommend Nick and in the process put their own career in the hands of an uncontrollable force. And also this: who would be the guy or gal gutsy enough to make initial contact? That would be a great way to catch a bullet or three from a man with a hair trigger.

CHAPTER 8

The man crazy enough to finally approach Nick was reconsidering his sanity.

"Mexico, you say?" Nick asked. "You need my help in Mexico? I thought our wars were in Iraq, Afghanistan, and a half-dozen countries in Africa and the Middle East. What the hell are we doing in Mexico? The drug cartels mostly leave us alone."

"Our focus *is* on most of those places," the CIA man said, "and that's where our resources are. But, recent events tell us that Mexico is about to completely destabilize. A drug cartel leader named Hernan Flores has nearly toppled the government. President Roberto Rivera has almost been pushed from power by Flores and this Godesto Cartel. And the country's largest businessman – or at least largest lawful businessman – is about to exit the country, removing his family and all his assets. Our analysts and strategists do not believe the country can survive his departure, so we're offering serious aid."

Nick nodded. "And this aid involves that major dust-up with the Navy SEALs down there and the attack on the Mexican Presidential Palace? The one you just told me about, which I should've seen on the news if I cared enough to watch it?"

"Yes," the CIA man said. "Hernan Flores hurt us badly. Wiped out much of an entire SEAL Team Platoon. He also simultaneously embarrassed and devastated President Roberto Rivera."

"Why not just kill this Flores fellow? How hard can that be?"

"We can't. He's beloved by most Mexicans and he owns several legitimate businesses, including numerous newspapers and TV stations. He's wiped his trail so clean that Rivera's government can't even get a warrant against him. Even if they did, most of the Mexican people would think it was because the President feels threatened by the possibility of Flores running against him."

"Are you sure he's not clean?"

The man looked exasperated. "Of course, we're sure. He runs his operations through several henchmen, who he claims are merely friends. But we're sure that Flores has an extensive network and is behind it all. He completely runs the Godesto."

"I still don't see what the problem is. Why not send down some military task force? Let them simply handle the problem?"

"We already did, remember?" the agent said. "We sent the SEALs. The best we had. And Flores wiped them out and we barely left a mark on him. Not to sound desperate, but the CIA literally lacks the resources to send our own task force down there. Our military units and intelligence assets are deployed all over the globe. We lack the manpower. And even if we had it, the same thing would happen. We'd send a team, the details of their deployment would get leaked, and they'd be dead in no time."

"And you think it'd be different if I went?" Nick asked. "That's the dumbest thing I've ever heard. There's barely an honest cop or merchant in Mexico right now. I'd be dead in no time, as well. Why in the world would I sign up for that? I don't need any money."

"We don't think they'd get you," the agent said. "You've led a hunter-killer team against the Soviet Spetsnaz in a country where you could trust no one. And just a few years ago, you evaded some of our best CIA strike teams for weeks and weeks with almost no external support. You have a nose for danger, unlike anyone we've ever seen. We think you're the best man we have available to go into Mexico."

"You want me to go alone?" Nick asked, nearly incredulous. "That's even more stupid than I thought. Hell, even in Afghanistan, I had a great spotter. Nolan Flynn, remember?"

"Of course I remember," the agent said. "We'd want you to develop a plan and come pitch it to us. You'd lead the effort.

We have the money to make whatever you want to happen, as long as we keep it off the books. And as long as we're not pulling men from our current ranks. The President wants this kept quiet."

"How do I know this isn't some scam?" Nick asked. "Just some trick to get me filleted. And to do so outside the country, at that?"

"If we wanted you dead, even as good as you are, we could have snuffed you out a hundred times by now. Drones. Snipers. Car accidents. Our opportunities have been endless and we haven't done a thing. No one wants you dead, believe me, but I understand after being betrayed so many times that you'll be fighting those demons for years to come."

"Why would I want to do this? You've read my file. I've got a lot of money stored away. I've got my guns. Why do this? I'm forty-seven. A bit old to be throwing myself into another war."

The agent smiled as if he already knew he'd accomplished his mission.

"Two reasons. First, you're bored. You know this. We know this. Secondly, you're a sucker for duty. Our country desperately needs your services and we intend to pay very well. But, it's duty that will eventually win you over. Our country can't allow Hernan Flores and the Godesto Cartel to win. We can't allow them to completely destabilize Mexico. We don't need a Third World country directly on our border and you're the best man for the job."

"You forgot the age thing," Nick said.

"Two years ago, you bested some of the greatest warriors our country had," the agent said. "You might not be ready to play line trooper, but you're fit to lead. You know it. I know it."

Nick turned, thinking about the enormity of it all. He knew they had him. The agent knew, too, and smiled.

"I knew I wouldn't need to tell you this," the CIA man said, "but it comes with a pretty good annual salary."

"I don't need money," Nick said. "Don't even care about it."

"It's two hundred and fifty thousand per year," the agent said. "Not a bad salary really."

"We've talked enough," Nick said. "What's the next step?"

CHAPTER 9

Three days later, Nick sat off to the side of a conference table, which was crowded with mostly men and two women.

An analyst was blabbing on-and-on about the background of the mission. Nick struggled to pay attention. He knew full well that he looked as out of place as a janitor carrying a dripping mop into the well-dressed crowd of a magnificent wedding ceremony.

The people in the room wore expensive suits and ties. He wore jeans, work boots, and a Carhartt duck jacket.

He'd been asked to remove his pistol from under the jacket, but there were some things Nick didn't believe in. Going for even one second without a piece of steel on his side was one of them. Two nervous agents had given up on trying to disarm him, but only because their boss had said it was okay.

Nick didn't know any of the names of the folks around the table. And he didn't care either. They probably didn't give two shits about the country bumpkin off to the side of them, whom they'd all flown down to hear. He was expendable. A tool for them. A piece of meat that would solve a problem. Or maybe not. They probably didn't care. All he'd do in the short term was keep the heat off their backs from on high.

Nick knew where he stood with them and he'd never again make the mistake of thinking that those above him gave two shits about whether he lived or died on some mission in some dirt-poor country. But the missions still needed to be done and someone had to do them. Nick, secretly, still enjoyed the work of actually doing them.

Duty truly was a bitch, and if you were born and raised in the South, you ingested that shit morning, noon, and night.

The truth was that it hadn't been hard to enlist him again

into another insane mission. Nick had no Anne. He had no life. And he missed command. And truth be known, he knew deep down that he was one of the best. One of the most battle-hardened veterans that America had ever produced. Or maybe that was vanity. But it was also the truth.

Besides, if he said "no," they'd send someone else. And that someone else might not be as good. And that someone else would probably have a wife and kids; or maybe a life worth living for. Nick had none of that. He'd go and it hardly mattered if he filled his will out before leaving.

He had no kids. No family. Nothing. It's what happened after you took part in a secret mission for the government and ended up having your death faked.

Truth be known, he barely thought of his surviving family down in Georgia. Even when he did, he had always worried that if he showed up and shocked them by announcing he was actually alive, they could be used as leverage against him by the government. No, better to have no attachments. That had been one of the painful lessons he'd learned after losing Anne.

The truth was that Nick was a cinch for the mission and he'd spent three days in a hotel room and at a local library in nearby Columbia, South Carolina.

Nick had been either brainstorming or conducting research nearly around the clock, limiting himself to four hours sleep per night and surviving on Diet Cokes, Snickers, and too much pizza and Chinese.

Now he felt weak from the marathon, around-the-clock effort, but he felt as alive and content as he'd felt in years. Hell, he felt happy, to be honest. In a perfect state of bliss. An old Samurai who'd been granted a chance to pull his sword one more time and go off to war.

The analyst was still babbling, but he appeared to be coming to the end of his remarks.

"This mission is critical," the analyst continued, "but we've got to keep it off the books. We think our best option is the plan Nick will present to you today. And we think he's the right man to lead this effort. With that, let me introduce you to the legendary Nick Woods."

Folks at the table started clapping. Weird, Nick thought.

Like he was a rock star or something. Nick stood and nodded to the man who had introduced him.

"You can sit down, hoss," Nick said. "I'll take it from here."

A few folks snickered and the man at the head of the table practically fled to his seat.

Nick looked at the man again and said, "I can't figure out if he's trying to date me or sell me a vacuum, but you keep that son of a bitch away from me."

More laughs.

He paused, knowing it was time to get serious. He looked around the table at the CIA bigwigs and analysts who had flown down, renting some high-priced conference room to hear what he had to say. They ranged in age from mid-twenties to high sixties. All looked soft and only one looked like he'd ever carried a weapon before.

Figures, Nick thought. These were the kinds of folks who had been sending men and women off to die for generations. They came from Ivy League schools and knew more about books than ploughs or weapons. Men of the stock Nick came from carried the rifles. Folks of the stock these people came from decided the fate of countries.

"Let's get to it," Nick said. "I'm not here to hear myself talk. And I hope you weren't expecting some kind of PowerPoint presentation."

A couple of folks chuckled.

He shrugged, then continued, "Now, you all described to me the problem of this man named Hernan Flores and the Godesto Carte. I've spent the past few days figuring on how he could be taken down. Out of curiosity, who here knows how we took down the Colombian drug lord Mr. Pablo Escobar, who at one time used to be public enemy number one?"

After ten seconds of silence, one of the men cleared his throat and meekly raised his hand.

"We used triangulation of his phone and radio signals, which he didn't realize we could track. We used everything from fixed sites to a plane flying overhead to make it happen, since the areas he operated in were usually mountainous or urban and densely populated. Wasn't easy, but that's how we finally got him. Triangulation of his radio signals, sir."

A few of the suits at the table smiled and nodded, impressed someone had remembered. That young man would get a promotion someday, Nick thought.

"Partly, you're right," Nick said. "Nice job. But if you remember correctly, all that triangulation stuff was hardly needed after the Colombian people got sick of him. Do you remember the death squads the Colombian people created?"

The man nodded.

"A vigilante group known as Los Pepes, short for Los Perseguidos por Pablo Escobar," the analyst said.

"Wow," Nick said. "Nicely done. For you non-Spanish speaking folks – myself included – that means," Nick looked down at his notecards he'd brought with him and continued, "the people persecuted by Pablo Escobar."

A few people laughed and Nick said, "Yeah, pretty simple name. But the point is the same. This group went after Escobar, his family, and his associates. They went all out. They used propaganda, threats to his associates, and broke numerous laws, same as he was doing. Hell, they even used car bombs, just like terrorists, which also killed some civilians in the process. That's how desperate they were to *finally* be rid of Pablo Escobar. But they basically are the reason why Pablo Escobar had to flee and go into hiding in shitty shanties and apartments, instead of his well-guarded compounds. And once he was on the run, it was only a matter of time before he ended up dead with a bunch of bullet holes in his body."

Nick nodded to the analyst and said, "That was where the triangulation came into play."

The analyst smiled.

Nick flipped to his next notecard. "And it's the same plan first instituted by the Los Pepes that I think could work in Mexico."

Nick explained his proposed plan, quickly summarizing it and answering some questions. Then, he was given a cell phone – somehow they knew he didn't have one.

They seemed to like it, but no commitments were made.

After a few more questions, one of the older men said, "We'll be in touch."

Nick nodded and left the room. He wasn't really sure that

they had bought into his plan, but he thought they had. If nothing else, it bought them time. And he was expendable.

Nick knew where things stood. And he also knew he needed some serious sleep after three nights in a row of barely any sleep.

Let the suits talk, he thought. It'll probably take them a month to make up their mind, the sons of bitches.

CHAPTER 10

But they surprised Nick again. It didn't take them a month, but only two days. That's when Nick Woods's CIA contact called him on the cell phone they had given him. The man on the phone was the same poor bastard from the gas station that Nick had promptly abducted.

The agent reported the mission was a go after Nick's plan had been passed up the chain of command. He also confirmed that Nick would head up the entire op.

"I get to lead it?" Nick asked. He was a tad skeptical of that part, even though he had been promised it. But he wasn't a boot licker, so he still doubted he'd be placed in charge.

"You get to lead it," the man said.

"Then, what's next?" Nick asked from his hotel room. He was wearing PT shorts and was covered in sweat from an intense hour of calisthenics and hand-to-hand – the thought of action had rebirthed his obsessive drive and determination.

"You pick your team," the agent said. "We assumed you'd never stand for us selecting your players, so you get to pick your entire team from top to bottom. It's entirely up to you who you pick. Someone will knock on your door in a few minutes and they'll have three boxes full of candidates. We assumed you'd prefer paper copies to review in your room rather than sitting in a cubicle and looking at a computer screen."

"You know me well," Nick said.

"You have no clue how well we know you," the agent thought, but he kept it to himself to avoid setting off the paranoid Marine. Instead, the agent said, "Don't shoot our man when he knocks on the door."

The knock came just seconds after Nick hung up. Nick

grabbed his pistol and walked over to the door, keeping his .45 down by his leg. A man in a suit, accompanied by two other men in suits, stood in the hall. Nick could see through the peephole that all three were carrying concealed weapons under their jackets. And the one in the middle balanced an overloaded dolly stacked to the top with legal boxes full of files.

Nick opened the door and the middle man wheeled the files into the room and then left with a nod. Nick noticed a look of respect from all three men and wondered if they had been told of Nick's new leadership position with the organization? O maybe these men knew of his past?

Either way, he figured it didn't matter. He bolted the door shut behind them and slid the chain in place.

With the door secure, Nick placed his pistol on the bed and walked to the fridge. He grabbed a can of Diet Coke and popped it open. He swallowed some down and unstacked the boxes off the dolly.

He pulled the cover off a random one and pulled out the first file he came to. He glanced at it and noticed a photo and probably twenty pages of information. He grabbed another one. It was the same, as were the next couple.

With that, he grabbed his phone and called the agent back.

"Yes?" the man said.

"Tell me about these files," Nick said.

"What about them?"

"I need to know how this will go down. I don't want to spend hours picking a team and end up with a dozen men who either aren't interested or haven't pulled any real duty for years."

"You'll be pleased to know," the agent said, "that every man and woman in those files have not only indicated a willingness to go on a top secret mission – the details of which were never shared with them – but they also agreed to fly to a training base and perform a recent assessment. And in the two days since we talked, while we waited on folks up in headquarters to sign off on you leading this mission, every person attached to a file in those boxes conducted a PT test and re-qualified on the range, with both pistol and rifle. All fitness and weapons scores listed in those files are from literally yesterday. The folks in those files folders are the best men and women we could find, who weren't already deployed."

Nick looked at the file boxes and imagined how much it must have cost to contact and then fly that many people to a location to be tested. He guessed there must be three hundred files in the boxes.

"You flew three hundred out for an assessment?" Nick asked. "That must have cost a ton."

"The cost matters little. We're talking about an entire country in duress. And who knows what kind of long-term effect it might create on our country if President Rivera's government falls? Old fitness scores would have been worthless, either to you or some other leader, had headquarters not signed off on you to lead this mission. Regardless of who was picked to head this up, all active operatives would have needed to be assembled and tested. It doesn't matter how good you were a year ago. It's all about what you can do now."

Nick considered what he'd just heard. It was still a little overwhelming. Being picked as a mission commander. Seeing the three men at the door, who were probably at this very moment helping guard him from some vehicle outside.

And now deciding who would be a part of the team. It was a lot to take in. And certainly too good to be true for an old warhorse who'd been bored out of his mind a few days ago, just driving the country.

"I'll call you the moment I've finalized my selections," Nick said. "Speaking of which, can you get me some pizza and more Diet Coke up in here? Maybe a salad, too. I need to start watching my carbs if I'm going to be sitting in this hotel for much longer. Looks like I'm in for a long night."

"You won't be sitting there long," the contact said. "We'll have you meeting your team soon."

Nick finalized his system for picking his team just minutes

after cramming down the majority of his new pizza, which was once again delivered by pistol-toting guys in suits.

Nick had gone over in his head a dozen times or more how he would want this to go down if he earned the chance to lead the effort, but now that he had it, he was less certain.

It was like running an op. You could never be too sure.

Nick scrutinized his plan from every angle, looking for a weakness, and still fell short of seeing any. So, with a full stomach and renewed confidence, along with some country music playing in the background off a cheap, ten-dollar alarm clock, Nick got down to work.

He sorted the files into two different stacks. One stack was made up of possible leadership material – men who were older and had served at least ten years. The other stack, which was a much larger pile and probably three-quarters of the files, involved younger, less-experienced men.

Nick ignored the big pile of straight shooters and focused on the leadership stack. He read and reviewed the files for hours, breaking up the monotony with sets of push-ups, sit-ups, and dry-fire shooting drills. He narrowed the stack of sixty-seven leadership files down to twenty, but no matter how many times he reviewed them, he could screen them down no lower.

He could find no weaknesses, no hints of buried problems, nothing wrong with these individuals. These men appeared solid, but Nick needed to whittle them down to just four men. He finally gave up. He rubbed his forehead, stacked the files, and looked at the clock. It was 3:18 in the morning, so Nick stood and decided to call it a night.

He'd call his contact in the morning and interview the twenty men by phone – or preferably in person if he could. He texted his contact asking if it was possible to do so and was surprised to get an immediate answer.

Maybe the guy didn't sleep? Or maybe the CIA had a duty officer who monitored the phone? Either way, Nick was told that he could interview the men and that he should be ready to leave the hotel at seven.

Nick awoke at six, showered, and called room service to bring up some eggs and bacon for breakfast. He put on a tight T-shirt, a clean pair of Wranglers, and his work boots. He followed that by stuffing his trusty Kimber .45 into a holster, strapping his back-up revolver on his ankle, and pulling a loose, button-up, long-sleeve shirt on to cover the pistol tucked in his hip holster. By seven, he was packed and carrying his duffel bag out the door.

Two men in suits were waiting in the hallway.

"We'll take that, sir," one of them said, reaching for the duffel bag.

"The hell you will," Nick said, yanking it back.

"Sir?" the man said.

"Don't 'sir' me either," Nick said. It was time to stop this "sir" bullshit, as he should have earlier. "You 'sir' me again and I'll knock your teeth down your damn throat."

Nick's contact came around the corner, hurrying toward them, dressed in a suit, as well. Nick wondered if any of the men owned anything other than suits.

"Nick," his contact said, "please let the men carry your duffel bag. You have an image to project. You're a task force commander now, not just some knuckle-dragging sergeant in the Corps."

"If you want a man who's willing to let someone else carry his gear, you folks done picked the wrong man. Now, which is it? You need to go back to the drawing board and find you another man to lead these boys? Or are you going to let me carry my bag?"

Nick had a stubborn, unmoving look on his face. And he was pretty sure he wasn't bluffing. He needed to control from this moment forward. His contact relented and turned to walk down the hall.

"You win," the man said. "Let's go."

Nick followed the CIA contact, with the two armed men falling in behind them. Nick felt uncomfortable with the guys acting as security, as if he were suddenly the President or something, but he knew he'd adjust to it eventually.

"Where we going?" Nick asked.

"They're going to drive you to the airport. We're flying you to Camp Lejeune. It's where the entire group is assembled."

"Good, but no need to drive me. I can drive myself, just like I can carry my own gear. My vehicle is parked at the side."

"I'm afraid it's not an option," the contact said. "Besides maintaining your image as task force commander, you also will be getting a police escort to the airport. I don't expect your driver to drop below eighty or ninety on the whole trip. This entire mission is time critical. And the plane is already warmed up and ready to go."

"What's the rush?" Nick asked. "This sounds ominous."

"It is," the contact said. "Your timetable has been moved up. Actually, make that moved *way* up."

"What gives?"

"President Roberto Rivera is begging our Ambassador for support and our intel says billionaire and good guy Juan Soto will rest easier when more Americans begin arriving. Even if it's only in small numbers, it will help reassure them. Don't forget how much unrest continues down there after the attack on the Presidential Palace. We've been screwing around up here for weeks while promising Rivera all kinds of support. Needless to say, Rivera's patience is wearing thin and our words are starting to ring hollow."

"He needs to put his big-boy britches on," Nick said.

"Too late for that, and respectfully, if you had lost as many men as he had, you'd be shaken, too. Remember, they went after him and his family while he was in his own protected compound. Not to mention how many of his forces they killed, plus wiping out that SEAL Team Platoon."

"Go ahead and get to whatever point you're trying to make," Nick said.

"The point is that our government has assured him that our first elements will arrive in three days. So again, the timetable has been pushed way up."

Nick stopped, realization finally starting to dawn on him on what had just been said.

"Wait. What the hell did you just say?" he asked.

"Our timetable has been moved up. We need to get our advance element on the ground in three days."

"What happened to me picking my men? What happened to the whole 'this mission being a national priority' thing? You're setting us up to fail before we even start."

"You know how the government works, Nick. And you're good enough to make this happen. We just need a few men to arrive in three days. They can just begin scoping things out. And in doing so, they'll get President Rivera and Juan Soto to calm down. We've told them help is on the way and they need so see that help."

"Unbelievable," Nick said.

"I'm sorry," the man said. "But we need to get moving. The plane is waiting and the clock is ticking."

CHAPTER 11

Nick Woods's contact dropped another surprise on him after he arrived at Camp Lejeune, North Carolina; the massive base that was home to the 2nd Marine Division and thirty thousand Marines.

Nick had been flown to Lejeune on a white corporate jet, where a few more suits were waiting on him by another black SUV.

Escorted by a local police department cruiser, the two vehicles raced into Jacksonville and approached the front gate of Camp Lejeune. The cruiser pulled off and headed back toward town, while the Marine MP checked some paperwork produced by Nick's driver. The MP waved them through and they proceeded to their destination.

Nick's contact had tensed up – Nick was learning to read the man.

"What gives?" Nick asked. "You're not nervous are you?"

The contact didn't answer, keeping his gaze out the window. Trees lined the road, but they weren't much to look at. Nick knew the man wasn't simply watching the woods.

"Go ahead and say it," Nick said. "I can tell something's bothering you."

"There's one more thing I have to tell you," the contact said. And he didn't meet Nick's eyes when he said it, keeping his head still turned away. Nick had come to realize that the man was a nice guy and that he respected Nick (maybe even admired him), so things had gotten complicated for the CIA contact. After all, the man was forced to play middle man between the Agency and Nick.

None of these surprises were new to Nick. He knew it was the job of the idiots in charge to constantly interfere, throw curve balls your way, and basically do all they could to keep you from succeeding, while doing everything they could do to cover their own ass in the process. Not that they meant to. It's just how it always happened with large bureaucracies.

The folks in charge wanted to avoid risks and owning responsibility for any screw ups. The folks at the bottom emphasized trying to stay alive and accomplishing the mission. Usually, the goals from up high and down below conflicted. Big time.

A good example was rules of engagement. Folks way up the chain wanted tight rules of engagement. No accidents. No dead civilians. But if you were the man leading the platoon or walking point on a patrol, you wanted looser rules of engagement.

"Go ahead and say it," Nick said.

"The unit you're leading is no longer going as a task force from our government," the contact said. "The unit is going as a private company."

"What do you mean? Like some kind of security corporation?"

"Yes. Precisely."

"Which means we're completely fucked if anything bad happens. If any of us are taken hostage, we're not CIA agents, who our government will negotiate for. We're just wannabe cowboys down there on our own."

"We said in the beginning," the contact said with a sigh, finally looking at Nick, "that the President wanted complete, plausible deniability. This will assure it."

"This charade wouldn't pass the smell test of even a local cop checking into it. Just where exactly did the 'great' Nick Woods get millions of dollars to form a company and hire dozens of people for this contract with the Mexican government?"

The contact looked over at him and said, "You've been awarded a twenty-million-dollar loan as part of your veteran benefits package. You presented a business plan for an SBA loan, which we typed up for you. It's been submitted and I'm happy to say you were approved today."

"So, on top of putting my ass on the line, I'm now twenty

million dollars in debt?" Nick asked, raising his voice. "That puts that annual salary of two hundred and fifty thousand per year in perspective, doesn't it?"

"No, effective today, you've been awarded a twenty-two-million-dollar contract from the Mexican government for consulting and security services. If you want to get technical about it, you've earned a two-million-dollar bonus over what we promised you a few days ago."

"I'll bet the American government just approved an emergency loan to the Mexican President?"

"Yes. It's a contingency, anti-drug grant signed by the President this morning."

Nick shook his head in disgust.

"All this bullshit loophole crap just to keep the President's ass out of a sling?"

"It's an election year, Nick. And all the personnel, as well as yourself, will receive the same salary and benefit packages you were originally promised. Basically, nothing changes."

"Yeah, basically nothing changes except if something bad happens, there won't be anyone to come and get us. The media will barely notice since they don't give two shits about private security companies operating in foreign countries. And don't forget, I'm suddenly an officer of a corporation and can be individually sued."

"We'd cover any legal fees."

"Sure you would, hoss. You all won't take credit for us if we do something good or something bad, but you'll ante up and help us defend ourselves in court if we get sued for civil damages. I doubt that. The opposition would have deposition powers and would see straight through this little charade you're creating."

"I'm sorry, Nick, but this is the deal on the table. We will worry about litigation if that happens, when it happens. We could always fly you to Britain or somewhere."

"So I'm losing my citizenship, too? Quite a deal I'm signing up for here. My old red Cherokee and a long, slow drive across the country is looking better and better now."

The contact said nothing.

Nick looked off and sighed. Then a thought crossed his

mind.

"I've been watching you. You haven't talked with anyone or taken any phone calls since we left Columbia. Why are you just now telling me this? That's quite the asshole move."

The man broke eye contact again and stammered, finally saying with complete embarrassment, "We felt if we waited to tell you this when you were just minutes away from meeting the troops, that you'd be more likely to accept the new reality."

The SUV had been taking a number of turns while Nick and the contact argued. It pulled up to an isolated barracks, where more than three hundred people were milling about. The candidates were in battle dress camouflage uniforms, with boots and boonie covers; no patches or identifying names or ranks.

"Those are my candidates, aren't they?" Nick asked, completely disgusted now.

"Yes."

"So, if I say 'no' now, I'm going to look like a bitch to every one of them? A quitter and a drama queen, right in front of the men."

"You still have both the option and right to turn this down. We're hoping you'll still accept the offer. Really, not much has changed. We'll even have an aide do all the corporate reports, put up a small company website, and help make this all look legit. We even have a name for it: Shield, Safeguard, and Shelter. Or S3, for short."

Nick threw his door open as hard as he could and looked at his contact, whose name he still didn't know, and said with a scowl, "Is there any other fucking thing you need to tell me? I've tolerated about as many surprises today as I plan to."

"There are none," the contact said. "I promise."

"Yeah, and your promises carry a lot of weight."

"I disagreed with waiting to tell you," the contact said. "I was ordered to handle it this way."

"You broke your trust with me, so save your whiny-ass excuses. You're no damn different than the rest of them."

That looked like it hurt, the contact dropping his head in shame.

Nick grabbed his duffel bag and slammed the door shut as

hard as he could. The big SUV rocked, despite its weight and armor.

All of the candidates were now looking at him and conversations across the barracks courtyard had stopped. A few pointed. The vehicle, and the grand entrance, had grabbed their attention. Probably also the fact that they had been there for two days doing all kinds of testing while this late arrival clearly implied he wasn't in the same boat as them.

This man wasn't another candidate. He was their leader, they quickly guessed.

Nick walked six feet away from the black SUV and stood straight, head held high, chest pushed out, eyes measuring and studying the people in the square.

He was in blue jeans and work boots, so he hoped none of the folks were expecting a man in a suit.

He threw his duffle bag to the ground, looking disgusted, and then with a scoff and a look of derision, yelled out, "Pull it in close. And don't take your time about it."

The clusters of people closed in, forming the half circle so commonly found in military units. Those in the front squatted. Those in the back stood.

"Listen up and pay attention," Nick said. "I'm only going to say all of this one time. Name's Nick Woods. I'm the man in charge here and some of you are going to be lucky enough to go on a nice little hunting trip with me. Rest of you will be changing diapers and cleaning gutters. Or whatever the hell you do when you're back home."

A few people laughed tentatively.

The ranks pulled in a little closer. Nick could tell he was making an impression and embraced the moment. There was an intoxicating high that came from being in command. From having men watch your every move, looking for weakness. Or inspiration. It all depended on the leader and Nick hadn't felt this thrill for far too long.

"Now," Nick continued, his voice growing bolder and more confident. "I can't say where we're going on this here hunting trip until the final team members are selected, and it's obviously classified until then, but I *can* tell you they speak Spanish, it's to our south, and it involves drug cartels."

Nick paused.

"Of course, that could be just about any country to our south."

Several people laughed harder and Nick saw one guy nudge another man with an elbow and a smile. Nick made a note of his face and tried to memorize it.

"I'm telling you now." He paused for effect. "The folks we're going to tangle with? They're meaner than hell. They're poor and don't have a lot to live for. And they're really well equipped. We'll be out-numbered, we'll be on their turf, and they'll know our every move – damn near every person down there will be sharing our location and activity to the cartel. Some out of fear. Some for money. And probably damn few of them even like Americans. We're kind of loud assholes compared to the rest of the world. Can't even say I blame them. "

Nick paused to stare down a few of the people around him. He continued, "I'm here to tell you. There are going to be a bunch of us who don't come home, so leave now if you have much to live for. Me? I don't have a damn thing to live for, so I'll be leading from the front. You can bet your ass on that.

"But I ain't got time for no babysitting and if I catch anyone in the corner crying and feeling sorry for themselves in the middle of a nasty firefight, I'll shoot you myself. I'm not kidding on that point and I'm not kidding about how dangerous it's going to be.

"My number one priority will be accomplishing this mission. I will achieve this or I'll die trying. My number two priority is bringing home as many men as possible, so if you're hunkered down in the middle of a firefight, then you're not helping us achieve either priority number one or priority number two. And for that, they used to shoot men. Used to call it cowardice. Or dereliction of duty. Some shit like that. I'm not much of a book man."

More people laughed.

"Whatever it's called, it doesn't matter. You hunker down like a coward while we're in the middle of the shit, and I am telling you right now that I will shoot your ass. I might shoot the ground in front of you first, but you need to be more scared of me than you are of the enemy.

"As Americans, we've gotten soft the past hundred years or so, but I'm old school, and being old school has pulled my ass out of some places where I wasn't supposed to make it out of. And where we're going, there won't be any outside observers."

Nick looked the crowd over with the icy eyes of a man who'd killed dozens of men. The men he saw were a bunch of hard-asses. He could tell. And yet still many of them broke away from his gaze. Maybe he still had, forty-seven or not.

Nick was tougher than rawhide leather and he didn't intend to back down from a single man in the square. And he for damn sure didn't intend to have to use rank to keep the men in line. He didn't stay sharp on all of his hand-to-hand stuff for nothing.

Having made his point with his steely, cold look, he finished by booming, "When I walk away from here in a few seconds, if you're having any second thoughts, just head on home. Nobody will hold it against you. Hell, it's the smart move. There's going to be a lot of us die, and you guys have been around long enough to know that there isn't anyone in America who's going to give a shit when we do."

He looked the group over again and said, "Whoever decides to stay, I'll be interviewing some of you in a bit."

Nick took a final look at the men who had pushed furthest forward.

"Who's in charge here?" he asked.

No one said anything.

"I said," Nick continued, raising his voice louder, "who the fuck's in charge here?"

Some of the group looked down, while five or six looked toward a big, black man standing near Nick. Nick, who stood a very lean 5'11," guessed this man to be 6'2." And besides the height, he carried loads of thick muscle. A definite bodybuilder, but not the biggest man in the plaza, Nick had already seen. There were some big boys in the group.

"Are you Marcus?" Nick asked.

"Yes, sir," the man said.

It hadn't been that hard to guess Marcus correctly. The man named "Marcus" had stood out in Nick's mind as he reviewed the leadership files. None of his files had the actual names of the operators – just their nicknames.

Nick figured Marcus would be the natural leader of the entire group, having reached the rank of gunnery sergeant in the Marine Corps, while also having done a three-year stint as a drill instructor at Parris Island, South Carolina. Parris Island was the bastion of discipline and hell, which consistently forged some of America's greatest warriors.

Marcus had been a football standout at the University of Florida – a ferocious middle linebacker and team captain, who most analysts pegged as a guaranteed first-round pick in the NFL, should he leave at the end of his junior year. And he'd have certainly been a first-round pick if he waited until after his senior year and remained injury-free.

Instead, the massive event that would come to be known as September 11 intervened and Marcus dropped out of college and walked straight into the Marine Corps recruiting station. His dad had been a Marine, so it was the natural thing to do.

Marcus had done several tours in Afghanistan and Iraq as a rifleman, then squad leader, and then platoon sergeant before heading to the drill field to become a drill instructor.

Marcus had the size, charisma, and intelligence to be an officer, but his records indicated he turned down offer after offer from his superiors to go to Officer Candidate School. His file quoted him as saying he'd rather be behind a rifle on the line than in the rear behind a map.

Nick pointed toward the men who had looked at Marcus when Nick had asked who was in charge.

"Those men say you're in charge," Nick said.

"They didn't put anyone in charge when we arrived," Marcus said. "I led some exercises, a couple of runs, and settled some disputes. I'm happy to lead, but I'm betting you're not looking for leaders. I'm betting you're looking for trigger pullers instead. So," Marcus said, stepping forward, pointing his finger at Nick, and coming across as intimidating as anything Nick had seen in awhile, "mark me down as nothing but a rifleman and pick me to go. You won't regret it."

Nick instantly liked Marcus. While Marcus held the rank of

gunny in the Marine Corps, his file stated that the man had grown tired of the politics of the upper-echelon ranks, which had led him to apply to the CIA. Now, even at the age of thirty-three, Marcus had the build and tough look of a hard-nosed sergeant, not some older gunny beaten down by hard deployments.

Marcus hadn't allowed the higher rank and increased benefits to soften him, like so many others had.

"Congrats," Nick said, reaching out his hand. "You made the team. Now step over here and talk to me alone."

Nick walked with Marcus a good thirty feet from the men. Nick stopped and angled around so that he could see the crowd, leaving Marcus's back to them. Nick didn't want the men to hear what Marcus would say.

"I need your help," Nick said. "We don't have much time. In fact, we need to have some men land in Mexico in just a few days – our timetable got pushed forward that much – so I'm not going to be able to interview and test the men the way I'd want. Hell, we're barely going to have time to even train together."

"I understand," Marcus said, "but I'm still in. How can I help?"

"I need to know who you'd pick if you were in my shoes," Nick said. "You've been with the men for two days or more, and while I've studied their files, you've been around them, so I'd like to lean heavily on your recommendations."

"They're all a solid group, but I've noticed some standouts," Marcus said.

And with that, Marcus began discussing some of the superstars he'd seen. And just like that, the early skeleton of the unit that would eventually become known as Shield, Safeguard, and Shelter was born. S3 might have been born prematurely, but Nick intended to make sure it survived its hasty formation and birth.

CHAPTER 12

Hernan Flores paced behind his desk. Things were going well, and he knew he shouldn't be pacing, but it was hard not to be a bit antsy when you had a meeting set up with the Butcher.

Flores had been working with the Butcher for nearly five years now and the crazy little bastard still made him uneasy. Flores had brought him on board once he was already a force worth fearing. Once he was already a force worth owning.

Legend had it that the Butcher – no one knew his name (or at least spoke of it) – started like most Mexican youth: broke, discouraged, and underfed.

A small boy, he was bullied from the beginning and soon fell into the wrong crowd. He got arrested and sent to prison for theft and grand larceny of a vehicle at the age of sixteen. While in prison, the Butcher learned there were far worse things than being harassed and bullied by older, fellow gang members.

Such a small man, and lacking any cartel connections or protection behind bars, he was beaten and regularly sexually assaulted. Even as he took to weights and tried to defend himself, he discovered he was too small to add enough muscle to win any fights with force. None of the boxing or punches he tried to teach himself proved effective.

Discharged six years later, and knowing that he would eventually end up in prison again with his career path, he dove headlong into martial arts; something that wouldn't discriminate against his small size. Something that would actually be even more powerful *because* of his small size and speed. Fueled by the painful memories of so many nasty sexual assaults, he threw himself into karate. He studied it. Practiced it. Honed it.

When he wasn't stealing or selling drugs, he was obsessively pursuing the skills of the fighting arts. And not just karate – he branched off into dozens of styles. And while he developed skill, he never achieved the peace and enlightenment so many usually gained from it. He had been bullied, beaten, and raped too many times for that.

The Butcher wasn't seeking peace. He was seeking fire. Molten flame that would burn to the ground the many tormentors that still lived in his nightmares each night.

Once his newly-acquired martial arts skills reached a high enough level, the Butcher started hunting. He had a long list of every single person who had raped or backed him down. The rapes were bad enough, but he bore a deep shame from all the times he had been backed down by bigger, meaner inmates; times he had been too afraid to even fight back or stand up to them.

That shame was too much. No one would ever bully or back down again the short little man who would soon be called the Butcher. With his list in hand, the Butcher tracked down every single man who had made his list. Any man who had been released from prison, who had attacked or backed down the Butcher, was now dead.

In every case, he had used his martial arts skills and his affinity for a blade to kill the men. Sometimes, it was a full-sized Samurai sword. Other times, it was a short tanto blade about half the length of the full-sized blade.

Not that he was opposed to gun work; he knew they were necessary, and he certainly was practiced with them, as well, but he simply preferred blades and the fear they put into someone. Also, he loved how long he could draw out someone's death with a blade.

He didn't cut off limbs or drive the blade through a man's body, even though he easily could. No, he extended things, with short, fast cuts. He could cut and slice strike after strike, as the fear and panic grew on his opponent's face.

He lived for cutting a man as many times as possible. He had gotten so good that he could go as much as sixty or eighty times, watching them progress from resistance, to sheer terror, to submission, to begging for mercy, tears and shrieks of pain and fear bouncing off alley walls for blocks and blocks. Not that mercy was ever given. He was the Butcher, after all, and his heart and desire for mercy had been crushed under the weight of quite a few three-hundred-pound men.

No one messed with the Butcher. He was unstable, easily provoked, and completely sick in the head. He enjoyed hurting people and lived to practice new fighting techniques on people. Especially bare-handed karate moves intended to only be used as a last resort.

Kicks to the knee, watching the effects of a hyperextended leg. Swordhand strikes to the neck, hearing an opponent gasp desperately for air from a crushed larynx. Hand strikes to the eyes, feeling the soft tissue tear under the steel-like pressure of his hardened fingers.

Hernan Flores hated even thinking about the Butcher. He continued his pacing and took a swig of Jack Daniel's. He knew he should kill the Butcher (and soon), but the man was so valuable to the Godesto Cartel that it was hard to do. Under Flores's tutelage, he had gone from a psycho, who lived on minor drug sales and stolen valuables, to a hired hitman, good with a gun and blade.

Flores had asked for four of his best bodyguards to be at this meeting instead of the typical two, but it wouldn't matter. The Butcher would be armed and Flores sure as hell wasn't going to try to disarm him again. He had tried that once inadvertently and the results had been disastrous.

It happened the first time Flores and the Butcher were to meet. As was standard procedure, Flores's guard at the front door of his massive eight-story building had tried to take the man's weapons from him – no one entered the building to see the cartel leader without being checked and disarmed. It was standard procedure.

The bodyguard – a huge man, who had been a former cop fired for excessive force – carried a pistol under his jacket. The man also had an AK leaning in a closet, but he hadn't seen any threat worth taking seriously with the small man before them. So though his partner was in the bathroom – they usually manned the door in pairs – and though sixty more men were on call and could have been there in sixty seconds, the bodyguard decided to handle this little runt himself.

Partly, he was bored. Partly, he was overconfident. Partly, he didn't want to be seen as weak by calling for help from upstairs. So, the bodyguard decided to handle it himself.

Unfortunately, he hadn't been warned about who was arriving, which turned out to be a big oversight by Flores.

The guard noticed the black duffle bag the little man carried, and while the man looked unarmed with his tight black T-shirt and loose-fitting, black karate pants, complete with thin-soled martial arts shoes, the guard knew a weapon could be concealed in the heavy-looking bag. And so the guard had walked around the tall desk to check out the mysterious man after confirming the man had an appointment with Flores.

The small man – built like a gymnast and not a bodybuilder – had stepped back and said, "I'm not going upstairs or even another foot inside this building without this bag and the weapons it contains. This is Flores's headquarters and I have no idea why he has summoned me, so I'm not going without this duffle bag. But I'm just one man, and I'm coming at Flores's request, so I hardly think I'm a threat."

"It's standard policy," the guard said, bored, but with a bit of attitude creeping into his voice. He moved toward the little man.

The Butcher took another step back to keep his distance and said, "I'm sure it is your policy, but I'm not comfortable with it, and I decline to be disarmed. And again, I am here at Flores's request."

"Listen here you little shit," the guard said, stepping forward again. "If you think your karate and your fancy karate shoes can help here, you're sorely mistaken."

"Last warning," the Butcher said, taking one final step in retreat, his back now against a wall.

The guard had fought plenty of guys this man's size. Sure, most knew martial arts, but the guard knew a fair amount as well. He had learned some as a cop. And he knew as long as he avoided several joint locks and arm breaks, while also protecting his groin, throat, and his eyes, he'd be fine.

He'd manhandle this little shit and not only get rid of some pent-up stress, but also break up a job that had increasingly become too boring for him. Of late, the guard was increasingly missing his days of being out on the street and messing people up for Flores (while wearing a badge, half the time).

The guard reached for the Butcher with both arms, cautious to avoid any arm-break attempts. But the wannabe karate kid simply dropped the duffle bag, seemingly surprised. The guard gripped the man by the shoulders and was in the process of slinging him across the room into the other wall when he heard the sound of metal scraping against plastic.

The guard recognized the distinctive sound of a blade being unsheathed from a scabbard. And then the guard felt the sharp pain of a slice between his legs. He looked down to see a full-sized Samurai katana blade rip up in a sweeping arc, from between his legs, just as the pain of having his entire manhood slit open hit him with a sickening shock.

He screamed in pain and grabbed himself, witnessing more blood than he'd ever seen in his life explode out of his gashed-open suit pants. And bent over, trying to stop the bleeding – and going into complete shock as he imagined the damage to his manhood – he never saw the Butcher step to the side and swing the blood-covered katana in a full circular arc down. The blade struck him on the back of his neck at more than sixty miles per hour, landing with an immense amount of power. Without an ounce of trouble, the blade severed the guard's head right off at the base of the neck.

The Butcher watched it fall and roll, the blade still held in both hands, blood running down the length of the blade into a growing pool. The Butcher had entered his own personal Zen state; the moment of death. It was something he lived for, even if it only lasted a millisecond. Once it ended, life stress returned. But for that one precious moment, time stopped.

And then time returned. The guard's body fell hard onto the ground and the Butcher ran both sides of his bloody sword along the back of the guard's suit to get the long blade mostly clean. He sheathed the blade and replaced it in the bag, yanking out an Uzi and looking behind him to see if more guards were entering the lobby, rushing in as backup.

Seeing it was clear, he placed the Uzi back in the duffle

bag and exited the building, hailing a cab as if he hadn't just beheaded a man. Flores smiled as he recalled the taped footage of the slaughter.

He had watched the entire event dozens of times, pausing the silent video as the Butcher reached into a hidden sleeve of the duffel bag, where the sword scabbard was apparently stored in some kind of special pouch in the bag.

In the video, the guard had barely flinched before the surprise upward swing struck the man's groin. And then Flores recalled the splendid side-step and downward arc of the blade into the back of the guard's neck.

It had been sheer artistry and Flores had been captivated by it for weeks. It was like a real-life martial arts movie in HD, with the best special effects ever.

Perhaps the best part was that the Butcher had made Flores wait a full three months before agreeing to meet again. He'd ignored the repeated calls (and demands) of Flores's aides. He'd ignored the personal calls Flores made himself. He'd even turned down a number of gifts that Flores's men had delivered to his home, including a gold, 24-karat AK-74.

The Butcher had ignored (and stood up to) the Godesto Cartel. To Hernan Flores himself. Who, in their right mind, was that crazy? The truth was that no one in their right mind was that crazy. The Butcher wasn't in his right mind. The man was a sociopath. Or a psycho. Or something along those lines.

Flores had been top dog for so long that he had been intrigued by this man who ignored his power. It was absolutely suicidal. And also, well, interesting. Flores hadn't had anyone stand up to him for years.

Flores had come up from the lowest footsoldier to the leader of the Godesto. Back then, there had been six cartels and the Godesto was easily the weakest of the six. And Flores had risen to the top of the Godesto, built it up, and even managed to make it the most powerful cartel. These days, there were only three cartels; not six.

Even better, the Godesto was more than twice as powerful as the second most powerful cartel. Flores was in a truce currently with both it and the only other surviving cartel. So the challenge five years ago by the Butcher – to both kill one of

Flores's men and then ignore his messages to meet – had been interesting to Flores.

Flores's aides begged Flores to have the man killed – either blown to bits in a drive-by massacre or taken alive and slowly tortured for weeks and months.

But Flores wanted this man on his team. Anyone could kill with a gun, but this man had panache. He had guts. He lacked fear. He was a psycho. The best kind.

Flores reached for his glass of Jack Daniel's. He took a large swallow – far more than he meant – and slammed his glass down. My, what a difference five years had made.

The Butcher had gone from his golden boy, a superb hitman who acted as some kind of ninja-like assassin, to a right-hand man. The two had worked together well for a while, but Flores had heard that the Butcher had begun undermining Flores behind his back. Flores had heard that the Butcher thought Mexico's most powerful cartel leader was weak. That Flores was too concerned with his public image and women and money and food. Food, damn it! The Butcher had said Flores was fat!

Flores swallowed the rest of his drink and slammed the glass down so hard that this time, it cracked. Flores had conceived, planned, and executed one of the most horrific attacks in Mexican history and now this short little shit saw him as fat and soft. Nothing but a drunkard and sex addict, as he had heard his informers pass along to him.

Flores slung his cracked glass across the desk into the floor. He walked to grab another. He filled it half and half with Jack and Coke and took another swallow. How could the Butcher not give him credit for what he'd done?

His men had ambushed and decimated a Navy SEAL team that had been hunting down and harassing the Godesto. Flores had been planning this ambush for weeks, and once again, perfect intel, evil cunning, and brutal force had won the day.

You didn't build the most powerful cartel in Mexico or take down a SEAL team or strike brutally at the President while he's inside his own compound if you were soft. Flores couldn't deny the sex addiction or the fat remarks, but damn it, he was a great cartel leader. And the people loved him. Thought he was completely innocent. How could the Butcher not see the pure genius of how Flores had positioned himself.

Hell, he had the potential to become both Mexico's most powerful cartel leader *and* president of the country. Flores was so close. Oh so close.

Flores walked over to a desk drawer and pulled out a bag of Funyuns. He grabbed several out and shoved them into his mouth. He washed the chips down with a big swallow of Jack and Coke, nearly finishing off the glass, which would be his third of the day. It wasn't even two o'clock yet. He needed to slow down.

Flores ignored this thought; he knew he wasn't an alcoholic. He was just under a lot of stress. Stress that a mere hitman and number two like the Butcher couldn't possibly imagine.

Flores grabbed three more Funyuns, shoved them down, and threw the nearly empty bag in the drawer. Christ, I have to stop drinking and eating so much, he thought. He burped, leaned forward, and moved his big frame toward his bar to pour himself a new Jack and Coke.

Flores took a long drink and smiled. Damn, it felt good. Up in his eight-story building, he wondered what Rivera and Soto were thinking right now. Stupid idealists, Flores thought. How they possibly thought they could stand up to the three remaining cartels, which operated under Flores's command, was beyond him.

But, President Rivera and Mr. Goody-Good billionaire Juan Soto were not immediate concerns. For now, Flores needed to focus on the Butcher, who'd be arriving at any moment. Or he should be.

The little asshole was supposed to have arrived twenty minutes ago, Flores noticed, glancing at the clock on the wall. Oh, that little shit... He was pulling one of his power moves.

The Butcher made his way up to Flores's office. He had four of Flores's guards around him in the elevator, but he wasn't scared. He knew he intimidated the shit out of them. He had enough martial arts skills to disarm and kill each of these men with no problem. Plus, under his straining arm, he had his duffle bag with all his weapons in it.

These men were barely a threat to him. He knew it. They knew it.

The elevator arrived at the top floor and they moved toward Flores's corner office. The Butcher smiled at Flores's busty secretary and walked with the four guards past two more armed sentries, who opened the doors for them. The Butcher noticed the heavier-than-usual security and smiled. The old man was letting his fear really show.

Hernan Flores waited behind his desk, and the Butcher knew the man had been pacing. The old Flores used to make a habit of forcing the Butcher to wait outside his office. Sometimes for fifteen or twenty minutes, appointment or not.

Now, the situation had turned. The Butcher walked straight in, late or not.

Yes, the Butcher thought, looking at the fat man before him. Indeed, this man had fallen far. Even in near total victory over the Mexican government, at what should have been the height of his power, Flores appeared soft and weak, both physically and mentally. It was as if the man's ascent to the pinnacle of power had exhausted and drained him.

Flores may be on the cusp of victory, but he was crawling across the finish line. Ready to be put out of his misery and the Butcher was just the man to do it.

The Butcher remembered a quote from Alexander the Great, which he completely accepted as truth. The quote was, "An army of sheep led by a lion is better than an army of lions led by a sheep."

The Butcher was the lion. Just the man the Godesto and the Mexican government needed.

The Butcher inspected the man who'd gone from a suave middle-aged man to a fat, dumpy grandpa. The Butcher noticed crumbs on the shirt of Flores's protruding stomach and he knew that Flores had been eating his favorite food prior to his arrival.

He'd probably just eaten an entire bag of Funyuns, the Butcher thought. And by the look of his flushed, red face, he'd probably drunk enough to get three men wasted.

The Butcher put aside his repulsive feelings toward Flores and got down to the point of the meeting.

"Have you made up your mind about the attack?" the Butcher asked. "I've had two additional sources confirm that the president will be there. He will be vulnerable and we can take him down."

Flores smiled and sat down in his chair. The Butcher never changed. He always acted how he fought – straightforward, economical, and aggressive.

"Would you like something to drink," Flores asked, "before we get started? Why don't you have a seat?"

"No, we need to move quickly if we're going to pull off this attack," the Butcher said.

"Ah, yes, the attack," Flores said, turning and looking out over the capital city of Mexico as he swallowed down more Jack and Coke. He wondered how to explain an elaborate, grand strategy to a simpleton such as this man.

Yes, it was true that an opportunity lay before them.

Multiple sources reported that President Roberto Rivera would be meeting with the mayor of Mexico City in an outdoor ribbon-cutting in just a few hours. Rivera had confirmed it himself through his most trusted source, just to be sure.

But how did you explain to this brute that one had to balance the use of force? And that though an incredible opportunity stood before them, now was not the right time?

Attack and appear too heavy-handed and pride might persuade the people to fall in behind the country's colors. Nationalism was a powerful force, and no one – even a poor Mexican peasant – wanted to live in a weak country.

Flores had spent years pushing propaganda that made Rivera and his predecessors appear corrupt, uncaring, and ineffective in providing services to the people. And so, the people had come to care little about their government.

But if they made the government appear too weak, and if the cartel suddenly appeared as some heartless bully pushing around the weak, then they might lose the people. It was a delicate balancing act and a mighty hard thing to explain to a man who never left home without a duffle bag full of weapons.

Flores turned back forward and studied the small man, who stood surrounded by the cartel leader's four bodyguards. He had to admit that the Butcher had come far, trading in his ridiculous ninja-like attire from a few years ago for sharp suits that he wore with an open collar.

But the man's aggressive nature was as present as ever, so Flores finally opted for the direct answer.

"No," he said. "We're not moving against the President today."

"Why not?" asked the Butcher. "We know he's going to be there and even if we fail to kill him, we will further show the people that their government is powerless."

"You're correct. That's why we're not going to do it. What if the people rally behind the government after this attack? Have you not seen the footage of the thousands who have gone downtown to view the damage on the Presidential Palace? They've placed flowers along the outer walls and some have even cried for those we killed. This isn't the government raiding people's homes or taxing them too much. This is us attacking a government that, in case you've forgotten, is necessary."

The Butcher wanted to scream at the weak man before him. They were so close to complete victory. He decided to make one final pitch.

"But we could have so much more power without any central government," the Butcher said. "We don't need a federal government. What does it actually do? They can't stop crime, they don't take care of the poor, they are too corrupt to even enforce their own laws. All of these things, the cartels do better. We don't need a government at all."

Flores sighed.

"Don't you see?" Flores asked. "If we topple the entire government, there would be consequences. Probably America would invade or send forces here to support pro-democracy forces. It would be better to have a weak government as it currently is, but with one of our men in power. Or maybe myself. Then our cartel would have a truce with the government and our profits would be maximized. We could live without fear for our families."

"I have no family," the Butcher said.

Flores turned away from him, exasperated.

The Butcher threw his bag down, lowered his voice, and growled, "We're missing a huge opportunity here. It's a big mistake. A huge one. We may never get another chance to take out Rivera this easily."

The Butcher looked at Flores with disgust, then reached down, grabbed the handles of his duffle bag, and growled, "Call me if you change your mind."

And with that, the Butcher turned, shouldered the nearest bodyguard out of the way, and exited the office.

CHAPTER 13

Two weeks had passed since Nick Woods had been introduced to Marcus and the other candidates. In those fourteen days, a lot had happened.

Nick had selected his team, outfitted them with the help of the CIA, and deployed an advance party of four men to scout their operating area.

The men of Shield, Safeguard, and Shelter were the real deal. Bad-ass trigger pullers, who wanted to get into the shit regardless of the odds. For some men, action beat boredom, and Nick had found men of that mold.

These men were fearless, tenacious, and hungry for revenge after being briefed on the exact details of the SEAL team ambush. Sixteen SEALs had died and these men wanted payback. And blood. Lots of it.

They had seen pictures of Lieutenant Commander Steve Todd and Master Chief David Adair. They had read short biographies of the two SEAL leaders, as well as of their team members and the flight crew.

A lot of great men had died that day and when you killed Americans, you paid a price. That was just the way it was.

For transportation, Nick's CIA contact had suggested that Nick's company "lease" armored Yukons from the federal government. He'd even had ten of them delivered to Camp Lejuene, where S3 was training. The contact was convinced that Nick would agree.

"They're 'surplus,'" the contact said, raising his fingers and putting quote marks around the word surplus. And he even smiled with a big shit-eating grin. "And the lease paperwork has already been filled out and approved. We just need your signature."

Nick stared at the man.

"You're getting them at a great deal, too," the man said, smiling, and throwing in a wink for good measure.

He apparently had misread Nick's look, but Nick wasn't amused.

"We going to put American flags on them?" Nick asked.

Immediately, the contact sensed trouble.

"No, why?"

"We might as well," Nick said. "Thanks for the offer, but we'll pass. We'll purchase vehicles ourselves and if I need anything else from you, I'll let you know."

And with that, Nick walked off. He then delegated the task of acquiring vehicles to a few of his men. He wanted various styles – SUVs, compact cars, even a couple of old trucks. And he wanted them in different colors and in various exterior conditions. The overarching idea was that they not stick out in any way, shape, or form.

No fancy wheels. No dark tint. Nothing sporty or aggressive.

Nick knew the contact thought the Yukons would be a welcome gift – they were armored, after all – but Nick didn't plan on rolling to his destination in a formation of matching vehicles, impressive though that might have been.

Instead, Nick wanted his men to infiltrate Mexico without Hernan Flores ever learning of the team's existence or entry. Not that this was easy to do. The contact had "suggested" that the entire convoy show up at the border at 2 p.m. one day. And an American government representative and a foreign diplomat from Mexico's government could get them through the checkpoint with all their weapons and gear.

Nick thought the idea bordered on sheer lunacy.

"If we want Flores to know we're coming so badly, why don't we just issue a press release?" Nick asked.

Nick fought with the Agency for the next two days and finally convinced headquarters to obtain vehicle passes that could be handed out to the men. The passes were dated with a three-day window from the Mexican government and would allow entry of a vehicle through any Mexican checkpoint without it being searched. The passes operated like diplomatic pouches, except they were for the entire vehicle and its occupants.

In Nick's mind, his plan was KISS simple, though he couldn't imagine how much hand-wringing had gone on while the deal was negotiated, since no such thing as a vehicle pass that operated as a diplomatic pouch existed. But that was a problem for the bureaucrats. It was their job to negotiate and create such a thing. Not his.

His goal was to get the team in safely and under the radar. He knew there was no way the Godesto Cartel would have enough men to watch every border crossing along the two-thousand-mile border, especially since his men would be entering in unmarked, impossible-to-profile vehicles.

And even if the Godesto could watch that many crossings – Nick figured there were probably hundreds of them across the border – Flores's men would be too spread out to strike any of the vehicles. Flores would have too few men to go toe-to-toe with the well-trained, well-armed men of S3.

But on the off-chance that Flores and the Godesto could take out a vehicle, Nick's plan would survive. Nick was bringing thirty-two men to this fight. Four squads of eight men, plus some support staff and leadership element. Nick could afford to lose a vehicle – or even two or three of them –as they crossed over.

But saying he was bringing thirty-two men to the fight wasn't exactly accurate. Besides the thirty-two men, he was stuck with three others, all of whom he had argued against.

Problem number one was his contact, who was the original CIA agent that had volunteered to approach Nick. The CIA had insisted that Nick had to keep the man as a part of Shield, Safeguard, and Shelter. Furthermore, that Nick had to take him with them to Mexico.

Nick had bitched to no end but lost that battle. Nick was instructed to "hire" the man. No exceptions. The contact could reportedly shoot and fight, but Nick still considered him dead weight.

Problem number two was worse. Nick had blown a gasket when he was informed that besides his CIA contact, he'd also have to bring along a cultural expert.

"We're there to hunt down Hernan Flores and destroy his organization," Nick said. "Why the hell do we need a damn 'cultural expert?'"

"We've reviewed your plan," the contact said. The man was now, unfortunately, a full part of S3. "And the strategists at the CIA believe you're going to need a cultural expert to prevent saying or doing something offensive. Public opinion is crucial in this operation. You've said so yourself."

"He better be able to shoot and take care of himself," Nick said. "I'm not babysitting any damn paper-pushers. And I'm definitely not assigning men to protect his ass."

"Actually, he is a she," the contact said.

"What did you say?" Nick said, advancing toward the man.

"I said he is a she. It's a woman. Not a man."

"No way," Nick said. "No way in hell are we taking a woman on the front line. Are you out of your mind? The last thing these men need is the distraction of some hot little filly."

"She's the best cultural expert we have," the contact said.

"Then we don't need the best. Give me the second best. Or third best. As long as it's a man."

"There are no second or third bests," the CIA contact said. "There may be a thirtieth best, but all our other experts are already working with the State Department, ATF, or DEA. There's no way we can get our hands on any of them. She's the best option we have. She was raised in Mexico and spent most of her life there."

"I'm not taking on some native," Nick said. "How do we know she'll be loyal?"

"Her father was killed by a cartel and her brother died in a nasty street fight," the contact said. "He was jumped by a gang and stabbed to death. Just thirteen at the time."

"What's her occupation? Just a housewife or mom who sought asylum in America?"

"No, you'll like this," the contact said. "She's educated and began her career as a lawyer, but after corruption in the judicial field allowed some high-profile cartel men to go free, she dropped the legal profession and became a cop. Worked her ass off and made a name for herself. She was later promoted to detective."

"Why'd she stop being a detective?" Nick asked.

"The truth is pretty gray, but our DEA folks believe she came to think some police higher-ups were getting paid off. Some weird things started happening. Some cases were taken away from her. Some witnesses were killed when they were supposed to be protected. Some last-second getaways from folks she was on the way to collar with the SWAT team."

"She turned them in and then they turned on her?"

"No, even better. A couple of the police higher-ups died in suspicious circumstances. Drug deaths, they were listed as, but most in the police department believed she did it."

"How'd she end up with us?"

"The cartels put a price on her head. She had to flee to America or end up on the front page of the paper."

"Not bad," Nick said, "but she has to qualify in front of me and I get the final say on whether she's a go or not."

"Fair enough."

"What's the final thing?" Nick asked. "You said there were three problems."

"The final thing is we have to put a Mexican liaison on the team. A man who can coordinate with Mexican authorities so there's no blue-on-blue action. I know you already have men who can speak Spanish, but this man is to help keep the Mexican authorities informed of the unit's activities."

Nick started to protest but decided he knew a great way to handle this man. Besides, he was ready to get in theater and start hunting. There'd already been way too much talking, so he agreed reluctantly.

CHAPTER 14

Nick Woods and the men of Shield, Safeguard, and Shelter arrived safely inside Mexico without any drama. The special border passes demanded by Nick had worked perfectly and the thirty-two shooters of S3 – plus the CIA contact, Mexican liaison, and cultural expert –made it to the team headquarters without trading rounds with the Godesto Cartel.

Nick felt grateful that his first hurdle of sneaking across the border had been achieved. As part of their entry plans, he had made his Mexican liaison fly to Texas so they wouldn't have to link up with him in Mexico, where they could be followed or ambushed.

Similarly, the cultural expert was already with S3, having had to qualify and train with the unit before Nick would accept her. The contact had never left Nick's side. Nick wasn't sure he could ditch the man, even if he wanted.

Now, all thirty-five members of S3 had rendezvoused at a large, 200-acre farm, roughly an hour south of Mexico City, after drifting in from every possible ingress route over a three-day period.

Nick's advance team of four men had finalized the lease for the farm prior to leaving America. Upon arriving, they confirmed the site was secure and began getting familiar with the area.

By the time Nick and the rest of his team arrived, the advance party had found the best defensive positions on the farm where security should be set up. Nick reviewed the security plans with the team leader once he arrived and with a couple small adjustments, they were now fully implemented.

A small dirt road led to the farm and a locked farm gate would stop any curious person at the end of the road.

Behind it, four men waited in an ambush position. Any intrepid salesman or thief too stupid to ignore the locked gate and "no trespassing" sign would most certainly never bother anyone again.

The men stationed in the ambush position would apprehend anyone that crossed onto the property. Nick and the men of S3 wouldn't be calling the police for anything. Hell, none of them trusted anyone down here. Not even supposed salesmen. Anyone could be an informer for the Godesto Cartel.

If someone came on the property, they'd be spending a few weeks under the hospitality of S3.

Nick trusted no one down here. In fact, Nick had even stripped the Mexican liaison upon his arrival in Texas and put his cell phone and all his clothing in storage, before having one of his men accompany the man to a store to buy new clothes. Nick didn't want to take a chance on any kind of tracking or listening devices.

Additionally, once they came within two hours of Mexico City, Nick had the men traveling with the Mexican liaison blindfold him and force him to lay down on the backseat of the car he was riding in until he was inside the farmhouse. That would leave about a three-hundred-mile radius that the farm could be located in, just in case the Mexican liaison ever slipped away to an open computer with internet access.

Better safe than sorry, Nick figured.

Nick had set the security as tight as he could. Besides the ambush team on the road into the farm, Nick had placed observation posts on each corner of the large farm. He personally oversaw positions that were in wooded locations or thick brush spots.

The place would look like a farm to any passerby, but it was a well-guarded hornet's nest, if anyone tried to attack it.

Nick had organized the thirty-two shooters of S3 into four squads of eight. One of the squads, the one with the most experienced and best shooters, was called the Primary Strike Team. Nick and Marcus would serve on it. And both agreed that the Primary Strike Team would do most of the fighting. As such, Nick and Marcus felt the Primary Strike Team should always be rested and ready to move at a moment's notice, so they wouldn't be pulling any security shifts at the farm.

It wasn't necessarily fair, but that's how life goes sometimes. It was more about the mission than anything else.

With everything set on the farm, only one thing remained: it was time to start focusing on that bastard Hernan Flores and his Godesto Cartel.

Nick's first move against the Godesto would take place in one of the bedrooms of the farmhouse.

"How close are we to being ready?" Nick asked, walking into the bedroom.

Marcus stood just inside the door, his hands on his hips, an M4 slung across his chest. Once a drill instructor, always a drill instructor, Nick thought, noticing how the man stood.

"Should be ready in five minutes," Marcus said.

Marcus was the XO, or executive officer, of S3, and as the unit's second-in-command, Nick had been leaning on him heavily.

Nick watched the men, standing next to Marcus. Men were sliding furniture to one side of the room. The bed, the dresser, the nightstand, everything, had been shoved to one side. And against the wall, men stood on chairs and hammered nails into a plain white sheet spread across the wall.

"We're going with a plain white backdrop," Marcus said to Nick.

Nick nodded.

A folding table stood in front of the sheet, with two M249 machine guns lying on the table. Called SAWs, or Squad Automatic Weapons, the light machine guns rested on their bipod legs. One of the men of S3, whose name Nick couldn't remember, adjusted a video camera that stood on an extended tripod.

"Get it right," Nick said to the man.

"Yes, sir," the man replied.

"I don't want anything in that frame except for the sheet. Not even one inch of that wall. We don't want to risk Flores or his men recognizing anything that might give away the type of building we're in. We give these guys the smallest clue and they'll figure out where these types of buildings were constructed and then they'll descend with so many spies asking for information that we won't be able to buy milk without being discovered."

"They won't see anything but the sheet and table," the man said. He looked back down and adjusted the camera one final time.

"Not even the floor," Nick said.

"Not even the floor," the man confirmed.

Nick exited the room and strode down the hall, his boots pounding the hardwood floor. It felt good to be in charge again, something he hadn't felt since he was a foreman working construction. And before that, back when he was in the Corps, where he had served as a squad leader and scout sniper team leader.

"Isabella," Nick boomed as he walked into the dining room.

Isabella, the cultural expert and only female in S3, looked up from a stack of papers spread across a wide dining table. Despite the skills she had shown qualifying and in training, Nick still wasn't happy about having her on the team. Two Latino men, both Americans whose parents had emigrated from Mexico, flanked her.

Isabella had been asking them their opinion on the message she'd spent days preparing. And with their collective Mexican heritage, they had helped her polish the message so that it was as perfect as possible.

"Camera is set up," Nick said to Isabella. "You ready?"

She grabbed the stack of papers and stood.

"Yes, sir," Isabella said.

"You sure?" Nick said walking up to her and putting his hands on his hips.

"Absolutely," she said.

"You better be," Nick said.

"We're ready," she said.

"Let's get one thing straight," Nick said. "This is on you. There is no 'we're ready' bullshit. This statement is on you, not those two guys, or anyone else. It's either you're ready or you're not. And if you're not, then you've got about three minutes to get ready. Are we clear?"

"Yes, sir," Isabella said.

"So, are you ready?" he asked.

"I'm ready," she said, adding more confidence to her voice this time.

Nick's eyes bore into her. He expected her to turn away, but she held his look. Former prosecutor and cop, he reminded himself. Probably a killer, too, if it were true that she had killed some dirty cops who'd served above her.

Nick said, "What are you waiting on? Get the script in there."

Isabella exited, walking down the hall.

Marcus walked up beside Nick and said in a low voice, "Don't you think you're being a little hard on her?"

"I need to know if she's going to crack or not," Nick said.

"She shoots as good as half of the men. And the woman may not have made the SEAL team, or been in the Marine Corps, but she's been a trigger puller in one of the most dangerous countries in the world," Marcus said. "I think she's earned some respect."

Nick glared at his second in command.

"We may be in the twenty-first century, but I don't believe women should be in a unit like this. Not when we're behind enemy lines. It's going to cause problems."

"I understand, sir, but we need her," Marcus said. "Are you an expert on Mexican matters?"

Nick turned from Marcus and saw several men stop and watch Isabella as she walked down the hall. Isabella was definitely a beautiful woman. Even Nick had noticed – as much as he hated it – that she had quite an ass, as well. Even in fatigue pants. It certainly turned heads, which was precisely the problem.

"I'd rather have a male expert who was average," Nick said, shaking his head. "Not one who looks like that," he said, pointing. "And capable or not, that woman looks too good to be isolated with us. She's going to cause problems."

"The woman lost her father and her brother to the cartels," Marcus said. "She wants to take down the Godesto as bad as you or me. And the men are professionals. They'll be fine. And any who aren't can deal with me. Now, if you'll excuse me."

Nick considered Marcus's words as he watched the 6'1', 240-pound beast walk down the hall. Why the man needed an M4, Nick didn't know.

And maybe Marcus was right. Maybe Nick was worrying too much about having a woman in the unit.

I'm going to have to catch up with the times at some point, Nick thought.

Ten minutes later, Nick supervised the first major strike against Hernan Flores and the Godesto. With arms crossed, Nick watched his men as they executed the performance they'd rehearsed.

Ten men stood behind the table and the two M249s lying on it. Each of the ten men carried intimidating weapons. Some held M4s. Others held up heavy, M240 medium machine guns.

They looked like irregular militia, wearing a variety of clothes. Mostly, they wore blue jeans and T-shirts, with hats ranging from boonie hats to ball caps to watch caps.

Nick had ordered them to look like a rag-tag group and they had achieved the effect. Additionally, each man wore a bandana to cover his face. Some red, some blue.

Marcus and Isabella had picked Latino men to be in the video, but none of them wanted to have their actual identity out on the internet for the rest of their lives, so the hats and bandanas left as little of each man's face exposed as possible.

The men knew that even if they knocked off Flores, they could still be at risk from remnants of the Godesto. Or even at risk from whichever cartel replaced the Godesto.

Cartels, like the mob, had long memories.

In front of the ten men sat a single man. After getting a nod from the man behind the camera, he began to read from a white paper held before him. Nick hoped the man's accent matched that of Mexico City. All of his Hispanic team members said the man's accent was the best of any of them; it lacked any trace of a life in America and the Marine Corps.

Nick hoped it was good enough. He had considered getting

a local native speaker, blindfolding him, and bringing him to the farm to read the statement. That would make it absolutely authentic. But, unless the guy was a dimwit, he'd know there were a large group of mostly Americans somewhere in Mexico with really bad intentions and that was knowledge Nick didn't want Hernan Flores to have.

Nick's whole plan was based on turning the population against the cartels and it was one thing for Mexicans to support fellow Mexicans. It was another thing altogether for Mexicans to support a bunch of gringos from up north. That was something that would never happen.

The man seated at the table read the following, but in Spanish: "I speak for the men behind me, and for dozens of others who have had enough. We are citizens of Mexico – bankers, butchers, and farmers. For decades now we have watched as our country has been torn apart by drugs and the cartels.

"For most of us, the violence began elsewhere. Other states, other cities, other neighborhoods. But it moved in on us in the night. And soon, what started as a few delinquents standing on street corners turned into organized gangs.

"Threats, intimidation, and corruption followed and before we knew it, our neighborhoods and cities were no longer ours.

"Since recognizing this threat, our military has tried to fight these oppressors, but they, too, have failed. Their officer corps has been infiltrated or paid off. Sadly, many brave Mexican soldiers have died fighting in a cause they cannot win.

"There's only one way to win this war and that's through us: the people of Mexico. We, the people of Mexico, will no longer tolerate these cartel pigs with their wealth and their cavalier attitude toward law and order. We will no longer accept their abuses and crimes. We will fight fire with fire. For every drop of blood they draw, we will draw ten more.

"We are the people of Mexico. And from this point forward, we will call ourselves – and those brave souls that join us – the Vigilantes. We are the true defenders of Mexico.

"The first target for the Vigilantes is Hernan Flores. This man may say he's clean and may claim to be a harmless grandfather and businessman, but we know differently. And you out there watching us today know differently, too, at least in your gut.

"This man has wrecked thousands of lives climbing to power and now he's killed dozens of Mexican soldiers and attacked our very own Presidential Palace. All within just the past few weeks. He has humiliated our country and nearly brought it to its knees. But no more."

The man dropped the paper and looked up at the camera.

"Mr. Flores, you murderer of thousands of good and decent people, we are coming for you. Your days of poisoning our country and our youth with your drugs and your guns and your wads of cash are coming to an end.

"We will cut your head off and stick it on a stake. We promise you this. We will match your violence and we will show no mercy."

The man nodded and the camera was turned off.

Nick couldn't understand what the man had said – it was in Spanish, after all – but he'd read the message in English and thought it was perfect. Isabella had outdone herself. Maybe having a cultural expert wasn't the worst idea after all.

Not that Nick would admit that to his CIA contact.

The next step was to distribute the video to several major news stations in Mexico City. With luck, it would go viral within hours.

Nick smiled and thought, "Thanks, Allen Green. I owe you for this one."

And indeed Nick did. Allen Green, the veteran reporter from New York, was a master of public opinion and had taught Nick much of what he knew. It had taken a while for Nick to come around to believing in the power of public opinion and social media, but he was on board with Allen's arguments about media strategy now.

Nick turned so the men wouldn't see his face, but he was smiling. Round One just went to Team USA. Or, Team Mexico, really. Nick shifted the .45 on his hip and anticipated the upcoming fight between the Godesto and S3.

Now with their opening media strategy complete, it was time to start spilling blood. And Nick? Well, he couldn't wait for that to begin. There were sixteen SEALs that Nick planned to soon avenge.

Lieutenant Commander Steve Todd and Master Chief David Adair, this is for you, Nick thought.

CHAPTER 15

Hernan Flores finished watching the Vigilantes' homemade broadcast and threw the remote as hard as he could against his widescreen TV, which was built into a cabinet inside his office. The remote cracked the screen and Flores slammed his hand on the desk.

Despite the cracked screen, the television now showed a foxy news anchor discussing the newly formed Vigilante group with a university professor, who was supposedly an expert on the cartels. Flores just wanted to turn the damn thing off and cover his ears, but realizing the remote was now ten feet away, he grabbed the coffee mug off his desk and hurled it as hard as he could at the TV.

The mug flew through the glass, penetrated two inches, and the TV popped in a shower of sparks. The widescreen now smoked and Flores stood still long enough to ensure no flames climbed from the guts of the worthless piece of scrap. Confirming there were none, he collapsed into his chair and buried his hands in his hair.

Who were these people? These Vigilantes?

He hit his intercom and said, "Maria, how many stations played that tape?"

There was a considerable pause, and then his secretary said, "We're still trying to figure it out, sir, but we think all of them did."

Flores jumped to his feet. He grabbed the phone from his desk and threw it as hard as he could toward the wall.

"Fuck!" he screamed.

The phone made it four feet before the cord stopped its progress and jerked it back in Flores's direction. He attempted to lift his arms in time to block it, but it caught him in the front of the shoulder and he yelped in pain.

Maria heard the curse and howl of agony. In any other circumstance this might have been funny, but in her case, she worked for an insane cartel leader. And when the fat man grew angry and then topped it off by getting hurt and embarrassed, people usually died.

Maria, assuming she could be on some hidden camera, showed nothing and continued her work, pretending she hadn't heard a thing. The pay was too good, and the fear too great, to do anything but that.

Flores rubbed his shoulder and sunk into his chair. He sat there for a moment and decided to pour himself a drink. He realized he was hungry, too, though it was only a couple hours after he had eaten breakfast. Well, a few Funyuns wouldn't hurt.

Drink poured and new bag of chips opened, he sipped and munched at his desk. In between bites, he considered this new problem. In truth, outlaws such as this group presented the greatest threat a cartel leader could face.

The public was vital in one's war against the government. After all, the government dominated the cartels in terms of troops, dollars, and vehicles. Plus, the government could operate in the open with armored cars and heavy weapons. But the government also had to keep the public happy.

The cartels struggled under the requirement to stay below the radar. They couldn't tote long weapons out in the open or assemble in groups near their targets or bases, except in some of their mountain fortress areas. And even there, it was best to not attract attention.

The cartels needed the public's support. It was crucial. Other than public support, the only other weapons wielded by cartels were loads of cash and out-of-this-world, extreme violence. Violence that topped what the government could bring. If you could create sheer terror among individual police officers and prosecutors, then you could thrive and survive.

But Flores had pushed too far with the violence, he now saw. He had lost the public's support and this group calling themselves the Vigilantes had sprung up. Flores needed to win back public support quickly. Even if he discovered who these Vigilantes were, he'd need to be careful. Attack them too ruthlessly and they'd only multiply like weeds.

Flores recalled the footage of the wrecked Presidential Palace and the convoy of shot-up Mexican troops. No one in Mexico had cared about the dead Navy SEALs, but the news footage of the Palace and bullet-riddled convoy littered with dead Mexican soldiers had played for days.

And the Palace had looked terrible in the TV footage and front-page newspaper photos, even after the bodies had been removed. Smoke plumes rose from the riddled, pock-marked Palace walls. And blood stained the street among the charred ruins of the convoy.

The Mexican people were poor, but proud, and the sight of their government power center shattered and their military embarrassed on a city street had proved too much. And Flores had known it before the day's news ended. The media pounced on the footage as if it were war coverage from World War II.

Flores, sensing the rising public anger and humiliation, immediately offered his assistance to help insulate himself. He publicly donated $10 million to the federal government's campaign to rebuild the Presidential Palace.

Best of all, Flores earned some great news coverage after President Roberto Rivera refused to be pictured with Flores. Rivera claimed to be too busy overseeing the defense of the country and its war against the cartels, but several media outlets slapped him on the wrists for not appearing with Flores.

"What better way to help raise funds than to appear with those who were donating so generously?" the papers asked.

But the attacks had done more than turn public opinion against the Godesto. It had also inspired the straight-laced billionaire Soto not to leave the country. That was what sources were not reporting to Flores.

Flores knew that President Rivera could not survive without Soto's support and Flores had been so close to driving Soto out of the country. Now, that opportunity was gone. Flores gulped down the final half of his drink and refilled his glass. He'd conveniently brought the bottle from the cabinet to his desk.

What to do with the Vigilantes...

He had a record of achievement. Of overcoming nearly insurmountable hurdles. He'd climbed to the top of the Godesto Cartel from the very bottom. And he had taken the Godesto from one of six major cartels in the country to the strongest one of three. By far.

Mexico had gone from six cartels to three within a decade. Now, there was only the Godesto, the Red Sleeve Cartel, and a newly formed upstart that at some point he would squash like a bug.

The Godesto had an alliance with the Red Sleeve Cartel, which controlled almost thirty percent of the country. And the upstart cartel held roughly four percent.

Fores controlled seventy percent of the country. He had suffered a setback with Soto deciding to stay, but he had just decided how to deal with the Vigilantes.

They might have pushed back the timetable of his plans, but he had endured setbacks before.

He'd destroy these Vigilantes no differently than he'd destroyed his prior enemies.

He reached for his phone and realized he'd totaled it in his earlier tirade.

"Maria," he yelled. "Call the TV stations. I'm holding a press conference in two hours."

CHAPTER 16

"Nick, you better get in here," Marcus said.

Nick pushed into the command center. He and Marcus had decided the small study/library of the farmhouse would serve this function.

"What is it?" Nick asked.

"Hernan Flores is about to hold a press conference," Marcus said. "Isabella was scanning the news channels about our video and came across it."

Nick looked at the TV and watched as Hernan Flores exited two massive doors from the entrance of the eight-story tower from which he worked. He cautiously walked toward the cameras and looked up and down the road, as if he were worried.

"He's putting on an act," Isabella said. "I've watched hundreds of hours of footage of him, and he's usually confident and loud."

"He's hamming it up for the cameras," Nick said.

"As if he doesn't have about forty armed men in a cordon around the media," Marcus added.

"I thought he always wore Hawaiian shirts?" Nick asked, looking toward Isabella. "He looks like a stuffed pig in that suit."

"He normally does," she said. "I don't like this. He hates wearing suits. He doesn't even wear them to black-tie fundraising galas, but no one cares because he donates so much that half of the galas are named in his honor."

Flores trudged up to a podium. Dozens of microphones and tape recorders were propped or standing on the podium. A hungry crowd of reporters with cameras and notepads stood eagerly awaiting. Flores looked up and down the street again and leaned toward the microphones.

Nick tapped Isabella on the arm and said, "You translate what he says."

She nodded as Flores began to speak.

"I appreciate you all coming out today and I apologize for my men having to search you a few minutes ago," he said.

Flores took a handkerchief out and wiped his brow, which had already begun to sweat. The man was a fat piece of shit, Nick thought, and hardly looked like a formidable adversary. And yet that's what made him so dangerous. He was a chameleon. He changed his colors to whatever was necessary.

Businessman and philanthropist by day, mobster and murderer by night.

"As you might have heard," Flores said to the cameras, "a group of law-breaking citizens has stated they intend to hunt me down."

Flores paused and looked down. He swallowed, brushed his forehead again, and continued. "I can't tell you how distressing this is. I'm obviously taking these threats very seriously, as you can see by the security around you. I have made arrangements to fly my family out of the country. And I'm trying to determine if I can manage to leave the country myself."

He looked up and down the street – really playing the scared angle, Nick thought – before continuing.

"As you all know, I own dozens of legitimate businesses, contrary to what the Vigilantes claim. And while I can afford to cash out today and close them all down, I cannot bring myself to do that for the sake of the thousands of employees and families who depend on those jobs. Not to mention the ongoing contributions those businesses provide to several charities. I'd hate for it to come to this, but I must say that if I can't move freely or even stay in the country without fear of harm coming to me or those I love, then that giving will have to decrease."

Now Flores leaned into the microphones and Nick detected the first hint of violence that he'd seen yet. But it was subtle and probably most of the public would miss it. Nick only caught it because he couldn't understand the language and focused completely on every gesture and action. Looking straight into the cameras, Flores said, "I call on President Roberto Rivera to crack down on these Vigilantes. And while I've been a big supporter of his – including my recent donation to rebuild the Presidential Palace after this horrific attack by cartel terrorists – I sadly cannot continue to endorse a leader who so blatantly is losing control of his country. I don't want to endorse a government changeover in the middle of his presidential term, but if he cannot bring these people to justice and cannot stop the attacks on our brave government forces, then we will have to consider whether a handover of power is not the right course of action."

"Wow," Isabella said in disbelief. "Did he just say he's been a big supporter of President Rivera?"

"Probably most folks don't know how much he funded and worked for Rivera's opponent," Nick said. "All they see is this old, scared businessman. The man who reminds them of their grandfather and who they've seen hundreds of times on TV during various charity events. They see a businessman and philanthropist who's reasonable and fighting for them."

"Nice bit of reverse psychology that he's using," Marcus said.

"He's a pro," Nick said. "That's for sure."

"It's all bullshit," Isabella said. "He's not sending his family out of the country. They have a mountain enclave and have complete control of the city he was raised in. No way is he letting them leave the country where he can't guarantee their safety as he can here."

Nick didn't respond. He needed some quiet to think over Flores's power move. Without a word, he turned and exited the room.

The blowback from Hernan Flores's performance in front of the country reached Nick Woods the next day.

His CIA contact rushed into the command post, where Nick and Marcus hovered over a map. He held a brick-sized phone that was some kind of super-encrypted, satellite phone, Nick had been told.

"It's for you, sir," his contact said. "It's headquarters and I warn you they're pissed."

Nick noted that his contact had his hand over the mouthpiece of the phone and looked as flustered as an eight-year-old about to get a spanking.

"It'll be okay, Hoss," Nick said. "I've dealt with headquarters before."

The contact handed Nick the phone and darted from the room, looking relieved, as if had just handed off some kind of radioactive device that might explode at any moment.

Nick looked over at Marcus, shook his head, and smiled.

"Kids," Nick said. Marcus laughed.

Nick paused and made headquarters wait a full fifteen seconds. He lifted the heavy phone, but Marcus stopped him.

"I'm going to walk the lines," Marcus said, holding up his M4.

Nick nodded and leaned into the phone.

"Nick, here."

"This is Smith. You mind telling me what the hell you're doing down there?"

Nick smiled. Smith was the high-level CIA official who was truly in charge of Nick's operation. Or, so Smith thought. Of course, the pencil-neck piece of shit didn't want anyone to know his name in case the whole mission went down in flames.

A real courageous man, you might say.

Nick had called him Mr. Smith once the man had said it was best if he didn't share his name with Nick. It wasn't like the man would have told Nick his real name anyway, so at least the name "Mr. Smith" was easy to remember.

"You know exactly what we're doing," Nick said. "Your contact updates you at least twice a day. Of that I'm confident. He's too scared not to."

"President Rivera's popularity has dropped another ten points since Hernan Flores responded to the Vigilante's video. Do I need to remind you that he already has a low approval rating and doesn't have a lot of room to give?"

"Do I need to remind you that you approved of our plan prior to our departure?" Nick asked. "Best I remember, you thought us producing and releasing that video was a great idea. A quote 'way to win over the people,' I believe was what you said."

"The plan wasn't to release the video and do nothing while Flores destroys the movement in the press before it really even begins."

"I didn't realize we were doing nothing," Nick said. "I bet that's news to all the guys patrolling the compound and spread all over Mexico City pulling surveillance in this god-awful heat."

"You need to make something happen soon. I've got the CIA Director on my ass and you-know-who on his ass."

Nick knew he meant the President, but that wasn't his problem. He wouldn't risk a single man rushing his plans.

"I said before I accepted the post that I would work at my own pace. I'm not risking any men because you or your boss can't take an ass-chewing. Your job is to run interference so that we can get the job done, so go run some interference. Create some kind of an excuse, whatever the hell you want."

"Listen here," Smith said, but Nick didn't hear another word. He hit the "end call" button and tossed the phone into a chair. He'd heard enough from headquarters on this day.

Marcus, whose first name was Dwayne, moved about the farmhouse's interior, his M4 cradled in his arms. He peeked out windows and surveilled the lines from inside the home. Satisfied with what he saw, he leaned his M4 against the wall near the door and confirmed his .45 was concealed under his untucked shirt.

Nick had set strict rules for S3 that no one was to be seen outside with a long weapon of any kind during daylight hours. Though the farm was pretty remote and the population surrounding it mostly sparse, nothing was supposed to be done that could arouse suspicion from outsiders. Or that could cause a passerby to call the police.

Not that long weapons weren't out at the positions, but they had been moved there during the dead of night and were

STAN R MITCHELL

kept concealed during the day.

Nick had also mandated that only street clothes were to be worn outside while in the compound. He didn't want anyone to know that this small farm had been transformed into an outpost for a large group of armed men.

"I want us to look like regular ol' field hands," Nick had said. "Or maybe local workers."

Marcus glanced down to confirm he was in blue jeans and T-shirt and stepped out of the home. Marcus took his time and walked the perimeter in a nonchalant manner. He certainly didn't want to look military in his bearing, but at the same time, he couldn't shake how happy he felt to be in an armed camp again in a foreign country.

This was what he was built for: leading men on dangerous missions. And as he talked with the men in various hidden positions around the perimeter, he couldn't shake how fragile it all felt. How worried he was – already – that when this ended, he'd have to return to an administrative leadership position in the Marine Corps. Or, even worse, have to leave the Corps and move on to some shitty civilian job.

And nothing scared Marcus more. He'd known nothing but guns and forced marches since the day he dropped out of college and left his lucrative destiny with the NFL for something grittier, scarier, and tougher. But just like the NFL, which stood for "Not For Long," in the military – even in the blood and guts Marine Corps – the opportunities to serve in harm's way were few and far between. Units rotated. Orders changed. You got promoted too high to be on the front line.

You only got so many chances to see real combat and Marcus didn't plan to take this one for granted.

Nick Woods had given him the opportunity to experience it all again, and there hadn't been a moment since he signed up that he wasn't almost euphoric.

The men of Shield, Safeguard, and Shelter were completely on their own. Just three eight-man teams, plus eight more counting Nick and Marcus in the Primary Strike Team. Thirty-two members in S3, plus the CIA contact, Mexican liaison, and cultural expert.

It was hardly an army or task force and they were about to

130

tangle with the billion-dollar Godesto Cartel, which probably had a thousand trigger pullers, a couple hundred police-department moles, and maybe as many as five thousand people on their payroll as snitches. It was why Nick had insisted on telling the Mexican government practically nothing.

The Mexican government had only one form of intel on S3, their Mexican liaison, and Nick kept that poor man so in the dark that the man didn't know a damn thing. Besides blindfolding him for hours prior to his arriving at their farm, Nick also kept a 24/7 watch on the man.

If you had the watch and needed to use the restroom, you had to get another member of S3 to watch him. Nick's orders were clear: the man was not to be left alone for even a minute. He was not to go near a phone, computer, or other electronic device at any time.

The man couldn't even hang on to his own phone and was only allowed to report into his superiors when a squad leader – or Nick and Marcus – stood near him. Each squad leader had been instructed to rip the phone from his hand if he crossed any lines.

Marcus still laughed at that. He felt sorry for the guy, but Nick had made clear that S3 wouldn't endure the same fate of the SEALs.

Nick mostly kept the man quarantined in a room with a TV, some books, and an S3 member on duty. Nick was straight stone-cold, Marcus thought, and coming from a strict drill instructor, that was really saying something.

To serve under a man like Nick, one of the most capable warriors Marcus had ever met, there was just nothing like it.

Even for a giant former linebacker like Marcus, who had yet to find someone he couldn't handle, Nick Woods caused a deep sense of unease. He screamed grit and determination with everything he said and did. And he looked like a man you didn't want to get on the wrong side of.

Not in a loud way like some kind of puffed-up meathead, but in a quiet calculating way. His eyes seemed to cut through you. Eyes that said they had seen deep shit and were willing to pay the necessary price again if you pissed him off.

Of course, all the men of S3 knew Nick's story. They hadn't

at first, but the CIA contact told the men that their leader was the very same Nick Woods who had exploded across the world's headlines a few years earlier. None of the publications had ever nabbed a photo of him, but the story of Allen Green and the mysterious Marine Scout Sniper had grown to legendary levels.

Once the men of S3 knew who was leading them, they immediately committed to following him. And Marcus had, too, if he were honest.

Marcus finished walking the perimeter of the farm, which was bordered by a simple barbed wire fence of three strands, meant for cattle. After checking on all the troops watching the line, he headed back for the house.

Marcus needed to do some push-ups and pull ups. No way would he let his body get soft, even while on deployment. And he also knew his example would inspire the men to stay fit, as well.

In the farmhouse, Isabella sat at a computer desk and rubbed her temples. She'd been surfing news site after news site, as well as dozens of forums that talked about drug beefs, gang battles, and rumors of crime.

She stood and stretched, lifting her arms. She wanted to take a break and at least leave the room. Get some much-needed caffeine, but she worried Nick would catch her.

Yesterday, Nick had caught her on just such a break. She had stopped to talk to a few of the guys after grabbing a bottle of water from the refrigerator and Nick had managed to walk by at that very moment. She still seethed at the exchange that had followed.

"Did you find every piece of intel there was to find on the internet?" Nick asked.

"No, sir," she said. "I just took a break to grab something to drink and stopped to say a few words on my way back."

"I see," Nick said, looking at the three men who had been talking to her. Each looked down and Isabella turned red with embarrassment.

"You men have anything else you need to say to Isabella?" Nick asked. "She has work to do."

"No, sir," they said.

"Then quit wasting her time," Nick said, dismissing them with a wave of his hand.

They scurried down the hall and Nick turned to Isabella.

"You are aware that we're counting on you to help with intel *and* plan our PR campaign, right?" Nick said.

Isabella didn't appreciate the scolding. She had been working her ass off, whether Nick knew it or not.

"You are aware of the double-standard you're imposing, right?" she asked, nodding her head back toward the men walking off.

She knew she shouldn't have back-talked Nick, but the attorney in her just wouldn't let his remarks go.

Nick was really the only thing that she didn't like about S3. She liked her new team. She was on the Primary Strike Team, composed of Nick, Marcus, and five more shooters named Truck, Lizard, Bulldog, Preacher, and Red.

Nick said he only wanted Isabella on the Primary Strike Team because she spoke Spanish, which put two people on the Primary Strike Team (counting Lizard) with that ability. Nick had also said he didn't want her on some other squad where the men would be distracted by her tits. His word, not her's.

But Isabella knew that one of the main reasons she was on the Primary Strike Team was because she could shoot and hold her own. And she also knew Nick wanted her close so he could draw on her language skills, even if he was in the middle of a firefight.

Sure, he treated her like shit, but she had been "brought into the fold" so to speak far more than she would have expected after first meeting Nick. She was literally on the unit that would see the most action.

When the Primary Strike Team deployed into the field, Nick left the CIA contact back at the base. Nick explained that it was to protect the contact from possible jail time in case Nick needed to break the law.

But Isabella relished this truth: the contact was left at the base because Nick only wanted operators on his Primary Strike

Team. And he trusted her to watch his back in the field, though he had never admitted it out loud.

Isabella knew that though he might never admit it, Nick was impressed with her shooting and the way she was handling the pressure from him and Marcus. She also knew that her records had informed him that she had killed her share of men.

Not near as many as Nick – or even most of the other men – but they were all some of the most experienced warriors that America had.

Isabella, on the other hand, had been in different circumstances while on the police force and as a prosecutor. But she had shown courage – just as much as the men Nick and Marcus had selected.

She looked out the window and saw Marcus walking toward the house. She again thought of how vastly different he and Nick were.

Marcus marched places (at least when he wasn't outside at this ranch, where he tried to blend in with a bored shuffle). But typically? He walked with perfect military bearing. Ramrod straight posture. S3 utility uniforms pressed and immaculate, when he wore them in the house or back in the States. The man was a drill instructor to the end, even in jeans and T-shirt, as he wore now.

Nick couldn't have been more different. He was a hard man. Cold. Of few words. His eyes looked straight through you and he so rarely spoke that you were always curious as to what he was thinking.

Marcus worked hard to balance Nick out. Marcus was a motivator, always quick with an encouraging word or a positive thought. He could be hard on the men, like Nick, but he had just as many words to cheer them and lift their morale.

The way Isabella saw it, Nick didn't really fit the role of commander of the unit. He was more of the hard-nosed sergeant, but with Marcus filling the gap by playing the officer role, it still worked. At least so far.

Of course, that could change in an instant if Nick pushed her too far. She smiled as she imagined kicking him upside his head. He probably so underestimated her that he'd never see it coming.

"Doubt he'd act like such a bad ass if I knocked his ass out," she thought.

But then again could she pull off such a surprise against his discerning eyes? The man noticed everything. He missed nothing. And he feared absolutely nothing, but failure. He'd clearly rather die and go out in a blaze of glory than ever fall short.

And while he didn't say much unless he was giving her hell, she couldn't deny that his strength did something to her. He was here, in a foreign land, to do what Mexico's bravest and smartest men had failed to do: take down Hernan Flores.

But more than that, his tall, lean frame called her in a way she hadn't thought about in years. Of course, most of the men she had been around in law enforcement weren't at the level of Nick. They were practically cowards, who donned masks on most raids for fear of being recognized or remembered.

Many had given up on any serious fitness routine and had gained too much weight. They had grown soft, both in body and in concern with staying alive.

Nick didn't fear death. He courted it – practically dared it to come his way. He had already taken too many risks and they were barely getting started. He was constantly going out on scouting patrols, where the unit sent vehicles out to recon target areas.

Nick was a real man in a world where few men still roamed. And he was good-looking, and strong, and, well, available. Isabella blushed a bit at the thought, but she had a track record with men.

Good or bad, she usually caught her man. The evil ones ended up dead or behind bars. A few lucky ones learned she could be as passionate as she could be tough. All the rest ended up chasing her like lovesick teenagers.

Nick might prove her biggest challenge yet, but, well, that was a nice thought to consider, too.

And with that thought, she opened up another news website to look for clues about the Godesto Cartel. She'd go get some caffeine in a few minutes, whether Nick scolded her or not.

But with that idea, a thought occurred... Perhaps he was playing up the asshole angle because he couldn't handle being around her?

Now that was an interesting thought. Something she'd have to ponder on some.

CHAPTER 17

Nearly a week passed before S3 made its first strike as the Vigilantes. It had taken longer than Nick would have preferred, but the unit was severely outnumbered and operating in a foreign country, in a land he didn't know. Nick figured it was better safe than sorry.

Nick felt real excitement at the prospect of action. Finally, he and his boys were off the farm. That was the good news. The bad news? They were definitely in the deep end now.

It was two o'clock in the morning, or 0200, as Nick still thought of things.

Nick and the Primary Strike Team waited alongside the back of a mid-sized passenger van. His men looked like a bunch of anti-government rebels, dressed in jeans and boots and hoodies and bandanas. And like any good group of anti-government rebels, they were armed to the teeth.

The best part of playing "vigilantes" was that their weapons needed to vary and not be uniform, so the team members got to pick their weapon of choice. Tonight, they were packing everything from 9 mm MP-5s to 5.56 mm M4s to 12-gauge shotguns, stacked full of buckshot.

The van they stood by looked like it had once been owned by a small business of some kind. The team had paid cash for a used van and painted over its commercial markings, using a cheap coat of white paint. And with the dings and scrapes, the van fit in nicely in the rundown part of town they were currently in.

Mexico City, like every other metropolitan area in the world, had its share of shithole neighborhoods, and the Primary Strike Team sat waiting in probably one of Mexico City's worst slums.

It felt scary as hell, just to be in the neighborhood.

Nick's Primary Strike Team was staged by the mid-sized van, waiting. They had backed the van into an alley between two abandoned buildings. The only downside was a twelve-foot-high, brick wall at the rear had them trapped. On the one hand, Nick didn't like not having any exit but forward. On the other, the alley provided great concealment barely one block from their target. And it would take a lot of Godesto shooters to take down the eight of them.

Plus, Nick had two squads of S3 reinforcements who could arrive quickly. Probably within about two minutes. The key would be to strike the target and get the hell out of the area quickly.

Tonight's target was a small cathedral. The target had been brought to Nick's attention by a tipster.

As part of the plan to take down the Godesto, S3 had set up a simple website called "The Vigilantes." Quite a few tips had come in, which Isabella had monitored and translated for Nick and Marcus.

Both men had been immediately intrigued by a few tips about this cathedral. The moment the cathedral was mentioned, it had stood out.

Nick appreciated the sheer genius of the location. It was precisely the spot he would have chosen to store tons of cocaine. The building wasn't a factory or warehouse or even storefront. No, it was exactly the place where you would least expect a ton of cocaine to be. A religious structure, supposedly sacred and off limits.

The building had been under surveillance by snipers for days.

Marcus was the one who first suggested they ask the CIA to bring in some snipers to help round out S3.

"Let's not wear our men down doing both surveillance and security at the farm," Marcus had said.

It was a good idea, so Nick requested his CIA contact to ask for six Scout Sniper Teams to be transferred from active duty in the Marine Corps to S3.

Two of those Scout Sniper Teams had been watching the target they planned to hit tonight for five days, 24/7. They had been watching the building from two different angles, gaining tons of intel.

The Scout Snipers – buried deep in the corner shadows of nearby buildings – reported odd vehicles coming and going in the middle of the night. Strange deliveries. Ferocious-looking men who wore unnecessary, loose, baggy coats on hot nights, overseeing the loading and unloading of boxes.

Nick shifted his feet. He was eager to hit the building.

They were waiting on a single thing: final confirmation that the cathedral was loaded with cocaine. It should arrive at any moment.

One of the two nearby S3 squads was trailing a vehicle that had departed the cathedral moments ago. The Scout Snipers had reported that several boxes had been loaded into the car, right on schedule.

"This is it," one of the Scout Snipers had said into a radio.

Nick looked over at Marcus.

"Man, I hope we're right," Nick said.

"We'll know soon whether they're delivering drugs or Bibles," Marcus replied with a grin, having heard the same thing through his earpiece.

"They don't deliver Bibles this time of night," Nick said. "Ain't enough demand."

"There might be," Marcus said. "Country's a shithole."

The two men laughed.

The eight-man squad to their west – Second Squad – would ambush the car.

Nick had some ideas on how it should be done, but he believed in delegating as a leader. As such, he had told the squad leader to get with his men and create their own plan.

The plan they came up with was excellent.

One car would follow the vehicle from the cathedral. The Scout Snipers knew which route the vehicle would take, so an S3 car would block the road up ahead at the last second. Gunmen would take positions behind the car while another S3 vehicle would rush up on the flank.

Nick knew it was happening at this very moment.

Moments later, a staccato of automatic gunfire carried across the city. More isolated shots followed.

STAN R MITCHELL

Nick imagined the scene. Darkness. The blinding flash and roar of gunfire in a black night. The zipping of passing rounds and the slapping of rounds tearing into bodies.

The screams of terror.

Nick wished he was there.

"Second Squad, report in," Nick said into his throat mike after the echoes of gunfire had ended. His men wore throat mikes, which wrapped around your neck, because the microphones worked better in high wind or extremely noisy environments. Situation when typical microphones amplified mostly wind.

They may be operating as Vigilantes, but they were wearing top-of-the-line spec ops radios, which they had hidden below bandanas.

"Roger," his squad leader reported. "Target occupants killed. No friendly casualties. Currently, collecting evidence."

"Move fast," Nick said.

He looked up at his Primary Strike Team and said, "Get ready. Double-check your weapons and get your head in the game."

None of them had their heads out of the game, but Nick was a big believer in the power of absolute focus. Nick double-checked that the van hadn't been turned off and was running as he had instructed. Turning off a vehicle – especially an older one like they were driving – in a slum like this seemed foolish. Their van had to be fifteen years old.

He watched his Strike Team prepare. They wore various types of web gear over their civilian clothes and the operatives confirmed follow-up magazines were accessible and grenades securely attached.

Marcus, his second in command, played leader and checked straps and pockets of those around him. Isabella, who was quite a shooter herself, double-checked her MP-5. She could hit a dime at thirty feet with the thing.

Lizard, a small Puerto Rican guy, who had served nine years in the Corps, looked nervous. But that was normal. The man looked timid and scared no matter what he was doing. Even when he was fighting in hand-to-hand, at which he was nearly unbeatable, he always looked like he was on the verge of losing.

But Lizard was a black-belt, Brazilian Jiu-jitsu grappler, and Nick had seen him wrestle with several team members from the other squads. He had never lost.

And even though Lizard's commanding officers had all remarked on his pessimistic attitude, he never lost his cool. He always thought every mission would prove a failure, he always showed real fear, he always wanted to get out of the Corps, and yet he had two Bronze Stars, and he'd *always* re-enlisted once his contract ended.

And even stranger, he had volunteered to try out for Nick's unit, even though he'd told several of the men that he had "a bad feeling" about it.

Nick liked the quiet Puerto Rican and had served with many men like him. Men like Lizard didn't break. They may seem too humble, they may seem too quiet, and they may look shaky, but they'd move heaven and earth once the chips came down. And Nick preferred men who hated danger over men who craved it. Only crazy men would enjoy regular gun work.

And, well, Nick was crazy. And so was the rest of his Primary Strike Team.

There was Truck. Truck was the nickname of a former Army Special Forces operative who had probably seen too much action. Unlike much of the team, he wasn't a gym rat. And he wasn't the typical, optimistic soldier either. Frankly, he was a constantly complaining cynic, but Nick appreciated him.

Truck had been kicked out of the Special Forces after he had beaten the shit out of an officer. He had avoided brig time by lying and citing PTSD as the cause of his outburst. His citations for courage, which his defense attorney had read aloud to the jury at his trial, had probably helped.

But Truck couldn't avoid a discharge after hurting an officer so badly, so he'd left the Army in disgust, applying for a military contractor job the same day. Men like Truck lived to carry a rifle, so he had done several more tours as a security contractor in Iraq and Afghanistan.

Eventually, he had lost that job, too, after abandoning his heavy diesel truck, which was loaded down with cargo. Truck had gone running up a hillside in pursuit of insurgents who had ambushed his convoy. This had been in Afghanistan.

It didn't help his case that his leadership had found him with three dead Afghans near him, shot at close range. Bottom line, the security company determined that Truck had abandoned his vehicle and recklessly charged a hill. The company cared little about winning a war of killing insurgents. It wanted supplies safely hauled from one base to another. Nothing more. Nothing less.

The contractor company fired him. And he couldn't get hired on with other military contractors after that; the liability was too high.

Worse, police departments wouldn't hire him either due to his record and PTSD symptoms. So, without further employment opportunities available, he became a truck driver back in America.

He had driven a heavy truck in Afghanistan, after all.

Nick had some concerns about Truck when the man applied, but he interviewed him following Marcus's recommendation. Marcus had a good feeling about the guy, having spent several days with him prior to Nick's arrival.

Nick asked dozens of brutal questions and fell practically in love with Truck. Turned out that the officer was a prick that Truck had assaulted – Nick had his CIA contact do research on the man – and that Truck had the perfect defense for his contractor work.

"Why'd you leave the vehicle and charge the hill?" Nick asked him. "No support? Disobeying orders? Leaving valuable equipment unguarded?"

"Ah, hell, I didn't give a shit about the truck. And I'd lost a lot of buddies over there. Those Taliban shitheads started firing at us, same as they always did, and I just decided that I'd had enough. To hell with ignoring them and dealing with the same thing again the next day, like we'd been doing for weeks. I just decided I'd rather off them."

Nick imagined the battle, looked over the photos provided by the company's investigators, and concluded that he'd have done the same. And just like that, a "disgraced" former Special Forces operative was picked up and given a second chance with S3.

Besides Marcus, Isabella, Lizard, and Truck, the eight-man Primary Strike Team also had Bulldog, Preacher, and Red in its ranks.

Bulldog was appropriately named. A former Navy SEAL from the brutal streets of Baltimore, he was a giant black guy – 6'4," 250. The biggest man, by far, on S3 and there were some huge guys that Nick and Marcus had hired.

Bulldog wasn't just big, he was also a workout freak. He always lifted and his only apparent weakness was an inability to grow hair. So, he shaved his head bald and was such an intimidating beast that no one asked him a single question about it.

Preacher was the most religious man on Nick's team. His parents had been missionaries and the 5'10" man had felt "called" to join the Marines. Nick didn't know about being "called," but Preacher had done four hard Marine deployments, two of them with MARSOC. And Nick knew from experience that men who joined and stayed because they felt called to do something didn't know how to quit or run when things got heavy.

Finally, there was Red. Red was a short little shit. He was 5'5" on a good day, red-headed, and covered in thousands of small freckles. About the ugliest man Nick had ever seen, but he was so confident that he had a way with the women.

Red was divorced, said "let's do it" a lot, and loved to fist fight. In fact, absolutely loved to fist fight. Red had boxed a lot and Nick was always trying to keep him from jumping Bulldog or any other giant that should be able to rip him in half. But, Nick had seen him in action and wasn't so sure.

Red was crazy and he had small man's syndrome. He'd come from his fourth Marine infantry unit – he transferred as much as he could to outgoing units headed off to war – and had done seven tours between his stints in Iraq and Afghanistan.

He was a tasmanian devil, if there ever were such a thing, and Nick was ecstatic to have the man in his unit.

This was the eight shooters Nick had with him tonight. All members of the Primary Strike Team. All killers. All ready to take on the Godesto.

The radio tsk-ed, tsk-ed.

"Command, this is second squad actual," the squad leader said. "We have loads of cocaine in the SUV. The target location is definitely a Godesto drug facility."

"Roger," Nick said into the radio. "Clean up and get out of there."

Nick looked at his Primary Strike Team.

"We're a go," he said. "Let's move."

The eight members loaded up into the van. The van doors slammed and the vehicle's driver – one of the regular squad members from the squad not taking part in tonight's op – roared out of the alley, headlights still off. The cathedral's entrance was only two blocks away, but the van hit nearly fifty miles per hour on the dimly lit road before it screeched to a halt near the front steps. The van doors sprang open and Marcus's four-man fire team rushed the entrance, with Nick's team following not far behind.

Marcus's team had Lizard, Red, and Preacher, while Nick's team had Isabella, Truck, and Bulldog.

The van driver lifted his radio and said, "Primary Strike Team at the door. Snipers, be alert."

The snipers were cleared hot to engage now, if necessary. Their task was to keep enemy combatants in and reinforcements out.

Marcus's team stacked at the entrance. At the door, Preacher checked the handle to confirm it was locked. He placed a demolition charge on the doorframe and backed up four feet with his team. Nick's team waited behind them.

Preacher clicked the detonator and the charge exploded, setting off dogs barking for a two-mile area.

Red, the number two man in the stack, threw a flashbang over Preacher's shoulder right after the door blew off its frame. The flashbang boomed and lit up the entire church. Marcus's team followed the incredible concussion and blinding flash, entering the building with controlled speed.

Preacher, the lead man, turned the corner first and saw

two armed men headed toward them, trying to react to the assault. They were partially blinded and their equilibrium shot from the flashbang. Preacher stitched them both with his MP-5, firing two to the chest and one to the head of both men.

Red, just behind Preacher's shoulder, caught movement from a more alert tango. This man had been far enough away that he hadn't been affected by the flashbang. The man let loose with an AK in their direction before Red dropped him with four shots from his own AK-74.

Of course, Red dropped the barely-trained man with ease. He hadn't made the mistake of firing while running forward. He had the advantage of an Aimpoint red-dot sight. He also had seven combat tours as a Marine under his belt. Red's four rounds punched fatal holes in the man and dropped him hard.

Marcus's team finished securing the sanctuary, while Nick's team pushed past them and moved to the lead. They broke into pairs – Nick with Isabella and Truck with Bulldog – and started busting into rooms down a hallway past the sanctuary.

Each room proved empty save one. Truck and Bulldog heard movement inside a room they were about to clear. They hit it with a flashbang prior to entering.

They followed the explosion a millisecond later.

Inside the room, two cartel men were holding their ears and reaching for weapons they'd dropped from the explosion. Truck could have taken his man alive, but Truck didn't take prisoners unless explicitly ordered, so he fired two rounds of buckshot from his twelve gauge into the man's chest. The man's chest was eviscerated and much of his innards now painted the way behind him. Truck was all trigger.

Bulldog, at 6'4", 250, loved nothing more than getting his hands on someone and using his strength that he spent hours each day improving in the gym. He dropped his weapon to the slung position across his chest and rushed his opponent, grabbing him by the shoulders and flinging him across the room into a wall.

The man's head bounced off the concrete block wall and before the man could react, Bulldog kicked him in the back of the knee with one of his massive legs. The man dropped to the ground and Bulldog shoved his head into the wall again.

This time, the collision between concrete and bone yielded an instantly knocked-out opponent, the man's face altered permanently with a broken nose and shattered facial bone above the eye.

Bulldog flexcuffed the man's hands and fee and Truck threw the men's weapons out of the room into the hall of the cathedral.

No other men were on the top level, but downstairs seven men surrendered without firing a shot. The one-sided fight on the top level had convinced them of the futility of resistance. Gangsters didn't do well against practiced assault teams and flashbangs.

Alongside the men in the basement were hundreds of crates full of cocaine.

The priest, assuming one was even attached to the church, was nowhere to be found.

More men from S3 arrived behind the Primary Strike Team. They shot loads of video of the cathedral, its drugs, and its armed cartel men lying dead throughout the place. Nick, Marcus, and the rest of the Primary Strike Team waited outside while the video and photos were taken.

"Can you believe with all that shooting – even all those explosions – that the police haven't even responded?" Preacher asked, disgusted.

"The cartel would have agreements in place," Isabella said, "for the police not to respond or investigate anything that happens at this cathedral. It's a way of life down here and the people in the neighborhood are aware of it."

"They probably didn't even bother calling it in," Nick said.

"It's just sad," Preacher said. "These people have no hope."

Red spit, his anger obvious. "They had their chances and they have additional chances every day. I'm not throwing them a damn pity party. They can pick up a gun and do something about these bastards."

Preacher looked at the short, hot-headed infantryman and swallowed down any response. Before Preacher had joined MARSOC, he had been as agitated and angry as Red. But Preacher had calmed down a lot. Plus, he had his faith and strong religion.

Marcus stepped next to Nick and said, "You sure you want to burn it down?"

"We're not burning anything down," Nick said, winking. "Place caught on fire during the firefight with the Vigilantes."

What to do afterward had been discussed prior to the mission, but Isabella hadn't given up on swaying Nick.

"We should call President Rivera and turn in all this coke," she said. "Let him take partial credit for its seizure. Or he can pretend a raid elsewhere seized it. It would buy him political capital with both the American government and his people."

"You missed the part," Nick said, "where I said I could give two shits about President Rivera or the Mexican government. We're here to take down this asshole Hernan Flores and the Godesto Cartel. Nothing more. Nothing less."

"Nick's right," Marcus said. "We give this stuff up and it's just a chance for some police informer to get a look at us or pick up a clue when we do the handoff. We don't need that risk. Plus, you know damn well that this coke would disappear from the evidence room and be back on the streets in two weeks."

"Not everyone in Mexico is dirty," Isabella said.

"And there aren't many naive Boy Scouts in our unit," Nick said, "except for Preacher there. And he'd cut your throat in a heartbeat. Just might pray for you as you died."

A couple of men laughed and Nick said, "Burn the place and let's get the hell out of here."

"What about the prisoners?" Truck said.

Nick wasn't to the point of executing men who were unarmed and bound.

"Marcus, get some of the men to load them up and drop 'em off at some landmark," Nick said. "We'll get our Mexican liaison to call President Rivera's chief of intelligence and let them know where they are. I'm sure they'd enjoy the opportunity to interrogate them. Isabella says not all the Mexican government folks are dirty, so we'll throw them a bone. See if they can chase down some leads themselves and help amplify the pain we're going to bring down on the Godesto."

"Everybody load up," Marcus said. "Red, burn the place down."

"With pleasure," Red said, walking back into the building with a lit cigarette in his mouth.

The next day, the Vigilantes uploaded a video and distributed a press release about the church raid. Besides footage of the cocaine, dead bodies, and weapons in the cathedral, they also inserted loads of evidence against Flores and the Godesto Cartel in the video.

Isabella had spent hours finding pictures of him online in various news clippings and websites involved with the church and its priest. And she provided images of Hernan Flores attending the church and articles describing him donating loads of money to it.

Plus, there were about a dozen photos of Flores and the priest together at various events.

In the end, it was a damning and compelling video against Flores and it exploded and spread virally online and across dozens of news stations across Mexico.

Best of all, analysts and commentators broadcast and discussed the video to no end and chat rooms across the internet began to say that perhaps Flores truly was corrupt.

Score one for S3. But Nick knew not to be overconfident. This war was just getting started.

CHAPTER 18

It wasn't just the Vigilantes making progress. It was the government, too, regaining its legs following the devastating attacks on it.

The next day, billionaire Juan Soto arrived at the Presidential Palace just a few minutes after twp in the afternoon. Soto hated to arrive late to any meeting, especially one involving a friend, but the capital city had rings of checkpoints, blocked roads, and vehicle barriers on all routes in.

Security remained ramped up.

Juan Soto's limousine and two SUV escorts – both crammed full of heavily-armed bodyguards – had to be checked and allowed through each of these security precautions and this lengthy process had Mexico's number one businessman running late.

The convoy finally pulled through the front gate, which was the most heavily guarded of all. Beyond the gate, a hive of activity was happening.

The Presidential Palace had dozens of men on numerous scaffolds along its exterior, all painting and patching its heavily damaged walls. Soto observed the workers with practiced eyes. He had overseen hundreds of building and renovation projects, and he wanted to confirm this was an all-out effort, not some dog-and-pony show for him and the media.

Soto stepped from his limousine into his crowd of bodyguards and felt certain this was no matter of pretense. This was a well-organized, effective undertaking, complete with foremen yelling out directions, architects studying plans, and workers rushing to finish assignments.

The restoration task had been given to a rival company,

despite the reality that Soto owned the country's most prestigious and sought-after construction firm. But Soto had agreed with President Rivera that it would have looked terrible to outsiders for Soto's company to have won the job.

It did chafe Soto a bit that he was donating $10 million toward the work and that his money was going to pad his competitor's wallet, but such was life. Plus, he had bigger things to worry about right now. He ran his hand over his custom-fitted suit jacket and straightened it, entering the Presidential Palace in a hurry.

A top aide for Rivera greeted him at the door, but four security men waved Soto's bodyguards to stop. Soto looked at them and said, "It's all right. Wait outside."

The aide escorted him down numerous halls and switchbacks to the President's private office. The aide opened the door for him and motioned Juan Soto in.

President Roberto Rivera sat at his desk, a phone to his ear.

"Yes, General," Rivera said, his voice slightly strained. He looked up and saw his friend and held up a finger. "That's exactly what I want you to do. Now, I must go."

Rivera hung up the phone and stood. Soto saw a sense of frustration and weariness in his friend before Rivera broke into his smile and covered his weary state with a practiced veil wielded by all great leaders – both in business and in politics.

"It's so good to see you," Rivera said.

"And you, as well," Soto said. "I know you're extremely busy, but I wanted to stop by and congratulate you on the magnificent first strike against Hernan Flores. The Vigilantes taking down the cathedral was great and the video was even better."

Rivera's practiced, fake smile went wide into the real smile Soto knew so well.

"It has only begun," Rivera said. "Can I get you something to drink?"

"It's a bit early, but we do have something that needs to be celebrated," Soto said with a grin.

Rivera avoided calling a staffer and walked to a cabinet and poured the drinks himself.

Soto didn't try to stop him. He had attempted to stop the

President the first couple of times that Rivera had rendered stiff drinks, insisting that no leader of Rivera's stature should serve a constituent, but Rivera had practically ordered him to stand back and allow him to do it.

"You're a friend and I wouldn't be here without your support," Rivera had said back then. "Plus, I must do something to keep myself humble. I can feel this power already going to my head."

So on this day, Soto bit down any objections and watched Rivera pour the drinks. Soto thought back to other drinks they had shared. The one they shared at three in the morning on the night of his victory. They both wanted to celebrate Rivera's election as President alone before returning to their wives.

They had repeated the private occasion on the night that Rivera won re-election against a top-notch opponent, who all had expected to win. The man had been the head of the Congress of the Union. No one expected the shaky, first-term President, even with Soto's support, to pull off defeating their older, more statesman-like rival. Many of Rivera's first-term supporters had dumped him in favor of his opponent.

His rival had pushed for peace with the cartels, especially the Godesto Cartel, and the polls showed that the Mexican people desired that, also. And his earlier backers had grown lukewarm in their support of him as the violence in the country escalated, following Rivera's strong moves against the Godesto. But Rivera's sincerity and charm had pulled in barely enough of the older Mexican voters who felt pursuing peace with the cartels was nothing short of naive and hopeless.

Rivera, the two term-president, handed Soto a glass and lifted his own in a toast.

"To the defeat of Hernan Flores," Rivera said.

"No. Rather, to the death of Hernan Flores," Soto said. "We cannot allow this man to end up behind bars. He will run his cartel just as efficiently from there as he does now."

Rivera said nothing and they both swallowed their drinks.

Rivera, with a look of gravity, said, "You know I can't say that."

"I do," Soto said, "but had he tried to abduct your daughter, you might feel differently."

Rivera nodded, looking down and remembering the near abduction of Soto's daughter.

"How is she?" Rivera said.

"She's still seeing a counselor five days a week," Soto said. "She was scared out of her mind and she was close to several of her guards who were killed. They went with her everywhere. Recitals, school activities, etc. They probably knew her as well as me."

Rivera couldn't meet Soto's eyes. The near-kidnapping of his number one supporter's daughter still caused him great embarrassment. And Rivera couldn't imagine how a kid was supposed to get over seeing men blown apart right in front of their eyes.

"How's Camilla?" he asked lamely.

Soto shook his head.

"She still thinks we should leave the country," Soto said. "Camilla's a good woman, but we've seen a lot of death and too many close calls to count. For God's sake, I'm traveling in an armored limousine these days, and keeping two SUVs with eight men around me. That's far more than I've had in the past. Every day is like leaving for a war zone. She worries to no end."

Soto saw the words cutting into Rivera and knew he didn't need to add more pressure. Being President in Mexico in good years would be a brutal job; the country was so poor and underdeveloped. But, facing down one of the most powerful cartels in the country's history would prove too much for most.

Soto walked over and put his hand on Rivera's shoulder.

"I'm sorry I said that. Just get this bastard as fast as you can, Roberto, and everything will be fine."

"I will, Juan. I promise you."

They shook hands and hugged and both men ended the meeting feeling guilty. Soto, because he had placed additional stress on his friend. And Rivera felt guilt because he had fallen so short to date in his war against Hernan Flores.

Just fifteen miles away, their opposition likewise wrapped up a meeting.

Hernan Flores and the Butcher had discussed and argued about their response to such a devastating loss at the cathedral – both in cocaine product and in Flores's reputation.

In the end, they came up with the perfect response. They polished the idea and finalized their plans.

"Let's see if we can fight their fire with fire," Flores said, as they both stood to leave.

The Butcher smiled his sick smile and picked up his duffel bag, crammed full of gear, including his Uzi and katana swords.

CHAPTER 19

The next day, the Godesto Cartel struck back and struck back hard. Their target was an isolated police station in Coyutla, a medium-sized city of 20,000 that lay nearly five hours from Mexico City.

The small municipality lay alone and miles from help, in the central part of the state of Veracruz. The city of Coyutla supported a department of fifty police officers. On a late afternoon like today, there'd be as many as twenty of them in their headquarters. But that wouldn't matter. Not today. Not against Flores and the Butcher.

Flores had assigned the attack to the Butcher, his best man for leading attacks. This irritated Flores to no end, but it was the truth. And for the moment, Flores would keep the Butcher alive and continue to use the little man.

The Godesto had already infiltrated the area, waiting around the police station, sitting in cars, trucks, and SUVs.

The police department headquarters was in the heart of the city, but the Godesto didn't flinch from such trivial things. They had incredibly precise intelligence. Two of the officers from the department had been paid one hundred thousand dollars to give detailed information about the target. How its headquarters was laid out. What the shifts were for the officers. And what the department's contingency plans were.

The building was hardened because of the threats from the cartels. It was more like a secured bank or armory than a building that was open to the public. The walls were mostly brick. The entries were solid steel doors, which opened outward, instead of inward.

The Butcher was sitting in the passenger seat of a Toyota 4Runner, a mere block from the police department. He turned

MEXICAN HEAT (NICK WOODS BOOK 2)

to a man in the back, who held a video camera ready for use.

"Are you ready?" the Butcher asked.

The man nodded and the Butcher pulled up a bandana from his neck to cover his face. The rest of the men in the vehicle covered up, as well.

The Butcher pulled a Motorola walkie-talkie up and said, "Begin operation. Let's kill all of the bastards."

In the back seat of the 4Runner, the cameraman flipped the simple Sony camcorder on and aimed it at the man across from him. The man, wearing a low baseball hat and speaking from behind a bandana-hidden face, said, "We are the Vigilantes and this is our second operation, against the evil Hernan Flores and the Godesto Cartel. These officers of this district are all corrupt and they will die for their crimes against Mexico."

The speaker directed the cameraman to look over his shoulder and the man turned the video recorder in time to catch a massive garbage truck speeding toward the door to the police headquarters across from them.

The giant green truck had its dumpster lifted over its cab and as it closed the distance to the rear entrance, it slammed on its brakes and bounced to a stop. The truck lowered its big, brown dumpster right in front of the door before any officers could react to the sound. The dumpster doors had been welded shut so there would be no climbing through it. And with the massive, one-ton obstacle in place, the door was utterly blocked unless someone had a couple of blocks of C4 on the inside.

On the left side of the building, a second garbage truck placed its welded-shut dumpster in front of that exit. Now, two doors to the square, brick building were blocked: the one facing the Butcher and the one to his left at nine o'clock. That left a door at twelve o'clock and three o'clock.

"Let's go. Let's go!" the Butcher screamed. His driver gunned it and the 4Runner peeled out, racing into the street. As the two garbage trucks departed the scene without their cargo, and without taking a single round of return fire, the Butcher's 4Runner and several other SUVs descended on the primary entrance, which was at three o'clock.

Another truckload of men – four gunmen – attacked the building's twelve o'clock entrance. They jumped from their vehicle and ran to the opposite side of the truck for cover. They hoisted AK's and M-16s, aiming them at their target. Their only job was to suppress this side of the building.

None of the police officers inside saw this, though, as nearly every one of them had run toward the two opposite doors to investigate the crashing sound they had heard through the walls. Was this possibly an attack? Or an innocent vehicle crash that had happened against the side of the building?

The four men from the first vehicle opened fire, pouring rounds into the door and windows of the building from the twelve o'clock. The Butcher's vehicle slid to a stop on the building's three o'clock side. While the bullets raked the other side of the building, the Butcher and his men jumped to the street and rushed behind their 4Runner for cover. Other Godesto vehicles slid to a stop around them.

All the men deployed from their vehicles, took up positions on the opposite side, and opened up with their weapons gleefully.

The plan was working perfectly. The police officers were taking automatic fire from two sides and their two exits were blocked by dumpsters.

There would be no escape. The Butcher had made sure of that. From his earlier study of the building, the Butcher had discovered that the windows of the police department headquarters were narrow, long slits. They were maybe six or eight inches wide and eight feet tall.

The Butcher had assumed a man couldn't slide through them to escape, but he'd left a couple men watching both of the sides blocked by dumpsters just in case. But anyone trying to escape there would have no chance. They would have to bust out the glass, clear out the shards, and slide out sideways. And in all that time while they were focused on the windows, they'd be sitting ducks for the Godesto men watching the rear.

No one was getting out of this building alive.

Inside the building, rounds slammed into walls, skipped off metal lockers, and zinged off the tile floor. Officers dove for cover and slid behind desks and file cabinets.

"What the hell is going on?" one screamed.

"We're trapped!" yelled another, who came running down the hall from one of the blocked entrances. "There are dumpsters in front of both doors out back!"

Another officer, this one a rookie, screamed, "There are about a dozen of them on this side!"

From the other side of the building, another answered, "There's probably four or five on this side."

Panic spread as officers waited to hear what they should do. They lay about, service pistols drawn. Fear spread and increased as bullets snapped by and pieces of wall and metal rained down on them.

No manual or training exercise told what to do if an armed group waged an all-out assault on the police department. After all, who would be that crazy? Well, the Godesto would be.

A fat, soft captain, who by rank should have been in charge, lay curled up in the fetal position, screaming his head off.

"God help us! God help us!"

And perhaps he could be forgiven. It wasn't like he could call for reinforcements.

The city of Coyutla was too isolated for any help to arrive. Reinforcements would have to come from the state capital of Xalapa. But that was seventy miles away. Absolutely best case, it would take thirty minutes to arrive.

Every officer inside the building also knew that while some police officers in Coyutla were out on patrol, no way would many of them respond to such an overwhelming attack from men so heavily armed.

Given morale (and the low pay) among the officers, some might even abandon their car, shed their uniform, and rush home for safety. Many were so scared for their family's safety that they never showed their faces. Instead, they wore balaclavas to cover their faces for their entire shifts.

Besides the captain curled up in the fetal position, other officers were hiding for their lives. They lay sprawled under chairs and desks. A few clustered in groups in the halls, hoping for safety in numbers.

But there was almost no shelter anywhere.

The rifle fire from the two sides formed a perfect L-shaped crossfire that cut through walls, obstacles, desks, torsos, and limbs. The full-size battle rifles used by the Godesto (with their military-designed ammo of ball ammunition) were doing precisely what they were issued to do: cut through reinforced buildings and wound or kill the occupants inside.

Screams and shrieks spread inside the building as more cops died or absorbed insanely painful wounds.

Panic set in. A few officers crawled toward windows to return fire with their pistols, but those who did found themselves prime targets for the well-armed men on each side of the building.

It was a turkey shoot and it was completely one-sided. A few officers, seeing the ease with which their enemies' bullets cut through the walls, decided to fight fire with fire. They aimed at the walls at the same level of the entry holes and shot back in an attempt to mount at least some defense.

But their smaller, slower pistol rounds – 9 mm – barely penetrated the walls. Plus, they lacked the accuracy of the long rifles firing from outside.

A former soldier, who was only a low-ranking police officer and had been hired four weeks ago, couldn't take it anymore. If their pussy, paper-pushing captain couldn't lead, and if their scared-shitless, sack-of-shit sergeants wouldn't lead either, then he would.

"Let's go!" he yelled. "We need to get to the storage lockers and grab the rifles. The SWAT Team has M-16's stored there."

No one responded, so he screamed it again. Louder, and with more authority this time. Several officers near him crawled toward the locker and he stood to encourage others.

"Let's go!" he screamed. "It's our only chance!"

It was a good idea that no one else had even thought of. And like that, with the herding instinct taking hold, other

MEXICAN HEAT (NICK WOODS BOOK 2)

officers jumped to their feet to join the others.

They scrambled for the desperately needed weapons. M-16A2's. These long rifles provided a measure of hope. At least now it was long weapons versus long weapons.

Out in the street, the Butcher yelled, "Phase two! Commence phase two and spread the word down the line."

Some of his gunmen ceased firing and snatched duffel bags from vehicles. Three men from the Butcher's side of attack, and two from the other flank, rushed toward the building. The remaining shooters switched to single shot and more carefully fired at the building, taking care to avoid hitting their own men.

The police officers couldn't see the action on the outside and in the horror of the attack, they never noticed the reduction of fire.

In fact, they were finally rallying. The prior army soldier had twelve of the officers rallied, assembled, and fitted with M-16A2s.

"All right," the former soldier said. "Pair off and set up on windows. Work together to fire back and find targets. We have to get them off us. There's no one coming to save us."

"Hell yeah," one officer said. "Let's get some."

The former soldier liked the spirit he was seeing. They might just make it out of here after all.

The officers split up and scurried toward firing positions, hunched over and low. They even looked like soldiers, the former soldier thought.

Even better, the former soldier noticed that the battle appeared to have slacked off. Rounds still snapped through, but with less frequency. Maybe their attackers were running out of ammo, the former soldier thought.

The officers throughout the building – those still alive – moved forward with purpose and confidence with their M16s.

One officer, a woman, crawled to a window and found a target. She fired, but saw no reaction from the man, who continued to fire slow, aimed shots toward the building.

She fired again, aiming lower at the man's stomach. With this shot, the man's head yanked back and he fell to the ground. Instantly dead. It was her first kill. Ever. She shifted to her next target.

In other rooms inside the building, other officers – armed with M-16s – engaged their enemy. The fire from the previously silent building was surprising and deadly to the Godesto.

The Butcher's men recoiled from the lethal and savage return fire. The momentum was shifting and a wave of relief passed through the building. Panic shifted to elation.

Some grinned. Some shouted. "Come on, you bastards. Come get some more."

And then, then it happened.

A grenade floated into one of the rooms inside the police headquarters and bounced about. Other grenades followed in other rooms, as the Butcher's men, who had rushed the building, threw M67 fragmentation grenades through the narrow, shot-out windows.

The baseball-like weapons exploded with massive booms, hurling fragments in all directions. Officers died. Officers panicked.

Officers broke. Completely hapless now.

The Butcher emerged from behind the cover of his vehicle and laughed maniacally. Ah, hahahahaha!! He roared in an insane cackle.

"Stay down, sir," one of his men warned, but the Butcher held his position, roaring in amusement. He was bent over laughing so hard that he held his side. He coughed and said, "You stupid bastards thought you were going to be okay with your rifles. Well, we'll see!"

And he laughed even harder, while his men at the vehicles picked up their rate of fire to cover their half-mad leader.

The cartel men against the building realized they had driven their defenders back with their frag grenades and they switched to their final weapon: tear gas grenades.

The CS grenades looked like tall coke-cans. The Butcher's men pulled pins and tossed them in windows already spewing smoke and dust from the frag grenades.

The cylindrical grenades were designed for riot control, but in an enclosed building, the tear gas from them was designed to produce coughing, vomiting, and difficulty in breathing.

They also created a thick smoke that was impossible to see through, even if tears weren't pouring out of your eyes in a feeble attempt to purge the burning chemical.

The officers had trained against CS and they rushed away from the CS fumes.

"Grab our gas masks," someone yelled.

They knew it would be more difficult to fire their M16s or pistols accurately with gas masks on, but they had trained for that. At least some.

A small group of officers huddled around the gear locker and the former army soldier saw that his group had dwindled from casualties. Worse, some of those around him bled from shrapnel.

"We're going to be all right," he said, trying to reassure the men, all of whom were coughing and choking through the haze of the growing CS fog. The chemical haze creeped down the hallway. Closer. Thicker. Harder to breathe through.

"We'll get our masks," the former soldier said through tears, "then we'll regroup and hang together."

An officer removed the lock and jerked the doors open to the gear cabinet. The locker was bare. Completely empty. A sheet of paper taped to the back of the wall said, in thick black magic marker, "The joke's on you!!!"

One officer screamed "Noooo!" in horror, while two others leaned back against the hallway wall and slid to the ground, their weapons clanging to the floor. They buried their heads in their arms to try to offer relief from the tear gas. A couple of officers cried. They cried hard. The sort of crying you do when you know you're going to die.

"We can't run," one said between gasps. "They'll murder us if we run out those doors."

"Come on," screamed the former soldier, trying to lift the man. "We can't give up."

And then they heard the maniacal laugh, one they had heard moments before off in the distance, but it sounded closer.

The Butcher couldn't stop laughing. His right hand held his cross-slung Uzi, which was aimed at the ground, while his left hand rested on the handle of his katana sword, which hung from an assault harness on his left hip, handle facing forward.

To his left and his right, two of his most trusted gunmen stood protecting him, their AK's aimed down the hallway and their eyes probing for danger. The fog was too thick to see through and they couldn't see the officers huddled around the empty gear locker farther down the hall.

The Butcher roared with hysteria as he stared at the thick fog of CS.

He had once been gassed by the police before an arrest and he knew whoever was still alive, they would be struggling to breathe or see. They would be functioning at a level of ten percent of their capability. Unable to breathe. Blinded. Choking.

The Butcher strode toward them, laughing gleefully.

Men exactly like these police officers had arrested him, when he was a young man merely trying to earn a living. And officers no different than these in this hallway had failed to protect him in jail full of muscle-bound animals, who hadn't seen the light of day (or a woman) in years.

Instead, the officers had allowed him to be molested and raped hundreds of times in the six years he was in prison.

Now, it was payback time... He laughed harder at the thought. He wouldn't feel an ounce of remorse for the one-sided slaughter he was about to finish.

The Butcher paused at the door. It was time to get serious. His laugh was gone. His grin and eyes transformed into a psychotic mask of anger. He had been told he was bipolar, but he had never bothered to confirm that.

He choked and coughed as CS tear gas emerged from the hallway. The man to his right leaned into his AK to fire at any movement they might see, but the Butcher used his Uzi to push the man's weapon to the right and off target.

"No!" said the Butcher. "Give me a mask and wait on me. If I don't come out in five minutes, grab the men and come in and kill anyone who's still alive."

The man on the right reached in his backpack and handed the Butcher a gas mask.

The Butcher turned his head and coughed, spitting out phlegm and snot caused by the CS, even at this distance. He put the mask on and blocked the filter with his hand, blowing out the small amount of CS that had crept into the mask. He removed his hand and inhaled the clean, filtered air. Blinking his burning eyes, he allowed his tears to remove the remnants of CS under his eyelids.

He cursed himself for walking so close to the building and getting hit by his own shit. But then he remembered that he didn't give a shit if he died.

He lived every night with too many nightmares and too much anger. Only a heavy dose of sleeping pills even allowed him to sleep. To hell with whether he lived or not. You didn't go through what he'd gone through in prison without coming out completely nuts.

And as he thought of the injustices and horrendous acts he had endured, rage took over. He checked the Uzi and confirmed it hung in its cross-chest sling, falling to the right side of his right leg thanks to a half-foot extension strap that he'd added. It lay against the side of his right quad, out of the way, but also where he could grab it quickly with his firing hand if needed.

The Butcher reached for the handle of his Japanese katana on his left side. He pulled it from its sheath and entered the building like a ninja moving through the smoke of war.

The Butcher moved down the hall, staying close to the wall. He didn't want to catch a bullet moving down its center, but no shots came from the building. Likewise, his men had ceased firing. A signal had been passed that their leader had entered.

It was eerily quiet, following all the gunfire. The only exception was the gagging and choking from surviving police officers. Thick CS clouds drifted outward, searching for the opened door that he had entered.

The Butcher tiptoed down the hall, his rubber-soled boots silent on the tile floor. He saw an open door on his right. He quietly sheathed the sword so that he didn't enter the room with it extended before him.

He gripped his Uzi and slowly pulled it up, aiming it from the hip and creeping through the door.

The room looked devastated. Glass fragments littered the

bloody floor. Wood splinters, concrete chunks, and scattered papers added to the mayhem.

An officer lay dead near the window in a bathtub-sized pool of blood, an M-16 lying under him. Standing behind him, oblivious to the approaching danger, stood another male police officer. The man was bent over at the waist, choking and wiping at his burning eyes.

The room was otherwise empty. The Butcher released the Uzi and it fell back soundlessly to the side of his right leg. He grabbed the sword sheath with his left hand, gripping the katana handle with his right. He slid the blade out without a sound, grasping it in a powerful two-hand hold, the blade pointed directly ahead.

The Butcher shot forward, his boots now making a lot of noise on the glass shards as he sprinted forward. The officer turned at the noise, but could see nothing through his burning eyes.

The Butcher plunged the sword into the man's side with a straight thrust, burying it to the hilt. The sword burst out the man's other side and the officer screamed in pain, a shriek more like that of a pig mortally wounded than that of a man.

The Butcher drove his shoulder into the man's shoulder and stopped suddenly, yanking back on the sword to free it from the man's body.

Blood cascaded down the blade's shaft, adding to the already blood-soaked floor. Pounding footsteps racing down the hall broke him from his trance.

Someone was running toward him and it had to be one of the officers.

The Butcher slipped away from the bleeding body and watched where he stepped, avoiding pieces of plasters and chunks of wood. He had to remain silent.

The Butcher stepped behind the door, lifting his sword high and waiting for his target.

"Eduardo!" a man screamed, before coughing and sliding to a halt on the debris-covered floor. "Eduardo, are you okay?"

It was the former soldier, who through his leadership had rallied the cops in this building. He entered the room, cautious now, a Glock 9 mm pistol stretched before him. A T-shirt was wrapped around his mouth and nose and his eyes looked red and severely irritated.

The Butcher admired the man's resourcefulness and chalked up the man's ability to respond so quickly to this one small improvisation. The officer turned his eyes from the empty part of the room before, to the corner on the left side that he instantly knew he should have cleared first.

His mistake was the last one that he would ever make.

The Butcher made his move. He stepped forward, dropped his entire body weight six inches, and swung the sword with all his might down from its maximum height to the floor. It was a practiced move. It was a deadly move. The blade raced downward in a powerful arc, striking the police officer across both arms, roughly at the elbows.

The forged-steel katana cut through the man's left arm at the elbow, while on the right arm it burrowed two inches deep, shattering bone in the forearm before stopping. Both men watched the left forearm hang for a moment because of its grip on the pistol, before falling to the floor.

The officer knew he was badly injured – probably mortally wounded – but he was completely immobilized by the sight that his arm had been sheared off. He couldn't believe it. Didn't even think such a thing was possible. But he was looking at it.

That was his last thought before his opponent struck again.

The Butcher stepped from behind the door, aimed the sword's blade to the rear, and drove the handle into the man's face. It crashed just below his eye and fragmented bone as if it were a pool cue. The cop screamed in pain.

As he toppled backward into the hall, he realized that his right arm couldn't even hold the pistol, which had clanged to the floor.

He kept screaming as he fell hard back in the hallway, landing on his duff, but somehow staying upright. He was completely defenseless now, a dead man still breathing, but he tried to use his one remaining arm to help him to his feet.

"No!" he screamed, still in the sitting position. But the Butcher was rushing forward with blinding speed. He swung the sword to the rear, as if it were a baseball bat, and then swung as hard as he could at the man's neck. The Butcher fully intended to behead the man – a feat he knew to be possible since he'd done it to the guard at the ground floor of Flores's office.

But his boots slid on glass and blood and he failed to gain enough torque, so the blade cut through the side of the man's neck and stopped after it hit the spine. The blow effectively ended all muscular control and the officer slid to the ground.

The Butcher heard movement down the hall and turned to see a cluster of officers. The CS fog had cleared some and the officers could see him. They reached for weapons to open fire.

The Butcher ran away while he could, yelling, "Cover me!" through his gasmask.

Two of the Butcher's men appeared inside the doorway and fired down the hall through the smoke. It was well-aimed, long-rifle fire from their AK's and the accuracy of their shots provided the Butcher with the cover he needed.

He raced out the door and to the flank, out of the cone of danger from the hallway, and ripped off his gas mask, sheathing his sword.

"The army is coming," one of his men said, as other Godesto men ran forward to fire down the hallway.

The Butcher needed no further urging. He yelled to his men, "Finish it."

More than a dozen Godesto gunmen came running toward the entrance. They quickly donned gas masks, organized themselves, and redistributed ammunition and grenades. Then with a nod from one of their leaders, they lobbed a frag grenade down the hall, waited for it to explode, and followed the screams of pain and panic into the building.

The Butcher heard the muffled yells of his men and the screams of wounded police officers as his killers worked their way methodically through the building, room by room, grenades first, then half a mag into some unfortunate soul.

The Godesto finished their bloody work, assembled in a convoy, and exited the city of Coyutla. They didn't even drive away in a hurry.

CHAPTER 20

Dwayne Marcus appeared as shocked as Nick Woods felt.

Isabella had grabbed Nick and Marcus for a leadership-only meeting and shown them a local news station report that she had recorded.

With the two leaders of S3 in the room, she hit play and watched a busty newscaster in a low-cut dress begin speaking with a graphic over her shoulder that said "Cartel." The newscaster stopped speaking and the camera switched from her to an amateur video.

The video showed a bandana-wearing man in the back of some kind of SUV. He began speaking and Nick and Marcus couldn't pick up the Spanish.

"What's he saying?" Nick asked angrily.

Isabella translated. "'We are the Vigilantes and this is our second operation, against the evil Hernan Flores and the Godesto Cartel. These officers of this district are all corrupt and they will die for their crimes against Mexico.'"

Nick looked at Marcus.

"I know this isn't possible," Nick said, "but just to be sure, we didn't have an operation happen that I didn't know of, correct?"

"Of course not," Marcus said. He looked offended.

They watched as the video – uncut and unedited by the news station – showed parts of a vicious firefight against a police station.

"Did this actually happen?" Nick asked. "We need to find out from the police or someone in government if this actually happened."

Isabella nodded. "I'm on it."

"Oh," Nick said, "and gather the Primary Strike Team in a

room with a TV and get this set up to play."

Isabella nodded and Nick noticed her hips as she walked off, despite trying not to. He turned quickly and refocused his attention on Marcus. Damn it, why had he allowed a woman into a war zone?

Ten minutes later, the Primary Strike Team was assembled and watching the video, with Nick and Marcus standing behind them.

The nearly identical look of "the Vigilantes," as well as the brutality of the strike on the police station, had shocked the team members the same way that it had shocked Nick and Marcus. Unfortunately, the gunmen in the video looked precisely as the members of S3 had appeared in their first video.

Whoever put the video together had made sure their men looked the same, recorded the video in the same style, the whole nine yards. And the worst thing was that nearly every news station in the country was playing the video of "the Vigilantes" assaulting the police station in Coyutla.

"Is this true?" asked Lizard, who looked scared. "Did it really happen?"

Isabella assured him that it did.

Nick knew the background to Isabella's answer; he had personally followed up with her. On the one hand, he'd wanted to confirm the information. But more than just that, he had wanted to see Isabella again. Watching her walk off had awakened something in him that he hadn't thought much of since Anne's death.

Nick needed to be careful of how her body called him and how those big, brown eyes pulled him in.

Suddenly, Nick came back to the present and realized that Isabella and the rest of the team were looking at him and that his mind had drifted from the task at hand.

"I'm sorry," Nick said. "I've got something I'm working over in my mind. Marcus, would you take care of this?"

Marcus moved through the group and stood in front of the

TV.

"Our Mexican counterparts," Marcus said, "have confirmed that this raid did in fact happen. They're confirming the body count and making sure no officers, who were on duty at the time, were abducted instead of simply killed."

Marcus was in what Nick called his drill instructor stance. His legs were spread shoulder-length apart, his fingers clasped together in front of him at stomach height. Nick had never met anyone with such a 24/7 bearing and Nick knew he was lucky to have such a man helping command this group of talented killers that comprised Shield, Safeguard, and Shelter.

The men were so skilled and experienced that it was easy to be intimidated by the task of trying to set the example and not look a total fool.

Truck, with his shaved head, big arms, and slight gut, was nursing a beer, but he cleared his throat and said, "Nobody ever said those sons of bitches weren't smart."

Nick knew he had to keep an eye on Truck and his drinking, but alcohol was just one thing that often went with being a warrior. You usually turned to alcohol, like Truck, or seclusion, like Nick, or faith, like Preacher. Preacher was sitting off to the side and had been visibly angry during the video footage of the bloody, wrecked police station. Preacher hated bullies and the assault on the police headquarters had been an entirely one-sided affair with heavily armed assailants on one side and barely trained, mostly pistol-armed cops on the other.

"Fuck it," Red said, starting to stand. "Smart or not, I'm ready to tangle with these assholes. You got a target we can go out and hit?"

Marcus shook his head "no" and Red sat back down.

Nick loved the cocky, smallest member of their Primary Strike Team. And he appreciated the fact that Red was sitting on a couch next to the biggest, most intimidating member of the team: the giant powerlifter Bulldog.

True to character, Bulldog sat on the couch in a tank top that showed off his eighteen-inch arms and had a protein shake in one hand and a grip trainer in the other. He was squeezing the grip spring mercilessly and Nick hated to think how bad the Navy SEAL from the rough streets of Baltimore would mess someone up in a hand-to-hand fight.

Correction, Nick remembered, the man had already fed one Godesto Cartel member a concrete wall, rearranging the man's face for good.

"We need to immediately air a response denying this," Isabella said. "Claim it wasn't the real Vigilantes, but some copycat attempt by the Godesto."

"Great idea," Nick said from the back of the room. He was a little pissed that he hadn't thought of it first. "Make it happen, Isabella, and grab whoever you need to help you get it done. Besides releasing it to the media, make sure we get it up on the website. We don't need our name trashed by this bullshit. Lizard, get your gear on and grab a bandana. We'll need you to do the talking."

Lizard and Isabella hurried out and Nick looked to the front of the room.

"Marcus, go walk the lines," he said. "Make sure everyone is alert. The rest of you either need to be practicing assault drills or getting some PT in. We need to be as sharp as we can be for when we finally figure out where this piece of shit Hernan Flores is hiding out."

Nick watched his Primary Strike Team leave the room and felt the strength of the men and women selected for this task. They were as smart as they were talented. Nick didn't know where old, fat-ass Flores was hiding, but when they found him, the man would be in a heap of trouble.

CHAPTER 21

Nick Woods and his team members weren't the only ones upset about the tape.

Juan Soto and President Rivera were meeting again. It was just the two of them, in yet another conference room.

The mood of this meeting was less pleasant than their most recent congratulatory visit after the raid on the cathedral. They'd already been arguing back and forth for five minutes.

"This is a catastrophe," Soto said. He'd already said it several times, but he was avoiding saying what he wanted to say. What he needed to say.

"I *know* it's a catastrophe," Rivera said, saying it much too hard.

"I tried to support you on the Vigilante idea, but already they've gone too far."

"This wasn't the Vigilantes," Rivera replied. "How many times do I have to say that."

"Great!" Soto snapped, slapping the palms of his hands loudly on the table. "So, we have more than one group of vigilantes out there, operating on their own, outside of the law. What the hell, Roberto?! The goal was to bring the country back under the rule of law, not the opposite! We can't have bands of armed citizens fighting it out against cartels and corrupt police officers. How will this lead to tourism and future business investment? How? Just how?"

"This wasn't the work of citizens, Juan," Rivera said again. "And this wasn't the work of the Vigilantes. It was Hernan Flores, using his own people in a strike against law enforcement. He knows he must turn the people against the Vigilantes. Flores knows what a threat they are to him. He's actually scared. He's terrified and acting out of desperation."

"The people don't know that the Vigilantes didn't do this. Don't you see that?" Soto said, his voice still loud.

Rivera turned away, his anger rising. He took a deep breath and turned toward his friend.

"What do you want me to do, Juan?"

"Tell the Vigilantes to go away," Soto said. "They're American Special Forces, aren't they? Send them away. Ask America for continued assistance in weapons and training, but that's it. We can win this fight on our own. Our military. Our own police. This needs to be a Mexican victory. You need to maintain your legitimacy and the rule of law."

Rivera leapt to his feet.

"We tried to solve this on our own for five years, Juan! Have you forgotten that? Have you forgotten how we nearly lost our re-election bid? Or the ambush and attack on our Presidential Palace? They assaulted our government headquarters. How much closer must we let them get? They're in our capital city and at our front gate."

"How dare you accuse me of forgetting," Juan said, though he managed to keep his seat. "It's not your daughter who was nearly abducted."

Both men turned away, fuming.

"I'm sorry," Rivera finally said.

"Don't apologize," Soto answered. "I didn't mean to lose my temper either."

"These are hard times," Rivera said.

"Of course they're hard times," Soto said, snapping again. "When hasn't it been hard times?"

"What do you want me to do, Juan? Please, say what you came to say."

"At a minimum, bring these Americans into the fold," Soto said. "Force them into Mexican uniforms and under your control."

"They won't do that," Rivera said. "I've tried that already. They operate independently and I've heard their leader is crazy."

The president of Mexico looked off at a painting from the war that had gained Mexico independence from Spain. The war had happened in 1810 and lasted eleven years, costing more than 250,000 lives. This painting showed men and horses charging forward into smoke and cannon fire. Rivera looked back at his friend.

"Juan, they lost most of a Navy SEAL Team just a few weeks ago. They're not going to come in again under Mexican authority. They know we have too many leaks. And honestly, I don't blame them for not coming in."

"Then ask them to leave," Juan said, standing as well. "And issue a warrant for Hernan Flores's arrest. Let's follow the rule of law, whether Flores does or not."

"That won't work," Rivera said.

"It *has* to work," Juan said, his voice raised again.

"He will just run the Godesto from inside. You know we barely control the prisons. The jailers are the most corrupt law enforcement that we have. I haven't even tried to fix the problems there. It's that bad."

"We have to follow the law," Juan said, holding his ground.

"We are at an impasse," Rivera said.

"Think long term, Rivera. Do we want Mexico to only be a country that follows the rules only when it's convenient?"

"I'll think about what you have said," Rivera said, turning his back on his friend. "I may consider issuing a warrant and I may ask the Americans to stop working as Vigilantes and at least put on Mexican uniforms."

Rivera stared at a painting on the opposite wall, this one from the Mexican-American War.

"My aide will show you out," Rivera said, ignoring his friend. He was still wounded from the fight.

Soto didn't want to leave with such a cold feeling between them. He walked up to Rivera and put his hand on his friend's shoulder.

"I believe in you, brother. We must do what's right. We must return to the purity you campaigned on. The people believe in you and thousands of officers do, as well. Give them something to believe in. Issue a warrant, go public with a big reward, and arrest this monster."

"I will consider your counsel," Rivera said, but refused to look back at his friend. Soto exited the room, feeling unhappy about how the conversation had gone down, but hopeful about the possible outcome.

CHAPTER 22

President Roberto Rivera strode up to the lectern. He approached it in a rehearsed walk that his advisors believed displayed grave seriousness, with just a touch of confidence. Cameras flashed. Every network station cut from their regular programming to show the presidential press conference.

Rivera reached the microphone and stood tall, staring out at the media horde with his head held high and his chin up. It was his command look, and advisors, focus groups, and women – that most important demographic of all – claimed the expression was their favorite. It was his display of command and it donned posters, websites, and billboards. Rivera practiced it often and he nailed the position again on this day, holding it for a long second before beginning.

"I come before the Mexican people today to make an important declaration.

"When I decided to run for president, a single issue compelled my candidacy: crime. Specifically, cartel violence, since it is the root of most crime. Cartel money and influence leads to untold amounts of violence against the Mexican state and Mexican people.

"I made reducing this plague against our country my number one goal during my campaign – no matter the cost – and you, the Mexican people, saw fit to elect me to right this wrong. We spent the better part of my first four years cleaning out our government offices of those who were corrupt, weak, and without morals. The cartels had informants that ran the gamut from our police departments to our military units to our judicial courts. My government could literally make no move without the cartels being two steps ahead. Sometimes three.

"But despite the limited success of those first four years,

STAN R MITCHELL

you, the people, placed great faith in me. You, the people, saw fit to re-elect me, despite a strong opponent running against me on the precisely opposite platform. My opponent ran on peace and I ran on war. My mind remains unchanged. This is a war we must fight. It's a war we must win. My re-election platform, just like my initial election platform, was for a single cause: to right this wrong.

"I have focused on the dangers posed by cartels every single day of my presidency and it is with great pride that I say today that we are announcing our biggest blow to our enemies yet. This case will prove to be a major strike against the cartels that threaten both our government and our way of life.

"As we speak, officers from the attorney general's office are filing charges against businessman and philanthropist Hernan Flores. While I know many of you may be shocked to hear this news, we have clear and convincing proof that Flores is the head man of the largest cartel in Mexico. The Godesto Cartel. This organized crime organization has significant influence across seventy percent of our country.

"The Mexican attorney general will step out in a moment to lay out all the charges against him and I assure you they are many. They range from treason to murder. More than three hundred murders, in fact. Yes. I said three hundred.

"I know Flores has always maintained his innocence. To him, I say that if you are truly innocent, then come forward and stand trial. You will have the opportunity to prove your innocence. You will have a chance to clear your name once and for all.

"Unfortunately, I feel confident that Flores will not stand trial. I think Flores will react differently and I think his actions to this news will confirm what we in the government have known for years: Flores is no philanthropist or business leader. He's a maniac who threatens the very existence of what we hold dear.

"In fact, we think he will either go on the run or hide out. Therefore, the attorney general and I have agreed that setting a reward for information on his whereabouts is appropriate. Thus, the government of the Mexican people is offering a $10 million reward for anyone that has information that helps lead to his arrest.

"Now with that, let me allow my attorney general to share with you a detailed presentation against Hernan Flores and answer any questions you may have."

President Roberto Rivera stood tall again, raised his head, and looked off in the distance. He allowed the photographers to snap some final shots. He then turned and walked away, shaking hands with his attorney general as the man approached the lectern.

Rivera mentally congratulated himself for nailing the press conference. Juan Soto would be pleased, and actually saying the words – and doing what the law required – felt immensely rewarding. And right.

Soto had been correct about following the rule of law and Rivera felt so much better now that he had decided to recommit himself to that rule of law. Part one of his deal with his billionaire friend was over. He had issued an arrest warrant and was now on the way down the road to incarcerating him.

Part two might be more difficult. How was he to tell the Americans he had changed his mind? That he no longer wanted them in his country, risking their lives, as Vigilantes? He would have to put some thought into how to do this. It wouldn't be simple.

Back at the farm where Nick's unit was based, Isabella received a text about an upcoming press conference involving the President. She set out to alert Nick.

As she walked down the hall to pass along the news, she secretly hoped Nick would be alone in his office.

Things had changed. Nick had removed the formidable wall between the two of them and she had finally understood his gruff behavior was a means to keep her at a distance.

She then had a better idea and stopped, heading back to her room. Inside her room, she took off a loose, button-up dress shirt, which she liked but which was too conservative for what she now envisioned. The button-up dress shirt was good for wearing around the men, who were always ogling her, but not the right top for what she had in mind with this opportunity – a rare chance to be alone with Nick, in a room with no spectators. And if she were lucky, no Marcus there either.

She looked at her thin, toned body in the mirror, then hung the shirt on a hanger and put it in the closet. She pulled a small, white knit shirt from a dresser drawer and wrenched the shirt on, tugging out the wrinkles – it was definitely tight.

She glanced in the mirror again and saw her figure highlighted by the tight shirt and her upper arms showing as well, below the short sleeves.

She smiled, opened the door, and stepped off for Nick's office. She rushed down the hall and thankfully avoided any of the men. She took a deep breath and knocked on the door.

Nick Woods was in the middle of his fifth set of pull-ups. He had asked some of the men to find the studs in the wall and install a pull-up bar shortly after they moved into the farm. He was on his thirteenth rep of the fifth set when someone knocked on the door.

"Hang on," he yelled, then eked out two more. He dropped to the floor and flexed his hands – his hands bothered him as much on pull-ups as his arms did. Nick slapped his hands together a few times and in his command voice said, "Come in."

The door opened and Isabella stood there. She wore a tight-fitting white top and her typically tight blue jeans.

"I'm sorry to interrupt," she said, "and I should have found a different top to throw on," she added, crossing her arms in front of her breasts. "I was in the middle of exercising when I got some important news that I wanted to get to you as quickly as I could," Isabella said.

The shirt was so tight that Nick could make out the curve of her breasts. He wiped his arm across his forehead and said, "I understand. I was doing the same." He nodded back to the pull-up bar.

She smiled, a bit too wide, and Nick saw her perfect, white

teeth. He hated how much he enjoyed her being in the room like this. He broke his eyes away and looked down, noticing he wore a pair of shorts and a tight T-shirt that wrapped around his chest and arms tighter than he remembered.

"I guess," he said, pointing down to his clothing, "as long as you don't mind, I don't mind."

"I don't mind," she said, quickly. She closed the door and walked toward him.

"What's the news?" he asked, fully aware that the door was closed and she stood mere feet away.

"A media contact of mine texted me to say the President would be holding a press conference in," she looked down at her watch, and Nick couldn't miss her breast moving when she did, "about forty-five minutes."

"Do we know what it's about?"

"We don't," Isabella said. "But this is an unscheduled press conference with the president. It'll be a big deal."

"We should round up the Strike Team and watch it together."

"Agreed," she said, turning to leave.

"Isabella?"

She stopped.

He hesitated. "Uh, thanks for getting me the news so quickly."

She smiled. "Was there anything else?" she asked, raising her eyebrows provocatively.

Nick stood there like an idiot. He couldn't take his eyes off her. He'd never dated a Latina woman; had barely even been around many in the backwater part of East Tennessee where he'd been raised. But her bronze skin, full hips, and nice breasts were a sight he didn't want to forget. And she was *more* than just any woman. The woman could shoot. She was smart as a whip. She was a serious asset to S3.

Nick looked down, embarrassed.

"It's all right," she said.

He looked up at her, hating that she had so perfectly followed his eyes. And worse, his thoughts.

"Sorry," he said. "It's just been a while since I've been around many women. Spent a lot of time alone in Montana after I lost my wife."

"I know," she said, walking toward him. "Marcus told me your story. You're quite famous. And heroic."

"I just did what any man would do who saw his wife gunned down. And while my story is famous, my face isn't. Allen Green made sure no photos were ever published of me in his book and on all those interviews."

"Well," Isabella said, dropping her eyes down his body, "if they had published any pictures of you, then you'd have been much more famous than you already are."

Nick tried to ignore her gaze.

"Well, long while or not since I've seen a good looking woman, it still ain't right, me being a commander and all, looking at a person in his unit like that. They call that fraternization in the American military. Strictly against the rules."

"It's okay," Isabella said.

Nick turned from her.

"Ever since my wife died, I just –" He shook his head. "Well, I tried to get away from it all by living in Montana, but then learned that I needed to re-emerge and be a part of society or I would go crazy." He stopped and looked back at her. "I just." He paused. "I try not to –"

Isabella raised her eyebrows with a slight smile.

He shook his head with a laugh. "I try not to even notice women. I stupidly thought that if I threw myself hard enough into duty, I could forget about them for good."

"Can't live with us, can't live without us," Isabella said, crossing her arms and shrugging, moving her breasts in a way that Nick felt confident was no accident.

"Right," Nick said, turning away again. He felt himself blushing. He swallowed, tried to regain control, and faced her again. "Thanks again for the news and call together the team," he said, back in his typical Nick voice.

She was looking at him again. Her eyes dropped from his face down to his chest. They didn't stop there.

Nick stepped back. If he could have gotten behind a desk without looking like a coward, he would have.

"Sorry I made all this get weird," Nick said, taking yet

another step back and putting his hands on his hips. He felt more in control now, the danger averted.

"I need to knock out another set of pull ups and we can't have this in a unit," he said, his voice deeper and more like the voice he was familiar with. "We need to pretend this didn't happen." He made the last statement definitive.

"Or, we can acknowledge that it did," she said, stepping toward him. She walked up and placed her hand on his forearm.

Nick stepped back, but he hit wall this time. He was taken aback by her aggressiveness and wondered how he'd never noticed her signals before. Perhaps he'd been too much of an ass, trying to keep his distance. Somehow, he had missed the clues.

"For a man who doesn't miss much," Isabella said, "you've missed everyone of my looks and signals."

"I'm not ready for this," he said, but he didn't yank his forearm back. Her hand felt *too* good. "I just need you to understand that it's been hard for me to get over Anne."

"I understand," she said, "but at some point you need to move on. Even she would want that."

Nick met Isabella's brown eyes and she slid her hand further up his arm, to his elbow. Her fingers felt light, soft, and inviting.

Isabella could barely control herself. He stood there, so tall, so magnificent, so rugged. And his clumsiness made him even more attractive to her. This was a real man. The kind of man who'd work all day in the fields and come home with a six-pack of beer, not a dozen roses.

Men like him weren't much for words or romance, but they understood grit. They understood loyalty. And they'd stick when things went south. In a world full of men who whitened their teeth and shaved their chest, this man appealed to her like old, worn leather. He was from a different age.

A lion, still fierce, but a drifter. He had nothing left to prove – he had already lived a dozen lifetimes – and he carried the physical and emotional scars like a weight around his neck. And yet, he had so much fight left. Even a passing glance at him would tell a stranger of how much fight he had left.

A man like him didn't know how to quit or retire or back down. Like a wandering lion, he was okay avoiding the confrontation of other males eager to prove their strength, but he would not back down if challenged. Or if a large pack of hyenas threatened the pride.

They didn't make them like Nick Woods anymore and Isabella couldn't shake the thought of what a man of his strength would be like. It was something she wanted to experience more than she could possibly explain.

He appeared to gain control of himself, after the surprise of hitting the wall.

"I can't do this with a woman I'm in command of," he said.

Isabella smiled. She knew she had him. She stepped forward again. "And in six months, you won't be in command of me," she said.

She stepped against him and ran her hand from his elbow up to his upper arm.

"I'm not ready for a relationship," Nick said.

"And I'm not looking for one."

She moved her face just inches from his and she could smell the light sweat of his body. She placed her hand on his chest and moved in, kissing him lightly. She pulled back and allowed her hand to drift down his chest to his abs.

She lightly kissed him again and then turned and walked away, as if nothing had happened. But, as she opened the door, she looked back at him and smiled – a smile so wide and inviting that she couldn't possibly have faked something so real.

"I'll round up the men," she said, lowering her eyes to his firm stomach (and even lower). She laughed and raised her eyebrows again.

"Commander," she said, winking before leaving.

Nick stood there, completely floored. He could feel every

single place her fingers had touched, from his forearm, to his elbow, to his arms and chest and stomach. And the way she had just looked at him… He shuddered.

His senses felt as alive as they had felt in a long time and he stood straighter, feeling better about himself than he'd felt in years.

"Nothing like a little romance to get the confidence back," he thought. Then he tried to suppress the thought. "Enough of that. Get your head back in the game, Nick."

But he couldn't shake a single thought: If the opportunity arose, he might just go for it.

Forty minutes later, the Primary Strike Team finished watching President Rivera's press conference. Nick stood as far away from Isabella as he could and he wondered if any of the men could read the thoughts he had running through his mind.

This new attraction to Isabella was the last thing he needed. They were in the middle of a war, for Christ's sake.

When the press conference ended, Dwayne Marcus said, "This isn't good."

"I'm not sure what's going on," Nick said. "But I for damn sure don't like being surprised like this. I thought we were on the same page with Rivera, but no plan I'm aware of involved an arrest warrant for this piece of garbage."

"He needs a bullet to the head," Lizard said, "not a pair of cuffs."

"We won't have to wait long to find out," Marcus said. "Probably either Mr. Smith or someone from the Mexican government will be contacting us soon."

Truer words were never spoken. S3 was about to hit a wall that none of them could have seen coming.

CHAPTER 23

Marcus's prediction proved true. Mr. Smith called Nick on his secure, encrypted phone three hours after the press conference.

"President Rivera wants to meet with you," Smith said.

"Tough titty," Nick said.

"Nick, don't be this way."

"First of all, I don't do diplomacy," Nick said. "Secondly, we're in a secure base of operations and we're not giving up our location so we can be followed back – either by President Rivera's police or Hernan Flores's people."

"President Rivera wouldn't follow you," Smith said. "You're forgetting that he invited the men of S3 to his country. You literally have a contract with his government. He needs you. Their government needs you. Their people need you. Don't forget that."

"And you're forgetting," Nick said, "that he is way off the mark with this public call to arrest Flores. Truth be told, we don't know what he's thinking. He could be up to anything."

"You're starting to sound paranoid again," Smith said.

"And you sound like a guy sitting behind a desk in Washington, without a thousand cartel men trying to hunt you down."

"We need you to meet with him."

"I'm the wrong man. Believe me on that. If he wants to meet, then you meet with him. Or send someone else from the Agency. Send the CIA contact you've got down here to babysit me. Believe me, it would be a mistake to send me."

"You represent the Agency," Smith said, "in case you've forgotten."

"Wrong. I represent a private military contractor named

Shield, Safeguard, and Shelter, which won a government contract to help train Mexican security forces. You all dumped that on me, in case you forgot."

"Come on, Nick. It's a single meeting. You can handle getting out of the capital without having someone follow you.."

"Clearly," Nick said, "you forgot about the Navy SEAL Team that got slaughtered down here. I'll bet you don't even know how many died."

"Nick, calm down."

"You don't, do you?"

"Nick, I'm not playing this game with you. No, I don't know off the top of my head how many died, and no, I have not killed as many men as you, and yes, I am a pencil pusher. You win. But remember, guys like you – even such a big-time, freaking hero as you – need guys like me, providing intel and support and –"

"You've been sending intel?" Nick asked. "I must have missed that."

"Nick, you *are* to meet with the President and you *will* represent the Agency well. He wants to meet tomorrow at –"

"He needs to be meeting with either your boss or our President," Nick said. "I'm not the one who's off script on this one."

"And you need to remember that you are in Mexico at the invitation of President Rivera. You piss him off and this mission is done. And with the mission off, you can kiss your two million dollars goodbye."

Nick laughed.

"You think I'm doing this for the money? How fucking stupid are you? I'll tell you what, though: I'll meet with him, but we do it on my terms."

Nick turned off the phone and dropped it on the desk.

"Marcus," he yelled.

Marcus, who had been standing in the hall in case Nick needed him, stepped into Nick's office.

"Yes, sir?"

"Marcus, get our Mexican contact to find out when Rivera wants to meet. Let's start planning how we get there early – and safe – and how we leave and get out without being

185

followed. Oh, and assign somebody to buy about five more used vehicles, for this ridiculous dog-and-pony show I'm going to have to attend."

"Will do," Marcus said. He turned to head out.

"Oh, and Marcus? Get with the squad leaders. I want back-up squads strategically located nearby and on exit points along our exfiltration route. This may be the most dangerous thing we've done since we've been here."

"Agreed," Marcus said. "I don't trust hardly anyone in their government."

"I don't either," Nick said.

"What made you decide to meet with him?" Marcus asked.

"I'm hoping I can change his damn mind," Nick said. "Otherwise, I'm out of here. And that means we're out of here."

The following day, after a marathon night of planning, Nick arrived at the Presidential Palace. He had to leave his Primary Strike Team – Marcus, Isabella, Truck, Lizard, Bulldog, Preacher, and Red – outside the gate by their two vehicles.

Nick proceeded inside alone. He allowed security forces to search him and confirm he was unarmed – a feeling that he did *not* like at all. Once they were done, an aide walked him down numerous hallways and corridors.

Nick hated the absurd amount of decor and splendor he saw as he made his way to the meeting. Gold lined the walls, priceless paintings hung, and stout, plush furniture unlike anything Nick had ever seen occupied waiting rooms. He wondered if the president had any idea how poor most of the Mexican people were.

"All politicians are the same," he thought to himself. "Stealing from the poor to line their own pockets."

They finally reached their destination. Nick knew it was the final barrier because it had the hallmarks of any big-shot executive's inner sanctum. First, it had the hottest receptionist he'd ever seen in his life, who sat behind a boat-sized executive desk. Secondly, it had a foreboding wall, thick door, and impressive security. The impressive security in this case was composed of two stout secret service agents by the door.

Nick wondered how many secret service agents were hidden in rooms and basements throughout the complex. Probably a couple hundred, if he had to guess, after the most recent attack on the Presidential Palace.

"Please, wait right here," the aide said, pointing to a massive couch.

"I know how this works, young man. The president makes me wait an hour to prove his power and then we talk."

The aide frowned. "Actually, the president is looking forward to meeting you. He will be with you very soon. As soon as he finishes his meeting, in fact. Please," he said, pointing, "please be seated."

"Sure, hoss. Sure he is."

Nick noticed the two agents staring him down like he was a criminal. They knew when a fellow shooter was in their midst and their senses screamed danger. Nick waved and smiled. Then he sat down and sunk into the couch, which was too big and plush to be comfortable.

He looked around for a magazine to read, saw none, and smiled at the receptionist who kept looking him over. Nick glanced down at his jeans and cowboy boots and realized he probably wasn't dressed to code. Yet, he *had* put on a long-sleeved, button-up shirt, so there was that.

A couple minutes later, the door to the Presidential Suite opened and five men in business suits shook hands with President Roberto Rivera and exited the room. Rivera noticed Nick and moved toward him.

Nick rose to greet him. The president was tall, like most politicians. Nick guessed his height at about six feet – a tad taller than Nick, but not nearly as lean. Nick had clearly spent more time running miles and shooting lead on the range instead of sitting in meetings and reading reports. But, still, the president was a good-looking man and he would definitely still qualify as fit. If Nick were a woman, then he'd definitely consider the man handsome. No wonder the man had never lost an election.

"A pleasure to meet you," Rivera said. "Thank you for coming in."

Nick nodded.

"Please, step into my office."

They walked in, Rivera pointed to a chair, and Nick sat, watching Rivera take a seat behind yet another gigantic executive desk, except this one was more elegant and distinguished. It probably came from some historic, wooden battleship or something. Nick knew the drill.

Rivera steepled his fingers in front of his chin.

"Normally, in a meeting like this," Rivera said, "you don't want to be the first to speak. It's a sign of," Rivera waved his hand, "weakness, if you will."

"You wouldn't want to try to outwait me," Nick said, remembering the time he had once outwaited an enemy sniper for hours. That man was dead. Nick wasn't.

"So I hear," Rivera said, smiling.

Nick didn't.

Rivera noticed the lack of a return smile and said, "You're obviously upset about the meeting and I understand from my aides that you're afraid that coming in for this talk will give your operating base away to the Godesto Cartel?"

"Seems to be a trend."

Rivera shook his head in reluctant agreement. "Unfortunately, drugs and money stacked higher than your wildest imagination have indeed corrupted many in our government. But, we have ferreted out many of these who have sold out their loyalty."

"It only takes one," Nick said, "but I'm not here to listen to excuses. What did you want to meet about?"

"I feel, respectfully of course, that you need to give more credit to those who resist the pressures of the Godesto, as well as understand better those who can't."

"I don't see me respecting anybody who sells out their brothers for money," Nick said. "Save your breath."

"How would you feel if you were a police officer or government official and you came home one day from a hard day at work, only to have someone stop and offer you a bribe?"

Rivera paused and reached for a cigar. He clearly worked on his storytelling. "Of course, your first thought would be to arrest them or turn them in."

Rivera offered Nick a cigar and Nick declined.

"As I was saying, your first thought would be to arrest them." He lit the cigar and puffed on it to get it burning right. "Maybe even shoot them. But, that would quickly disappear once the cartel man mentioned that they knew where your wife worked and where your daughter went to school. Can you imagine that?"

"I've actually lost a wife in a similar situation, so yes, I can."

Rivera stopped, like he had been punched in the nose.

"I'm sorry," he said, surprised. Rivera didn't like walking into a trap like this and he reminded himself to chew his aide out later for not providing him with a better history on Nick. A mistake like this killed the momentum of a debate and this was a discussion he needed to win.

While Rivera paused to recover from his misstep, Nick thought of Anne, bloody, in a nightgown in their backyard. He remembered the dew on the grass, the FBI agents standing over her, and him running his fingers through the dirt, swearing he would avenge her.

"As I was saying," Rivera said, trying to get back on course, "many of these officers will have their families threatened, in addition to being offered untold amounts of money. The temptation to assist the cartels comes as both a carrot and a stick, as you Americans are fond of saying. The temptation is very great."

Nick couldn't help but sympathize.

"I understand, Mr. President. And I need to remind myself that your country has been at war with the cartels for more than ten years."

"It's been longer than that," Rivera said, "though the casualties were lower and the news coverage much less in the past. Truth be told, we tried to keep it out of the news as much as we could. Didn't want to hurt tourism, as you know, which is crucial for our economy."

Nick nodded again and wished the man would make his point.

"Respectfully, Mr. President, you didn't ask me to come in to give me a history lesson. I'm not much on sales pitches. Just get to your point."

"Indeed," Rivera said. He took another puff on his cigar, exhaled a cloud of smoke, and continued. "But I am in the presence of one of America's greatest warriors? Am I not correct?"

Nick said nothing. He knew most of America's greatest warriors were in graves – marked and unmarked – across the globe, but you couldn't waste your time trying to educate everyone.

"A moment like this," Rivera said, "in the presence of a man of your reputation, needs to be savored. Just like a great cigar," he said, raising the cigar and smiling.

Nick half-smiled. The man was certainly charming. No wonder he'd been elected.

"Nick," Rivera said. "May I call you 'Nick'?"

Nick made the smallest of nods.

Rivera stopped smiling and turned serious. He smashed his cigar into a silver ashtray and leaned forward.

"Nick, I need you to change tactics. To stop the Vigilante act. Take down the website, stop making videos, and end the whole charade."

Nick said nothing.

"I know I initially approved the creation of the Vigilante unit, but things have changed. After the assault on the police station in Coyutla, we can do this no more. I must ask that you stop operating in such a way."

Nick stopped him.

"You don't seriously think we did that?"

"Of course not. But that attack hurt your effort. It hurt our effort. And I've since come to realize two things. First, acting as a Vigilante unit encourages other residents to act out as vigilantes. At some point, this will lead to lawlessness and innocent people being wrongly killed without benefit of even a trial. Secondly, I've come to realize that it's important for the prestige of Mexico to have government forces finally take down Flores and his cartel."

Nick sighed and Rivera stopped.

"Wish you had come to this realization before my team packed up and came down here," Nick said.

"I understand you're upset, but I'm prepared to offer a

compromise."

"Not much to compromise on, is there?"

Rivera ignored the snide comment and said, "I'm not asking you to take your team out of the country. I confess, as much as it hurts my pride, that we need your help. I'm simply asking you to operate under the guise of being Mexican forces. Wear our uniforms. Keep a low profile. No one will ever know the difference."

"I suppose," Nick said, "that I should tell you I need some time to consider your offer."

"I understand if that's necessary," Rivera said, holding his hands up in a conciliatory gesture and smiling as if he had won.

"It's not," Nick said.

"I'm sorry?" the President asked. "It's not what?"

"It's not necessary."

"I'm afraid I don't understand," Rivera said.

"I reject your offer. Or your request. Or demand. Or whatever cute political word that you want to call it. The original deal was we stay off the radar, we keep our homebase and operations off the government's radar, and that we operate as the Vigilantes. That was the deal, which you approved before we entered the country. I reject any renegotiation of it."

"But, Nick, surely you understand. Things have changed. The Godesto appropriated your idea."

"Nothing has changed," Nick said, his voice loud. "Other than perhaps your resolve or independence, apparently."

Rivera slammed his hand on the desk, then winced, immediately regretting it. He recovered quickly and stood. "I'm sorry you feel as you do. Please, take a couple of days to reconsider. Your contact can call his liaison within my government with your decision."

With that, Rivera turned away from Nick and looked out the window.

Nick laughed to himself. *Looks like diplomacy really isn't my strong suit*, he thought.

CHAPTER 24

Nick Woods left the Presidential Palace with a deep sense of defeat. The last thing he wanted to do was pack up the men of Shield, Safeguard, and Shelter and leave Mexico. But President Rivera was giving him no choice.

The selfish side of Nick wanted to keep going. Just put S3 in Mexican uniforms and loosely – with a lot of distance and care – work with Rivera. Nick enjoyed being in command and carrying a gun again.

Nick loved war. He loved the stress. The tension. The feeling of being alive. He lived for it and now he was going to have to leave it again. Possibly for good, given his age.

While Nick's mind raced, his unit zigged and zagged out of Mexico City. They swapped vehicles at busy locations (once in a packed mall parking lot and another time in a dark downtown garage) and reversed course several times. They traveled north for an hour before making a wide loop and driving south.

As they drove south, Nick tried not to dwell on the fact that all this was going away. These superb warriors. This incredible opportunity to make a difference. The chance to defend the weak. To do what the men of S3 were all born to do.

He tried to shake these thoughts and realized at this point, about the only thing he wanted was a cold Diet Coke, a Snickers, and a moment alone with Isabella. If this was all going away, then he wanted to explore whatever existed between them before he left.

Nick tried to stay alert for threats on their route home, but it proved difficult. His mind was simply racing too much, trying to find an angle to keep S3 in the country and thinking about Isabella more than he should. He hated that both of these opportunities could be ripped from his hands before they really had even begun.

Back at the farm, Nick's various units returned. The squads and six sniper teams came from different directions and spread out their arrival times. Once everyone returned, Nick called a meeting of his leaders.

The three squad leaders arrived, along with Marcus and the leader of the six Scout Sniper teams. Nick briefed them on his meeting with President Rivera. (Nick had already met with Marcus and discussed their options privately.)

With the full leadership team in place, Nick relayed Rivera's two demands: drop the Vigilante act and come in under the authority of the Mexican government.

"No way," said the second squad leader. "I'm not trying to undermine you, Nick, but there's no damn way I want to be a part of going under Mexican governmental authority. And I'm confident I speak for my men. They don't trust hardly anyone down here and one of them is Mexican himself, so that is saying a lot."

"Same with my men," said the first squad leader.

"Jimmy?" Nick asked, nodding to the third squad leader.

"The same."

Nick glanced at Marcus.

"Good," he said. "Then we're all on the same page. Marcus and I have decided we're not game for this change in plans. We feel it would be a death wish to come in under Rivera's control."

"Damn right," his second squad leader said. "We know what happened to the SEALs. And as they proved, it doesn't matter how good you are. If the enemy gets intel on you, you're as good as dead."

"Where does that leave us?" the leader of the Scout Snipers asked.

"Probably unemployed," Marcus said.

"We assumed everyone would favor safety over salary," Nick said.

"Agreed," said Jimmy. "It's one thing to put your life on the line. It's quite another to take a stupid chance because of the idiocy of a politician."

Nick saw several heads nodding.

"Then we're in agreement. Go brief your men with the news and let's meet up again in an hour to decide how we're going to exit the country. And just a heads-up, we plan to do so without alerting either Rivera, Flores, or Smith at the Agency. Once we're back in Texas, we'll let them know we're no longer here."

The entire group reconvened an hour later and spent more than three hours planning their exfil. It wasn't going to be simple.

Even after racking their brains, the best they could come up with was something extremely risky and arguably very dangerous. But it wasn't a cakewalk these days getting across the border. After years of griping from the American people, Washington had listened. All the easy ways across were a thing of the past.

Now, a formidable obstacle awaited them. Walls. Cameras. Agents. All working in concert to stop most of those illegals attempting the famous crossing of the Rio Grande. Tunnels were your best hope, but Nick's team could hardly call up the Godesto Cartel and ask them to allow a crossing through one of the cartel's tunnels.

Marcus had joked, "Maybe if we promise to leave Flores alone, he'd grant us passage."

"Fat chance," Nick said.

The problem mainly lay in all the weapons. Each member of Nick's team had legit passports, but trying to cross the border with enough weapons for a small army would certainly create some attention. And they couldn't just use their company credentials from the fake corporation, since that would instantly alert Smith as well.

"So we're left with leaving our weapons and gear?" the second squad leader asked.

"Not an option," Nick said. "If these weapons were ever used by the cartels, it would make Operation Fast and Furious, the walking guns case, look like nothing."

"I'm not game," Marcus said, "for a bunch of Congressional hearings and dealing with all those assholes in Washington."

The Scout Sniper leader cleared his throat and asked, "Blow them up? Keep only our pistols?"

"We're not putting this all on Nick," Marcus said.

Nick knew that tactically it made sense to destroy the weapons, but he feared the repercussions. Smith and his folks would be pissed enough to learn they had refused Rivera's request and left the country without alerting anyone. But to blow up several million dollars' worth of weapons, too? That would be too much.

"Look," Marcus said. "This is going to be complicated, getting our extraction planned out. Why don't you ask Rivera for a couple more days to consider how we could work safely with his government? Meanwhile, we figure out how we're going to do this. And by the time Rivera is ready for your answer, we'll already be gone."

Nick liked that idea and nodded. "Sounds like a good plan." And with that, he left the room to make the call.

CHAPTER 25

Hernan Flores and the Butcher were in the middle of yet another ugly meeting. Shockingly, they were standing in the same room, something that didn't happen much these days.

Partly, it was due to risk. Flores now had a ten-million-dollar reward on his head and there were plenty of impoverished Mexicans who'd like to have that kind of money dropped on them.

But the bigger reason for not meeting was crystal clear in the dingy warehouse office in which they met. Flores had increased his entourage to eight guards in the room with him instead of four. And he had more than thirty heavily armed men in the warehouse outside the room. The Butcher had upped his armament as well. He had his ever-present duffel bag on the floor next to him and a grenade, unbeknownst to Flores, in his right-hand coat pocket.

Neither man trusted the other and the Butcher didn't plan on hesitating. If Flores tried anything, he'd pull the pin on the grenade in his pocket and rush him, tackling and holding him close as the grenade blew them both into shark meat.

"What are you smiling at?" Flores asked.

"Just thinking about something," the Butcher said.

"If you don't mind, I'd prefer you pay attention," Flores said, standing up from behind his desk – a desk that had to be the cheapest one he had ever sat behind. "We need to plan our reaction to President Rivera's move to try to incarcerate me."

"We need to kill him," the Butcher said. "Ambush his convoy. Attack the Presidential Palace. Whatever. Doesn't matter."

"In case you've forgotten," Flores said, "attacking the Presidential Palace is precisely what got us in this situation."

"No, failing to kill him is what got us in this situation. We need to take out both him and Juan Soto. It's really a simple equation. They're the backbone of those who oppose us."

"We've discussed this before," Flores said. "We don't want to completely decapitate the Mexican government. We just want to get the man we want in power as the country's president."

"While we've discussed this," the Butcher said, "we clearly are not in agreement about the strategy, nor have we ever been. The way I see it, we take the government out and you don't have a reward for ten million on your head. You'll be able to come out of hiding again. And ride around in Mexico City and attend your dinners and balls and galas. Life returns to normal."

"Nonsense," Flores said. "The Mexican people are too proud to accept such a reality. They'd rather have a weak, corrupt government than a government that's been overthrown by drug runners. Even those who support the cartels want to at least have the appearance of having a country with its own independent government. Plus, our country needs tourism to survive. You can't have a country this big without at least the appearance of a government in place."

"Believe what you want," the Butcher said. "I stand by what I said."

Flores sighed. He knew his number two man was talking behind his back and undermining him in increasingly regular intervals. Flores had hoped to win him over, but the Butcher wasn't going to budge.

The Butcher wanted the government overthrown. Flores wanted the government left in place, but with a Godesto man in charge.

This much was clear: neither were budging. And with that clarity, Flores decided he would take out the Butcher, once and for all.

Unfortunately for him, the Butcher had come to the same conclusion.

Exactly one hour later, before Hernan Flores could move to yet another hidden location, cops and SWAT members descended on the warehouse where the meeting with the Butcher had gone down. President Roberto Rivera dispatched more than three hundred officers to conduct the raid once a tip on Flores's location came into the government hotline. The fear of Flores and the Godesto had been so strong that this had been one of the few tips on the location of Flores since the press conference offering the reward.

Armored trucks, vans loaded troops, and five helicopters swarmed the building from four different directions.

No one would escape.

Flores's guards fought at first, but the well-trained, fully-decked out assault officers cut them down with little fanfare. The snipers from the helicopters picked off others. And within thirty seconds, the shock of such a force of three hundred men hitting the building convinced those inside to surrender.

Flores watched his men as they looked about and decided to give up. He didn't blame them. His men didn't have armor and helmets and weapons with sophisticated sights. And certainly very few of his men had fired thousands of rounds in practice.

Flores's men folded like a bunch of kindergartners and he knew he was screwed. He'd have to surrender since this warehouse lacked a tunnel system or any other viable escape option.

But as he walked toward the officers with his hands held high, he surrendered knowing there was no judge and no jail that could hold him. He'd re-emerge soon and he'd be stronger than ever. Of that he had no doubt.

Less than half an hour later, President Roberto Rivera confirmed his men had the great Hernan Flores in hand and called an emergency press conference with the media once again. He gave the details of the raid and then provided a short speech he'd been working on in his head for too long.

On the way back to his office, he paused behind a bullet-proof window and looked over the skyline of Mexico City. This. This was the pinnacle of his presidency. Mexico's greatest days now lay before it. Only two weaker cartels remained and Rivera decided he'd offer more rewards to take down their leaders, as well.

Rivera smiled. This had all gone down on his watch. The history books would sing his praises for literally centuries to come.

He could imagine the entry about his presidency:

President Roberto Rivera entered office in the middle of Mexico's darkest days.

Yeah, this wasn't bad. Not bad at all, he thought. Maybe all the emotional stress and fear would prove worth it. Maybe his nearly failed presidency was worth it after all. And with that, he turned and walked back to his office to celebrate with Juan Soto.

CHAPTER 26

While President Roberto Rivera celebrated the capture of Hernan Flores with Juan Soto, the Butcher took the reins of the Godesto Cartel. He had two of Flores's most loyal lieutenants killed and immediately began telling a few men to spread the message that Flores had been shanked in prison and was already dead. That would be the truth soon enough anyway.

At the same time, he promoted two of his best men to fill the spots of the lieutenantshe had killed. He also pulled his men together to begin planning their assault on the government.

Flores, the fat, over-weight pig, had been too weak to do what needed to be done. Not so with the Butcher. He would show President Rivera and Juan Soto what the Godesto could do once you fully turned them loose.

While the Butcher ramped up his planning, the exact opposite thing occurred in the operating base of Nick Woods's unit. The press conference by President Rivera halted the frantic planning of how they'd exit the country under the nose of Rivera and Smith. The press conference and news of Flores's arrest also led to mixed feelings in the ranks of Shield, Safeguard, and Shelter.

Some wanted to celebrate. Flores was down, they'd get bonuses for completing the mission, and each was returning home in one piece. Not a bad couple of months work, training and deploying to Mexico. But the cynics in S3 warned that Flores would probably be released. Or that he would just run the Godesto Cartel from prison.

But as the debates about Flores's demise (or lack thereof) raged, in the end each member knew it didn't matter. President Rivera had sent word to the American Ambassador that with Flores now in custody, he no longer needed S3 operating in his country.

This had been another suggestion by Juan Soto and Rivera eagerly agreed with the idea. He was drunk – literally – from the success of Flores's capture and the splendid operation of his Mexican police who had raided the warehouse.

Rivera had watched the entire operation on video from three drones flying high above. He had never seen three hundred men move with such synchronization and force. And witnessing it had restored his confidence in the power of the Mexican government. Why had he ever feared Flores so much? That seemed remarkably strange now. And distant, too.

The American Ambassador sent word of Rivera's wishes to the CIA Director, who sent a secure message to "Mr. Smith." Nick Woods got the message ten minutes later from his CIA contact.

Nick discussed the situation with Marcus and they cancelled the planning of their own top-secret extraction. Convinced the mission was over, they decided they might as well light a bonfire and get everyone shit-faced drunk. Or most everyone.

As the news spread through the unit, Preacher and a couple of other men, who didn't drink often, volunteered to stay sober and pull duty, just in case. Marcus decided it would be wiser to split the men up. For each squad to have its own bonfire since they had plenty of room on the farm.

"Don't want any fights," he said. "And too many alpha males from rival squads around the same fire is bound to cause that to happen."

Nick agreed and told Marcus to grab one thousand dollars of petty cash from the Shield, Safeguard, and Shelter cash box and send someone out for all the beer and hotdogs they could carry.

But not everyone was celebrating. One man waited alone, anxious and nervous. Miles and miles away from the Presidential office and the field dotted with men from S3 throwing down beer and hotdogs, Hernan Flores awaited his arraignment. He sat in Mexico's most secure prison – the Federal Social Readaptation Center No. 1 – and he knew all too well how many miles away he was from the center of Mexico's power. But with luck, they would have him arraigned soon.

Thankfully, they had him in isolation, which suited him fine. He felt confident his high-priced attorney – the best defense attorney in Mexico – would have him in better quarters in no time. Maybe even out on bond, but that seemed a stretch given the charges against him.

Still, Flores was restless for a meeting with his attorney. And for a chance to plot out his counter attack, which he knew would prove a brilliant defensive strategy.

There were several non-profits whose executive directors owed Flores big-time. If he could get a message out through his attorney to a handful of them, they could go before the media and call the charges absurd. Yes. That's what he needed. A few high-profile humanitarians standing behind him and defending his character in some media interviews.

These non-profit CEOs would also confirm that Flores was in the process of multi-million dollar donations to their respective nonprofits. Yes indeed. Flores could imagine the interviews and the doubts they would sow in the people's minds… After all, would a true cartel leader honestly be giving so much money to nonprofits? And look at this man's track record over the past ten years as a giver and businessman.

This wasn't a new thing for him that just began after the Mexican government charged him publicly. He had been giving away millions for years, they'd say. And it was true. There were tax records to prove it.

Flores could imagine the interviews airing on TV. He smiled and laughed at the thought. Heh. Rivera may think he had the upper hand, but Flores still had plenty of cards that he planned to play.

As he mulled over the situation, he put his chances at getting out and free from incarceration within five years at better than fifty-fifty. And if the sentence was longer than five years, he'd be breaking out. For sure. Even here, in this high-security facility, he calculated his odds of escape as at least twenty-five percent. You could never fully comprehend the sway the Godesto Cartel wielded.

But none of this could happen until he met with his lawyer. He went to glance down at his watch and remembered they had taken that when they stripped him down and placed him in prison attire. Flores paced back and forth in his small cell. What the hell was the hold up with his attorney? That asshole better not be moving slow, he thought.

Flores speculated which judge his case would fall under. Several names came to mind as strong possibilities, but he wasn't too worried about this part of his dilemma, either. He knew many of them and most of them were in his pocket. Or in the pocket of some other important businessmen, who *was* in Flores's pocket.

These businessmen could help sway their opinion. Flores laughed, his voice echoing in the small isolation cell. The ironic thing was that most of the judges' wives were friends with Flores's girlfriend. And with these other businessmen's wives, as well.

If the public knew about all those connections, and how close everyone was, there'd be riots in the streets. The number of get-togethers they shared was truly staggering. Christmas parties for various civic groups. Non-profit galas. Political functions. And they all sat together and asked about each other's families and personal lives. It was truly a tight and small circle.

Flores shoved the thoughts down and wondered again just where his attorney was. Besides the PR strategy with the nonprofits, Flores wanted to find out the latest news and send a few quick messages to the Godesto Cartel.

Flores's biggest worry in the coming months – besides a possible conviction – was the threat posed by the Butcher. That bastard might be moving against him in a coup attempt from the outside, but as long as Flores could get some messages out to a few key people, he felt confident his men would remain loyal.

Men almost always fall into line under decisive leadership. And hearing the PR plan and Flores's orders would relieve everyone and keep anyone from stepping out of line. Surely they understood that he might get out on bond in a day or two. And should he not, then he'd eventually be released after his conviction. He simply needed them to know that they'd better not double-cross him. Flores was still Flores. You double-crossed him at your own severe peril.

But as the hours passed and no one approached his barely lit cell, Flores's confidence began to drop. Surely President Rivera wouldn't deny him a chance to meet with his attorney? He bristled at the idea. Could he, legally speaking?

Would he?

Flores struck the wall with his palm. Even without using his knuckles, it hurt his hand, and he instantly regretted doing it. Damn, he was getting soft. And clearly his confidence and control were not what they once were. He swallowed down a creeping and growing fear. Something was happening outside of what he expected. And that something couldn't be good.

While Flores paced and nursed his hand, the Butcher scrambled to kill him. Unfortunately, it was proving harder than he expected.

First, most of the Godesto Cartel and other cartel leaders still feared Flores would return to power, so they doubted the Butcher's claims that he had completely wrested control of the cartel from Flores. And since the Butcher wasn't as well-known as Flores, and considering Flores was the most powerful man in Mexico – some said North America – the Butcher was getting nowhere with his idea.

None of the officers in Federal Social Readaptation Center No. 1 would kill Flores. Nor would they so much as release a prisoner for a few minutes time to kill him. But finally, after spending ten million dollars in bribes from the Godesto Cartel's flush accounts, the Butcher got enough people on board to make something happen.

Yet it wasn't going to be simple. No one in the prison would move against Flores. The danger was too great. Plus, Flores had loyal prisoners in the facility. If someone did kill Flores, that man was as good as dead.

The Butcher was about to give up his attempt when one guard mentioned in a phone call that they would allow a man in, but his safety would be up to him; they couldn't guarantee his survival. And that man would have to take care of some guards, who were too straight-laced to be bought.

The Butcher knew just the man for such an assignment.

Two hours later, the Butcher was on his way to Federal Social Readaptation Center No. 1.

He was wearing cuffs and in the back of a police van. Earlier, a police lieutenant on the Godesto Cartel payroll had sent in a memo to prison officials saying that another inmate was being hastily transferred to their care, under cover of night. The memo stated the prisoner had very important information on a crucial federal case and his life had been threatened, thus no one was to know about his transfer.

This included the warden. The inmate was to be kept away from the other prisoners and off the electronic record, since it was feared the enemy had informants on the lookout for him. The VIP prisoner was to be placed in isolation until the next day. Nothing more. Nothing less.

It was a strange memo, but when you live in a country that's lost fifty thousand lives to drug violence, weird things occur more regularly than you'd think. And one doesn't live long, let alone move up through the ranks of law enforcement, by asking questions.

While the memo was distributed to those who needed to know, the two police officers delivered the Butcher to the castle-like facility. The Butcher had his head covered in a sack and wore a bullet-proof vest over the prison garb that he'd been handed by the officers. The paperwork was a bit of a stretch, but given the secrecy surrounding the "transfer," they felt it just might work. At least for a few hours. And that's all the Butcher needed to kill Flores.

He had learned that fortune favored the brave and besides... He felt no fear of a prison. He'd been incarcerated before and he knew that none of the inmates could intimidate him now. And certainly not touch him. Not even six men could take him now. And if anyone made the mistake of trying, they would be the ones who needed the officer protection, not the other way around.

The Butcher's days of being tortured and abused by bigger men were done. For good.

The officers drove him to the facility in the back of a prison van. He was handcuffed and had been searched. Since he would be searched again upon his entry, the officers had made clear that he couldn't go into the prison carrying weapons. There were, after all, several important police officers putting their careers on the line to get him in. They needed this to succeed as much as the Butcher did.

The officers handed him off to the prison authorities and the Butcher was ushered through gates, doors, and halls, all of them running together in his mind. He tried to keep his bearings, but it was impossible.

The Butcher talked to no one, as he had no idea which of the guards were in on his plans and which weren't. He noticed no signals or clues from any of the guards, so he kept his head down and his shoulders hunched to appear as nervous and submissive as he could. The last thing he wanted was to appear threatening.

After probably forty minutes of moving about and processing, three guards escorted him to a cell and pushed him inside. The heavy door slammed behind him and he stood in the empty cell alone.

So far things had gone as planned. But, the joke might be on him, he thought. Could they know his real identity? Could they know his value as such a high-ranking member of the Godesto Cartel? Could this be his home for the next twenty or thirty years?

The Butcher didn't have time for these thoughts. He took a deep breath and blew out the air forcefully. Then he repeated this process ten times, just as he'd learned in his martial arts training. He followed the breathing with some push-ups and light stretching. Whether things went smoothly or his plan went awry, he wanted to be ready. Lithe. Warmed up. Prepared for anything.

His cell had solid walls on both of its sides and rear. Only the front had bars. There'd be no prisoners reaching in from the side cells to grab you or stab you in this place. Someone had designed it wisely.

Taking his eyes from the concrete walls that encased him, he looked across the hall, into the only cell he could fully see. There, a prisoner lay under the covers. Otherwise he could see nothing and hear only remote sounds of men talking, laughing, and cursing.

The isolation felt crushing, especially when he'd just left the protection afforded by hundreds of gunmen and millions of dollars.

He shook the thought from his head and stretched some more. He inhaled deeply a few more times, trying to swallow down the idea that he might literally be the most stupid criminal ever. Who breaks into a prison? Voluntarily? And the most secure one in Mexico, at that?

He pushed the thought down and started shadow boxing. Throwing some kicks and strikes. Nice and loose. Maybe thirty percent power.

Perhaps Flores knew about his attempt to take over the Godesto Cartel and plan to enter the prison to kill him? How would Flores respond if he did? Did Flores have the power to have guards enter the cell and beat him to death?

The Butcher *did* fear a bunch of guards with nightsticks. He had skills, but not the kind of skills to fend off multiple men with clubs and decent training. Especially if they came with shields, helmets, and shin and elbow pads.

The lights in the hall clicked off and darkness flooded the corridor to his front. Small night-lights barely lit the hallway. He wondered how long he should stay up waiting? Perhaps he should catch some sleep in case he had to fight for his life tomorrow in the general population against twelve or fifteen of Flores's men?

As he debated this, he kept bouncing from foot to foot. Nice and loose. Then a sound caught his attention. He recognized footfalls walking down the hall. No, it was two sets of footfalls. Wearing boots.

Then they were there and he saw the silhouettes of two

guards stop in front of his cell in the dark hallway. They looked up and down the corridor before unlocking the door and waving him forward.

The Butcher rolled his shoulders a couple of times and prepared himself. It would happen soon.

The guards led him down several corridors and gates. After pushing through yet another gate, the Butcher knew he was there. These cells weren't like the other cells. Their front doors weren't iron gates with bars that you could see and reach through, but steel doors that you couldn't see out.

This must be their isolation unit, the Butcher thought. The guards led him about three-quarters of the way down the hall and then looked back up the corridor behind them one more time to make sure the path was clear.

"Make it quick," one of them said in a low voice, finally looking at him.

They placed a massive key in the lock and turned it a full turn, then yanked the heavy door open. Before the Butcher walked in, the officer who hadn't said a word put a hand on his shoulder to stop him. He turned and the man reached in his pocket and handed him a handmade shank.

The Butcher looked down at what had once been a flathead screwdriver, but was now a ground-down piece of metal, its handle removed and replaced with tape, its point like a sharpened shark gaff.

The Butcher entered the dark cell.

Hernan Flores heard men approaching and finally relaxed. He was still reeling over how long it had taken his attorney to arrive. But, "Better late than never." He started moving toward the door and blinding light, then stopped. Silhouetted in the door was a short man, who was clearly holding a shank.

"Miss me?" the man asked. Flores instantly recognized his voice.

"You bastard."

Flores rushed toward him with every intent to knock the little bastard out. Just knock him down, get the shank from him, and take him out. The Butcher was so small that Flores knew he could handle him. He had size and he'd been in his share of fights in his day, so to hell with all that bullshit martial arts the Butcher always practiced.

But as his fist swung hard and wide, he saw his nemesis step to the side as easily as if he were Bruce Lee. And as Flores's momentum carried him forward, the little bastard kicked him in the ribs with a side kick that drove him twice as fast toward the wall. Instant, earth-shattering pain in his ribs screamed through his nerves, so intense that he never felt the pain in his head from the wall.

The Butcher knew he had kicked him hard. As the fat asshole had come at him, he had simply side-stepped him to the left and leapt forward into a flying side kick. With Flores on the ground, holding his side and stunned from the impact with the wall, the Butcher closed in to finalize the deal. He skipped forward – light and fast – and mounted Flores's back, pinning him just in case he somehow tried to rise up. Without a moment's hesitation, he drove the shank into his right ear. Deep.

The entire attack was smooth, fast, and flawless.

It was less a fight and more an execution.

The guards watched the whole thing go down, shocked and stunned at the little man's skills. The entire thing lasted two seconds. Not a moment of fear as the big man rushed him, just a Zen-like calm, a simple sidestep, a powerful flying kick, and cheetah-like speed as he darted forward, jumped on the man's back, and drove the shank into his brain.

The little guy yanked the shank out of Flores's head and wiped the blade on the back of the dead man's prison uniform.

"Who's next?" the man asked, a sick smile on his face.

The guards looked at each other, shrugged, and then pointed him toward his final destination. They walked him down a hall and guided him toward where their sergeant had instructed them to go next. There were three guards who weren't involved in the bribes and this nighttime excursion.

They needed to be killed before the Butcher could successfully get out.

As they led him down yet another hall, the guards wondered if the little man could pull off this final challenge. In all, twenty-one guards were in on the bribes from the Butcher and the Godesto Cartel. That much the Butcher knew. And he'd been told before entering the facility that nearly one hundred and fifty additional guards on the night shift didn't need to be involved, as they were either in different parts of the building, stationed in guard towers, or stationed in reserve as reaction squads.

But there were three guards too straight and honest to even approach, so the lieutenant in charge of the night shift had worked around them up to this point. But the Butcher could never leave in the middle of the night without these three knowing or asking questions, so they'd have to be taken out. And none of the guards were up for taking care of this nasty part of the plan themselves.

"We know them too well," the lieutenant had said. "Plus, we can have you take them out in an area where there are cameras. That will lend credence to the story we must concoct after you're gone. After all, we must think of our own protection, as well."

"And these men," the Butcher asked, "will have billy clubs?"

"Yes," the lieutenant said.

"And radios?" the Butcher asked.

"Yes. There's no way we can get their radios off them without them knowing something is up. From day one in training, guards are taught to keep their radio on their body. Even when they go to the restroom. It's their lifeline. There's no getting their radios off them without putting them in high alert and possibly causing them to send out a warning."

"So, three men with three billy clubs," the Butcher asked, "and I have to take them out unarmed?"

"Yes. Because if you used a weapon against them, the investigators would have to figure out where you got it. Any guard who lost control of their weapon would be mercilessly questioned. His finances watched for years. He might be jailed based on suspicion alone. But these men's guards should be down. I'll ask them to meet me in the break room," the lieutenant had said, "so they won't be expecting anything."

"All right," the Butcher said. "I'll take care of the men, unarmed. But what if they get a warning out on the radio?"

"You can't allow that to happen."

"You can't block the signal or get them on the wrong frequency?"

"They're already wary. And they barely trust me as it is."

"And if they get a call out before I take them down?"

"All is lost."

"Meaning?"

"I mean these officers you've paid off can't ignore a distress call. Obviously, that involves more than the twenty-one men who are in on this, but those twenty-one can't be seen as not responding. That would look very suspicious. If one of those three gets a call out, a response force will come and they will beat you half to death."

"And I'll be thrown in a cell and you won't be able to get me out?" the Butcher asked.

"Correct. Probably, the warden will be here within twenty minutes of it happening and there's nothing I or anyone else can do at that point. Plus, with any call out at this prison, an alert goes out to the Presidential Palace. There are just too many VIP prisoners here. Without question, they'll figure out who you are and you're toast."

"Toast?"

"Yes, toast. For the rest of your life."

That had been the conversation the Butcher had shared with the lieutenant prior to his entry. As the Butcher neared the task of killing the three straight-laced guards, those words seemed far more real. He now fully understood the risks he faced. There was a very good chance he'd never leave this prison.

He had to kill these men before they got out a distress call.

The two guards by his side walked a bit further, and then they stopped. The guard on the left put his hand on the Butcher's arm and leaned toward him, placing his mouth mere inches from his ear.

"We can't get any closer as we'll soon enter one of the

areas under video surveillance. But, go down this hallway and it's the second door on the right."

The Butcher nodded and looked at the man for any final instructions.

The guard said "good luck" in a low voice. The Butcher noticed the man had sweat on his forehead and looked very nervous.

The Butcher leaned back into him and said, "Don't worry. I'll be right back."

The guard nodded and the Butcher turned and took a deep breath. He kicked off his prison slippers. He'd prefer to do this with boots on, but they were right that it would look suspicious if the video later showed him wearing footwear that someone had clearly provided. Thankfully, though the prison uniform was itchy and bright orange, it did have the advantage of being loose enough for him to kick high.

He rolled his shoulders, made several tight fists, and squatted down, doing a couple of quick splits. He was ready.

He slipped down the hall soundlessly, his bare feet silent on the tiled floor. He stopped at the door and debated peeking through a small window on the upper part of it. But his gut told him that probably at least one of the three guards was facing the door and would see him, so he decided to go with the element of surprise. It was his only chance.

He placed his fingers around the handle, took a long and deep breath, and turned it slowly. It twisted without a sound and he opened the door slowly. He didn't want to alarm them by yanking it open.

He entered the room at a normal pace – just a guard entering the room – and then saw the startled faces of the men as they looked up. They were the only ones in the room, sitting in a circle around a table that seated four. All three faced the door at nine, twelve, and three o'clock on the circular table. The table wasn't a large one at all, but more of a round cafe table than anything. It was one of four round tables in the otherwise empty break room.

As the men started to stand, the Butcher sprinted across the distance between them, his barefoot feet gripping the floor nicely. It was maybe twenty feet and the men hesitated as they stood, too shocked to know what to do. Should they reach for their night sticks on their right hips or the radios on their left hips.

The Butcher never wavered and used their indecisiveness against them. At full speed now – an all-out sprint – he leapt into the air, cleared the empty chair in front of him, and kicked out a flying side kick across the table. It was aimed at the man now trying to stand at the twelve o'clock position. The Butcher skimmed over the table and hit the man at twelve o'clock with his bare heel right in the chest.

Unfortunately as the man flew back into a counter, doubtlessly compounding whatever injury he received from the kick to the chest, the Butcher lost his balance and missed his landing, falling into the man he'd just kicked. From the ground and lying on his side, he threw an elbow into the man who had yet to recover and knocked at least three teeth practically down his throat.

He leapt up and grabbed the chair that the guard had been sitting in, which now lay on its side. He hurled it at the man who had been at three o'clock, but was now positioned behind him and on his left.

It was the one man the Butcher couldn't see and he had learned from long experience in fighting that it's the man you can't see that you must worry most about. The light,plastic and metal chair flew nearly six feet before the man who had been coming toward him with a billy club caught it with his face and arms. The man had tried to block it at the last second. Of course, he didn't actually catch it. He practically ate it, shattering his forearm and taking a hard shot in the face. The combined effect knocked him off his feet.

That left the third guard, who had been at nine o'clock but was now on the Butcher's right at three o'clock. He stood close by, but was wisely bringing his radio up to his mouth.

The Butcher took a fast step to close the distance and leapt up, throwing a hard front thrust kick forward. It landed into the man's elbow just as he pressed the button to sound the alarm. The arm flew backward and whipped the man around, his radio bouncing across the floor to the other side of the room. As the man tried to recover, the Butcher glanced back at the two other guards.

The one he had attacked first with the flying kick and elbow on the ground, was trying to stand, but blood poured from his mouth and he held his chest with his hand. At a minimum, the guard had had the breath knocked out of him. But the Butcher felt confident he'd cracked his sternum and possibly ruptured his heart with the all-out, almost twenty-miles-per-hour kick.

The guard who had "caught the chair" held his elbow with one hand and his bloody face with the other. He hadn't recovered from the shock of such a hard hit. The Butcher marked him as having a shattered elbow and probably a fractured orbital bone. Maybe a broken nose, too.

The glance had taken a half second, but the guard still standing had yet to pull out his nightstick – his one remaining weapon since his radio was thirty feet away. The Butcher stepped toward him and faked a punch toward his face. The man raised his arms to block it and the Butcher stopped the strike and kicked him with a front snap kick to the groin. It was fast. It was impossible to block. Just a fake strike with your hand, the opponent looking up, and BAM, a fast kick to the nuts. The Butcher had probably practiced the strike twenty thousand times.

The guard doubled over and grabbed himself. The Butcher slapped his palms to the man's ears. Before the man could react to that additional pain, the Butcher pulled the guard's head down into a powerful knee. The man took it right in the face, his legs giving out instantly.

The Butcher glanced back around and was stunned to see the man who had taken the shot from the chair was actually pulling his radio out. He stood eight feet away, which might as well have been a mile.

Shit.

The Butcher panicked for a millisecond, then remembered the billy club on the man he had just dropped. He reached down, slid it from the belt of the downed guard, and turned. The guard was still raising the radio when the Butcher hurled the heavy bludgeon as hard as he could toward the guard.

The guard saw the Butcher start to hurl the club and

stopped his attempt to radio for help. He ducked and raised his arms, but it was too little too late. The billy club slammed into his arms and shoulder, cracking bone and tendons like they were fragile eggs. The guard dropped his last hope for salvation like a panicked six-year-old infielder trying to hang onto a line drive.

The radio clanked and bounced on the ground. The Butcher rushed toward the man, not wanting to give him another chance. As he ran to the guard, he looked to confirm the man he had kicked against the counter still lay barely moving. The man was a little more alert, but appeared badly shaken and in pain. Still no threat. Yet.

The Butcher moved toward the man he'd just clocked with the billy club and grabbed an outstretched leg. He lifted it to keep the man from standing. With the officer's leg high in the air, the Butcher stomped his foot into the man's open groin. As the man reacted, the Butcher held his outstretched leg and drove his heel into the side of the knee. It cracked and broke sideways, the man screaming. As the guard reached for his knee, the Butcher drove a sword hand strike right into his throat. The Butcher's hardened fingers drove a couple of inches deep, hitting all kinds of arteries and necessary tubes in the throat. It was probably enough to kill the guard, but the Butcher needed to be certain. He grabbed the billy club lying nearby and smashed the man's head twice, just to make sure.

That was definitely like the sound of an egg cracking.

The other two died the same way: billy club strikes to the head, though the one at the counter tried to block the first strike. The Butcher expected it and never slowed his swing. The first strike broke the man's arm and the man couldn't lift it again. The Butcher showed no mercy, finishing him with similar strikes.

He checked the pulses of all three men and confirmed he had fractured their skulls and killed them. He had.

He took a deep breath and noticed his hands were shaking. My, that was quite a rush, he thought. Too bad he hadn't been able to sneak in his sword. His katana would have made the entire business far more fun.

But he needed to run back to the guards waiting outside of

camera range. He was ready to be out of this prison, as quickly as possible. It was starting to make him anxious.

CHAPTER 27

Back on the farm, Nick Woods's unit struggled to wake up and get moving. In the post-dawn hours of early morning, most of the men were still hungover. Beer cans and hot dog wrappers littered the grounds where the men had spent the night drinking and laughing among their fellow squad members.

With the capture of Hernan Flores and the word from President Roberto Rivera that Shield, Safeguard, and Shelter was no longer needed (or welcome) in Mexico, the men and one woman had spent the night relieving some much needed stress and pondering their future employment options. Without question, Nick's one thousand dollar purchase of alcohol and food had been a big hit.

Nick had spent most of the night with his Primary Strike Squad, hanging out with Marcus, Isabella, Truck, Lizard, Bulldog, and Red. But like any good leader, Nick had also stepped away to spend time at the other squad fires across camp – the three squads and the six-team Scout Sniper squad. Nick had learned many of the men's names and backgrounds from the other squads and managed to play the role of funny, wise leader as he walked about.

Nick had also walked the perimeter and checked in with Preacher and the other men who had volunteered to stay sober and play guard so that the rest could enjoy their final night in the country. Nick appreciated that these men had volunteered for duty and he spent quite a while speaking with them.

As he walked back to his own fire and the members of the Primary Strike Team, he couldn't shake the thought of what good men they all were. Without question, Nick dreaded giving up command of Shield, Safeguard, and Shelter.

By the time the night ended late into the morning, Nick realized he had enjoyed the evening, but he had been frustrated that he hadn't managed to get any time alone with Isabella. He had caught her eyeing him across the fire several times when he hung out with the Primary Strike Team. Once, their eyes had met while the rest of the men were distracted by a story. She had smiled deeply and he had found himself smiling back, harder than he meant. She had looked beautiful sitting there with the firelight dancing across her face. Nick had known that was not a sight he'd forget any time soon, even if he never saw her again.

And by the looks of things the next morning, he wouldn't.

The men were stirring from their drunken slumber and Dwayne Marcus and the squad leaders were rousting those not already up. It was time to get cleaned up and begin the process of packing.

And in truth, there wasn't a lot to pack, so they'd be leaving in no time at all. Shield, Safeguard, and Shelter was a small unit, living out of sea bags, footlockers, and truck beds, on a small, simple farm. They carried light weapons and didn't have heavy vehicles and all the required tools and parts that went along with them.

Sadly, there just wasn't any way for Nick to stretch it out to get more time with Isabella. Today was their final day and it would be the last time he'd see her.

The unit would drop her off at the capitol and she would go back to serving the Mexican government.

And Nick would go back to what? Driving around the interstate in his red Grand Cherokee, looking for answers he'd probably never find?

Nick sighed at the thought. He wasn't sure what he'd return to and he honestly didn't even want to think about it. But things were happening that Nick and S3 couldn't even dream of. This mission wasn't over and the unit would soon realize it probably should've packed up a bunch of body bags.

The Godesto Cartel was not a critically wounded dragon. It was a growing monster that was about to strike back hard.

In the capital city on this morning, President Roberto Rivera hung up the phone as if it were a fragile piece of glass. He placed his head in his hands and just rested his weight on the desk.

He was in absolute shock.

He had been woken up earlier that morning at 5:15 a.m. by a watch officer, who had patched in a phone call from the head of the prisons bureau. Rivera still reeled from a deep drunkenness as he tried to make sense of what he was being told by his head of prisons. It seemed impossible, but the man was telling him that Hernan Flores was dead, shanked in his cell not even twelve hours after being arrested.

Rivera wanted to believe he was dreaming but his headache and shaky thoughts reminded him that he was totally awake. No. He wasn't dreaming, but this was a nightmare all right. A real-life nightmare.

"How did this happen?" Rivera managed to ask in his stupor, during the initial wake-up call. "Flores was supposed to be kept in isolation without any visitors, even his attorney. My orders were explicit."

"We're not sure yet," the administrator said.

"I want a full report by ten a.m.," Rivera said, and then slammed his phone down.

He had crawled back under the covers, but found it impossible to fall back asleep, despite the fact he'd only gone to bed at two in the morning – an incredibly late time for him. Now he regretted the heavy drinking he and Juan Soto had done following his news conference that announced the arrest of Hernan Flores.

The death of Flores inside Federal Social Readaptation Center No. 1 would no doubt be a blow to his presidency. A serious, and possibly fatal, one.

First, many would assume either he or Juan Soto were behind it. Not that the idea hadn't crossed his mind, but both were committed to the idea of following the law. Had they wanted to ignore the concept of justice, they would have allowed the Vigilantes to skin Flores alive. But that wasn't what they wanted. Besides, they had a solid, strong case against Flores. Coupled with an honest judge they'd selected, it was clear that they didn't need to kill him.

But many of the voters wouldn't believe any of this for a second. He would be looking at a blitzkrieg of innuendo and whisper campaigns, practically around the clock.

Secondly, for those who didn't assume he or Soto were behind it, they would certainly fall back to the next most logical position: the government of Mexico couldn't be trusted. It was either corrupt or incompetent, both of which meant it was hopeless. If the government couldn't keep Mexico's most wanted fugitive alive, then what could it do?

Rivera hung his hat on the hope that in a few hours, at ten, they would know what had happened. With a small amount of luck, there'd be an elaborate story behind Flores's death that placed the murder squarely on one of the cartel's shoulders. And with just a little more luck, Rivera could get out in front of the story. He'd schedule another emergency press conference with the media, lay out the absolute truth, and announce a major investigation.

Those thoughts provided some comfort. With luck, the investigation would root out corruption from his prison system. And with newly announced resignations and prosecutions, Rivera's reputation could be restored. His legacy might even be reinforced. The columnists, the historians, and the people would all say in one voice: Roberto Rivera would not tolerate corruption or cartels of any kind. It was the complete focus of his presidency.

But the ten o'clock phone call from the head of the prisons bureau had been worse than he expected. It was why his head was buried in his hands. That ten o'clock phone call had left him in shambles.

After a couple of moments, he sat back in the chair, completely defeated, looking at the phone.

How could it be?

The prison bureau had nothing. Well, actually, they had tried to pull together some small threads to make it appear as though they had something, but Rivera knew better from his years in government. They had nothing.

Somehow, Flores had been killed. Three guards had died, as well. This was a disaster of epic proportions and Rivera saw no way out of it. His dream to crush organized crime, the legacy he had worked to build throughout his career – all of it was over now.

Or would be soon once the media learned the news.

The Butcher was on the phone with the prison lieutenant who'd helped arrange the takedown of Flores. Both took protective measures to avoid government surveillance, with the Butcher on a throwaway cell phone, while the lieutenant was on a pay phone deep within one of Mexico's most dangerous drug slums.

Yet they knew they could discuss precise details and names and not be caught. Mexico was not America. There was no NSA to record and sort and filter every phone call on some massive supercomputer.

"Was everything taken care of?" the Butcher asked.

"Yes, sir, it was," the lieutenant said. "The fake memo has been shredded."

"Are you sure?"

"Yes. I shredded it myself."

"And the rest of the story?"

"It fits well. We had your man rough up a couple of other guards and his fellow cellmates, so it looks like an actual escape."

This was the best part of the Butcher's plan. Since they needed to hide the late-night transfer, the two of them had decided that one of the Godesto Cartel's most evil men would "escape" and kill Hernan Flores on the way out.

It would seem a little odd that the man wouldn't rescue other Godesto Cartel members, but the story being pushed to investigators was that Flores had planned to eliminate the man, claiming he was a snitch, who had caused the great cartel leader's arrest as part of a deal for a reduced sentence.

But the man had caught wind of it and made his move.

He'd beaten up his cellmates, roughed up some guards, and shanked Flores first in a pre-emptive strike. Then, as he escaped, he caught three guards unawares and killed them, as well, before finally completing his escape.

So, in one clean sweep, the Butcher had killed his number one nemesis and earned the release of one of the cartel's best shooters: a man named Felipe.

"The investigators seem to be buying the story?" the Butcher asked the lieutenant.

"Yes, sir. They do. The story has been bought hook, line, and sinker. And we've edited videotapes, cleaned up records, which showed the entrance of a prisoner last night, you name it. And I talked with the cops who made the delivery and they've taken care of covering up their log entry of transporting a prisoner to Federal Social Readaptation Center No. 1. Believe me, everything is taken care of. I wanted to make sure this was the case as much for myself as for you."

"I'm glad to hear it," the Butcher said.

It had cost him ten million dollars for the entire operation, but it had been well worth it. Now, the Butcher was focused on his next big target: Juan Soto.

CHAPTER 28

The Butcher wasn't the only one on the phone. President Roberto Rivera was discussing the death of Hernan Flores with Juan Soto.

"How could this happen?" Soto yelled after hearing the news shortly after the 10 a.m. report from the head of the bureau of prisons. The phone call to Soto, Rivera's closest advisor, had been the first call Rivera had made.

"I told you," Rivera said, sighing. "We're still not sure yet."

It was the third time that Rivera had said they weren't sure how it happened and he was beginning to wonder how many times he'd have to say it before Soto understood that they truly weren't sure how the killing occurred.

"And why didn't you call me this morning immediately after you learned the news?"

"I told you why," Rivera said, sighing. "I was half drunk, you were half drunk. I figured you'd rather sleep since we had no facts anyway. I know if the situation were reversed I'd have wanted to sleep."

"You don't become a billionaire by sleeping while something big is happening," Soto said, an intense anger in his voice.

Rivera may have known that his political career was likely over, but he didn't want to put up with Soto's shit. Not with this little sleep. Not on what was likely the worst day of Rivera's life.

"I think," Rivera countered, "that someone is forgetting that we followed their plan. I never wanted Flores arrested in the first place. It's why I called in more American support after the Navy SEAL Team was wiped out. Flores should have been killed by the Vigilantes and then the Mexican people would have felt empowered. Now, thanks to your brilliant plan, the Mexican people think we're either corrupt or incompetent. I'm not real sure which is worse."

"Oh, you're now placing this on me?" Soto asked.

"No, just reminding you of the facts."

"Why didn't this man have thirty guards around him? Was that really asking too much? Hell, you could have placed members of your Presidential Guard around him. They've got a much higher security clearance and I guarantee you that if you had used some of them, there's no way he'd be dead. I just can't believe he's dead."

"Well, he is. I've seen pictures of the body."

"You still should have called me when you first learned of this. I don't even care how early it was."

"Why?" Rivera screamed, slamming his hand down on his desk. "What would that have served? What could I have done? It was already too late!"

"Bullshit," Soto fired back. "You could have called up your elite Special Forces Battalion and rushed them there. They could have been there in thirty minutes and secured the site. And then you could have arrested every guard in the prison, separated them, and secured them in holding cells. We could have interrogated and sweated them and probably come up with what really happened."

Rivera couldn't help but see the merit in this idea. Damn, why hadn't he thought of that? Well, being half-drunk hadn't helped.

And why hadn't any of his advisors thought of it? Ah, that's right. He hadn't called an emergency cabinet meeting, instead deciding to try to get a little more sleep. Could he have even managed a meeting in his impaired state? Who knew? And shit. Just the thought of not calling the cabinet meeting made him consider the oversight hearings his opponents would demand in the Congress of the Union (Mexico's congress) once news broke.

What did Rivera know and when did he know it? What was his response and why didn't he react differently?

Rivera sighed. He needed more aspirin. He even wondered if he should just resign. Maybe even flee the country, so the

Godesto couldn't hunt him down anymore.

Soto knew by the delay in any response from Rivera that his remarks had hit home.

"Next time just call me," Soto said, deciding to drop it and move on.

Rivera swallowed and said, "I will," like a bloodied kid who'd just been pummeled by a bully.

"What do we know about this number two man – the Butcher, I think they call him?" Soto asked.

"We're pulling together all we can on him, but already we know an impressive amount of information, mostly from informants. Let's see..."

Rivera pulled a file toward him and opened it.

"Looks like he started out as a nobody. Just a small kid who got bullied. Fell into the wrong crowd, got busted for theft and grand larceny of a vehicle. Prison apparently really sucked for him. He made several formal complaints about being sexually molested."

Soto interrupted him.

"Which reminds me," Soto said, "we have to get that under control. Our prisons should be safe for both the guards *and* the inmates."

"We have a lot to get under control," Rivera said, his voice icy. "Worrying about prisoners is pretty low down my priority list."

"That's the wrong attitude to have," Soto said, "but we can argue about this some other time. Like, when your entire career isn't hanging by a thread."

Rivera ignored the remark. He didn't feel like fighting anymore, so he scanned the memo further.

"Continuing where we left off, the Butcher gives up on alerting the prison authorities about the sexual abuse he's enduring and takes to weights and boxing."

Rivera flipped a page and continued, "Um, I'm assuming the weights and boxing didn't work because he left prison and went on to develop a fierce reputation as a martial artist."

Rivera scanned some more, then said, "Hmm. Interesting. So, he apparently takes these newly acquired martial arts skills and tracks down nearly every man who had raped him in prison or bullied him as a kid."

"What did he do?" Soto asked. "Beat them up?"

"No," Rivera said. "He killed every one of them, supposedly. Either by beating them to death or slashing them up with either a short tanto blade or long katana blade."

"My God."

"No, it's worse than that. He didn't just put them away with a swift killing strike. Rather, he would cut and slice them up, often as many as eighty or ninety shallow slices until they bled out, according to the medical report."

"And why was he never arrested for these killings?" Juan Soto asked.

"Warrants were put out for his arrest, but no luck in arresting him. At one point, one officer called in a suspicious person driving a vehicle he had been linked to, but before backup arrived, the officer was killed by heavy nine millimeter fire. Detectives suspected it was an Uzi used on the officer."

"So, that may not have been him?" Soto said.

"No, it probably was. Says here that his second favorite weapon after his katana sword is an Uzi."

"Well, there's little doubt that the man is a serious killer," Soto said. "But can he lead? Running the Godesto Cartel would challenge even the strongest leader. It's a huge organization with tons of people in it. That's a lot of details to keep up with."

"Wow," Rivera said. He hadn't even been listening to Soto. The report was simply too interesting. "Looks like, according to one informant, he once famously killed one of Flores's guards who tried to disarm him."

"But can he lead?" Soto asked louder.

"Hell if I know. Guess we'll find out."

And find out they would, though it'd cost one of them their lives. The clock on their final hours was already ticking...

CHAPTER 29

At the farm where S3 was located, Isabella said, "Nick, the president is holding a news conference. Something big has happened."

Nick looked up from his desk, where he had been making some notes for a final report to submit to his boss, Mr. Smith.

"Hurry," she said, waving her hand impatiently.

He stood and followed, noticing as he caught up to her that she wore tight green fatigue trousers and a black tank top that stretched across her chest tighter than anything he'd seen her wear.

Nick didn't know if it was Isabella's goal to torture to death every man (including himself) until they departed the country, but she was doing a damned good job at it. Well, their time was limited and running out, so what the hell, Nick thought.

They walked into the living room where most of the Primary Strike Team and probably two dozen others from the three squads stood around a television. Dwayne Marcus looked up from it and saw the two approaching.

"Make way for Nick," Marcus said, his deep, drill instructor voice carrying across the room like a wave.

The men shifted a bit and Nick slid into the half-circle. Marcus picked up the remote and rewound the TV five minutes backward.

"Wait until you see this, Nick," he said, dropping the remote to a chair. "This is unbelievable. Or on second thought, maybe it's not."

The show resumed and Nick recognized the Mexican Presidential briefing room. Seeing that room was becoming a theme. Did the president hold an emergency briefing for the country every single day down here?

The Mexican President walked up to the podium and looked down at a notecard he carried. He looked grim and Nick felt just a touch of uneasiness in his stomach.

"I've come out today to make a statement and I apologize to the members of the media present today, but I will be unable to take any questions," Roberto Rivera said, nodding to the reporters who stood around him, hovering like a flock of vultures.

Nick noticed the man directly to his left – Bulldog, the huge Navy SEAL from Baltimore – stepped away from him. He wasn't sure why until Isabella slid into the circle. She moved in close, placed her hand on his lower back, and pushed her breast against his crossed arm.

Nick assumed no one was behind them because Isabella immediately began sliding her hand up and down his lower back, her nails tickling his back seductively. He tried to pay attention to the press conference, but it was taking all the focus he could muster. Between the feeling of her breasts and the sensation of her fingers running up and down his back, he was about to call the entire unit outside into formation while he took care of more pressing matters.

"I am as shocked at this news as you are," Rivera said, and Nick wondered what he was talking about. He focused harder.

"While Hernan Flores was no friend of either mine or the Mexican people, he deserved better than to die in a prison."

Nick came fully to his senses. Flores? Dead? What the hell?

"Make no mistake," Rivera said, "this was not justice. And while we were going to seek the sternest of sentences, this is not an equivalent punishment. Flores should have faced a judge. The Mexican people should have witnessed the cruel acts of this man, as the government presented its case against the most dangerous man in North America.

"I regret that at this time we're not more sure of what happened yet, but our facts *do* show that Flores was killed by another prisoner. I want to emphasize that point. This was not a corrupt guard who killed him. Of that we are certain.

"In fact, my press secretary will distribute the name and photo of the prisoner who executed this vicious attack and who also in the process managed to escape from Federal Social

Readaptation Center No. 1. As you will note in the profile we will hand out, this man is a member of the Godesto Cartel. We're not sure if this is part of a coup inside the organization or personal revenge taken by this man. We intend to find that out, though, and once we do, we will alert you, the public immediately. It's crucial that the Mexican government have your assistance in this fight against the Godesto Cartel and the other elements of organized crime.

"Now, before I step away, I want to address two misconceptions that I've already heard. Some have said the Mexican government, or possibly even myself, had a hand in Hernan Flores's death. I want to assure you this is false. Quite frankly, had we wanted him dead, then we could have killed him in the raid that netted him. Our officers could have claimed it was self-defense. Thus, you can be confident that neither I nor the Mexican government wanted this man killed in prison.

"The second misconception I'd like to address is that Hernan Flores's death is either proof of the Mexican government's incompetence or our corruption."

The President looked down and swallowed.

"It is true that we still struggle with these issues, but I'm proud of our record and the improvements that we have made to date. Our government is more competent and less corrupt than when I took office. And I want the Mexican people to know that every day we improve the quality of our police and military and root out more corruption. But this remains a monumental task. Nonetheless, I –"

Isabella had removed her hand at some point and Nick turned to look at her. She looked pale and had crossed her arms protectively. Nick remembered that these news events mattered a heck of a lot more to her than they did for the other members of S3, who'd soon be leaving this tumultuous country.

He reached around and pulled her against him in a protective hug. And as he held her, remembered her dead father and brother. She had lost a lot in this fight. Not to mention the honorable officers, prosecutors, and judges she had known, who'd been killed by the cartels.

Nick turned and saw that none of the men seemed to notice that he held her. They were all focused on the TV as their entire lives hung in the balance of what Rivera might say. Their focus was complete.

Nick knew he was dropping the ball as a leader, falling short of every military standard he had ever held himself to, but he didn't let go.

A few men turned and saw them, but Nick decided to hell with it. It was their last day. He'd never see the members of S3 again.

Nick was beyond caring.

Nick wrapped a second arm around her and she pulled herself closer. Rivera prattled on, but Nick had stopped listening long ago.

"Want to share a beer?" he asked.

"Yes," she said, desperation in her voice.

Nick grabbed Isabella's hand and led her toward his office. There, they shared two beers, in fact, talking for almost two hours about her family. About Nick's past. And also the future, which neither was sure about.

Nothing else happened. The impending separation kept an insurmountable gulf between their physical desires.

They might have been ignoring their desires, but one hundred miles away, another man was following his: The Butcher's plan to topple the Mexican government was already under way.

CHAPTER 30

S3 had no way to know about this move by the Butcher and the Godesto. They were wrapping up their exit. Nick sat in his office, dejected. In the corner, his bags and footlocker waited, packed and ready for the trip home. His locked and loaded M14 stood propped by his gear.

Nick knew this was the final hours for Shield, Safeguard, and Shelter in Mexico. He had called a brief formation earlier behind the farmhouse. He had thanked the men for their service and diligence, and wished them all luck wherever their paths took them once they returned to the States.

Now Nick wanted to talk to his Primary Strike Team members one-on-one. Most likely, they would separate at the border and this would be his last chance to take his time and talk with his men, man-to-man.

"Send the first man in, Marcus," he yelled.

Truck walked in, wearing a ratty T-shirt that was half tucked in and did little to improve his look. And the look wasn't much – a bald, middle-aged man with the start of a gut.

But he did have a look of ferocity in his eyes and a pair of hulking arms and chest to back them up. Nick had a natural affinity for the man who had given so much to America and fallen so far in his sacrifices. Nick smiled at the man who probably struggled with more demons than anyone could ever guess.

"Well, thanks for not beating me up," Nick said, a smile on his face.

Truck shrugged and gave an embarrassed smile.

"Ah, hell, I'll never live that down. Beat up one dumb-ass officer and it follows you the rest of your career."

Nick laughed.

"Well, it cost you your time in Special Forces. And then you had to go charging up the hill in Afghanistan instead of just driving on."

Truck shrugged and smiled. "I'd do it again. Lost too many friends over there and I don't take kindly to getting shot at day in and day out by the same jackasses."

Nick stood and reached out to shake his hand. They shook, two strong grips, and Nick said, "Truck, it's been an honor to serve with you. I just wanted to say thanks for all you've done and if I'm ever lucky enough to get in the shooting biz again, I'll be giving you a call. You're a damn fine man."

"Thank you, sir."

And that's the way it went with each Primary Strike Team member. Nick wanted just a few words with each of them.

Lizard, the small Puerto Rican, who always seemed nervous and scared. But just like his nine years in the Marine Corps, the little Jiu-jitsu black belt had never backed down or shied away from danger.

Bulldog, the 6'4", 250-pound Navy SEAL from Baltimore. He was always motivated, even once the mission end was announced. "There's always a need for good trigger pullers. We'll be fine, men," he had said after the formation broke up, while so many others seemed crushed, like men that had lost a bloody skirmish and left quite a few comrades on the field of battle.

Preacher, the quiet, religious man of average size, who had done four tours with the Marine Corps, two of them with the special unit MARSOC. He had lived up to his billing. Devout. Avoider of nicotine and alcohol. Rarely found without a small Testament in one of his cargo pockets.

Red, the crazy 5'5" Marine, who wanted to fight everyone. He also wanted to go on every mission and stand every guard post. The thin man seemed to live on Marlboro Reds, which powered him through impossible levels of sleep deprivation. Nick wasn't sure if Red's name came from smoking Marlboro Reds 24/7 or the red, short-cropped hair that topped his freckled face. Nick had seen the action-addict side of Red since they had left the States and he understood why the man transferred from one Marine combat unit to the next deploying one, while he served in the Corps.

"It was an honor," Nick told him.

"I just wish there had been more shooting," Red said.

"Me, too," Nick replied, having no idea how soon he'd regret those words.

Nick had decided not to call in Isabella for any final words. They had exchanged phone numbers the day before and Nick didn't want to deal with talking a final time to a woman he had feelings for.

Nick also spoke with the three departing squad leaders and the Scout Sniper squad leader, since he had gotten to know them all pretty well. Nick encouraged each of them to talk with their men as he had – to say a few words and thank them individually for their service.

He said a few final words to his CIA contact, whose name he still didn't know. The man had proven as loyal and faithful as one could ask.

Finally, Nick called in Marcus.

The 6'1", University of Florida football star was among one of the greatest men Nick had ever met. He was all-Marine and full of courage and skill, but he also had the discipline and charisma that only a drill instructor carried. The man never looked flustered or unprepared. He was the textbook example of what a Marine leader should be and Nicked thanked him to no end for how much work he'd shouldered.

Marcus had taken it all in the position of parade rest and ended the conversation by only saying, "Nick, it's been an honor to serve with you."

And with all the goodbyes said, and the hour of departure approaching, Nick sat back in his chair and felt a deep sadness come over him. In just a few hours, he'd have nothing again: no mission, no Isabella, no men to joke with, no command to challenge his wits and determination.

Nick looked over at his secured footlocker and considered pulling out his bottle of Jack Daniels, but knew he should hold off. At least for a little while longer. But something told him he might just drown in the bottle in the months to come.

"You've seen too much and done too much, Nick," he said to himself. "Pretty soon, you'll just be a washed-up old man down at the VFW."

He remembered his time in Afghanistan. His betrayal by a man named Whitaker. His dead spotter, Nolan Flynn. Evading more than a thousand Soviet troops. A changed identity and his time as Bobby Ferguson. Anne and all the sweetness and beauty that went with that name. Her death. Meeting Allen Green. Hunting down Anne's killers.

Nick shook his head and stood. He had to get these thoughts out of his head. And with that he reached for his footlocker.

"Just one drink, Nick," he told himself. "Only one today and no more thinking about Anne or what you're going to do tomorrow when this is all done. Just one, small drink."

And with that thought, he reached for the bottle.

CHAPTER 31

While Nick Woods said his goodbyes, the Godesto Cartel went after Juan Soto.

With the Butcher in charge, the cartel carried out one of its most ambitious operations since the three-pronged nighttime attack on the Navy SEALs, their reinforcement column of Mexican troops, and the Presidential Palace.

After all, the Butcher reasoned that if Soto's mere departure from the country would cause a national emergency and American intervention, then what would Soto's actual death cause?

The Butcher had been looking forward to this attack for months and months. Few last-minute preparations were needed, as the operation had been planned for more than a year. But the attack hadn't gone down because Hernan Flores – the soft bastard – wouldn't green light it.

But now Juan Soto would die.

The man resided on the top floor of an eight-story building in Mexico City. Soto owned the building for security measures.

The Butcher watched the building, waiting with eight Godesto gunmen in a mid-sized van, parked in an alley near Soto's building downtown. The eight men were jammed in tight, three bodies per bench seat in the back, with the Butcher sitting in the passenger seat up front. The six men in the back were mostly hidden behind the dark-tinted windows of the white van, and the van provided adequate camouflage on the busy streets of Mexico City.

It was just a white, industrial passenger van. Unmarked. No business logos. It could have belonged to a hundred different companies or simply been a rental.

All eight gunmen wore SWAT uniforms and full battle gear.

Helmets, assault vests, and MP5s slung just like they carry them on SWAT teams. Their uniforms failed to precisely match Mexico City's SWAT team, but they were close, including the black combat boots and the patches on their shoulders.

"Let's go," the Butcher said.

The eight of them climbed out as calmly as they could and made final checks of their weapons. Their 9 mm MP-5s wouldn't do at long range, but they were perfect for the kind of close-in work planned for today.

"Ready?" the Butcher asked.

His men nodded in affirmation and made final adjustments of helmets, slings, and assault vests. With the van parked deep in an alley between two tall buildings, and behind three dumpsters, they weren't concerned with being seen.

The Butcher double-checked his MP-5 and confirmed that his M9 Beretta was strapped down on his thigh holster. He didn't need it falling out during any ducking and rolling he might have to do. Behind him, his men racked slides and checked magazines. Other than the sounds of metal clicking on weapons and rocks grinding under boots on the pavement, the late afternoon was quiet.

Traffic passed down the busy road in front of them, but it was rush hour in the middle of Mexico City and commuters had one thing on their minds: getting home. Looking for odd sights like a van disgorging SWAT guys just wasn't high up on their priority list.

The eight men formed up in a single file with the Butcher taking the third position. He preferred to take point, but he couldn't lead and make sound decisions if he was looking for targets and other dangers. The eight men exited the alley at a leisurely pace, their weapons hanging loose from their slings and aimed toward the ground.

In their planning, the Butcher had reiterated numerous times that they were to seem as relaxed as possible when they broke cover from the alley. And as expected, the moment they stepped onto the sidewalk and started down the street, they came under intense scrutiny from passersby and residents living in apartments up and down the street.

"Stay calm," the Butcher said, his voice just loud enough

for his men to hear.

They only had a block to cover before they would arrive at Juan Soto's building. And if their recon was accurate, they wouldn't come under observation from any guards inside until they were about fifty yards from the front door. It was one of the few security weaknesses of the building.

The group walked in a file toward their target, heads mostly down and bodies seemingly relaxed. The eight men looked unalert and disinterested. A few people on the streets noticed the group, but barely. Seeing well-armed Mexican police or soldiers on the street was all too common in the cartel-riddled country. And this group didn't seem concerned about danger, so people went about their business without fear of being blown up or caught in a massive firefight with drug runners.

They strolled right up to the front of Juan Soto's building with shocking ease, thanks to the cover of the uniforms. And once the first man opened the massive glass door, the Butcher knew there was no stopping them now. The SWAT uniforms had served their purpose well.

Up on the eighth floor, Soto was reading a good book, far more relaxed than usual. He had eight men – all prior SAS, Special Forces, and Navy SEALs – protecting him, which always made him feel pretty safe. But today, with Hernan Flores dead, he felt safer than he'd felt in years.

It seemed a lifetime since he had called President Roberto Rivera and threatened to leave the country and close all of his businesses. And while he didn't know what Flores's replacement was like, it was inconceivable that he was more of a concern than Flores had been.

Hernan Flores had posed a special kind of danger because of his ability to win over public support, thanks to how he played the role of businessman and philanthropist. And Flores, having come from the depths of poverty, could relate to the poor. During his reign over the Godesto Cartel, he had often enjoyed more popular support than the President.

Now, with the Godesto Cartel back under the control of a much more common thug, it would be easier for President Rivera to rally the people and the country's law enforcement agencies. Finally, the tide against the government would be permanently checked and momentum turned against the country's parasites.

Soto turned the page, sitting back in his most comfortable reading chair.

There had been too much violence and political drama of late. Rivera still had to work hard to win back the support of the people, but the press conference where he promised full transparency had helped.

Soto lay the book down for a moment. Tomorrow, he would start catching up on all the work he had ignored of late, due to the political drama in his country. Soto had asked his executive assistant to cram as much into tomorrow's calendar as possible.

From here on out, Soto would mostly be focused on business. And when you were a billionaire, you had a lot of business to focus on.

Top of his list tomorrow was one of his rock quarries, where production was down and there'd been a curious, deep drop in profits. But Soto's chief financial officer suspected profits hadn't fallen, but rather the plant manager was pocketing increasing amounts of cash.

After dealing with the quarry manager, Soto had to meet with his braintrust about a wealth management firm he was in the process of purchasing. Soto wanted to make a decision and either buy it or move on. He hated over-studying issues and letting them divert his focus. His team of advisers had been considering purchasing the firm for nearly three months, which Soto figured was probably two months too long.

It was time to either buy it or forget it.

Finally, the last thing on his day's schedule was the final touches on planning a symposium on economic development with the Mexican Chamber of Commerce. Soto, Rivera, and other top Mexican leaders planned to host a three-day economic development summit for Middle East leaders. It was time to convince Arab countries to invest a portion of their vast sums of cash into beachfront real estate along Mexico's coast.

Soto picked his book back up, a sense of bliss returning. He loved running his businesses. And it was an added bonus that in doing so, he helped Mexico. He hoped his grandfather could see him now. That single fishing boat had truly multiplied far higher than the ten he had passed down.

Suddenly, the sound of an explosion rocked Soto from his thoughts. It had sounded close, very close, and he walked to his bedroom door – a four-inch thick vault-like slab – and opened it.

"Gordon, what was that?" Soto asked.

Gordon, an SAS veteran dressed in a suit, stood with his finger pushing his earpiece further in.

He held up a finger and then said, "Sir, we're still trying to figure that out. Not sure how close to us that was."

But Soto could tell the decorated veteran with tours in Iraq and Afghanistan was far more on edge than usual.

Gordon noticed Soto looking at him and said, "Sir, please step back in your room."

Soto resisted and said, "Has anyone alerted the authorities yet?"

"Sir," Gordon said, with tension in his voice, "we don't even know what it was. We've got this, sir. Let us do our job."

Soto stepped back in his room and slammed the heavy door. He'd deal with Gordon later. The man was good, but he was too confident. And only a year into working security in Mexico, he seemed in Soto's opinion to consistently underestimate the power of the cartels. It was as if all his deployments into combat zones, and the insane talent he had in close quarters battle, had created too much confidence in the man.

Soto walked to his eighth floor window to look for a rising smoke plume. The explosion had definitely been close. But as he looked out his four-inch bullet-proof window, he saw no smoke anywhere. He rushed to the window at the other side of the room and saw no smoke there, either.

His peripheral vision caught movement and he looked down in the street below him to see several SUVs and cars squealing to a stop, men jumping from them carrying

STAN R MITCHELL

automatic weapons and rocket launchers.

"Gordon!" Soto yelled.

He raced across his bedroom for the door. The door opened and Gordon no longer looked like a dignified bodyguard in a suit. Now he was cinching down a tactical vest loaded with pockets, magazines, and grenades. He pulled a submachine gun sling across his body and looked up at his billionaire VIP.

"Sir, we've got a problem," Gordon said.

"No shit," Soto said. "Call the police." He pointed back toward the bedroom windows. "There are dozens of them down there!"

"We're on it," Gordon said. "But we need you in your room."

Gordon pushed Soto back into the room and stepped in it with him. He slammed the thick steel door, locked it, and then turned a foot-wide aluminum wheel in the center of the door that pushed eight-inch steel posts into the reinforced floor and upper wall. Soto's room was essentially a vault, encased in four inches of steel. It was fireproof, bombproof, and definitely bullet proof.

Its only weaknesses were the two windows, but even they were four inches thick and could handle anything up to a fifty caliber round – or at least a couple of them. If they got hit with a steady stream, they'd be screwed.

In truth, Gordon knew there shouldn't have been any windows, but billionaires get what billionaires want, and Soto refused to spend his nights in a room where he couldn't look out over Mexico City.

Gordon tossed his submachine gun on the bed and balled his hands into fists.

"Shit!" he said.

"How bad is it?" Soto asked.

"They've breached the building," Gordon said. "Killed our two men at the door and will be having it out with the rest of my men soon."

"How many men do you have left?" Soto asked. "Five, right?"

"Correct," Gordon said. "They should be able to hold them off. These men are the best. I just hate that we lost Sherwood and Craddock at the front door. And I hate that I'm stuck in this room as a last line of defense and not out there with my men, where I belong."

Gordon was pacing and frantic. Not scared, but just furious he wasn't on the line with his men.

Soto walked back to the window and saw a derelict school bus screech to a halt below. Gang members carrying AKs and pistols rushed off the bus and into the street. There were dozens of men running about and taking up positions, hiding behind newspaper stands and metal trash cans.

This wasn't a raid. This was a war.

Soto sat heavily on the edge of his bed.

"Gordon, your men will never hold off this many," Soto said, a deep dread in his voice.

Gordon walked over and looked down at the street below. Seeing the look of horror spread over the stoic man's face, Soto grabbed for his phone.

The moment Rivera picked up, Soto blurted out, "Roberto, they're coming for me."

Hearing the shakiness of his own voice made Soto realize how scared he actually was.

Sounds of machine gunfire and explosions roared in the background.

"What?" Rivera asked, hearing the sounds of battle, as well. "Hang in there, Juan. Let me call for help. I'll call you right back."

Hands shaking, Soto slid his phone in his pocket and moved back to the window. Why didn't Soto have a gun in this room? Or about a dozen?

He looked outside again. His attackers had parked their cars horizontally in the road, completely closing it off. And the gangsters and thugs had lit tires on fire in the road. Smoke rose from the tires ominously and Soto saw weapons pointed outboard from half-hidden men kneeling in shadows and behind pieces of cover, waiting for anyone insane enough to approach.

What was this? What had happened?

Soto wasn't sure, but he was quite certain he was on the losing side right now. By quite a bit. And vault or not, he didn't feel safe. But he prayed it would suffice until a quick response from the Mexican police or Army broke through.

Back downstairs, before the situation exploded and flooded with armed cartel members in view of Soto's bullet-proof window, things had been quiet and calm, same as any other morning. Then Soto's two security men at the entrance to the building noticed the SWAT team out front walking toward them.

Soto's building, privately owned, was about half glass, like most of the other skyscrapers downtown. The difference was that Soto's building didn't just have massive glass windows that could survive a bad storm. No, his windows had all been replaced and were bullet-proof.

Additionally, since Soto had purchased the building, he had turned it into a fortress. No tenants. They were moved out. And no visitors, except by appointment.

Visitors had to come through a single entry point, and even then, they had to be buzzed in. Most weren't. Under any circumstances. Soto's security was too important, and threats too many, for any kind of other security posture.

So when Soto's two security men at the bottom level saw the SWAT team, they stood and walked out from behind a desk for a better look. The SWAT team looked unalarmed and casually walked up to the door. The lead man pointed at the door and one of Soto's suited security men buzzed them in.

"How can we help you?" the smallest guard said, raising his hand to stop them as the eight men walked through the door. "No one called us with an alert so I'm afraid I'll have to stop you here."

The uniforms and calm demeanor had clearly worked. Then suddenly the point man for the faux SWAT team quickly raised his MP-5 – it had just been hanging from its sling and directed toward the ground in as non-threatening manner as possible. He brought the smaller guard's face into his sights and fired four rounds on automatic into the man's face. It happened smooth and fast, the rounds shattering the relative silence of the morning.

The larger guard was reaching for his weapon when the second man in the stack fired a round through his knee. The bullet shattered the man's knee and he shrieked in pain as he tumbled to the ground. He slid backward on his hands and good leg, dragging his lifeless limb behind him, desperate to gain some distance from the threat. Somehow ignoring the pain, the guard moved his hand to his jacket, reaching for his gun a second time.

The Butcher, shoving men out of his way, charged forward. He kicked upward, catching the man in the bottom of his jaw with the toe of his assault boot. Teeth crunched and the man's head lifted. Blood poured from his mouth.

The Butcher grabbed the guard's lapels, lifted him off the floor, and removed the .45 from its holster inside the man's jacket. He handed it to a cartel member near him, who shoved it in a pouch on his web belt. The Butcher then released his grip, shoving the man's body back to the ground.

The man looked half out of it. Definitely in serious pain from the the wrecked knee and remodeled dental work. The Butcher figured he was a prior Special Forces soldier.

"You're going to tell us what we need to know," the Butcher said, "or you're going to be wishing you had. Either way, I don't care."

Two cartel men grabbed the guard by his arms and yanked him back to his feet. He stumbled on his good leg, leaning on them for support. One of the Butcher's other men circled behind the guard, checking him for more weapons and found a revolver strapped to his ankle. He ripped it off the man's leg and threw it away from them. It skidded across the floor.

The Butcher looked out the front entrance and saw SUVs and cars sliding to a halt in front of the building. He smiled at how easy this would now be. Juan Soto's guards had never stood a chance. And now that his men had made their breach into the building, Soto didn't stand a chance either.

The Butcher watched his men deploy in the streets in front of the building. The rest of his men would be here soon, riding in SUVs, sports cars, and even a bus – basically, whatever form of transportation they could get their hands on. The Butcher hadn't sweated that detail and it ultimately wouldn't matter. They'd be abandoning many of them and they could steal or buy more vehicles later.

What mattered wasn't how they got here, but *that* they got here. They'd have to fight their way out of the city and they needed sheer numbers of fighters for that. Of course, sheer numbers weren't a problem for the largest cartel in North or South America.

Not only did the Butcher have nearly two hundred of his own men streaming in from various directions, he had also ordered the various gangs affiliated with the Godesto Cartel to do a single task: kill at least one or two cops in their sector. Ten thousand dollars if they killed one; twenty-five thousand if they killed two, which provided a nice incentive for attempting to kill two, since $25k for a street gang was a lot of money.

The Butcher needed chaos, and a lot of it, across the entire city. And if these gangs wanted to keep profiting off the high-quality coke that only the Godesto Cartel could provide, then they would start shooting at cops in their area beginning at five o'clock this afternoon – and not a minute earlier; the orders were clear.

His men out in front of the building looked confident as they rushed from vehicles and looked for targets. He knew they fed off of having their leader actually taking part in the operation. Not some fat ass, wannabe politician safely waiting in some giant tower, cramming down Funyuns. No, now they had someone who would share in their victories and defeats. Who'd put his own life on the line on every mission from here on out.

And he knew they were especially excited that a bank heist would be going down once the police had committed to responding to the assault on Juan Soto's building. The men appreciated the boldness and the promised bonuses they'd be getting from the bank robbery.

The Butcher turned from watching the street and refocused on his SWAT team. They had put the wounded guard back on the floor and pinned him down. One of them was screaming questions into his face while another one was stabbing a Kabar knife through the man's hand and into the tile floor. He'd need a new knife after this, but it looked like an effective technique to the Butcher, who knew a thing or two about sadistic torture.

"Hurry up," he said to his men, looking down at his watch. They had a short window of no more than twenty-five minutes to finish this. And he wanted Soto's head on his wall, not some overpaid guard who fancied himself a former war hero.

The Butcher looked at the screaming man and wondered if the big salary he earned protecting Soto was worth it now. But then the knife slammed through the hand again and the Butcher got his answer through the man's ragged screams. No matter how much you made, sometimes no amount of money was enough.

The Butcher pulled out a tactical radio to check in on his teams outside the building that he couldn't see. The government forces would be coming soon and the Butcher wanted to be ready.

Juan Soto watched the scene below in the street in sheer horror. He felt hopeless, but couldn't force himself to stop watching. Gordon was pacing, calling into his sleeve mic for updates from his men.

Three men alive upstairs, plus Gordon. That's all that stood between Soto and the army below.

Twenty minutes ago, eight expensive men had seemed overkill. Now, it seemed ridiculously shortsighted.

Juan's cellphone rang. He looked down and saw it was President Rivera's number.

"Juan, hang in there," Rivera said. "You're going to be fine. We have an armored SWAT truck on the way. It has thirty men in the back who are armed to the teeth."

Rivera sounded a little too shaken for Soto's liking, as if something else was wrong.

"What is it?" Soto asked.

"Nothing."

"Tell me, damn it," Soto shouted. "It's my life on the line here!"

Rivera sighed into the phone.

"The Godesto Cartel is doing more than just attacking your building," Rivera admitted. "Apparently, there have been dozens of cops murdered across the city in what must be a coordinated attack of some kind. We've got all law enforcement pairing up into groups of four and they're breaking out shotguns and assault rifles until we figure out what's happening."

"Meaning?" Soto asked, frustrated.

"It's affecting our response time," Rivera said, his voice quieter.

Soto felt a deep, sickening feeling that he hadn't felt in a long time. Actually, since he filed bankruptcy as a young businessman, twenty-plus years ago. Yet panicking and screaming at Rivera would not help the situation, only make it worse.

"Do the best you can," Soto said. "We'll find a way to hold. But, you better send more than just a SWAT truck and some officers. There are tons of armed men in the street below and thirty won't be enough. We're going to need the army."

CHAPTER 32

Nick felt an anger and sense of remorse in him. It was time to go and the SEALs would not be avenged. Nick wanted to destroy the entire cartel. Sure, the head of the Godesto Cartel was gone, but Nick had been aiming for more than simply Hernan Flores's head on a platter. He had wanted to tear apart the Godesto, limb-by-limb,returning home, knowing his men had made a difference.

And with the victory, he could've made made Mexico, and thus America, safer.

The sound of approaching footsteps shook him from his thoughts. The steps stopped at his office door and a fist rapped respectfully on the door. His hopes of a soft knock from Isabella died right there.

"Come in," Nick said.

His CIA contact stepped in the room, holding up a phone.

"It's Mr. Smith," the man said.

Nick looked up at his CIA contact. He was in no hurry to hear Mr. Smith, jerking his chain about this or that. Or yelling about how they should leave the country in this manner or that manner.

"We've been through a lot," Nick said, holding the eyes of his CIA contact and ignoring the outstretched phone.

"Sir?"

"You and me, we've been through a lot. From you volunteering to make contact with me at that gas station by the interstate, to me abducting your ass and taking you hostage, to all the planning and nasty surprises you dropped on me before we ever left the country. Remember all those? Remember the early departure date and the fact that we'd be a corporation instead of a government unit?"

"Sir, that wasn't on me. I told you–"

"I know," Nick said, holding his hand up and cutting him off. "I was just reminiscing before you knocked and I wanted to say to your face that I haven't given you enough credit. Hell, I don't even know your name. But, I wanted to say thanks for all you've done. I hate that our mission down here is ending, but it's still better than if it had never happened. And I owe you for that. So, thanks. For everything. Especially volunteering to approach a half-nuts, crazy-ass sniper like me. I'm glad I didn't shoot your dumb ass."

The CIA contact stared at Nick flabbergasted.

"Seriously," Nick said, "had you not volunteered, I'd have still been driving the roads and I would have never had the chance to command again, so in all seriousness, thank you. I owe you."

"Thank you, sir. The honor's been all mine. But I think you better take this call or I'm not going to have a job when we get back."

"Don't sweat him," Nick said. "I don't really give a shit about what your boss thinks."

The CIA contact reluctantly extended the encrypted phone and Nick accepted it. "Now get the hell out of here."

Nick waited for the door to close and then lifted the phone.

"To what do I owe this pleasure?" Nick asked.

"I wouldn't be such a smartass if I were you," Mr. Smith said. "You're going to put me on your Christmas list when I give you this news."

"Don't count on it," Nick said. "You forget, I really don't like you, plus I don't even know your real name."

"Cut the crap," Mr. Smith snapped, clearly eager to re-establish his authority over the situation. "What I'm trying to tell you is you may get to hunt a little longer."

"What do you mean?"

"Juan Soto, Mexico's most influential billionaire –"

"I know," Nick said. "I've done my homework. He's President Rivera's most important ally."

"Of course," Mr. Smith said, irritated at being interrupted. "But what you don't know is that his building is currently under assault."

"Say what?" Nick asked.

"You heard me. A large number of armed men have infiltrated his building, with dozens more surrounding the area."

"So, we going to go play SWAT now or what?" Nick asked.

"No," Mr. Smith said, "but something serious is going on. Besides the assault on Soto's building, nearly seventy cops have been killed this afternoon and a bank has been robbed. And we've been informed by the NSA that they have intercepted messages that show some advisers in Rivera's government are suggesting martial law be implemented."

"Holy shit," Nick said. "What do you want us to do?"

"Nothing, for now," Mr. Smith said. "But you're not leaving. We expect President Rivera will soon be asking for your help. Tell your team to change gears and forget about returning home. They need to mentally prepare for war again. And this one might be longer and uglier than we expected."

"This might be the best news I've heard in at least a year or two."

Mr. Smith hung up and Nick would eventually find himself recalling these words, as well, as S3 stacked bodies of men under his command for burial.

A shot rang out and the Butcher flinched in surprise. He ignored the radio he was talking into and turned. Smoke rose from the pistol of one of the men standing behind him. A big splash of blood from the guard's head was sprayed across the area.

"He told us what we needed," the man said, shrugging in confusion at the look of anger on the Butcher's face. A shell casing rolled to a stop on the marble floor.

"I'll get back with you," the Butcher said into his radio. "Where are Soto's men?" he asked the man with the smoking pistol.

"Top floor," the man said. "There are five more of them, just like we had been told. They're covering the elevators and fire escape, as we expected. Plus, one locked in the room with Soto."

The Butcher nodded to his man. They don't stand a chance, he thought. So far, their intelligence had been correct. He lifted his radio and said, "Bring up the assault teams. Quickly."

A couple minutes later, more than twenty men sprinted through the doors. They were a rough-looking bunch of rough dudes. Piercings, tattoos, and bad haircuts abounded. Just as importantly, they seemed eager for the task before them. Each had killed and most had been stabbed or shot in their years of service to the violent drug life. They knew danger and they had been moving toward it since they were young men. These men had tasted the reward in cash and women that such a life could provide and today simply equaled higher pay than normal.

"Let's go," the Butcher said to the men. "He looked back to his faux SWAT team members and said, "Stay here. You know the plan."

The SWAT team was to be used in a counter-attack if police managed to fight their way through the defenders outside. The Butcher calculated that police would hold their fire instinctively for just a moment if they saw other men in blue running toward them. As long as the officers looked as if they were retreating, the real cops might not react. And that would be all the hesitation his men would need. His counter attack by "SWAT" officers would shock the responding forces and cause additional confusion and delay of any rescue attempts.

With the SWAT members moving toward the front door to stack in case they were needed outside, the Butcher and his assault team marched toward their starting point. There was complete confidence in their numbers and the accuracy of their plan so far.

"You two cover the exits," the Butcher said.

Two men stepped away from the group, to cover the only possible routes out of the building. One of them covered the two elevators and the other covered the fire escape on the other side of the building.

The building lacked the dozen-plus exits a building of eight stories would typically have. Several years ago, Mexico City authorities had granted Soto permission to seal off two of the fire exits and completely weld them shut after he had bought the building and reduced its occupancy by more than eighty percent.

Soto wanted a fortress, not a revenue-generating apartment complex. He had wanted fewer entrances and exits to guard as a matter of maximizing his security, but that decision would now cost him his life, if the Butcher had his way.

The Butcher checked his two men one last time to make sure they had the elevators and fire escape covered. They lay in the prone behind AKs and would certainly get the drop on anyone who tried to escape.

"Sir? Your gear?" one of the men said, holding up a black duffel bag.

The Butcher had almost forgotten.

"Yes," he said, grabbing the bag.

He took off the uncomfortable helmet and assault vest and threw them to the ground. He then pulled his katana and Uzi out of the bag.

He turned back to his assault team.

"Stay sharp and be alert," he said.

The Butcher could see final victory within his grasp. And he knew if they bagged Juan Soto, President Rivera would soon fall. Either through resignation, public demand, or countless investigations at how such a horrific string of events went down.

It didn't matter to the Butcher. There wouldn't be a government still in place by the time he was through.

But, help for Soto was on the way and the responding vehicles were closing in fast. They had raced from their police station, charging to the rescue. Now, barely two miles separated them from Soto's building and the convoy sprinted the final distance, sirens blaring and lights flashing.

The convoy contained four police cruisers – two officers per vehicle, following the horrific cop assassinations just minutes earlier – followed by a massive armored SWAT truck, which was loaded with thirty heavily-armed men crammed in the back.

The lead cruiser had the shift captain in it and he and the SWAT team commander were conversing over the radio, going over details of how they'd deploy their officers once they arrived. Intel on what was happening at Soto's building was sketchy, but apparently there were quite a few bad guys there. Even stranger, the president of Mexico himself had ordered their hasty deployment to help protect his friend, despite the lack of details on what was actually happening.

This violated department policy. Patrol officers were supposed to be on the scene before SWAT members arrived, but the police chief lacked the balls to stand up to President Rivera.

The convoy roared past vehicles pulled to the side of the interstate. Drivers frantically yanked their cars to the shoulder or braked hard in sheer panic – anything to avoid the screaming police cars.

But the streets were getting narrower as they worked their way through arteries that led into downtown Mexico City. The buildings pushed in tighter to the streets through here, the city growing denser and higher. As they closed the final distance, parked cars on the street made it even more precarious.

The shift captain in the lead vehicle was mid-sentence talking with the SWAT team commander about how they would deploy outside the building when a parked car next to his cruiser exploded, blowing the police cruiser across the street. The ferocious two-hundred pound detonation caused the car to somersault five times before it hit the building across the street ten feet in the air. What remained of the car skidded and shrieked down the side of the building, crumpling to the pavement and crushing two bicycles parked near a doorway.

The shift captain and his driver didn't just die; they vaporized. The explosion was so big that the three police cruisers behind the captain's had their windows blown out.

The police officers who were lucky enough to have survived the huge blast suffered ruptured eardrums from the shockwaves. Two of them were additionally blinded by flying glass. Those who managed to keep their eardrums intact and their eyes shielded sustained severe concussions that would most likely affect them for the rest of their lives.

The men in the armored SWAT vehicle fared better – they rode in an armored vehicle with bullet-proof glass enclosing the front cab. They were also farther away from the explosion when it detonated across the street. The only injuries to the SWAT members occurred when the truck decelerated so hard that the men in the back were thrown into one another.

The vehicle had fully stopped, bouncing up and down from the severity of the brake pressure applied. The men had just begun to untangle themselves, when the unthinkable happened.

An open-bed Toyota truck tore out of an alley two blocks back. The truck had lain hidden, waiting for the explosion.

And as the SWAT members tried to regain their feet and deploy on the street, the truck sprinted forward the two blocks, hitting fifty mph before slamming its brakes and stopping thirty yards behind the armored vehicle.

Three men popped up from the back of the truck and hoisted RPG's on their shoulders. They had a non-moving, defenseless target sitting in front of them and the SWAT members hadn't even opened their armored doors yet.

The first RPG ripped through the back of the SWAT truck, hitting right in the seam created by the two heavy doors. Two more RPG warheads followed, exploding among the mass of men.

After the blasts and explosions from the first three rounds, the three men in the pickup reloaded for a second volley. They fired again into the smoking, ripped-apart piece of metal that had moments before been a fully-functioning, armored SWAT truck. The screaming tangle of men, who were lucky enough to survive the first strikes, had begged for their lives through the smoke and fire. But they were all silenced by the second volley of three RPGs.

This hadn't been a firefight. It had been an extermination.

Back in Juan Soto's building, the Butcher snapped his web gear on and adjusted the straps so that they fit snugly. He had thrown off the SWAT gear, tossing the helmet and assault vest against the wall. Now, he wore his familiar web harness, his Uzi cross-slung across his chest, where it always fell to the outside of his right leg. His Japanese katana was sheathed on his left side, handle facing forward, comforting with its weight.

The Butcher gripped its handle and slid it out a few inches, making sure it moved freely. He really hoped he'd get to use it. Against Soto himself.

The Butcher picked up his duffel bag, which was full of more goodies, with his left hand and grabbed the pistol grip of his Uzi with his right.

"Let's go," he said to his men.

The men moved to the stairwell at the far end of the building and entered it cautiously. They didn't expect anyone to be waiting for them, but better safe than sorry. Seeing no one, they covered the open space above with their weapons and began their climb up the eight flights of stairs.

The men carried AKs, shotguns, and submachine guns; an assortment that varied based on each man's preference. The Butcher didn't care what they opted for. They had each killed and fought before. They knew the advantages and disadvantages of each of the weapons. The variety would probably prove an asset in the close-in fighting to come, depending on what they faced up top.

None of Juan Soto's men waited for them at the top of the stairwell. They reached the eighth floor without any problems. They paused to catch their breath and prepared themselves for the action that was about to commence.

They believed the top door would be locked. It was, after all, purely a fire escape for exit during emergencies from above. But they had brought explosives to deal with it, so the Butcher had no concern when he tested the door by slighting pushing on it. He was surprised to see it wasn't locked. That struck him as odd.

"Careful," he whispered. He pushed the door open.

He figured going first was a good way to take a bunch of bullets in the chest, but he didn't have a lot to live for. And building his reputation mattered more than anything else to him.

He placed his duffel bag by the wall and took a two-hand hold on the Uzi, leaning low over it. With that, he nudged the door open and edged around it, leading with his short weapon, which had been designed for close-in work like this.

An empty hallway was all that awaited him.

He could see a couple of waist-high plants and a lush carpet that probably cost twenty thousand dollars, but no bodyguards. His men rushed into the hallway behind him, weapons rattling as slings jingled and gear clinked.

Two elevators and at least one other fire exit could be seen at the other end of the hallway, but otherwise the corridor was empty. The Butcher reached behind him and picked up his duffel bag.

The Godesto assault group pushed down the hall cautiously, taking stock of their final obstacle. It was two doors, but to call them doors was almost a misnomer. They were massive, twelve-foot tall slabs that looked about six inches thick. Heavy, ornate wood, meant to be both spectacular and secure.

The Butcher noticed two small, black domes on both sides of the door. Cameras. Probably high definition and maneuverable, given that a billionaire had installed them. He cursed, stepped back, and blasted both of them.

The men covered the doors with their weapons and the Butcher yanked his long Uzi mag out, threw it into his bag, and pulled out another. He replaced it and looked back at the man in the rear of their group. He was a fat man carrying a huge pack and a shotgun. He was also the only man wearing a mask to conceal his face.

And for good reason. He was an active-duty army demolition specialist, a sergeant with more than twelve years of service. It wouldn't do for him to lose the lifetime pension he had nearly earned.

Though considering what he was earning today, the pension wouldn't be necessary if he got many more assignments from the Butcher and the Godesto Cartel. But the Butcher wanted the man's identity protected as badly as the sergeant did. If the man was recognized and arrested, it wasn't the imprisonment of the NCO that would bother the Butcher. It would be the loss of access to unlimited amounts of explosives.

This man had the rank to fudge paperwork and exaggerate the volume used in training exercises. The sergeant squeezed through the group of men and went to work. He pulled out a prepared explosive charge that was about twenty feet long and about two inches wide. The man had prepared the charge prior to their arrival at Juan Soto's building. And as he attached it around the doorframe, the Butcher suddenly remembered that the sergeant had literally been trained by American Special Forces.

Oh, if only Congress and the American people knew about this, the Butcher thought. The sergeant positioned the explosives in about ten seconds.

"We need to move back," the sergeant said.

No one needed any additional encouragement. They all moved down the hall and back into the far stairwell, as the sergeant unreeled a length of fuse behind him. He fed the line under the fire escape door, and they closed it.

"Hold your ears," the fat man said to the group hunkered down in the stairwell.

He squeezed the clacker four times and a blast rocked the hallway, along with a heavy thud. The cartel members rushed the hallway, running through a cloud of dust and smoke.

One door had fallen and the other hung twisted and leaning, only the top hinge holding it up.

Juan Soto's guards inside the room hadn't known to expect the blast since their cameras had been shot out. Two of the guards crawled away from the doors, their heads rattled and their ears bleeding. The Butcher's men, who had raced in front of their leader, tore the two shook-up men apart in a deluge of barely accurate automatic fire. Flesh blasted apart. Blood painted furniture. Hardwood floors disintegrated.

There was a momentary feeling of victory among the cartel members, but then a snap sounded and a Godesto man's head exploded. Another man crumpled. A third screamed and jumped, as if he had been shocked.

"Get back, you idiots," the Butcher said. "They've got silenced weapons."

They scrambled back, but another man screamed in pain

and fell before they could retreat behind the cover of the wall.

At least one of Soto's guards had smoked them in a calm and efficient manner with his silenced weapon. Now, four of the Godesto men lay in front of the missing door. Two were motionless, already dead. One lay on the ground whimpering and clutching his wounds. And one held his neck, bleeding profusely.

Apparently whoever was left alive inside was fully coherent, despite the blast. They clearly had complete control of their senses, including their hearing. The Butcher knew Soto's men would be some of the best that money could buy, and they might even have submachine guns or assault rifles. Not just pistols.

But, the Butcher had planned for this.

His men, bloodthirsty by nature and angry at the loss of their friends, didn't need to be told what to do. They were already reaching into pouches and pockets and pulling pins.

Grenade after grenade was thrown, rolled, and bounced into the room. Explosion after explosion roared as the men ran back down the hall, away from the massive room. New screams joined the sounds of the Godesto wounded. None of the Butcher's men wanted to take any chances, so more grenades were tossed and hurled deep into the room.

After those explosions ceased, they rushed the room like a bunch of wild animals. They assaulted the room in typical cartel style. No fire control. No clearing of corners. No communicating.

In fact, it was the precise opposite of the organized, synchronized movement of elite forces. Instead, the Godesto charged in and shot up couches, counters, and furniture sets – anywhere anyone could be hiding. Their rounds tore through shaken and wounded guards.

One survivor was gleefully executed. The Butcher stood among his men, the smell of cordite, C4 explosive, and blood filling the air.

"How many are there?" he asked, too loud. "We need a body count."

He shook his head to clear all the cobwebs in it – damn, he hated how explosions shook you up, even when you were prepared for them – and he hoped his ears would stop ringing soon.

"We count five, sir," one of his senior men said.

"Good," the Butcher said. They wouldn't need to go searching through the building looking for any more of Juan Soto's men.

His radio beeped and his ambush team reported that they had destroyed the responding SWAT team. The Butcher shook his head in disbelief. He had been certain of the path the SWAT members would take during his planning and staging, but to actually have them do so? For the plan to be working this well?

It was almost too good to be true. With the destruction of the SWAT team, the Butcher knew they were in good shape, timewise.

"Get the demo man up," the Butcher said, nodding toward the final, imposing obstacle of Soto's vault door. "We need to finish this."

He wasn't sure what Rivera's next move would be. That was where his planning had ended. Would the Army be sent in? Other SWAT teams from neighboring cities?

Who knew?

"Hurry up," the Butcher said, feeling a touch of fear in his gut. Uncertainty was scary.

Again the fat sergeant pushed forward, digging in his pack and removing several shaped charges. He stacked them on the floor and began studying the vault-like door, estimating its weight and strength from up close. The man squinted, placed the charges, and stepped back.

"We better move way back," the sergeant said. "Into the hallway."

CHAPTER 33

Nick Woods waited outside President Roberto Rivera's office again. It was like deja vu.

He wondered what the president would say. The news reporting on the prior day's events had been brutal.

Juan Soto? Killed. A major bank? Robbed. A SWAT team? Wiped out.

And that didn't take into account the nearly seventy cops killed within a fifteen-minute period across Mexico City, in some kind of timed, coordinated hit. It was the bloodiest day against law enforcement in Mexico's history. Martial law had been imposed – a "temporary" martial law, Rivera called it in a late-night press conference – and the president's enemies in Congress were screaming for multiple investigations into the day's events.

To say that President Rivera was on the ropes was the understatement of the century. None of this really affected Nick. He hated to see the losses, but they were to be expected when you're at war.

He had watched much of the coverage the previous night with his team. Though the carnage was unfortunate, the team members of Shield, Safeguard, and Shelter were ecstatic that their mission would be extended. They were like a sports team that had traveled a long distance to play a championship game, only to be told the game was cancelled in the first quarter.

S3 was ready to get back in the game and even the score.

Once a summary of the day's events was mostly digested, thanks to Isabella's translation, and once the talking heads and analysts on the news started focusing on the upcoming investigations and political ramifications, Nick had called

Dwayne Marcus over for a private pow wow.

The two had agreed that with their extension looking imminent, the men should enjoy one last night of relaxation before things kicked back into high gear the next day. And with that thought, they planned a rotating security schedule that would allow everyone some time off and instructed each squad to spend some time together out by their own fire, cooking hot dogs and melting marshmallows. They also sent another couple of men out with one thousand dollars in petty cash to stock up on food and beer.

The only caveat this time was no fighting and a two-beer limit. The last thing they needed were men dealing with hangovers the next day, since there was a small chance they could be called to jump into action.

Nick had avoided mingling with the various squads of S3 this time, choosing not to rotate around the fires like he had the first time. Instead, he remained with his Primary Strike Team.

Dwayne Marcus, in typical fashion, lapped Nick in the physical and leadership category, asking permission to PT instead of hanging out with the Primary Strike Team. The former football standout from Florida then did a one-hour calisthenics session before showering and checking in on the other squads, like Nick knew he should have done.

Truck, the former Army Special Forces soldier, who had been kicked out for beating up an officer, stayed true to form and broke the rules. Nick caught him drinking four beers instead of two during the night, but didn't say anything. Mostly, because Truck drank twice as much as everyone else regularly, so the extra wouldn't faze him. But also because Nick didn't want to ruin the evening – for either himself or Truck.

Lizard, the Puerto Rican Marine vet of nine years, had looked nervous the whole night. He fidgeted and avoided drinking at all.

Bulldog, the massive, 6'4" Navy SEAL from the streets of Baltimore, had arrived late to the fire, having worked out for two hours prior to his arrival. He was easily the biggest PT freak in all of Nick's unit. He had doubled the amount of time that even Dwayne Marcus had exercised. And as if that wasn't enough, even once he showed up, he hardly relaxed. Bulldog declined the offered beer, hot dogs, and marshmallows, choosing instead a protein bar and some kind of gross-looking nutritional drink.

And of course, Red, the short, cocky, and reckless asshole, had scoffed at Bulldog's selection, asking the giant man if he was there for a war or a bodybuilding contest. Bulldog had threatened to crush the chain-smoking country boy, to which Red then said that he didn't fear men who shaved their legs and underarms and put on a g-string after lotioning up.

Nick had seriously thought he would have to step in between them, but Preacher played peacemaker and settled Red and Bulldog down.

Preacher had even enjoyed a couple of hotdogs with the team before retiring early.

Nick had spent the night around the fire mostly quiet and simply watching. He had relished the stories told around the crackling flames, tales that ranged from firefights in foreign lands to barfights in shitty ports throughout the world. The men had also indulged in some locker-room talk. And Isabella, the consummate team player and cool chick, hadn't minded.

The laughs and taunts had lasted for three-plus hours. Nick had watched his team, and especially Isabella, savoring the entire time as they sat out under the cloudless night, stars lighting up the night sky majestically.

If the night wasn't heaven on earth, then Nick didn't know what it was. But eventually, he had picked up his M14 and headed back to the farmhouse, exchanging a long look with Isabella before he left.

The night got better an hour later.

Nick heard a soft knock and put down the shooting magazine he was reading. He opened the door to see Isabella standing there.

"You wanted to see me?" she whispered, a coy grin on her face. She stood there in a tank top and a pair of shorts.

"More than anything in the world," Nick said.

Nick reached for her, yanked her into the room, and stuck his head out the door. Confirming the hallway was clear, he then gently shut the door.

"Most men would be more focused on what's in the room," Isabella said. She now stood against the tall bed, her hips leaning against it, her arms crossed in mock rejection.

Nick strode toward her, towered over her, and put his hand behind her neck. He pulled her toward him and said, "I'm not most men."

She resisted, leaned back again.

"I could find another," she said.

"You could, but you're in my room."

He pulled her close again, kissing the spot where her ear and jawline met. He slowly breathed in the scent of her hair, an intoxicating mix of strawberry and fire.

"You're awfully confident," she said. "What makes you so sure?"

"I hit what I aim at," Nick said, lifting her chin and kissing her lightly.

"And I always catch my man," Isabella said.

Nick pulled her to her feet, leaned forward, and kissed her. She responded and soon they were locked in deep kisses and passion that had been repressed for too long.

Nick picked her up and she wrapped her arms and legs around him, her hands in his hair.

They made love, ferociously the first time that night, and later made love again, slow and passionate the second time, before they drifted off to sleep with what little time remained.

Nick, thinking back on it, couldn't help but feel like he was on top of the world. A night with friends, by the fire; a night with Isabella, so full of passion; and now he was about to be handed a hunting license again by the president of Mexico.

Life was grand in his book. This was the life of a warrior. The thing every kid dreamed of: a brave man, a hot lady, and a phone call to save the day.

Now, outside the president's office, that same attractive secretary seemed to have looked at him differently this time. Not as some country weirdo in Wranglers. But as someone that could save them.

A quick fifteen seconds after he sat down, she hung up the phone.

"Mr. Woods?" the woman asked.

He broke away from his daydream and looked up.

"You may go in now," she said. "But, first?"

She paused, swallowed hard, then said, "Thank you so much for coming. We really need your help."

She walked him to the door and even hugged him before he entered. As if she knew he probably should run, but wouldn't. As if maybe she wouldn't ever see him again. It wasn't a lustful hug. It was, well, an anxious hug.

Nick walked into the President's office amazed at how much the man had changed since this mission to Mexico. The president looked nothing like he had the last time they met. In fact, Nick wasn't prepared for what he saw.

Rivera faced away from him, gazing out the bay window. The early morning sun shined through the glass, creating long rays of light over his shoulder, dust particles dancing through them at their own pace, oblivious to the somber mood of the room.

President Rivera wore a wrinkled white Oxford shirt with no jacket. The sleeves were pushed up carelessly and unless Nick was wrong, he held a glass of scotch in his hand. Nick wasn't sure what he should do since it appeared Rivera was unaware Nick had stepped into his office, but he heard the secretary close the door behind him. Nick eased up quietly to one of two chairs in front of the desk. Uncertain what etiquette dictated in such a situation, he stopped between the chairs and cleared his throat lightly to make his presence known.

Eventually Rivera averted his gaze, turned from the window, and took a big sip of his drink. He walked to his desk and sat down, placing his glass on the desk too hard, splashing some of his drink onto the surface. He nodded to a chair and Nick sat quietly. This felt spooky. And weird. Just plain weird. The confident, charismatic man who had greeted him mere days ago was gone.

Rivera poked at the pooled liquor on his desk and Nick realized that not only was he unshaven, his hair was greasy and his collar was dirty. It looked like the man hadn't showered since the day before.

"You look rough, Mr. President."

"I lost my best friend!" Rivera roared defensively.

Nick realized the man was already drunk and it was just a little after nine in the morning.

He took another swig and Nick raised his hand to stop him. "Sir, I think you need to hold off. Your opponents —"

"You don't think you'd be drinking if you lost your best friend?" he snapped. "I just got off the phone with Juan's wife. She's worse today than when I called her last night to break the news."

He sighed and said in a lower voice, "I fear reality is sinking in for her."

"Sir," Nick said, "I'm not trying to be critical of the fact you're drinking. I'm not even sure I'd show up to work the next day."

"Yes, you would," Rivera snapped. "You're like me: A workaholic who puts duty first."

Nick paused, thinking back through the years. He nodded, saying, "Been known to do that a time or two. You're right."

"I thought so," Rivera said, leaning forward. "I've researched your background more since we last met."

The man was slurring his words pretty bad, Nick noticed.

"I can't believe I didn't know you'd lost your wife. I bungled that detail last time. Her name was Anne, I believe?"

Nick nodded.

"But I know your story now. About Afghanistan. About the murder of your wife. About how you hunted down the men behind her death, killing every one of them."

"No," Nick said, "there's one left. But I promise you, once I figure out who he is, he'll get his due. You mark my words on that."

Rivera leaned back and crossed his arms behind his head, looking at Nick strangely.

It seemed to Nick like he was being sized up and measured, as if Rivera saw him as some strange animal. And now that Rivera had confirmed his past, the man needed to take it all in and think a moment before going on. Nick felt like a lion trapped in a cage at a zoo. Some strange creature that fascinated some member of a different species. But with Rivera's grief and unpredictability, Nick didn't want to say anything. So, he decided to wait and say nothing. Nick knew how to wait.

"I didn't call you to talk about your past, but I needed to get a better measure of you," Rivera finally said. "They've got me in a hell of a jam now."

"I can help with part of that jam," Nick said.

Rovera continued, as if he hadn't even heard Nick. "The bastards in Congress are launching multiple investigations. They say I hastily ordered a response from the SWAT team to save Juan Soto. They say a lack of planning led to their deaths."

Nick said nothing.

"The worst part," Rivera said, "is that it's true."

Rivera took another drink. Placed the glass too hard on the desk. Nick waited.

"They say I ignored intelligence reports that stated the Godesto Cartel was planning something. That's a complete lie, but it's a good one, I must say."

Rivera looked at the glass again, but it was mostly empty.

"They say I shouldn't have arrested Hernan Flores. That he was innocent. Or that he wasn't innocent, but was a decent human being, who gave to charity and all."

Rivera had waved his right hand when he said "and all" and now looked off again. Nick realized the man was completely, absolutely, drop-dead drunk. Drunk from both shock and liquor. And the lack of sleep wasn't helping. Rivera was struggling to stay focused.

"I'm going to get that little bastard, the Butcher."

Nick nodded. He had read up on the new leader, with recent information provided by the CIA this very morning. The little shit apparently had a thing for swords. Nick figured that meant he had a little dick.

Rivera looked off yet again.

Probably a full minute passed and Nick worried that Rivera might actually fall asleep on him, but suddenly Rivera turned back toward him.

"The bastard used a sword," he slurred, "and Juan's wife saw the footage. His daughter, too."

Nick had seen the video, as well. So had the rest of Mexico. The Butcher had taped the whole thing, being the complete bastard that he was. It looked like one of his men had followed behind him with the video recorder when they had blown the door off Juan Soto's safe room. The video showed a Godesto man in front of the Butcher fire a long burst from an AK toward the ground on the right, presumably at a final remaining bodyguard. The man on the ground hadn't returned fire in the footage, so it wasn't clear whether he was concussed or already dead. Regardless, he certainly died from the long burst.

And there stood Juan Soto, the camera jerky as it moved away from the man who had fired toward the corner and now focused on Mexico's richest man, who stood with his hands up in the international signal of surrender. He looked shocked. Dust covered his face and crisp, white shirt. Blood dripped from his ears. A book lay on the floor.

The Butcher asked him if he had any last words, but Soto merely shrugged in confusion, presumably deaf from the blast. And then with two men locked in on him with their weapons, the Butcher turned to the camera.

"This man," the Butcher said with a sneer pointing back at Soto, "is responsible for hundreds of crimes against the people of Mexico. For years, he has believed that money, the president, and this safe room could protect him from the repercussions of these crimes. But no more.

"This man is guilty of stealing billions from the backs of the Mexican people. He has practically forced people into slavery, paying them pitiful wages, all the while propping up a corrupt president after buying him the election. This man deserves no trial. His wealth alone proves his guilt."

And with that, the Butcher turned, letting his Uzi hang from the sling, and withdrew his sword ceremoniously. Soto either didn't believe what was about to happen or more than likely hadn't heard what the Butcher had said.

The Butcher pulled back the blade and chambered it far behind him, stepped into the stroke, and swung the blade toward Juan Soto's neck. He drove the sword through swiftly and beheaded Juan Soto as cleanly as was probably possible. The stroke looked crisp and perfect. Well-practiced, for sure.

The news channels had blurred out Juan Soto's head falling – at least partially; they still wanted their ratings.

The CIA had studied the footage that had been released to news organizations across Mexico. Several computer programs verified what the human analysts suspected: The culprit with the sword was most definitely the man known as the Butcher. The CIA had immediately compiled a file on the man and sent it to Nick by encrypted document. Nick had begun studying a frustratingly short file on him since he woke this morning.

"Mr. President," Nick said, "that sword isn't going to do him any good when I get him in my sights."

"I want him dead," Rivera said.

"We can get him," Nick said. "No problem."

"No," Rivera said, slapping the desk with both hands, as hard as he could. "I know you can capture him, but I want him dead. I do not want him taken prisoner under any circumstances. He will not rule from prison. He will not be shanked in prison. I want him killed in the take-down."

Nick nodded.

"I don't think I'll lose any sleep over failing to give him a chance to surrender," Nick replied.

"And, don't worry," Rivera said, "I'll deal with the coroner and after-action report. But this man beheaded one of the greatest men in Mexico. He murdered my friend. And he will die for doing so. Even if it's my last act in office."

And with that, Rivera stood, refilled his glass, and went back to his window. Nick waited a full five minutes, but Rivera never looked back again. Nick wasn't sure if the president had forgotten he was there or if that was all he had to say on the matter. That Rivera simply wanted his final request done.

In the end, Nick finally stood and walked out of the room.

CHAPTER 34

Nick Woods received a more-detailed briefing on the situation the day after his meeting with President Rivera. The situation was worse than either Nick or Rivera could have imagined.

But even without knowing that, Nick had decided to do what all warriors do in dead time: Sharpen the sword.

Once Nick returned from his meeting with Rivera, he had ordered the men of Shield, Safeguard, and Shelter to gather their gear for some much-needed training. The men of S3 had rehearsed immediate reaction drills, fired tons of ammo at a remote mountain range, and exercised with moderation – about three-fourths of their capacity, since Nick didn't want the men sore the next day. Just ready and relaxed for whatever was coming down the pike. And it would definitely be coming, Nick knew.

The entire team had trained hard, shot well, and completed their PT – a mountain run with full gear and weapons – with lots of motivation. Nick and Marcus were ready to move and that turned out to be a good thing. Mr. Smith called later that evening, a bit after 5 p.m., after the team had cleaned up and scrubbed down their weapons.

Mr. Smith shared that both the CIA and the Mexican Ambassador were afraid that Rivera might only have another day or two remaining in office.

"His poll numbers are in the teens," Mr. Smith said. "The public has bought into the fact that he treated Juan Soto special when he directly, and personally, ordered that SWAT response. And the cartels are really playing the poor-versus-the-rich card, dropping in some talking points about high unemployment and government corruption."

"And his opponents smell blood," Nick added.

"Correct," Mr. Smith said. "They see an opening and the first of several hearings starts tomorrow. Plus, Rivera hasn't done a very good job staying away from the bottle. But that's changing. He realizes he's in serious trouble. The NSA is intercepting the emails and phone calls of his opponents and our Ambassador will have him prepped as much as possible for the hearings. But we've role-played these hearings many times and Rivera is totally screwed. He has days left in office. Not weeks. And certainly not months or years."

"Where does that leave us?" Nick asked.

"Nowhere good. The head of the Mexican Congress, who will likely be sworn in after Rivera is gone, is already talking about a truce with the Godesto Cartel. He wants a return to how things were. Less war. Fewer military ops. More peace and stability."

"So, turning a blind eye to it all?" Nick asked.

"Precisely. The public is weary. It's what they want to hear."

"What does that mean for us?" Nick asked.

"It means you probably have two days to take down the Butcher and the Godesto Cartel, who still control seventy percent of the country. Probably more now."

"You're not asking for much," Nick said sarcastically.

"It's probably impossible," Mr. Smith said, "but it's reality. Get with your team and figure out how you can pull off the impossible in two days. We want the Butcher dead. We want the Godesto Cartel broken in half."

Nick didn't know what to say, so he said nothing.

"Look," Mr. Smith said. "You've got the talent and brains around you to pull this off. But know that if you haven't succeeded within two days, we will have to extract you, for both your safety and our country's relationship with the new president. There's no way President Rivera's replacement will sanction S3 being in the country. And we don't want that interim president leaking your info or using the Mexican military to arrest you all. You have two days. Period."

And with that, Nick had been left hearing a dead dial tone in his heavy, encrypted phone. It was a new experience to be the one hung up on. Nick glanced down at his watch and saw that it was 5:50 p.m. They needed to move fast. Like, immediately.

Nick and Dwayne Marcus mustered the entire S3 team, placing the need of garnering input from every single man over the need for security at the farm. Nick and Marcus wanted to hear every possible sound idea that might be out there among the forty-four team members.

The men formed up behind the house at 6:15 p.m., in a platoon-sized formation of five squads. All of the members of Shield, Safeguard, and Shelter wore uniforms and web gear, carrying their M4s that they had been issued before leaving America.

The S3 members had ditched their undercover civilian clothes and looked uniform and sharp, dressed in olive drab trousers, S3 T-shirts (with the logo on the left chest), black jungle boots, and OD green boonie covers. Despite their uniform appearance, Nick could name them all.

They had grown close, though their time together had been short. With no one allowed to leave the farm, they'd practically lived on top of each other in the moderately-sized farm house built for a family of four.

Given that each squad had to squeeze all eight of its members into a single bedroom, they practically slept on top of each other, using green, Army surplus cots placed just inches apart. Gear was stored mostly in sea bags and footlockers under their cots.

But Nick believed strongly in unit cohesion and the farmhouse had provided more than seclusion and anonymity. It had taken a bunch of superbly trained and experienced warriors and forged them into a tight unit. The men – and one woman – of S3 would take a bullet for each other, and they had created this tight fraternity in mere weeks together. And now they faced a completely unfair deadline that would doubtlessly cost several – or many – of them their lives.

"All right, everyone, listen up," Nick said, walking up with Dwayne Marcus to the assembled formation. His voice halted any light chatting going on in the loose formation.

Nick looked across the formation. They were a good unit. Some of the best men he'd ever seen assembled.

In the front row were the six members of the Primary Strike Team, not counting himself or Marcus, which made eight. Behind the Primary Strike Team were the three squads of eight. All good men, decorated veterans from the Marine Corps and Army.

In the fifth row stood the six Marine Scout Sniper teams he had requested. Quiet men, tall and lean, with service records showed that each of them had confirmed kills.

Not in the formation, but inside the house was his CIA contact, who he had still failed to name. Nick had asked the CIA contact to keep watch on their Mexican liaison, so that the man wouldn't hear what was said and thus couldn't possibly sell them out.

Nick took a deep breath and put his hands on his hips, standing tall and pushing his chest out.

He knew he had earned the men's respect, but he needed to nail this set of orders and squeeze every ounce of love and respect he could from them. They'd be knee-deep in shit in just a matter of hours and the lives of everyone depended on each of them trusting him enough to die for him.

"Men, there's no need beating around the bush. We're in a hell of a situation. Again."

A few men laughed, remembering how they had been forced to deploy early before their training was complete and then nearly had the entire mission yanked from them just a couple days earlier.

"Good point," Nick said, acknowledging the laughter and thinking about what a disaster this whole gig had been to date. "Well, the good news is we don't have to leave immediately. We finally get a chance to complete the mission. There is one catch though and it's a big one."

Nick paused for a long time, then continued, "The bad news is we have a very short timeline to complete the mission."

No one said anything or complained, so Nick continued.

"We, no shit, have two days to wrap this up." Nick let that sink in as he looked them over. "Two days to kill this bastard who calls himself the Butcher. Two days to rip the balls off the

Godesto Cartel and turn them from the most powerful cartel in North America to nothing but a bunch of crying Boy Scouts.

"The CIA believes President Rivera only has two more days left in office, and that means we also only have two more days. His likely replacement would love nothing more than to arrest a bunch of gringos operating in Mexico to score some easy political points with the public. But the main point of me yapping here in front of you is we need all hands on deck on this one. Marcus and I need every idea and brain cell that we have in this unit.

"And we need whatever solution we can come up with fast. You guys will break into squads, brainstorm how best we can take the Butcher out, as well as wreck the Godesto Cartel in only two days. Then, your squad leaders will report to Marcus and me in forty-five minutes. Time is of the essence men. No screwing around in these brainstorming sessions. We'll probably be locked and loaded and hunting in just a few hours, so get your game faces on."

Nick looked back. "Marcus, you have anything to add?"

Marcus shook his head and Nick said, "Squad leaders, take your men and make it happen. Dismissed."

It took three intense hours, but Nick and Marcus crafted together a plan from the combined ideas of everyone in S3 that they thought just might work. It was their best chance and there was no time to improve it. Already, they were racing to get everything into position.

With the plan as complete as they could make it, Nick stepped away to call President Rivera. Nick had assumed Mr. Smith with the CIA would want a briefing, but the man had said he didn't want to know the details when Nick had called him. Nick could sense the growing feeling of "plausible deniability" starting to happen here. Well, fuck it. Being sold out was pretty typical behavior for "warriors" who led from behind desks.

Nick looked down at his watch and saw it was 9:13 p.m.

Late or not, Rivera had asked to be kept personally in the

loop, since Nick didn't trust reporting his info to any other Mexican official. Well, maybe Juan Soto, but he was no longer an option.

Rivera had persuaded Nick to call him personally in part because the President had felt confident that Nick would need his help. The President could move men and material, or gather last-minute intel through his generals without explaining what it might be used for. Nick felt comfortable with this arrangement and promised to call once his team had devised some plans.

With it now nearly 9:15, Nick pulled out a throw-away cell phone and called Rivera on the man's personal cell phone. If Nick and Marcus's plans were going to work, then they would need some big favors from Rivera. But as the phone rang in Nick's ears, he remembered the vengeful mood he had seen the man in… Rivera would come through.

And with Rivera's help, they would kill the Butcher and rip the balls off the Godesto Cartel, breaking it for good.

CHAPTER 35

Just minutes after President Roberto Rivera approved Nick's plans, the majority of Shield, Safeguard, and Shelter left the farm in SUVs, compacts, trucks. S3 was on the hunt. And it was a good night to do it. It was black out – darker than normal.

"Good night for hunting," Nick said into his radio.

"Oh, yeah," Marcus answered, riding in a vehicle further back in the convoy. "We're going to bag our limit tonight."

In many respects, this was the most dangerous part of the operation. The entire unit of S3 was moving toward Mexico City. All forty-four of them, minus their Mexican contact and CIA liaison, who they had left back at the farm. But otherwise the entire unit had grabbed as much ammo as they could carry and loaded all of their vehicles.

Now the convoy of mixed vehicles, all purchased with the idea of not standing out, was dispersed over a two-mile distance. They had waited a couple minutes between each vehicle departing to avoid moving as a large pack. Had they been bunched up together with that many headlights traveling as a group at night, they would have likely been called in by some police officer worried they were a cartel group rolling out in force.

Nick couldn't afford a delay if they were stopped by cops. President Rivera would have gotten it sorted out eventually, but the delay might still last an hour or two. And their element of surprise would be totally gone once the police department started talking about the large formation of men that had been pulled over and then released, following a call from the President.

Nick swallowed down an uneasy feeling as they drove

north. Just another hour or so and they'd be at the pick-up point. Then the mission would really get interesting.

President Roberto Rivera stood in front of his bullet-proof window and stared out over the massive city. The Presidential Palace was still mostly wrecked from the attacks it had sustained.

He knew his time as the leader of Mexico was coming to an end. His testimony and removal might be happening soon, but he wasn't going out in a whimper. No. Not even close, he thought. He'd fix Mexico or die trying.

And with luck, his country's fortunes would change in a big way tonight. Rivera no longer cared if he survived his second term. And this was a bigger deal than he could ever explain. He had spent his whole life getting to this point, and yet he had come to grips with the fact that he'd gladly sacrifice that. His legacy meant nothing compared to the necessity of saving his country.

He stared at the cell phone in his hand. It was a burner phone. Rivera needed to make some calls with a phone that wasn't monitored.

And as Rivera looked over the city, he knew that now was the moment of truth. With the first of several calls he was about to make, he would break so many laws that he shuddered to consider how long he would serve in prison if Nick's plan failed.

But Nick had laid out the facts as only a non-national could do. Nick didn't care that he was speaking to the president of Mexico. He frankly and directly told Rivera that he was being told by CIA intelligence that Rivera probably had two days, which meant Nick and S3 had only that much time as well.

Rivera hated to agree, but the wolves were closing in. Congressional hearings. Close aides, jockeying for their own political careers. The media blasting him across newsprint, radio, and TV.

Nick explained that he and his team had devised some possible plans that just might crush the Godesto Cartel and

STAN R MITCHELL

put the Butcher in the ground, if Rivera was game for helping them.

Rivera had listened and Nick's ideas were brilliant. They were outside the box and the Godesto would be completely surprised. Rivera had added some suggestions and Nick agreed the additions added to the strength of the plan.

Once Nick realized that Rivera was on board, he asked the man – the president! – to take out a memo pad and write down some detailed instructions, as well as what time they needed to happen.

Rivera had complied and now he was seconds from completing step one.

He looked up from the burner cell phone and shifted his eyes north toward America. If Nick and his men failed to pull this off, he and his wife, as well as the remainder of Juan Soto's family, would be flying to America to seek asylum in just a couple of days

At that point, the fate of Mexico would no longer be his problem.

Maybe one of the bastards in Congress ripping him on 24-hour news channels at this very moment could find out what it felt like to be looking out this window into the dark night, wondering if an RPG would come flying toward you from the apartment complex across the way. He wished they could see what it was like. To go to work wondering if your family or the families of your supporters would survive the day. To have to decide whether to stand up to the cartels or look the other way.

He glanced at his watch. It was time for the first task Nick had assigned him.

He typed in the numbers he had looked up earlier.

The phone rang three times and then someone picked up.

"Police Department," a man answered. "Is this an emergency?"

"No," Rivera said. "I need to speak to–" he looked down at his memo pad to find the name of the duty officer, "Captain Millan. Immediately."

"Who is this? What is it regarding?"

"This is a Class 5 Emergency. Password J587IWM."

A pause ensued, doubtlessly as the person fumbled and looked up the numbers.

"One moment, sir. I'll get him."

So far, so good.

Thirty seconds later, a captain picked up the phone. He sounded like he had been running.

"Captain Millan, you don't need to know my name, but I am a high-ranking official who works at the Presidential Palace and is in the know, you might say. I wanted to warn you that you will soon be getting a call – approximately thirty minutes from now – that will come as part of an emergency set of orders from the Presidential Palace. And I wanted to warn you that you might want to get twelve of your standard, green police trucks fueled up and ready to go. The ones with rails in the beds for troops. Trust me on this. Gas tanks, fully fueled, as they should be, but often aren't because officers are too tired at the end of their shifts."

"Why are you telling me this?" the captain asked.

"My father was a police officer," Rivera said, telling a lie, but for a good cause. "Now, I must go before I'm busted for alerting you, but make sure you fuel those twelve trucks up. You're going to thank me, believe me."

Rivera hung up, then picked up his own cell phone – government issued and probably tracked – but necessary. So be it, he thought.

He had to use it for these calls, or things would seem too odd to those who picked the phone up this late at night. And ultimately, either he and Nick would succeed and that would give him a shot at retaining his presidency and saving the country. Or they wouldn't. And if they failed, then none of it mattered anyway. He'd be on that plane to America.

His first call was to the head of his Secret Service.

"Herrera, this is President Rivera. I apologize for calling you so late, but I need you to call up two hundred of your men. Full battle gear, get them to the Presidential Palace as fast as they can get here. And I need your shift leader in my office in the next five minutes. Please, no questions. I must go now and will fill you in later. Just do it."

Rivera hung up and called his Chief of Staff.

"Mateo, this is President Rivera. I apologize for calling you so late, but I need to call an emergency Cabinet meeting. Get everyone here immediately. And then get with the stewards and bring us food and drinks, since everyone will be here for a while."

Task one, complete.

Thirty minutes later, the entire cabinet was assembled. A police escort had accompanied each of them, so their arrival was unimpeded. And since there had been an earlier Cabinet meeting that afternoon, all of them were in Mexico City instead of out touring their departments across the country.

Rivera kept his distance as they arrived. He stayed in his office and ignored them while they muttered and waited anxiously. Many of them texted him, hoping friendship would supersede his plans, but he ignored their queries without an answer.

He also knew a few would try to meet privately with him to find out what was going on, so he had stationed twelve Secret Service officers in full battle gear, including M4 assault rifles, to stand at his door and admit no one. Absolutely no one.

Given that he had told the shift leader that a possible coup was under way, these men would listen to no one but Rivera himself, no matter how high ranking a Cabinet member might be.

Once his Chief of Staff texted to inform him that the last member had arrived and all were seated and ready, Rivera took a deep breath and charged into the conference room. If the door flying open uncharacteristically didn't get their attention, then the eight men entering behind him in full combat gear did.

All chatter ceased around the conference table and Rivera stopped behind his seat at the head of the table, his hands on his hips. He didn't plan on sitting down. He stared down at them and said, "Tonight, I'll be issuing a number of orders. I expect them to be executed immediately and without comment."

No one said a word.

He pulled a folded yellow sheet from his pocket; the notes from his conversation with Nick. He would burn it soon, but for now, it supplied the blueprints for his and Nick's war plans.

He turned to his head of Federal Police – Mexico's equivalent of America's FBI.

"Luis, call the Mexico City Police Department. A Captain Millan is the duty officer. Instruct him to immediately deliver twelve police trucks to this address."

Rivera popped one of his business cards face down on the table and slid it toward the head of federal police.

"The address," Rivera said, pointing to the back of the card on which he had scribbled down the address, "is an abandoned warehouse. There will be a number of men there and these men are Americans. The police officers are to say nothing to these men, but simply confirm there's a full tank of gas in them before they drop them off and leave the keys in the ignitions when they depart."

Luis shook his head in confusion.

"I don't understand," he said.

"You don't have to," Rivera shot back, cutting him off. "Tell Captain Millan to have his men drive a couple of vans down with them so the officers have a way back to the police station once they've dropped the vehicles off. Oh, and if there are reports of twelve police trucks running throughout the city with their lights on later tonight, inform the police department that they are to leave them alone and ignore the call."

The Secretary of Interior, Marcos Sanchez, jumped to his feet. He was in charge of Mexico's internal security.

"This is absurd," he roared. "Why don't I know of these Americans? Are these the men of your S3 or some other group?"

"Sit down," Rivera said.

"I will not sit down," Sanchez said, slamming his palms on the desk. "This is how blue-on-blue situations occur. I command all security operations inside this country and I will not allow something to be done without my knowledge."

"Fine," Rivera said. "Step out of the room and type up your resignation letter. These two officers will take your cell phone from you and then escort you to one of my offices. By the way, don't plan on going anywhere. You won't be allowed to leave the premises for at least the next thirty-six hours. Probably forty-eight."

Rivera shifted his view from the stunned Secretary of Interior to the rest of his Cabinet.

"Nor will any of the rest of you."

No one said anything. Good, he had them where he wanted them.

"Now may we proceed?" he asked.

Sanchez eased back in his chair.

The attorney general spoke up.

"Sir, if there are Americans here and if they're going to be impersonating police officers and driving around in police trucks, then we better discuss the implications immediately. You are quite likely breaking a number of laws by this action."

"You seem," Rivera said, "to always forget that I attended the same law school that you did. I'm aware of what laws I may or may not be breaking. Your suggestion has been noted and declined. With witnesses, at that. So you can breathe easier."

The Secretary of Finance, a reasonable man and friend of Rivera, said in a humble and respectful voice, "Mr. President, what is going on? The armed men in here. The tone of your voice. The statement that we can't leave."

"Isn't it obvious?" Rivera asked. "We're at war, Lorenzo. That's what's going on."

"We've been at war," said Sanchez, the Secretary of Interior, though his tone was a bit more deferential than earlier.

"That's right," Rivera said. "We've been at quote war," he raised his fingers in the motion of quote marks, "for nearly five years now and we've gotten nowhere. My time as president could almost be up. I was elected to take care of the Godesto Cartel and I've tried to do so within the letter of the law since the day I took my oath. But we're no closer to accomplishing that task today than we were then. I campaigned on this goal and it's what the people wanted. It's also what they wanted when I ran for re-election."

He paused and took a deep breath. "Now, since my time is nearly up, we're going to move more aggressively."

No one said anything to that. Rivera's tone made clear it wasn't up for discussion.

The Secretary of Environment reached for his phone – probably to tell his wife it would be a long night – but Rivera said, "Don't touch that phone. No one is to use any phone or device unless I directly instruct them to. And if any of these security officers see anyone using a device, they have been ordered to immediately arrest them."

"Under what authority?" blustered Sanchez, the Secretary of Interior, in an almost weary voice.

"My own. I'll deal with the legal implications later, but for now, it's my personal opinion that some of you are working with the cartels and possibly even planning a coup."

"That's absurd," the Secretary of Education said.

Roberto knew it was probably unlikely, but he couldn't admit it in front of these officers.

"I must take the threat seriously," he said.

Rivera shifted his attention to the Secretary of Communications.

"Olivia, call your people. I want them to draft an emergency press release stating that the Godesto Cartel and the Red Sleeve Cartel have broken their alliance and are going to war with each other. We urge all citizens to be on full alert and as cautious as possible as we expect heavy violence because of this split."

Olivia was scribbling down Rivera's words on a legal pad before her.

"But, Mr. President," the Secretary of Tourism said, "that's not true. And such a baseless – and fear-based – claim will only give the American media more ammo to tell their people not to visit here. They may talk about this for two days, bringing up the background of both cartels and their history of reckless violence. We really don't need this hit on our already struggling tourism industry."

"I'm aware of that," Rivera said. "Your objection has been heard."

"Mr. President," the Secretary of Economy said, "this is irresponsible. Our country's finances are already gasping and our businesses are at their breaking point–"

Rivera held his hand up and stopped him mid-sentence.

"I don't want to hear it," Rivera said.

"Sir, if I may," the Secretary of Defense said, his tone so reverential as to prevent Rivera from cutting him off. As a former general, Ignacio Arango was the oldest and most respected person in the room. When he spoke, even the most puffed-up politician stopped to listen. "We really need not spread misinformation. You've said before that once you lose your credibility, you can't recover. If we say the Godesto Cartel and Red Sleeve Cartel have split and are about to go to war, we'll have no standing once it's proven false."

"We're going to make it true," Rivera said, causing several Cabinet members to gasp.

"But, sir," Arango, the Secretary of Defense, said, "we haven't provided you any counsel. Or approved any of these ideas. We're not even sure what you're planning."

"I haven't asked you for any," Rivera said. "I've been asking and receiving counsel from every person in this Cabinet for the past five years, not to mention hundreds of experts in our military, intelligence, and police forces. And if we're honest, we've had more setbacks than progress."

Rivera looked away from the table and pointed to a scarred wall that had been partially patched.

"Look at this building," he said. "Up to this point, we've been at war with the Godesto Cartel but only they've been doing the serious fighting. Tonight, that changes. And tonight, general, we're doing it my way."

The trucks sat parked right where they were supposed to be. Nick had entered the abandoned warehouse grounds alone, with just his vehicle and two Primary Strike Team members. If it was a trap, he wanted as few casualties as possible. The rest of S3 could split up and make for the border, with Marcus in charge.

But it was no trap. Twelve green Toyotas, with blue police lights across the cab and rails in the back for troops, sat in the parking lot. Keys rested in the ignitions and they had full gas tanks.

After Nick finished checking the last truck, he called in the rest of S3. As all the vehicles piled in, Nick could feel their strength. Like an angry army of wolves gathering in force in the night, ready to head out on a hunt.

With the trucks in hand, it was going to be a bad night for the Godesto Cartel. Nothing would stop S3 from its attack now that the trucks were here.

"Let's not mess around," Nick yelled at the men. "Move fast. Get those trucks loaded."

The men were already moving fast, but his words pushed them faster. Footlockers were unloaded and gear tossed into the bed of trucks.

Back at the Presidential Palace, the Cabinet meeting remained tense and uncomfortable, but President Rivera wasn't close to finished. The Butcher and the Godesto Cartel had backed him into a corner and could taste victory, but in doing so, they had created a desperate man. A man with absolutely no fear.

Rivera turned to his Secretary of Defense, Ignacio Arango.

"Ignacio, I want you to get with the head of the Army and ask him for his best hand-to-hand expert. One name. And I want this man delivered to the Federal Social Readaptation Center No. 1 within two hours."

Arango had a questioning look, but didn't say anything in reply.

Rivera looked to the Public Security Secretary, Gerardo Jimenez, who managed all the federal prisons. "Gerardo, by the time this hand-to-hand expert arrives, you will have it arranged so that he is accepted into the prison without notice and placed in the same cell as," Rivera looked down at the yellow legal sheet, "Edgar Argel. Make sure one of your officers provides him an authentic shank, as well. One that was actually made in the prison from scraps; that was seized recently."

"Why?" Jimenez, the Public Security Secretary, asked.

"This hand-to-hand expert will kill Edgar Argel, who, for those who don't know, happens to be one of the highest-ranking members of the Godesto Cartel that we have incarcerated. And once Argel is dead, then our man will slash the symbol of the Red Sleeve Cartel on his back. Have him study precisely how it should look according to prior times they've left their mark in the backs of other victims. I'm sure we have police photos of this."

"That's impossible," said Jimenez, thinking of how hard it was to get things into his prisons. "You can't just sneak someone out of Federal Social Readaptation Center No. 1."

Rivera slammed his hand down on the desk.

"That is precisely what the Godesto Cartel did to kill Hernan Flores. Surely, if the cartels can do it, then you can do it. Otherwise, you will hand in your resignation and I will personally lead the prosecution against your corruption and involvement in the death of Flores."

The Public Security Secretary said nothing. He appeared furious, but also trapped.

Rivera continued, "Finally, once we've removed our man from the prison, and provided him with a good ten-thousand-dollar bonus, Jimenez will issue a press release tomorrow claiming a member of the Red Sleeve Cartel killed Edgar Argel of the Godesto Cartel. And I expect a suspect from the Red Sleeve Cartel to be named. You all can pick whomever you want. Just make sure it's a bad guy because his days will probably be numbered."

"That's unconscionable," the attorney general chimed in. "You can't just frame someone for something they didn't do."

"I'm betting," Rivera said, "that the worst man of the Red Sleeve Cartel has probably done everything from execute people in cold blood to burn women and children alive. I don't care who's picked. Ask the warden to name the worst one. If it makes you feel better, pick one of them that raped little girls. It doesn't matter to me. Either way, I'll sleep fine. But we *will* have a name and photo of a Red Sleeve Cartel member to accompany the news release of the death of Edgar Argel. And that news release better have a good-sized picture of Argel's carved-up back in nice resolution and detail. I want everyone in the country, even those who can't read, to know the Red Sleeve Cartel killed Mr. Argel."

Rivera leaned over the conference table, placing both

hands on the table.

"In case it's not clear, I want everyone in the country to know the Red Sleeve Cartel and the Godesto Cartel have gone to war."

No one said anything and Rivera met every eye around the table. Sensing no further resistance, he stood again.

He looked over at the Secretary of Defense.

"Finally, I've got two other things for the military. To begin with, general, let's talk about a different prison than the Federal Social Readaptation Center No. 1."

The general looked nervous.

Rivera continued, "It's my understanding that the inmate population of the federal prison in Nayarit is mostly Godesto Cartel members. Some of their best men, all corralled off on their own so there's no prison violence with other cartels or prisoners. That makes sense, I know, but it also provides a unique opportunity. Given that more than eighty percent of their prisoners are Godesto Cartel men, you will create a disturbance working with Jimenez and his prison personnel.

"I want this disturbance to lead to a break out. I literally want you, Jimenez," Rivera grinned, nodding to the head of all federal prisons, "to open the doors of this correctional facility. Call it a malfunction in your after-action report. Or maybe gross corruption. Whatever plan you can concoct, I don't care. But Ignacio, as Secretary of Defense, what I do care about is this: I want a platoon of your coldest, hardest killers waiting a quarter of a mile away, standing by to move in. Once the doors are open and the break-out begins, your men will rush in to support the out-numbered nightshift of jailers, who will certainly be calling for help against this set of mad men."

Rivera leaned forward and stared as hard as he could into the steady eyes of the former general.

"And they will kill as many of the cartel members as possible. The cartel members will probably stop running quickly, once they see all the automatic weapons open up on them, so it's important your men kill them in a way that provides plausible deniability. No execution shots to the head. Instead, have your men lay in the prone and shoot into them sideways if the Godesto members immediately lay down to surrender. Or come up with a better plan. I don't care. But, I want at least seventy percent of them killed. Killed. Do you understand?"

Arango understood completely. And for the first time that night, he smiled. He hadn't felt this good about a set of orders since the day he had taken his oath of office as a young man, more than thirty years ago. Thinking of all the men he'd lost to the cartels over the years, the former general was eager to get started. His leash had finally been removed and the Godesto reign of terror and violence was about to run into an angry and vengeful Ignacio Arango. He would personally make sure that the best and most loyal men were selected for the task; men who also knew how to keep their mouths shut.

Then, the Secretary of Defense had another thought. With a slick grin, the former general said, "What if a fire accidentally started during their escape attempt and unfortunately killed the majority of them?"

"An even better idea," Rivera said, "but anyone running out gets shot down."

"Might look bad," cautioned Arango.

"Just some soldiers fearing for their lives," Rivera said. "Trying to corral a massive escape of dangerous felons."

He glanced down at the unfolded sheet of yellow memo paper that Nick had mostly created. He smiled, then lit it with a lighter. No way did he want these notes falling into anyone's hands. The paper caught, the flame rose, and he dropped it on the carpet, ensuring it burned completely before stamping it out. They could worry about the burn mark on the carpet later.

"One last thing, Mr. Secretary of Defense. You will call up your generals and devise plans to invade at least three of the Godesto Cartel's strongholds. I don't care which three, but they are to be surrounded, hit hard, and as many weapons and drugs seized as possible. Oh, and make sure cellphones among troops are seized prior to the orders being issued. The units are to be isolated so that no warning gets out before their departure.

"Meanwhile, our attorney general, you will get with our best intelligence experts tonight and by the time the banks open tomorrow morning, you will have judicial orders seizing every possible account that could be tied to the Godesto Cartel. Practically any account in Mexico that looks shady and has more than two hundred thousand dollars in it, I want it seized. Period. And I want it seized one minute after each of these financial institutions open. No warning to any of those affected, of course."

"Since you went to the same law school as me," the attorney general replied, "I'm confident that you know this isn't legal."

"I know," Rivera said, "and I don't blame you all if in a couple of days you all inform the media that I was acting like a madman and breaking dozens of laws. I'm okay with that, but I'm not okay with the Godesto Cartel ruling Mexico for a single day longer. I'm not okay with the Godesto Cartel being able to attack the Presidential Palace, kill influential citizens such as Juan Soto, or invade our capital with dozens of armed men at any given time. I know we'll have to release the funds in the coming weeks, once the courts order us to do so, but the Godesto Cartel can see what it's like to operate without them while we hold off their high-priced attorneys."

Rivera projected as much confidence and fight as he could muster. It was time to give his war speech. And perhaps his last instructions as President of Mexico. Make it look good, he thought, standing even taller. It was time to stand bravely in complete defiance of the Godesto Cartel and those in Congress who were trying to bring him down.

"Tonight, my esteemed Cabinet, we finally fight back and commence full-fledged war against the Godesto Cartel. Maybe it's true that if we destroy them, another will replace them, but we will set the precedent that no cartel can threaten the government of Mexico as the Godesto Cartel has done. Our entire focus will be on the Godesto Cartel. Leave the Red Sleeve Cartel alone. The other, smaller cartel, as well. If we have Red Sleeve men awaiting trial, let them out. We're going to shift the balance of power and we need the much weaker Red Sleeve Cartel to make as many gains as possible in the time that we have left. Just as a monopoly will damage a country, so too will a cartel that becomes too powerful. Tonight and tomorrow, before I am removed, we reset the balance of power."

Rivera walked to the door and looked back.

"As far as I'm concerned, this meeting is over. Those of you with tasks to do based on what I've asked, please jump on making them happen. Update me as you complete them. For the rest of you, I apologize, but you will need to place your phones and internet devices on the table before leaving the room. I've had rooms in the Presidential Palace prepared for you, but none of you will be leaving the building tonight. Some of you will be busy, others bored, but it's what the job requires for the next day or so. Staff members will call your families to alert them that you have been tied up in an emergency meeting, but none of you will be allowed to make outgoing calls except as duty requires. These calls, as I said earlier, will be in the presence of a witness of my guard force."

And with that, Rivera shut the door. Firmly.

CHAPTER 36

In no time at all, the members of S3 had crammed the trucks with equipment, boxes of ammo, and even jugs of water. The mission called for a two-hour timeline, but there was a good chance they could end up cut off and surrounded.

The entire team of S3 had geared up in assault vests, helmets, and full battle gear, which they had brought from the states. Everyone wore olive drab cammies, which would make them look like a police force to casual passers-by.

"Move out," Nick said over the radio, riding in the first truck as the "police" convoy as S3 headed toward the most dangerous slum in Mexico.

How many of them would survive this, Nick wondered. He honestly wasn't sure. They could end up fighting a thousand or more men in this fight, so there was a good chance that they all died. He remembered the speech he had given before the unit left the farm.

He had stood in the bed of one of a red Ford pick up truck, allowed his M4 to hang across his chest, and removed his helmet. The team members had pulled in close, forming a half circle around him.

"Well, gang, this is it," Nick said, fiddling with his helmet strap. "I can't deny that the whole shebang has been a clusterfuck up 'til this point."

Nick looked at his band of forty-four warriors.

"I'm not one for speeches and you guys aren't the type to need them. But I still wanted to say a few words before we go in. You all haven't given me or Marcus a lick of trouble and we've certainly jerked you around from the beginning. Most of it was beyond our control, but in war, a commander is supposed to protect his men from silly games and unnecessary stress. Marcus and I have failed you in that regard.

"But goat rope or not, this is exactly what we signed up for. Tonight we finally – *finally* – get a chance to really go after these bastards. We've been issued our hunting licenses and there's no bag limit."

"Hell yeah," Red said with a smile. Nick noticed how small Red looked, even in his combat gear.

"Now," Nick continued, "you all know the plans and you know it's 'hey diddle diddle, right up the middle.' This shit-hole slum we're going into – Neza-Chalco-Itza – is one of the largest slums in the world. Twenty-plus square miles of serious danger. And not even the Mexican government knows if there's one million or four million people in it. That's quite a variance.

"But we do know that practically the entire slum is loyal to the Godesto Cartel. It's the heart of their operation and we know it's dangerous as hell and rarely entered by police forces. Every time they go, they end up in a big fight, so they don't go much anymore. Haven't in years.

"I have no idea if we'll be fighting our entire way in or if we'll drive in, pull up to the Butcher's building, and just take it down. As you all know, we have no snipers providing intel and we aren't even sure if the Butcher will be at home. If he's not, we grab every computer and piece of intel that we see and we get the hell out of there. With luck, the intel will give us more clues on how to break the back of the Godesto Cartel and hopefully tell us where the Butcher might be hiding if he's not there. If we figure out from the intel where else we might be hiding, we immediately go hit that location with whoever is still alive and breathing."

Nick paused. He wanted the words to sink in.

"You don't have to be a genius to know this mission has about a hundred things that could go wrong. Hell, it has 'catastrophe' written all over it and with any lesser unit, I'd cancel the entire thing right now. But we don't have much time until they send us back home and tonight's our only chance to do what needs to be done. I think you all want this as bad as I do."

Nick looked down.

"We do," someone said.

Nick lifted his eyes and scanned the crowd, searching for who said it, but he couldn't tell. What he did see were determined eyes. Folks who wanted this opportunity as dearly as he did.

He soaked up that affirmation and continued, "Remember, we have no support. It's just us. If you get hit, administer self aid. If we're under fire, ignore your buddies who get hit. We'll need every weapon facing outboard so this doesn't turn into something like Blackhawk Down in Mogadishu. And don't think if we get in some deep shit that someone from the Mexican government will come rescue us. They won't. We're on our own. We know this is the reality before we even step off, so don't go expecting anything different. We fight in, we try to grab this bastard, we fight out."

Nick put his helmet on and finished the speech, raising his voice louder than necessary.

"Tonight is how this plays out. We either accomplish the mission or we all go down together in the middle of one of the biggest shitholes in the world. I suppose that's how most battles happen. It's been that way since the Romans marched off to war. Probably earlier than that. We are the well-trained force. We are the invaders. And we will enter Neza-Chalco-Itza and nab the Butcher. Or maybe we'll just go in there and remind them that there are men in the world that aren't scared of them."

Nick paused a final time and savored the moment. In war, it was these moments that you *had* to savor, because it could truly be his last.

"Anyway, if dying together is what it comes to, I can say that I'm proud to be your skipper and there's not another set of guys I'd rather go down fighting with."

Nick looked at each of his team members, from left to right, and nodded solemnly. Not a single one broke off their eye contact. They were as ready as him.

"Let's go kick some ass," he said.

A few of the men screamed war yells, while others said a few words to their buddies, embracing in hugs and handshakes. Others just had a look of determination that Nick appreciated.

What they lacked in numbers, they made up for in experience. They were older than most armies, had been blooded, and they'd definitely give better than they received tonight. Whether that would be enough in Neza-Chalco-Itza, Nick wasn't sure.

"Keep it tight," Nick said into his radio, glancing back at the trucks behind him.

The forty-four members of Shield, Safeguard, and Shelter roared onto the road, their police lights flashing. All of the trucks had rails that encircled the entire bed, and the rails had been well designed. Not only were they round and padded, they also rose about a foot higher than the top of the cab, stopping roughly chest high if you were standing in the bed. The height allowed the men to loop their arms over them to hang on or lay their rifles across them for additional accuracy.

Nick's vehicle was the lead truck, with Nick sitting in the passenger seat, two GPS's and several maps spread across his lap. His driver was Truck, the former Special Forces soldier who had a history of beating up officers and driving vehicles in challenging situations.

Nick looked back over his shoulder at the convoy. He pressed the push-to-talk button on his vest and spoke into the microphone that hung down from his helmet.

"Task Force Leatherneck, this is Six Actual. One final radio check."

Nick listened as each truck checked in. The formation was set up in a KISS simple formation. The Primary Strike Team provided the tip of the spear. The eight members of the Primary Strike Team were spread out in the back of the first truck.

Nick and Marcus had decided to place as much firepower as possible up front in case they needed to shoot through any roadblocks. Thus, Nick's vehicle had the most shooters in it.

Behind the first truck, the eleven other trucks would have fewer shooters. Some would have as few as two in the truck bed.

That wasn't ideal, from a convoy protection standpoint, but Nick had insisted on taking twelve trucks.

"That's overkill," Marcus had said. "We could get by with

six. Then bring an extra one or two in case something goes wrong."

"Nope," Nick said. "I want twelve. They're not armored like our Humvees. We'll lose a bunch. Busted radiators. Shot out tires. Maybe even shattered or leaking engine blocks."

Nick had won the argument because he was Nick, he was stubborn, and he didn't lose arguments when he knew he was right. Marcus maintained that Nick was being too concerned and cautious with that many trucks, and with fewer shooters in each one, they'd take unnecessary casualties. Nick stood his ground.

Thus, S3 departed with twelve trucks. Behind Truck and Nick in the bed of the first vehicle were Bulldog, Red, and Preacher. Bulldog manned a light machine gun, an M249 SAW, which rested on the rail above the cab, its bipod legs scraping back and forth on the top of the truck's roof.

Bulldog's M249 Squad Automatic Weapon faced forward to twelve o'clock. On Bulldog's left, Red stood with his M4 watching the nine to eleven o'clock sector, while Preacher leaned over the rail on the right watching one to three.

Behind Red, Bulldog, and Preacher were Lizard and Isabella. Lizard leaned out the left behind Red. Lizard was responsible for seven to nine while Isabella watched the right behind Preacher. Isabella covered three to five. And in the middle of the truck bed was Marcus. He was there for command and control reasons and to provide additional firepower to whichever side might need it.

Behind the crammed, lead truck – or, Truck 1, as it was named – came each of the three remaining squads, in their numerical order for the sake of simplicity. The squads were spread out among eleven trucks. And in the rear of the convoy, in Trucks 11 and 12, were the six Scout Sniper teams.

Everyone in S3, including the snipers, carried M4 carbines tonight. The M4s were the upgraded version of the long-serving, military-issue M16-A2s. These M4s were shorter and lighter than the full-sized M16s, and far better suited for close-quarters battle. They also had upgraded handguard rails that allowed all manner of sights, lasers, and attachments to be added.

S3 had night vision, infrared sighting lasers, and Aimpoint red dot sights. Its members would have a significant advantage over the Godesto Cartel members in combat in the dark. They could see and shoot in nearly complete blackness by pointing their infrared lasers. The Godesto? Not so much.

S3 also had the M249 SAWs, which were the standard for light machine guns across the world. The M249 SAWs fired 5.56 mm rounds – the same caliber as the M4s – but they had plastic drums attached with 200 rounds of ammo instead of a mere thirty-round magazine.

Nick figured he had enough men and firepower to allow the unit to get in and fight its way out, but he had ordered the six Scout Sniper teams to pack their sniper rifles and plenty of heavy 7.62 match-grade ammo just in case. If they were stuck in the middle of the shithole come morning, Nick wanted the snipers putting full-size hunting rounds through anyone dumb enough to lift their head.

The snipers, being good snipers, had brought hard cases to protect the rifles and scopes, since the weapons would be bouncing around in the back of the trucks with the rest of the gear.

They were ready, Nick knew. They had the guts, they had the weaponry, and they had enough ammo to invade a small island. Now it was time to see if they had enough skill and men.

There was only one small problem. Nick's gut feeling, which had always served him so well, failed him completely on this night. Maybe it was the necessity of having to strike before Rivera was removed from office. Or maybe it was something else. But whatever it was, it should have been blaring like a roaring siren.

Because S3 was about to walk into a hornet's nest. And even a man of Nick's bravery and sense of duty would have turned the convoy around and ran back to the farm if he could have seen what was going to happen in the coming hours.

CHAPTER 37

Meanwhile, deep inside Neza-Chalco-Itza, the Butcher went to bed early. His men had asked if they should send up some women to his room, but he harshly told them "no" and headed straight for his bedroom. He felt exhausted. Too tired to think straight. The past few days had drained him.

The infiltration of the prison to kill Hernan Flores. The huge assault on Juan Soto's downtown building. The distribution – and arguing that went along with it – of the money from the bank heist.

Then there had been the editing and formatting of the video of Juan Soto's execution – it had to be perfect. And coordinating with various members of Congress who were on the payroll of the Godesto Cartel. They sensed victory at hand, but were so incompetent and carried such huge egos that the Butcher could barely keep them on track and wrangled in. The Congressional members on the Godesto payroll had to execute their investigations and impeachment of President Rivera flawlessly.

All of this work had sucked every ounce of energy that the Butcher had. He'd had too little sleep, too many shots of adrenaline, and too many close calls.

Now, all he wanted to do was sleep. And nine o'clock or not, he had ordered silence among his foot soldiers. No partying tonight. No bumping music. No fighting or womanizing.

The boss man wanted to sleep in peace and the men knew to give him his way or face his unpredictable nature. Blissful or not from all the successful actions, the new head of the Godesto Cartel was just as likely to pull a pistol on you as the prior head had been to cram down a bag of Funyuns.

The Butcher undressed down to his boxers and pulled back the sheets. He kept his Uzi and katana next to his bed, but he felt mostly at peace. He had two hundred gunmen in and around the apartment building. Besides these men, he had dozens of low-level gangsters surrounding him on street corners for miles.

On this night, when he was a mere day or two from achieving his short-term goal of driving President Roberto Rivera from office, he didn't need a bevy of girls or a grandiose celebration with his men. He simply needed sleep. Just one good night of sleep.

His first step in what would be the total downfall of the Mexican government was nearly complete, but he had pushed himself too hard these past few days. He wanted to be fresh, so he didn't screw up his final assault.

Rivera would soon either flee the country or be hauled off to prison in cuffs for his role in personally giving the order that led to the death of the SWAT team members. The Butcher didn't care which fate occurred.

All that mattered was that the Godesto Cartel was on the cusp of achieving in mere days what Hernan Flores had failed to achieve in ten-plus years: a president allied with the Godesto, who would look the other way and allow them to seek expanded distribution into America. And with that alliance, they would explode in size and strength.

The Butcher smiled. That wouldn't be enough though. His ultimate dream? First, topple the Mexican government in a few years. And then in the civil war that followed, as states fought other states, he would create his own.

His own independent state didn't have to be big, at least not at first. But he wanted a place in which the Godesto Cartel could be truly safe. A place so thorny and strong that no foreign power would even bother with them.

And it didn't have to be good ground. Las Vegas had blossomed in the desert, after all. The Butcher would take a mountain stronghold, or a wet, marshy area. Didn't even Disney World sit in a swamp?

From this refuge, they would establish a puppet government, of course, since the people had to believe they had some power. But once such a state was established, then the power for him and the Godesto Cartel could really come. They could trade for military hardware with other countries. Only a few would recognize the new cartel-backed government. Maybe Syria, Iran, Cuba, and a few others. But that would be enough.

They could import tanks, anti-air missiles, maybe even some attack choppers. A country only needed one thing to fuel it and that was a strong income. The Saudi's had oil. Africa had diamonds. The Butcher would build his future country with drug profits from the U.S.

And with that thought, he fell into a deep sleep.

Roughly fifty miles away from the Butcher's bedroom, the twelve-truck convoy of Shield, Safeguard, and Shelter closed the distance toward their target, getting closer to their epic battle with the Butcher and his men.

The convoy had charged down an interstate and then a highway, the twelve trucks dropping their speed from sixty to twenty as they turned onto an exit ramp toward the slum of Neza-Chalco-Itza.

The police trucks worked their way through ten more miles of commercial and residential area, their flashing lights illuminating buildings and homes on the dark night. The team members could feel the area getting more dangerous and perilous. Empty, boarded-up commercial buildings, fewer working streetlights, nervous people darting across streets.

The convoy passed a sign that said "Welcome to Neza-Chalco-Itza" in Spanish and English below it. The team members knew the slum's stats. It was twenty-four square miles crammed full of one million residents. At least that's what the city claimed, but Mexican intelligence and the CIA believed more than four million people resided, hid, or barely survived there. Most of them had no identification, no job, no life.

Neza-Chalco-Itza had a crime rate higher than nearly any other part of Mexico and the city was so poor that trash collection was handled by carts pulled by donkeys in much of the city.

The city also boasted one of the largest landfills in the world. The sprawling landfill covered nearly four hundred acres and had approximately twelve million tons of trash, but had mercifully been closed in 2006.

That hadn't stopped the people from living there. Hundreds lived in and around the landfill, digging and looking for valuables to sell. Or seeking metal to salvage. And it was near this infamous Bordo de Xochiaca landfill that the men of S3 headed. Because just two blocks from one of the worst places on earth was a small apartment building that held fourteen units; one of which was the Butcher's.

From the outside, the apartment building looked as old as all the hovels and shanties around it. But numerous pieces of intel data had identified the place as one of the sites that Hernan Flores had used as a safe haven through the years. And with some helo fly-bys and foot intel, Mexican authorities had determined that the place had been improved on the inside, while keeping the rough exterior in its rundown state as a form of concealment.

Flores had reportedly hated the place, but kept it as part of a fall-back position in case of a worst-case situation. But since the Butcher had shanked Flores in prison and taken over the Godesto Cartel, almost all intel pointed to the Butcher spending most of his nights in the small apartment building. It was easily the safest Godesto hideout, surrounded by hundreds of foot soldiers on the cartel's payroll. And also by high-crime area that the police could barely penetrate.

According to the map on Nick's lap, they were roughly two miles from the Butcher's fourteen-unit apartment building. So far, so good, he thought. They'd seen some tough-looking men standing on a few street corners and the demeanor of those on the streets had changed, from a slight look of fear of possible arrest to increasing bravery and defiance at the "police" intrusion.

No longer was any fear shown of the convoy with its flashing lights and menacing weapons aimed out at the streets by mean-looking folks in truck beds. The last set of three men they had seen on a corner hadn't even budged at the sight of twelve police trucks roaring down the road. They stood defiant and cold, facing the trucks with a defiant, confident look; one only the most hardened of criminals carried.

"I'll bet them boys are Godesto," Nick said Truck as they passed.

"I wish we had time to stop," Truck said. "They wouldn't' be standing there so cocky after I got through with them."

Nick could feel the hair on his neck standing up and his senses on high alert as the convoy pushed deeper into the massive slum. They were in bad-guy country, for sure, roaring down the pot-holed road at forty miles per hour. It would have probably been safer to do the speed limit of twenty-five miles per hour, but they needed surprise on their side and they'd already been spotted at least a couple miles back. Nick just hoped the Butcher was still in the apartment complex.

Intelligence provided by Isabella, and backed up by analysts in the CIA, stated that if they could just take him out, the Godesto Cartel would probably fall in on itself and fracture into pieces. Losing Hernan Flores and the Butcher – two of its strongest leaders – in such a short time span would prove fatal, intelligence officials believed.

The Butcher had four lieutenants under him, but there was little trust or coordination among them.

Nick just hoped the former prison boy was at home when they arrived. Come on, big boy. Be home and let's make this our one and only trip into Neza-Chalco-Itza, he thought.

"Take a right up here," Nick said, looking up from the map.

Truck turned the steering wheel and the convoy pivoted deeper into the dark slum.

"I haven't seen any welcoming committee," Truck said. "I figured we'd have taken some incoming fire by now."

"Yeah, I'm a little surprised by that," Nick said. "We're about a mile out. Maybe half a mile."

"I spoke too soon," Truck said. "Looky here."

His headlights showed a group of men just a block ahead. Maybe about a dozen of them. Truck flipped his lights on bright and slowed to a stop.

The men stood facing the truck, long weapons held across

their body, but aimed at the ground for the moment.

"We've got tangos up ahead," Nick said into his radio. "They're not even scared of us."

Trucks 2 and 3 pulled up on the left and right of Truck 1, but the men ahead of them didn't flinch at so many weapons aimed at them. They stared at the flashing police lights with disdain and hatred.

"Looks like they don't respect the po-lice 'round here," Truck said in his redneck drawl.

Nick and Truck heard the Primary Strike Team behind them, moving forward in the truck bed and better aligning themselves toward the threat. The truck bed had a rubber mat in it to dampen noise, but they were close enough to hear their boots moving on it.

"Just hold this position," Nick said, putting his hand on Truck's forearm.

Nick opened the door, stepped onto the cracked pavement, and aimed his M4 at the group. With the headlights on bright, he could see the group pretty clearly through the red-dot scope.

He kept his eyes toward the men and felt only a minor level of comfort knowing all his men were aimed in on the group. Nick knew that it wasn't these men in their lights that he needed to worry about. They were acting far too confident to be alone. Far too confident. They probably had plenty of back-up fighters hiding in the shadows and in dark windows ahead.

"Isabella," he said quietly. "Jump down here."

He heard her land, but didn't turn his head. This was like cornering a rattler. You didn't take your eyes off him, so Nick kept his eyes looking through the M4's Aimpoint scope.

"What do you want me to do?" she whispered, now standing just behind him.

"Reach in the truck, grab the mic, and tell these men to disperse," Nick said.

Isabella leaned into the truck to use the built-in bullhorn.

"On behalf of the government of Mexico," she said in Spanish, her voice loud through the booming volume of the truck's speakers, "you are ordered to disperse."

None of the men moved their weapons, but they spread out a bit.

"Warn them again," Nick said.

Isabella did, repeating the same words.

Nick leaned into his rifle and said without turning, "Bulldog, scatter those men."

Nick knew the big Navy SEAL from Baltimore was covering the men with the M249 SAW. He hoped the Squad Automatic Weapon firing a burst over their heads would quickly show these punks that this convoy wasn't a typical police force who would be easily deterred by some thugs or cartel members.

The SAW ripped off a burst and two men jerked and danced and splattered under the deafening roar of the machine gun. Nick was shocked to see the bullets tear through the men, but those who weren't hit took only a second to react. Some tried to flee and others brought their weapons to bear.

Nick already had one lined up in his Aimpoint red-dot site, so as the man started to bring his AK up, Nick pulled the trigger. Since the men were in the headlights of three trucks, and since the Aimpoint sight did a wonderful job of picking up ambient light, the man's face looked fairly clear in the scope.

The bullet hit about an inch from where Nick wanted at the roughly fifty-yard distance and the man fell hard to the ground. That was the thing with headshots. You put a 5.56 round through someone's face and into their brain and they dropped and never stood again.

The entire team of S3 opened up, as well, firing over the tops of the truck cabs and using the padded railings to assist their accuracy. The roughly dozen men before them were cut down and chopped up before they even returned hardly a single round. A couple crawled and dragged themselves across the pavement until single shots ended any movement.

Nick wasn't sure who shot the survivors and while he wasn't a huge fan of shooting wounded when it could be avoided, he also knew they could roll out a grenade or get a weapon around and shoot you minutes later in the back.

"Clear," yelled Red.

Others responded by stating "clear," as well.

"Hey, Bulldog," Nick said.

"Yes, sir?" Bulldog answered, his head still lowered over the SAW, ready for any targets that popped up.

"I only meant for you to scatter them by firing a burst over their head."

That elicited some laughs, but then a burst of machine gun fire ripped down the street toward them. The bullets clanged into metal and glass on the truck. Immediately the men of S3 responded at the light of a muzzle flash further down the street, well into the darkness beyond the range of the headlights.

More bullets whizzed by, this from another side of the street ahead. Again, fire was returned.

"Contact rear," Nick heard over the radio.

And then a staccato of M4s started firing from Truck 12, the vehicle with the Scout Snipers.

"Contact left," Nick heard someone else say on the radio.

More firing erupted from the middle of the convoy toward an alley to their left. Nick realized they were not in a good defensive position strewn out in a long column, not to mention their mission was to grab the Butcher, not duke it out with the entire Godesto Cartel.

"Let's get the convoy moving," he yelled into the radio. Isabella jumped back into the truck and Nick retook his seat. He rolled down the window and leaned out with his M4. He spotted a muzzle flash at his one o'clock and sent three rounds toward it, firing on single shot.

"Let's go, Truck," Nick said, anger welling up in his voice. For all he knew, hundreds of fighters were running toward them right now. Staying in place meant certain death.

Truck stepped on the gas and knocked Nick back against the seat. The convoy roared forward while the Primary Strike Team engaged targets in windows, around corners, and on roofs. They hung to the bars built up around the truck bed and fired as best they could from the moving truck.

Truck yanked the vehicle left and right as bullets pinged off and through the glass. It appeared the Mexican Police Department hadn't sprung for bullet-proof glass, something Nick wished he had known a bit earlier in the mission.

"How many you figure there are?" Truck asked, his voice

strained.

"Maybe fifty already," Nick said, holding on to the door, and firing three-round bursts toward various shadows up ahead.

Unfortunately, Nick knew it was only going to get worse as more gunmen rushed to the sound of battle. It was feeling more and more like what the Army Rangers and Special Forces had endured in Mogadishu, when more than a thousand Somali fighters came at them in the infamous Blackhawk Down battle .

We might have bitten off more than we can chew, Nick thought. And unlike those who had fought in Mogadishu, we don't have any air cover.

In his dream, the Butcher was riding on a tank, with several Godesto fighters alongside him. They were armed with rifles and had several tanks behind them. In this dream, the Goesto Cartel was invading another town to expand the size of the Butcher's country.

But something was shaking him and it wasn't the rumble of the tank. He opened his eyes and saw a man shaking him. He had told them to leave him alone.

"What is it?" he yelled, pissed. "I said no interruptions under any circumstances."

"Sir, they're coming," one of his guards said breathlessly through the door. "They're coming."

The Butcher reached for his Uzi, katana, and black duffel bag as his feet hit the floor. Then he realized he needed to grab his pants and a shirt.

"How many? And where are they?" he asked, reaching for his clothes.

The twelve-truck convoy of S3 barreled toward their target, braking hard and squealing around corners, before revving up and roaring forward as fast as the eight-cylinder trucks would take them. Bullets zipped and snapped around them, with occasional pings as bullets smacked home against the trucks.

"I can't believe how ballsy these idiots are," Truck said, as he focused hard on the task of driving and leading the entire convoy. He yanked the truck around two burning barrels of trash that someone had hurled in the road to block them. The front bumper caught the corner of one of the half-burned, half-rusted hulks and knocked it across the street.

"Well, I guess," Nick said, flinching as two bullets smacked into the truck, "that we now know why the police won't come up in Neza-Chalco-Itza anymore."

"President Rivera should have sent a convoy of tanks and troops from the army through here years ago," Truck said. "This requires more than just police work."

"Agreed," Nick said.

In the bed of their truck, the members of the Primary Strike Team lit up shadows that moved and fools who silhouetted themselves. Their M4s, and Bulldog's light machine gun over the cab of Truck 1, blasted away, jarring the night and cutting into buildings and bodies.

"Stop the convoy," someone said on the radio.

Truck hit the brakes and Nick said into the radio, "We're not stopping for long. What's the situation? Give me a sitrep. Immediately."

"Truck 7 stopped," someone said. "I think they had a tire shot out."

Bullets flew by the cab and Nick flinched, despite his best efforts not to. Someone from the Primary Strike Team fired over the cab and Nick heard Red say, "Nice shot."

A garbled transmission came back. Nick hit the mic button and said, "Second Squad and Third Squad, ditch the truck with the flat. Put its occupants in another truck and make sure you grab any ammo or valuables from the back. We have to keep the convoy moving."

The moment Nick let go of the transmit button, a nervous voice came over the air. "Man down in Truck 8. I say again, man down in Truck 8."

The incoming fire was picking up as fighters from throughout the slum of Neza-Chalco-Itza closed in on the men of S3.

Nick thought of a thousand Godesto fighters rushing toward them. It brought some fear to him. Not so much for himself; he didn't care whether he lived. Matter of fact, he'd be glad to take a bullet if it saved one of his men's lives. But if a thousand fighters truly were heading for them, then S3 would be burying a lot of its members tomorrow.

Nick looked back down the road behind him. The convoy was strung out more than three hundred yards, with ten- or fifteen-yard gaps between trucks. Nick wrestled with whether they should push ahead and leave the supplies in the truck. Every second they sat, he knew other fighters would be zeroing in on their location and rushing toward them. Not to mention it was giving the Butcher more time to get away, which was the true reason for this insane thrust into this hornet's nest.

"Man down," another voice said on the radio.

"Damn it," Nick yelled, slamming the dash with his fist. They were sitting ducks in the vehicles.

"Dismount," Nick said into the radio. "Take cover no more than fifteen feet from your primary vehicle. Engage targets and be ready to move."

Nick felt the truck shaking as the Primary Strike Team members jumped from his truck and more rounds zipped by. He kicked his own door open and stepped out, aiming his M4 toward an alley up ahead where he had seen movement.

He was so angry. Coming to a full stop before they had even reached the target? This was *not* how he had drawn up the mission.

The Butcher and nearly two hundred of his men rushed toward the sound of automatic weapons. It sounded like a war zone up ahead. Automatic weapons roaring. Large hunting rifles booming. And pistols and Uzi's popping like small firecrackers.

His men had put away their sidearms and toted long weapons as they rushed forward. They carried everything from

AK's to H&K G3's to full-length shotguns. This wasn't the place for any sawed-off shotguns.

They looked like a band of guards you'd expect to see around some terrorist leader in the mountains of Afghanistan. An oval-shaped mass of men, alert, angry, and aggressive.

One of the Butcher's men came running toward them from the firing up ahead. The Butcher, and the nearly two hundred men around him, slowed and spread out, weapons outboard and aimed toward possible threats.

"What is it?" the Butcher asked the breathless scout.

"Maybe ten trucks or so. Who knows. Maybe fifty or a hundred troops total?"

"Why didn't you get a better count?" the Butcher asked.

"They are shooting anyone who shows their face. Not just those with weapons," the man said.

The Butcher had often wondered why the Mexican Army followed such strict rules of engagement. The cartels and gangs regularly used unarmed women and children to act as spotters. Looked like the army had finally learned its lesson.

"Are they army troops? Or Mexican Marines?" he asked.

"No, sir. They appear to be Mexican SWAT."

This made no sense to the Butcher. First, he had a great inside source with the Mexican police force and there was no way they'd have launched a raid without this man warning the Godesto Cartel. Secondly, it was nothing short of pure lunacy to launch a raid into the middle of Neza-Chalco-Itza with so few men. Only a hundred? Against a thousand, who knew the area and had pre-planned defense locations?

The Butcher looked at one of his lieutenants who stood nearby.

"And you talked with the other lookouts in the other sectors? No other units are coming from either the north or west or south?"

"Yes, sir. I just called them each again. All sectors are quiet."

"Call each of them again," the Butcher said, dismissing the man with a wave.

The Godesto Cartel kept advance guards posted for miles around, not to mention all the typical dealers and informants who called in suspicious behaviors for cash payouts.

It just didn't add up to the Butcher, though.

Ten trucks or so? Fifty or a hundred troops? And Mexican SWAT at that?

Why would so few troops so bravely raid Neza-Chalco-Itza? There were so many cartel members and addicts and gang members in the slum that they had literally stopped an army battalion of more than a thousand soldiers several years ago.

There were probably eighteen hundred gunmen the Butcher could call up with enough warning, though this group had managed to make the raid without advance notice from their informant network. But the Butcher worried that there had to be something else going on.

No way would so few SWAT members enter alone. Perhaps there were dozens of helicopters on their way in with more troops. Or maybe an army battalion stationed just outside the slum. Maybe two or three of them, actually. That's what the Butcher would do if he were in charge of Mexican forces: Send in at least three battalions of army troops. A thousand in each. Three thousand total. Clean out the entire Godesto stronghold.

President Roberto Rivera was certainly in desperate straits. Would he have called up an all-out assault of Neza-Chalco-Itza, the heart of the Godesto Cartel? That made more sense than sending in fifty or a hundred cops in unarmored trucks. Losing so many cops – or perhaps the entire SWAT unit– would only inflame the President's critics and opponents.

And then the Butcher had another thought. What if Rivera wanted all these cops killed?

It might very well create sympathy for the federal government and the embattled President. The media might cite it as another example of out-of-control ruthlessness by the drug cartels. More unnecessary deaths of the brave and honorable police, who were merely poor men trying to do their jobs, they would say.

This idea sealed the Butcher's decision. Either more troops were on their way or it was a huge public relations move by President Rivera. Either way, staying and fighting was a bad idea.

"Pull everyone back," he said to his lieutenant.

"Why?" a lieutenant asked. "We can take these guys. Let's kill them all."

His lieutenant still thought the way the Butcher used to think: you hit the enemy every time you had the advantage.

But, things were more complex once you were in charge of an entire cartel organization. And with the firefight roaring in the distance, the Butcher didn't have time to explain that more troops could be on the way. Or that this could be a well-planned political move to win the support of the people.

They were too close to toppling President Rivera to mess it up now by either a costly battle against thousands of hardened army troops or a terrible media disaster that could be spun out for days of public sympathy.

"No," the Butcher said. "Pull everyone back. Keep some scouts on the convoy and see where they go, but tell our men to pull back and leave them alone."

"Yes, sir," the man said, lifting his radio to pass along the new orders.

The stalled convoy attracted additional fighters and emboldened their enemy. Nick realized this and cursed his inability to right the situation. He was their commander. How had he lost control so quickly? His blood pressure continued to rise as the element of surprise drifted away...

Suddenly, an M60 blasted to their front – a fighter dispersing dozens of rounds down the street from the direction the convoy intended to go. The 7.62 bullets tore down the street. Nick and the rest of the Primary Strike Team dove for cover. The Vietnam-era medium machine shredded their truck. Several of the members tried to rise up and engage its brave – or suicidal – user, but the bullets were flying everywhere with complete unpredictability. And they came in waves, not like just some three- or four-second burp from an AK.

The gunner was probably firing it from the hip. Nick remembered being pinned down in Afghanistan and tried to will himself to lift his head and find the shooter. At least here he had a helmet, unlike in Afghanistan where he had just worn a boonie cover.

He pushed his M4 up above the car he lay behind on the side of the road. He thankfully had an engine block between him and the gunner, but already several rounds had walloped into the clunker he hid behind.

Nick lowered the barrel of his M4 above the hood to an angle that he guessed would be in the general proximity of the gunman. He then fired off a full mag in the direction of the shooter. Other Primary Strike Team members were doing the same thing, except for crazy-ass Red, who had his weapon up in his shoulder and was firing at the gunman using his sights. He was totally exposed like the insane madman that he was. No wonder the big guys left him alone. The 5'5" Red was batshit nuts, but Nick was glad he was on his side.

As the Primary Strike Team regained fire superiority on the front end of the convoy, Nick reloaded and popped up behind his carbine. He wanted to find the shooter in his Aimpoint red dot sight and put the punk down for good. And with the streetlights shining on the area to their front, he felt confident he'd nail the gunman.

Then he saw him, as the M60 opened up again with a fresh belt toward Red and some of the other team members. Nick could just make out the silhouette of the man behind the yellow flame of the bullets coming out the front of it. Nick placed the red dot on the target roughly eighty yards away and fired four 5.56 rounds into the man.

It was spitting distance for the M4. As easy as dropping a piece of crumpled paper in a trash can right next to you if you were a sniper of Nick's caliber. Not that there were many snipers of his caliber, but the bullets – even in the low light and hasty firing position – whacked into the man in less than a three-inch group. Not as good as the one inch group expected of snipers at this range, but it was night, he wore assault gear, and his breathing was out of control.

The shooter crumpled and Nick put two more rounds into the body, just to be sure he didn't get up anytime soon. Another cartel member darted out to the gun, just as Nick expected, and he mercilessly put three bullets into him without having to adjust his aim much. Nick kept the M60 and the two bodies in his scope for a few more seconds, but allowed his ears to hear the battle around him. Trying to get a feeling for how the rest of the members of S3 were doing.

Without question, his men were getting hammered. They were outgunned, outnumbered, and still probably half a mile from the target. Nick imagined the nightmare scenario of trying to surround the target building and actually enter it. It seemed impossible. And absurd, now that he saw the ground and resistance before them.

He heard someone slide up beside him, their clothing and equipment scuffing against the ground as they skidded up next to him.

"It's me, Nick," Marcus said.

Nick didn't turn, keeping his Aimpoint sight on the M60 and two bodies.

"We're in the shit, huh?" Nick said. "Having fun?"

"You know it."

"What do you think?" Nick asked.

"I just ran down the column," Marcus said, still breathing hard, "and we have nine wounded and five KIA."

Nick kicked himself for getting personally tied up in a small part of the firefight with the M60 gunner and not doing what Marcus had done. He should have known to not get locked into using his rifle, instead relying on his leadership skills and radio.

"Oh," Marcus said, "and we also have two trucks already out of commission. Maybe three."

Nick recalled the M60 chewing up the lead truck, right through the grill and into the motor when it initially opened up.

"Four trucks out of commission," Nick said. "That M60 out there hammered Truck 1 before we stopped him."

Nick cursed. "This isn't going to happen, is it?"

"That's kind of what I was hoping you'd say," Marcus said. "I know you're prone to stubbornness, but I think we collect ourselves and get the hell out of here. We've lost the element of surprise. Bottom line, we gave it a whirl, but they were waiting on us. No point in being stupid and losing a bunch more good men."

It burned Nick to agree, but facts were facts. And if a leader of Marcus's talent felt the same way as Nick, then they needed to pull back. And fast.

"All units," Nick said into the mic, "load up. We're turning around and heading back. All squad leaders, confirm you have all your men and report in. Leave any trucks that aren't running, but leave no gear. And there better not be a single man left behind."

Nick stood, fired half a mag down the street toward some movement on the other side, and moved toward Truck 1, which looked like it wouldn't be driving anytime soon. You just can't avoid the Mexican heat, he thought, even at night.

He started grabbing gear and maps from the cab to throw into another truck. His men fired and moved, fired and moved, covering each other, working in pairs as they had trained. Nick threw his gear into the cab of Truck 2 and watched as his unit moved and operated like pros. And in that moment, even in defeat, Nick felt pride in his unit. They had been repulsed, but not beaten.

CHAPTER 38

The day following the massive firefight in the slum of Neza-Chalco-Itza, the Butcher quickly wished he had never gotten out of bed. His assumptions about the convoy from the night prior had been wrong. No other army battalions had entered their slum and the government under President Rivera wasn't decrying the dead troops in the media.

Damn it. He had missed an opportunity to wipe out an entire SWAT team. He had missed the chance to show how strong the Godesto Cartel was under his leadership.

Now the Butcher felt numb, like he needed to puke. He was in the middle of an "emergency meeting" with his CFO; the skinny little puke sitting in front of him, wearing a three-thousand-dollar suit.

The Butcher couldn't stand the guy. The little shit had a finance degree, got weekly manicures, and played racquetball. Worse, he had never lifted a weight a day in his life and couldn't possibly imagine life in prison or anything else that the Butcher had gone through.

But you apparently needed a guy like this when you ran a nearly billion-dollar criminal enterprise. Same as you need an army of attorneys.

This little prick normally seemed so in control and calm. It drove the Butcher crazy, but he certainly wasn't that way today. Instead, the skinny, soft prick looked as shocked and scared as someone on the street, who had just been robbed and nearly beaten to death.

"What do you mean the money's gone?" the Butcher yelled.

The man shifted nervously and cleared his throat.

"I, uh, got a call at 8:01 from one of our banks. And I've

since checked the status on all of our other accounts, as well, and, um, most of it is gone."

"What do you mean it's gone? And how much are we talking here?"

"I've still got three of my assistants calculating out the exact figures, but my worst-case estimate is that ninety-one percent of our money is gone."

"And when you say 'our money,' are you talking about my personal money or the Godesto Cartel money?"

"The Godesto money, sir." The man flinched when he said it. The Butcher hadn't gotten his name from being a reasonable or forgiving person. And the man could see the duffel bag where he knew the new cartel leader kept his sword.

"That's worst-case," the Butcher said. "And what's your best-case estimate of how much money is gone?"

"Eighty-seven percent?"

"Eighty-seven percent?" the Butcher asked. "But you said the worst-case estimate was ninety-one percent. That's not much of a range."

"It's all digital and computerized these days," the accountant explained, "so there's not much guess work. Unfortunately, we're quite certain that most of the corporation's money is gone."

The Butcher ignored the man calling the Godesto Cartel a "corporation." He despised the man feigning ignorance at how they derived their income and had berated him about it before, but not today. No, not with the way this conversation was going.

"What did you do with the money that still remains?" the Butcher asked, trying to breathe and repress the panic seeping into his chest.

"We've moved it into new accounts, just to be safe. Although doing so does present some risks. Even at roughly ten percent, that's a lot of assets to be moving, but I deemed it the prudent course of action."

The Butcher gritted his teeth and scowled. This couldn't be happening. How had the Feds seized that much of the cartel's money without any of his informants warning them? It was inconceivable. The Godesto Cartel even had a man in

President Rivera's Cabinet. This just couldn't happen without notification.

"Forget the numbers for a moment," the Butcher said. "How much money will we have after we make our payouts and payroll checks for this week?"

The CFO cleared his throat and shifted in his chair.

"We can't make them," the man said, his voice barely a whisper.

"What?" The Butcher sprang to his feet and slammed his fists on the desk and then threw a side kick that drove a hole in the wall. "What are you saying?" he screamed.

The man flinched and shrunk down lower.

"I'm saying we're bankrupt."

"But we can get this money back, right?" the Butcher asked. "I'm not an attorney, but we have the best legal team that money can buy. In thirty days, maybe sixty, we'll get the money back. You need to figure out how to handle this until then."

"We owe too many suppliers, too many gangs, too many other cartels to wait that long," the finance man said, desperation in his voice. "Just the one shipment we moved north of the border today has a twenty-five million dollar payment that we owe the Venezuelan Brothers. They're expecting that wire transfer today."

"And how much do we have that's been moved to other accounts? That we could pay them with?"

"Eighteen point six million."

"So, not even enough to pay the Venezuelan Brothers?"

"No, sir, but we could require some advances from our various entities. Those who rent buildings from us and some of those who lease territories to operate from."

The Godesto Cartel allowed some gangs and organized crime groups to tax businesses in areas it controlled but lacked the manpower to effectively manage. These smaller groups paid a tax to the cartel, while the Godesto Cartel focused on international growth instead of petty, small-turf scuffles over mostly irrelevant amounts of money.

But, the Butcher could envision the rumors spreading among these armed groups and other cartels if they asked for an advance on money owed. These were men of the street. They could smell weakness from a mile away and they'd turn on the Godesto Cartel in a minute if they sensed that the tides had turned and that the mighty cartel that had ruled for so long suddenly lacked strength.

Especially since the Godesto had really turned the screws into many of these groups, requiring too much, if truth be known. And these groups knew the truth, but had been too powerless in isolated groups to act. But, if the cash started running dry, all of them would turn on their despised landlord.

It was no different than a pack mentality among a pride of lions. The moment the older male showed injury or weakness, he would be attacked and driven off by a rival. Leadership was only held by strength, poise, and confidence.

And this news of their accounts being seized by the government, combined with the news he'd heard earlier this morning about the Red Sleeve Cartel breaking their truce, was enough to make him ready to run.

One of his lieutenants had told him earlier that news stations were reporting that the Red Sleeve Cartel had declared war on the Godesto. The Butcher had immediately called the leader of the rival cartel on his direct line and the man had neither answered nor returned his call. Several immediate calls to the Butcher's subordinates across the country had led to reports that the members of the Red Sleeve Cartel were acting strange, packing heavy today, and ignoring nods and attempts to communicate from members of the Godesto Cartel.

The Godesto Cartel and the Red Sleeve Cartel had enjoyed a shaky alliance for years, but at their core they were rivals who had temporarily put aside differences for a more unified front against the government. It had been the biggest move pulled off by Hernan Flores and it had catapulted him and the Godesto Cartel to unprecedented levels of power. And it was this alliance that had first brought the Navy SEALs to Mexico.

The Butcher struggled to get his arms around the situation. Money seized. Reports of a declared war by the Red Sleeve Cartel. What the hell was happening?

One of his lieutenants knocked hard on the door and said,

"Sir, turn on the TV."

The Butcher ignored the CFO for a moment and flipped on the television. The news showed a man lying in a pool of blood. He turned the volume up when he saw the name Edgar Argel appear next to a picture of the corpse. A pretty news anchor had a look of concern on her face and she said with great gravity that the high-ranking man in the Godesto Cartel had been shanked in prison. And even the Butcher could clearly see the symbol of the Red Sleeve Cartel slashed into the man's back.

Photos don't lie, and Edgar Argel, who had several distinctive tattoos on his lower back and legs, was clearly the man who lay dead and carved up in the photo of the news broadcast. Already police were identifying, the cute news anchor said, one of the well-known Red Sleeve Cartel members, who was also housed in the same prison as the killer.

"Get out, both of you," the Butcher said.

They shut the door behind them and he collapsed in his chair. The Butcher cursed the fact that he needed to set in motion a reprisal for the death of Edgar Argel or be seen, once again, as weak by those on the streets.

The news anchor followed the report regarding Edgar Argel by talking about the catastrophe that had occurred in the federal prison in Nayarit.

What was this?

He pushed away the idea of reprisal against the Red Sleeve Cartel and focused back on the TV. For five minutes he sat glued to the broadcast. As the shock set in, fear started to grow.

He just couldn't believe what was being reported. The anchor said the federal prison in Nayarit had faced a huge breakout attempt, but the Butcher hadn't authorized any such escape. This, too, made no sense.

The population of the federal prison in Nayarit was mostly composed of Godesto Cartel members, so they shouldn't have attempted an escape unless he gave the order. And why would he? From this prison, the Godesto Cartel controlled a nationwide embezzlement operation of all the prisons.

The news anchor reported that a fire had broken out

during the attempted escape and most of the inmates had died. The Butcher couldn't believe it. These were some of the Godesto Cartel's heaviest hitters. Men who rotated out on parole to take primary shooter slots in the Godesto Cartel. Men who mentored young gang members out on the street and new prisoners who had just arrived. Men who younger members looked up to as examples of what they should aspire to.

And now they were gone. The backbone of the Godesto Cartel had died gasping in smoke or burned alive. Well, not that the cartel had the money to support them anymore, the Butcher reminded himself, turning the TV off with disgust.

He wondered if all this was propaganda, but the news station had shown a reporter on the scene. They had provided video of a burning prison, which looked exactly like the compound as the Butcher remembered it.

The phone on the desk rang, but he didn't have it in him to answer it. He gripped the back of his head and buried his face in his arms.

This couldn't be happening. It was just a bad dream.

But then someone knocked on his door and he knew it was real. The Godesto, and the Butcher, were in some seriously deep shit.

"Come in," he said.

One of his most trusted lieutenants stuck his head in the door and said, "I'm sorry to bother you, but we've got problems."

"What is it?" the Butcher asked, sounding more exhausted than he wanted.

"I'm hearing that the Mexican Army has entered Coacalco, Magdalena Contreras, and Allende."

The Butcher couldn't believe it.

Coacalco and Magdalena Contreras were two of the strongest footholds the Godesto Cartel had, after Neza-Chalco-Itza. Both were on the outskirts of Mexico City and they had helped provide the base of operations that had allowed Hernan Flores to take over the country. If they were being hit by the army in strength, then loads of supplies and men were likely going to be lost.

And Allende, the third city mentioned, was their primary northern base of operations. It was hundreds of miles away from Mexico City, just south of Texas, and was a linchpin in helping them hang onto the north, as well a great base of operations for excursions across the border into Texas.

"Are you sure?" the Butcher asked.

"Absolutely," his lieutenant said. "We're pulling together casualty figures now, and while our men are trying to get away with some of the supplies, they apparently hit us before six a.m. and our men were completely unprepared. We had no warning."

"Keep me up to date with the latest," the Butcher said. "Now, give me some space so I can process this."

The door shut and the Butcher pressed the button for his assistant.

"Gabriel," he said, "call our pilots and have them fire my jet up. And also, arrange transportation to the airport for me."

He hung up on his assistant before the man could say anything and took a deep breath. He just needed to get away from it for a few days. There might still be a chance. Perhaps he could still handle all of this. If a fat, Funyun-gobbling grandpa could run this organization and navigate an untold number of obstacles, then surely he could, too.

The phone buzzed back.

"What?" the Butcher asked, punching the button hard. Gabriel knew to leave him alone. What the hell was his problem?

"Sir, one of the calls that came in while you asked me to hold them is from one of our attorneys representing the aviation wing of our corporation. He said that he had been served with a federal warrant this morning and all aircraft had been temporarily seized."

"So none of our four aircraft are available?"

"Not according to him, sir. Though he said to inform you that they were drafting counter-motions that should be filed by this afternoon with the courts."

"And?" the Butcher asked.

"Well, he said with luck they'd be available for use again possibly as soon as four days, if the judge agrees with us and the motions are squeezed in on the court calendar as he hopes."

The Butcher felt his stomach roll over. He wasn't sure who he feared more, right then. The Red Sleeve Cartel, the Venezuelan Brothers who were about to get stiffed, or President Roberto Rivera and the government.

His mind was racing and thinking of an exit plan. There might be a way to salvage this sinking ship, but he didn't see it.

This was the final straw for him. He'd let someone else deal with it, since he had enough money to get a new start somewhere else. Or maybe hide out on a beach somewhere, living a life of leisure and martial arts.

But in no way did he see his future tied to the Godesto Cartel anymore. As a small boy bullied on the mean streets, he knew when it was time to run. And that time had come.

CHAPTER 39

The Butcher might have made a clean escape from Mexico City and all of his problems, but one of his assistants saw him acting strangely and heard him tell his assistant Gabriel that he'd be back and didn't need his security detail with him.

That struck the assistant as alarmingly odd, so he had made an excuse to get past Gabriel and into the Butcher's office. Then he checked the internet history on the computer. And there, in plain sight if you knew how to search someone's internet history, was a recent purchase of a first-class plane ticket at Mexico City's international airport.

And though it was the riskiest thing the assistant had ever done, it was obvious the Godesto Cartel was in shambles. Besides the news outlets practically cheering their demise, the assistants had been talking among themselves about the impending war with the Red Sleeve Cartel, money problems, and Army incursions into Coacalco, Magdalena Contreras, and Allende. Things didn't look good.

But there remained a ten million dollar reward on the Butcher's head from the government... And it suddenly looked like whoever turned on the man might actually live to tell about it. Especially if provided a new identity.

And with that, the underpaid and barely-recognized assistant decided to make a call about the Butcher's departure.

President Roberto Rivera stood to shake off his weariness. He felt exhausted, but alive. Very alive.

And very close to victory.

He had kept the entire Cabinet in the Presidential Palace, as promised, and while he had found time for a two-hour nap and shower, he could feel the Godesto Cartel falling to its knees right before them as he monitored incoming reports and media outlets.

And the Cabinet members could feel it, too. Most had slept very little and after the initial resistance, they had thrown their full support behind the effort and offered additional suggestions. Now, it was no longer a solo effort by President Rivera. Finally, when it was almost too late to matter, when Mexico had come up to and almost past the brink, the entire government was aligning itself against the Godesto Cartel as it had never done before. No longer did political gain matter for the members. Now it was about winning before their government fell apart in a dozen different investigations.

About the only shortcoming so far, from Rivera's perspective, had been Nick's mission into Neza-Chalco-Itza to capture the Butcher. Nick's group from Shield, Safeguard, and Shelter had been mercilessly ambushed and shot all to hell by the Godesto. They had failed to even make it to their target building.

But practically everything else was going Rivera's way, including some of the new suggestions now being made by his Cabinet members as they jumped onboard with his effort.

One of those ideas brought forward by a Cabinet member was to have all tips into the hotline involving the Godesto Cartel or the Butcher called directly into the Presidential Palace, where actual Cabinet officials would man the phones. It wasn't like there were that many calls anyway. And having the calls come directly into the Cabinet would throw a wrench into whatever informant system that the Godesto Cartel had set up, giving the government a new edge.

Rivera considered this a wonderful idea. Once the phone lines were rerouted away from the intelligence headquarters and directly to the Presidential Palace, three Cabinet members assumed the first shift.

Besides avoiding informants, the realignment paid dividends in terms of pace, since President Rivera and his security forces could react to tips faster. It also had one final huge benefit: with the Cabinet members in full control, they avoided informing command of a unit's destination. They simply ordered units to a certain location and waited until the units were a short distance away to inform them of what the tip actually was. And the new technique was scoring big wins.

But when the phone rang regarding a tip about the Butcher flying out of the country, Rivera knew that redirecting tips straight into the Cabinet had proven nothing short of genius. And he knew he only trusted one man to take care of this one.

Back at the farm, Nick Woods felt exhausted, despite a shower and shave. He stood on the back porch of the farmhouse – S3's humble but well-hidden headquarters – and looked out at the rising sun, wanting nothing more than a hard drink. Yet he knew he should settle for some breakfast instead. But the memories from last night wouldn't leave him alone and had killed his appetite.

Following his command to turn around, the unit had limped out of Neza-Chalco-Itza in only seven trucks. Three had been left smoking or burning, while two lay paralyzed with flat tires, like beached whales unable to move any further forward.

Nick and his men had rushed their wounded to a hospital in Mexico City and dropped their dead at the morgue before returning to the farm.

By then it was after three in the morning.

The final tallies from Marcus and the squad leaders were thirteen dead and twenty-three wounded. Even the Primary Strike Team had been bloodied badly. Preacher, Bulldog, and Isabella had all been wounded and were in the hospital.

The Lizard, who had had premonitions prior to the mission, had been killed with a bullet to the throat.

And for what? What had they accomplished? They hadn't even made it to their target building, much less nabbed the Butcher.

Hell, by not reaching the target building, they had done more than just missed grabbing the Butcher. They had also failed to even grab any intel by raiding the location that might have led to his whereabouts. No computers, no file cabinets

MEXICAN HEAT (NICK WOODS BOOK 2)

stuffed full of documents to scan for clues, no cartel punks to question for days and days in an effort to break them.

What had they accomplished? Nick asked himself.

Absolutely nothing. Nada. Zilch.

A lot of good men had died because of the foolhardy mission Nick had ordered. He knew the plan came from the input of his men, as well, and Marcus had reminded him this morning that each of them had gone out doing what they wanted to do, but Nick couldn't shake the gloom.

Why had he survived with nary a scratch? He had given the punks inside Neza-Chalco-Itza numerous opportunities to put a round in him as he had walked around and tried to play brave commander.

But his luck continued, as it had from the beginning. First, Afghanistan, against the Soviets. Then in his tussle with Whitaker and too many of his CIA commandos to count. And now last night.

He didn't understand it. Besides the thought of Lizard being dead and twelve others from his command, Nick wanted to see Isabella. She lay in a hospital bed drugged up and with two bullets in her, but Nick knew she'd survive barring any complications.

Marcus, who'd also survived without a scratch, was in classic Marine DI command mode. Nothing knocked that man down. He had ordered the men to line the trucks up in an orderly manner and spray the blood out of the truck beds and off the sides of them.

Then he'd had the men spray off and pack up the gear of the wounded. Then he'd ordered them to clean their weapons and get showered up. Nick had cleaned his weapon, as well, but he wondered for what?

His unit was hardly combat ready. They had organized the survivors into two ragtag squads in case some kind of mission was necessary, but his men had gotten the shit kicked out of them and failed to even accomplish their mission. They were experienced veterans who had all seen their share of war, but fifty percent casualties on a mission that in the end proved unsuccessful was pretty tough mustard for anyone.

Nick, leaning on the deck railing, spat onto the dusty

ground and fought the urge to go grab his liquor bottle. Last thing the men needed was a drunk commander, but boy, that bottle had a powerful call at this moment.

Nick had already reported the terrible mission results to Mr. Smith, who to his credit, had been up all night waiting for their call and relaying information about the Godesto Cartel from President Rivera, as well as intel that the NSA and CIA had picked up.

Other than the failed mission by Nick's men, things were mostly going swimmingly for Mexico and President Rivera, according to Mr. Smith. Maybe it wasn't all a waste, Nick thought. The men of S3 *had* come up with the plans that were now throttling and destroying the Godesto Cartel, so there was that. Plus, even with their heavy casualties, they had helped gut the army of the Godesto in the filthy streets of Neza-Chalco-Itza. S3 had probably killed upward of a couple hundred cartel gunmen. That was a lot of muscle to carve off any organization.

Nick's cellphone rang and he looked down at it. It was President Rivera's cellphone number. Now what, he wondered?

"How would you like to get your hands on the Butcher?" President Rivera asked.

"Go on," Nick said.

"He's headed to an airport to fly out of Mexico. He's fleeing, Nick, all because of your plans."

"They were your plans. You make sure that's how you phrase it to the public from here on out. Now, where is that bastard? I'd love nothing more than to get my hands on him."

And minutes after that question, Nick Woods and Dwayne Marcus raced toward the Mexico City International Airport, the siren on their green police truck roaring. As they flew down the interstate, Nick was glad that Marcus had asked the men to spray down the trucks.

They had to move fast for a chance to nab the little punk. President Rivera had decided not to stop the plane or alert other authorities. The Butcher was fleeing and the last thing

Rivera wanted was a court trial or to spook him and keep him in the country, where he might re-assume control of the remnants of Godesto Cartel.

Nick understood Rivera's thinking and he was glad that the President was giving him one final chance to get his hands on his prey. This was one final chance for Nick to avenge the SEAL platoon and all the men of Shield, Safeguard, and Shelter who had died or been wounded the night before.

He and Marcus had changed into civilian clothes and Marcus sported jeans, polo, and some kind of hip shoes that Nick couldn't place a finger on. Nick wore jeans, a tight Sniper shirt with the sleeves rolled up, and a pair of work boots. His look failed the undercover/CIA look, but there were plenty of rough-looking construction workers south of Texas and he was too square to go dressing like Marcus.

They had put a squad leader in charge of the entire unit back at the farm while they were gone and picked the truck with the fewest bullet holes punched into it. President Rivera had stated that the Butcher's flight would begin boarding in one hour and twenty minutes. Since they were well over an hour away at legal driving speeds, they needed to seriously cut down the driving time. After all, they would have to find him *before* boarding began, since there'd be no way to get him off the plane without attracting attention.

Now they raced toward the airport at a hundred and twenty miles per hour, siren blazing, in a truck that should only do eighty. The big tires and heavy steel frame in the back for troops made it hard to drive, but Marcus was handling it.

Nick was trying to control his rage. He had a .357 revolver in the floorboard, but knew he'd probably be going in unarmed on this one. And he was more than okay with that. The Butcher would be unarmed, too.

Nick wanted to get his hands on this bastard so badly he couldn't stand it. He'd somehow get him in a bathroom or hallway alone and then beat the shit out of him. And once the Butcher could no longer defend himself, Nick would choke him out and hold the lock until the man was dead. Nick wouldn't lose an ounce of sleep over this either. He was one hundred percent sure of this.

STAN R MITCHELL

They arrived in Mexico City without any problems. And as they rushed into the mass of parking lots and garages around the airport, Nick said, "Just pull up to the front doors."

"Roger that," Marcus said.

The truck's siren was off now, but Marcus kept the lights on as he raced past stalled traffic in front of him. He drove down the road into oncoming traffic, forcing cars to jerk off the road and up onto the curb.

Marcus spotted an opening in traffic in the correct lane and jerked the truck back over with the flow of traffic.

As more cars began to block their path, Marcus was forced to jump the curb and drive down the sidewalk the final half-mile. Marcus laid on the horn and pedestrians dove out of the way as the truck ripped down the sidewalk.

People jumped to the left and right and Marcus hit one large suitcase that exploded a pile of clothes across the truck and sidewalk.

"Like a damn movie," Marcus grunted, yanking the truck to avoid a mother with a stroller.

By the time they reached the airport entrance, two police cars were rushing toward them, sirens blazing.

"Ignore them," Nick said. "It might take half an hour to get the situation cleared up before President Rivera can intervene. Pull up closer and I'll jump out. Then punch it and take these two on a wild goose chase."

"No way," Marcus said. "I'm coming with you." He had come too far to let Nick deal with this alone.

"It's the only way this will work," Nick said. "If you come in with me, we'll be in handcuffs trying to make a phone call and the Butcher will be gone."

"We'll figure something out," Marcus said, anger in his voice.

Nick pushed open his door a few inches. "Marcus, that is a direct order. Drive the fucking truck away."

Marcus cursed and slammed the breaks. Nick slipped out the door. Marcus floored it and took off again. Nick hoped the two cruisers hadn't noticed him. It stood to reason that they hadn't. They were still a couple hundred yards away and there were dozens of cars and hundreds of people streaming in and out of the airport between them.

Nick avoided looking back and simply immersed himself in a large group of tourists headed toward the entry doors. He entered the lobby and saw a huge line in front of a security checkpoint up ahead. Being from the South, he hated to be an ass, but the Butcher's plane would be boarding at any moment.

He rushed down the line past the impatient travelers, walking fast and hearing people bitching and gasping as he moved forward. At the front of it, he said to a tired looking family, "I'm very sorry, but I have to break line. My seven-year-old son is up ahead and my wife has lost him. It's an emergency, please."

The wife shrugged, clearly unable to understand him.

"I'm sorry," Nick said, walking toward the two federal agents.

"Do you need help finding him?" a security agent said in barely understandable English. He was reaching for his radio with concern.

"She's already working with airport security," Nick said. "No need."

He placed his wallet and keys in the tray and said, "If you could just help me get cleared quickly, we're both really nervous about this."

"Of course," the man said. "I have a son, too. I can only imagine how terrifying it must feel."

Nick stepped through the metal detector and waited for his keys and wallet in the tray. They took forever to come through the slow-moving belt and he practically ripped them from the agent.

"Thank you," he said, "and I'm sorry, but I've gotta go."

He rushed away and headed for a directory. He found the wing where the Butcher's flight would depart and accelerated that way. He glanced at his watch and saw only fifteen minutes remained before boarding began.

Nick wanted to jog, but also knew that the Butcher might be waiting out of range of the departure area, wary and alert. Nick slowed and decided to keep his cool, walking as calmly as possible.

He scanned the crowd, ignoring old men, harried moms,

and screaming kids. There also seemed to be a huge percentage of well-dressed businessmen and women, who were looking down at iPhones, laptops, and papers they had brought with them.

And then he spotted a possible fit. A short man, walking away from him. The man carried a black duffel bag, walking as smoothly as a gymnast or ninja. Nick closed the distance toward him, taking larger steps. His gut told him this was the Butcher.

He caught up to him and slowed, staying just a couple feet behind him while his brain tried to work on the fly. He knew a fight in the open corridor would only lead to both of them being arrested. That wouldn't work. He had promised President Rivera that he wouldn't take the man alive.

"Juan Pelo," Nick said loudly, reaching for the man's shoulder and using his real name, which hardly anyone knew. It was also a name that no one in the Godesto Cartel dared called him.

The man tensed under Nick's hand and Nick knew he had the right man.

"Don't do anything stupid," Nick said, walking alongside him. "And don't act like you don't understand English. I've read your file. Trust me. For your own good, just keep walking like we're friends. I have an offer for you."

"Who are you?"

"Roberto Rivera sent me, but that doesn't matter. You see, I have a proposition for you."

"I don't need to hear your proposition," the Butcher sneered. "I could make one call and you'd be cut into fish bait within the hour.

"Well, you could," Nick said, emphasizing his Southern drawl, "but we already know you don't have your security detail with you. And I kind of doubt you could get your phone up and dialed before I ripped it from your little hand."

"I'm not worried about some redneck taking a phone from me. I could break your arm before the phone hit the ground. If you've read my file, you know that."

Nick chuckled.

"I know you're a little karate boy or something," Nick said.

"But if you did that, security would rush up and arrest us both. And frankly, I'm betting they'd probably figure out who you are without needing to break out the fingerprint kit. You're kind of famous now, you know? Worth $10 million to the government. So, if you want to leave the country in a few minutes, you'll listen to my proposition."

After a moment, the Butcher said, "I'm listening." But he was still walking toward the departure point, his mind racing through his options.

"Option one is I cause a ruckus and get security over here to arrest you. We know that gets you into prison after a painful and long court trial that will probably last at least two or three years. You'll be inside the pen that entire time. And once you're convicted, no parole for you. Ever."

"What's option two?" the Butcher asked.

"Option two is you step into an empty hallway with me without causing a scene. President Rivera wants you dead and he's looking to avoid a trial. He also doesn't want you enjoying the easy life in jail, like you cartel members always seem to do. Plus, he can't kill you in jail because after the Hernan Flores shanking incident, the public would come unhinged. Rivera can't have another cartel leader dying in custody."

"Get to your point," the Butcher said, his voice angry.

"So, option two," Nick continued, "is we mosey over into an empty hallway and see who walks out. I figure you have about ten minutes before your plane leaves, which gives you time to take care of me, clean up, and leave on schedule."

"How do I know I won't be arrested anyway, assuming I break your country-boy ass in half?"

"President Rivera would rather have you gone from the country than on trial or in jail, so that's why I'm here. I get one chance at you. And from your perspective, you only have one final obstacle remaining between you and your destination. And that obstacle is me."

The Butcher looked Nick up and down. The man was probably about six feet tall and lean, but he didn't seem like anything special to the Butcher. There was no way this man had been in as many fights and hand-to-hand killings as the Butcher had.

"This could be dangerous for you," the Butcher said, a smile creeping across his face.

"I'm accustomed to danger. Plus, I was paid good money by the U.S. government to come down here and deal with Mr. Flores and the Godesto Cartel. You took care of Flores for me, which I appreciate, but you still bear a right smart amount of blood on your hands. Besides all the Mexican people you've killed or leeched off of, you guys took out a bunch of Navy SEALs. And last night, you killed some of my men in Neza-Chalco-Itza. So, it's kind of personal, you might say."

"Hah," the Butcher laughed, as they continued to walk through the bustling airport. "That was you? I should have known only some cocky-ass American would enter Neza-Chalco-Itza with so few men. You're lucky we didn't kill you all."

Nick swallowed down his anger. He felt the fire and hatred building up.

"That one hit close to home, didn't it?" the Butcher asked. He could see the anger on this stranger's face.

Nick thought of Lizard. Of Isabella. Of how helpless he had felt, dragging and carrying his wounded men into the hospital. And then offloading the dead at the morgue, once they had stripped them of their gear to limit the questions from emergency personnel.

Let it go, Nick, he told himself. Focus on this little bastard. Nick flipped a switch.

"Hey shithead," Nick said. "Ask yourself this. How come President Rivera had barely made a dent against the Godesto in five plus years? And then magically, in just a single night and morning, you suddenly find your world turned upside down. And now you're leaving the country carrying a single bag. Ever wonder how that happened?"

Nick felt the Butcher tense again underneath his hand.

"That's right," Nick said, both of them still walking. "You can thank us cocky-ass Americans for tearing apart your entire organization in a single night. How long did you spend building that thing up? Thirty years? And poof." Nick snapped the fingers of his free hand. "Gone in one night. Accounts seized. A fake cartel war that we started. A slaughter of some of your best men as part of a fake prison break. And then three massive Army raids into some of the key Godesto strongholds. You didn't get any warning on those, did you? Whose idea do you think it was to pull the Cabinet into an isolated meeting, without even access to their cell phones?"

The Butcher stopped walking and said, "You're going to be wishing you had called those security guards in just a few minutes, country boy."

"Well," Nick said, "some say I'm not too smart. But I see a hallway up ahead. Want to see if you can do what so many others couldn't?"

"Gladly," the Butcher said.

Nick took his hand off the short man's shoulder and the angled toward a sign that said "fire exit" on it.

They entered the hall and Nick was relieved that no alarm went off. A chair sat inside the hall next to an old trash can with a pile of cigarette butts in it. Clearly some guard or janitor used the place to sneak a smoke. But it looked dusty and dingy and rarely visited otherwise – the perfect place for a fight to the death.

The Butcher moved down the hall and when he was a safe distance away, Nick grabbed the chair by the trash can and wedged it against the handle at an angle, blocking the door behind him. The last thing he wanted was a janitor, cop, or tourist trying to stop them. This would be a fight to the death. Period.

Thankfully, the hall was a wide one, built so that golf carts and other emergency vehicles could navigate it. Probably even wide enough for ambulances to drive through.

There'd be plenty of room to dance in here, Nick thought, and then he saw that the Butcher was smiling.

"You may be smiling now," Nick said, "but I guaran-damn-tee you that you won't be smiling in a couple of minutes."

The Butcher smiled wider and the little shit had the creepiest of looks. Nick couldn't read his face. It was the strangest damned thing.

"What's so funny?" Nick asked. "You really think your little goober karate moves are going to work against me?"

"Probably," the Butcher said, "but not as well as this."

And with that he yanked his katana from some kind of secret pocket in the duffel bag.

"Well," Nick admitted, "I wasn't expecting that."

"Turns out," the Butcher said with a smirk, "that ten thousand dollars won't get an Uzi through airport security, but it will get a sword through."

Nick was barely listening. He suddenly regretted that the hall was so wide. Or that he had blocked the door behind him with the chair.

No doubt if he turned his back to grab it he'd be a shish kebab. The Butcher would skewer him straight through his back like a piece of meat pierced by a stainless steel cooking rod.

Nick's brain raced, looking for something. Now it was the Butcher's turn to have fun.

"Ah," the Butcher said, "the over-confident American has made yet another horrendous mistake. Just like last night."

Nick stood facing him, his legs shoulder-width apart and his empty hands held out to his sides. What the hell had he gotten himself into? And how in the world did you dodge a swift swinging sword? Especially from a little karate dick who knew how to use it?

"I could kill you so quickly," the Butcher said, "like a stork stabbing a fish out of water, but I wonder... I wonder if you know how powerless it feels to be cut time and time again and not be able to do anything about it."

Here comes the sadistic, cruel side of the man, Nick thought.

The Butcher held the sword in a two-hand grip directly in front of him and he looked like he knew what he was doing. He had unsheathed it with ease and grace, then positioned the sword expertly. Yeah, he definitely knew what he was doing.

And there was something unnerving about a long blade. Much more intimidating than a pistol or submachine gun, despite the absurdity of such a comparison. Perhaps it was the slow death such a weapon would cause.

"I'll bet," the Butcher said, "that I have you giving up and begging for your life after just twenty or so deep slices. Sharp cuts bleed a lot and they burn. They're really no fun, I promise you."

Nick searched the hallway for anything. His mind raced through scenarios and calculated angles, distances, and possibilities. He knew he had roughly four feet to his rear that he could step back toward. On the wall just behind the Butcher hung a heavy, red fire extinguisher. That would be nice, but how to get eight feet forward against a man wielding a sword?

Nick cursed himself for not even having his Benchmade tactical knife on him, but he had abandoned it in the truck to enter the airport.

Shut up, Nick, he thought. You have your fingers. With a properly trained man, they're blades. And you have your boots. With a properly trained man, they're hammers. You're going to get cut no matter what, but if you start thinking too much or having regrets, you're going to die right here in this dusty, dingy corridor.

"Come on, you little shit," Nick said. "You've talked enough. You're the one holding the sword. Come get you some."

The Butcher rushed in, the sword aimed right at Nick's chest. Nick made himself wait. He knew moving too soon or reacting too early would allow the Butcher to alter the swing.

And so he held as the sword stabbed straight toward him, entering his guard. Nick was partly banking on the fact that if the Butcher planned on torturing him slowly as he had stated, then driving a sword through his chest or stomach hardly allowed that to play out. Sure enough, the Butcher lifted the blade at the last moment and angled it back and right, slashing it down in an angled cross slice to the left.

Nick leapt back, certain he had dodged the swift swing. But as the Butcher retreated following the swing, his shoulder started burning and he looked down to see a sharp cut and blood running down his arm. The moment he saw the cut, it burned worse. The wound was maybe a half-inch deep. Enough to need stitches, but not enough to sever an artery.

Frankly, an expert strike.

"Hurts, doesn't it?" the Butcher said, with a laugh.

"I've been cut worse shaving, you little bastard. Now come get you some more."

Nick guessed he had maybe two feet behind him to work with after his first retreat. The Butcher took the same stance as earlier: two-hand grip, sword held straight forward. He still had his evil smile plastered on his face.

Again the madman darted forward, the sword held straight forward, and again Nick held his open hand stance, thankful to not have to worry about a straight stab to the body.

This time the Butcher angled back over his left shoulder and swung it from left to right, high to low. Same stroke, but opposite side.

Nick tried to time the swing again, but this time he wasn't just ducking back. Instead, he dropped his body low, placing his weight on his left leg, while kicking out his right leg toward the Butcher's knee. Again he misjudged the little man's speed and the sword struck the side of Nick's head above his ear, instead of the targeted shoulder.

Nick didn't feel the strike, his adrenaline pumping and his pain sensors completely turned off. His life was on the line and his body didn't need much convincing from his brain to act and move with purpose and super-human speed and strength. And while Nick had taken a bad cut to the side of his head, the heel of his boot landed hard into the Butcher's knee, driving him back.

Nick had hoped to hyperextend the little punk's knee, but the nimble fighter had leaped back to avoid that fate. But what mattered more than the knee getting blown out was the jump back by the Butcher.

In the hasty retreat by the Butcher, he allowed Nick to complete his true goal. Nick turned in an instant and reached for the chair behind him.

Now Nick held the chair out in front of him in a guard position, with its four legs aimed menacingly toward his opponent.

"I figure," Nick said, "that if you're bringing toys to our little date, I'd bring one, too."

"You think a chair will help you against this blade?" the Butcher asked, again holding the sword aimed upward toward Nick in his guard position. "It's a thirty-thousand dollar sword.

It will pierce that chair or cut through its aluminum legs as if they are nothing."

But Nick was sick of the talking and rushed forward, thrusting the chair forward and twisting it at the same time. The chair's legs turned from their horizontal, square position (with two legs high, two legs low) to a diamond shape as they burst forward as hard as Nick could shove and lunge.

The move caught the Butcher by surprise and his brain struggled to change from finishing a sentence to reacting to a multi-point attack rushing toward him. In the end, his brain failed to deal with the speed of the attack. He basically tried to step back and block the thrust with his sword in a horizontal blocking position.

But the chair's twisting legs deflected the sword and the upper leg and lower leg of the diamond shape both drove into the Butcher. The upper leg's point smashed him in the mouth, while the lower leg missed his groin by about two inches, driving in just above it in the lower abdomen.

Both strikes seriously hurt and the Butcher stepped further back after the blow, wiping blood from his mouth and using his tongue to push lightly against his lower teeth. They wobbled loosely and he felt the first touch of fear. The soft muscles around his groin didn't exactly feel right, either, and he wondered if the chair's leg might have caused a hernia or soft tissue damage to the inner workings of his man parts.

"Hurts doesn't it?" Nick said with a laugh.

Nick knew he didn't look so great himself, and he could tell his head wound was bleeding like crazy down his back. It was part of why he hated head wounds.

But he had much larger problems than just a bleeding scalp. Without question, the Butcher was a skilled fighter and he'd solve the problem presented by the chair in no time. At that point, Nick would lose some fingers or maybe the little shit would duck down and slice Nick across the lower legs. Or maybe he'd just use brute force to cut the legs off the chair.

Nick didn't have time for these kinds of calculations. Some guys liked to study martial arts and spar and consider strategy for literally hundreds of hours. Not Nick. He practiced just enough hand-to-hand to be good with hard strikes, joint locks,

STAN R MITCHELL

and basic self-defense.

Rather than kicks or strikes, Nick preferred to put down his enemies with a Kimber 1911 .45, or even better, stand off at a great distance, estimate the range to the target, determine windage, and drop some fool from eight hundred yards with his M-40 .308 sniper rifle.

So, Nick wasn't about to wait for the Butcher to calculate how he might get attacked and how to respond appropriately. Nick acted instead. He took a step forward, reared the chair back over his shoulder, and threw it as hard as he could with both hands at the Butcher. Like he had just slung a baseball bat at his worst enemy.

The Butcher tried to react, but he couldn't possibly dodge the chair at that distance. The chair hit the Butcher hard in his chest, knocking his arms and sword back into him.

Nick rushed forward behind the flying chair and the surprise of the Butcher, grabbing the fire extinguisher off the wall. And as the chair bounced to the floor and the Butcher's eyes opened in surprise and serious fear at his own miscalculation, Nick yanked the pin out of the extinguisher and pulled the hose free from its holder.

"That won't help," the Butcher said, but before the man could say more, Nick sprinted forward.

And as the Butcher extended the sword to defend himself, Nick sprayed a massive burst of chemical foam toward the Butcher's face. The Butcher released the sword with his left hand and tried to block the spray with his outstretched palm, but he was too late.

Nick didn't let up, blanketing his face with chemicals. The Butcher turned away and blindly swung the blade around behind him in the hopes of catching Nick by surprise.

Nick ducked the sword and advanced further forward, keeping the deluge of chemicals flying into the back of the Butcher's head. The man was screaming in pain and Nick figured the stuff was hell on the eyes, mouth, and nose.

The Butcher stumbled and slid in the growing pool of foam. And as the trained assassin and leader of the Godesto scrambled to stand, Nick changed grips and grabbed the extinguisher around the top of the handle. He swung the thing like it was a thirty pound bat and walloped the steel weapon into the back of the Butcher's head.

Bone echoed, and possibly cracked, and the man screamed louder. The sword clanged to the floor and as the Butcher reached for the back of his head, screaming still louder, Nick stepped around him, switched his grip on the extinguisher, and sprayed a quick burst into the Butcher's mouth.

Fighting a blind man isn't hard, Nick thought.

This was finally getting fun.

The Butcher gagged and wretched, still blind and increasingly helpless. Nick grabbed the top of the tube again and retracted it back like a batter in the box above the plate. He then swung it down into the Butcher's right knee as the man held his face, screaming.

A horrendous, bone-crushing impact burst every bone and tendon in the Butcher's knee. The man dropped to the ground like he'd been shot, spinning in the foam as he screamed and cried in pain. He no longer held his face. Now, he held the knee in complete and utter shock and terror.

"Going to be hell walking any time soon," Nick said without an ounce of emotion.

The Butcher screamed and coughed and used his hands to feel the damage to his knee. It was natural instinct and impossible not to do, even if you were blind, barely able to breath, and in the fight of your life.

Nicked watched the wounded man, amused, and then the Butcher somehow came to his wits and searched along the foamy floor with his hands for his sword. He found it and turned blindly toward the sound of Nick's footsteps, the sword outstretched.

Nick laughed at the swordsman sitting on his duff, holding a sword toward him as if a blinded man could defend himself. Nick tiptoed two steps to his right and suddenly hurled the extinguisher toward the Butcher's face from roughly eight feet away. The man never saw it coming and it cracked into his face, the bottom of the steel cylinder punching into his face like a heavy torpedo.

"That was stupid," Nick said, "but I guess I don't blame you."

The Butcher had dropped his sword again and held his face, but now the white foam competed with loads of blood, and the blood was beginning to win.

The man was starting to cry among the screams of pain.

Nick picked up the sword and wiped his hands and the handle of it against his pants. The foam burned his bare hands so he couldn't imagine what it must be doing to the man's eyes, throat, and nose.

Wouldn't matter soon anyway. Nick wasn't one to dwell on topics like mercy and forgiveness. That was God's business and Nick wasn't in God's business. Or maybe he was, but Nick didn't dwell on such thoughts either. If God wanted mercy to be shown now, He'd have sent another man.

If Nick was God's tool, then may the Lord's will be done.

This evil thing bleeding and crying helplessly in the foam had killed or terrorized countless individuals. The man had killed probably hundreds that Nick didn't know about.

And what Nick did know about was bad enough.

Nicke remembered the video of the Butcher entering the police station and chopping up officers, who couldn't defend themselves because of the tear gas. He remembered the brutal decapitation of billionaire Juan Soto's head in his room by a sword. And he reflected on the helplessness he had felt just hours ago in the slum of Neza-Chalco-Itza, fighting off hundreds of rabid dogs, who were snapping at the convoy.

Nick tested the balance of the sword.

"Nice sword," he said.

"Please," the man muttered between shrieks. He was reaching out with his right hand in mercy, and trying to wipe out his eyes with his left.

Nick kicked the Butcher in the leg, but only with a light tap.

"Listen up, hoss. Quit your screaming and belly aching. I need to give you a little speech here."

He stepped toward the man, careful not to slip in the foam. The grip on his boots was doing far better in the foam than the Butcher's black tennis shoes.

"You see, in the Marine Corps, they teach you that if you're going to carry or use something, you need to do so responsibly. So, if you're going to deploy tear gas, you have to spend some time in a gas chamber finding out how bad it sucks. Same thing with tasers. Honestly, if it didn't cost so much to train new Marines, they'd probably test rifles out on you, as well. My beloved Corps can be a bit thick headed about things like that."

Nick stepped closer to the sprawled out punk.

"So, I figure," he said, stepping forward again as the Butcher tried to crawl back, "that if you're going to go carrying a sword around, stabbing people, you need to figure out how it feels. Seems only fair."

And with that, Nick Woods swung the sword horizontally toward the Butcher's head. The man had wiped the foam from his eyes and could half see, so he raised both forearms to stop the sword, just as Nick hoped.

Nick stopped the strike before it sliced into the man's forearms and switched his grip, inverting the blade so that it pointed down with the handle up.

And before the Butcher could place his hands on the ground to slide or reposition his legs, Nick thrust the sword down into the quad of the cartel leader's good leg. The blade drove straight through the thick muscle, ricocheted off bone, and slammed the concrete floor hard enough to chip out chunks.

"Oh, damn, that's got to hurt," Nick said.

The Butcher wasn't even screaming. His eyes were bugged out and he was hyperventilating, his hands holding the blade's handle to keep it from swinging side-to-side. Complete shock was setting in.

Blood spilled from below the cut, but not nearly as quickly as might be expected. Nick was glad he had missed the femoral artery. He had hoped not to hit it.

"I wouldn't pull that blade out," Nick said. "That's when the bleeding will really start."

Nick stepped back and pulled out his cellphone. He turned on the video camera and filmed the helpless, weeping man.

The blood, the foam, the look of sheer horror. It was a stark contrast to the man who usually looked brave and daring in the videos he emailed into the news stations. Nick stopped recording him and texted the video to President Rivera. He hoped the President would have someone upload it online anonymously, but that wasn't up to Nick to decide.

He confirmed the text had sent and put a hand up on his bleeding scalp. The thing was pouring blood out pretty fast and he felt a bit weak. He dialed the President's number and waited for him to answer.

Walking past the upturned chair, he stopped and righted it on its legs. He sat heavily and when Rivera answered, he said, "Your Christmas came early. The Butcher has been butchered."

Nick looked at the man, holding the sword blade with the utmost of care. The Butcher was afraid to move and afraid not to, given the blood draining out of his leg. Shock was creeping up on him and death approached with increasing haste. Nick had seen it in war and battle too many times to count. The Butcher wasn't dead yet, but he would be before help could arrive.

"Now, get some men here. We've got a mess to clean up. I need someone to get me out of here without being arrested. We also need to grab all video footage from the airport and have it seized for national security reasons. Finally, I'd imagine you probably need to get Marcus, my number two man free. I'd imagine he's probably in cuffs outside the airport somewhere."

Nick hung up before President Rivera could answer and he sunk back in the chair, relieved but exhausted. The fight with the Butcher, the lack of sleep from the night prior, the emotions from the battle in Neza-Chalco-Itza, the stack of fresh memories from seeing and hearing the wounded and dead men from S3, it was all too much.

He pulled his sniper T-shirt off and placed it against his head, keeping firm pressure against the deep cut. He lowered his head and tried to keep from passing out and looked down at the HOG tooth, or Hunter Of Gunman, 7.62 round hanging around his neck.

He said a silent prayer of thanks to all the Marine instructors who had trained and beaten him into the person he had become. Thanks, guys, he thought. You came through again.

EPILOGUE

In the days that followed the Butcher's horrendous death, the Red Sleeve Cartel hunted down the remnants of the Godesto Cartel, leaving it as nothing but a footnote of Mexican history. Those who were lucky enough to survive, switched sides.

President Roberto Rivera rode a wave of public support to fend off the Congressional inquiries. Suddenly, the public nor the Congress cared that he had intervened to send Mexican SWAT members to rescue billionaire Juan Soto. President Rivera was now firmly seen as the cartel fighter, his legacy and popularity secured.

The men of Shield, Safeguard, and Shelter packed up and convoyed back to America, some of their wounded left behind until a private medical plane could be dispatched from America. Dwayne Marcus handled the logistics and temporarily took command while S3's leader healed and rested.

Mr. Smith had told Nick there was good news and bad news.

"Give me the good news first," Nick said gruffly.

"The good news is you've worked yourself into a full-time job."

"What do you mean?" Nick asked.

"There's been a lot of discussion since you took down the Godesto Cartel and the Butcher," Mr. Smith said. "The administration is impressed with your results. You all have proven yourselves to be inexpensive, while providing plausible deniability to the U.S. government. Seems they have some more work for you as long as you're okay with keeping the current arrangement. That is, you're the head of, and owner of, S3. And you get security contracts through the foreign country

341

you're operating in."

"I'm sure that's not the only catch," Nick said. "You all dropped about three surprises on me before we even got to Mexico."

"I promise you, there's no catches," Mr. Smith said.

"You forgot the other bad news," Nick said.

"What's that?"

"I have to work for you," Nick replied.

"You're a funny man, Nick Woods," Mr. Smith said.

"What was the good news?" Nick asked.

"You're two million dollars richer," Mr. Smith said.

"I don't give a shit about money," Nick said. "I'm just an old country boy who drives an old, paid-for vehicle and already has more rifles than he knows what to do with."

"I just wanted you to know that we've sent the money into your personal bank account," Mr. Smith said. "We keep our promises."

"You have this time," Nick said. "Which I'm still surprised at."

"So what's the answer?" Mr. Smith asked. "Can America count on you to keep running S3?"

"Let me think about it," Nick said, hanging up on the man.

Bastard, he thought. The truth was he wanted to stay in command. But he was thinking of Lizard and the other men. And also thinking of Isabella. He didn't like that men like Mr. Smith and the other assholes in D.C. were ecstatic to have found another group of expendable men that they could send off to get killed at even lower political cost.

But on the other hand, he was born for this. No different than Michael Jordan was born to shoot a basketball and Mike Tyson was born to wear boxing gloves.

Still, he wanted to think on it a bit. To privately grieve the cost that S3 had paid in Mexico. In Neza-Chalco-Itza. And he also wanted to see Isabella.

He remained by Isabella's side as she recovered, helping her recuperate. They only talked about small things until the third day.

"You're going to leave me," she said.

"I haven't decided what I'm doing," Nick said.

"You're lying," she replied. "I can see the way you look out that hospital window. You're already detaching."

"I was made for this, Isabella. I can't change that. It's like I have this gift or something. And if I don't do it, they'll send someone else. Someone who's not as good at it. Or hasn't been around long enough to know everything that they should know. And that's going to lead to more young men dying who don't need to die."

"You thought about staying," she said. "I can tell that you did. That you were even seriously considering it until today."

"I did," Nick said, his voice low.

"But?" she asked.

"But I belong with my men," he said.

"It's more than that," she said.

He turned away from her, unable to hold her eyes.

"It is," he said.

"What?" she asked, her voice almost aching.

Nick looked her in the eyes.

"The only thing that scares me more than combat is staying here with you," Nick said.

She gasped.

"Come here," she said, reaching up from the hospital bed.

He held his ground. He knew if he walked by her bed, he'd never leave.

She saw him spurn her request, but said, "If this is the thing that scares you the most, then it's the thing that you should do."

"You deserve someone who's younger and not as used up," Nick said.

"I don't want someone younger," she replied.

"You're a damn fool," he said. "And you don't know what you're asking for."

"You can't tell me what it is that I want," Isabella said. "Or what I need."

"I'll be home in a pine box or all shot to hell in two years," he said. "You're not wasting your life waiting on me."

"What if I've been waiting on you for my whole life," she said.

"Then I'd say you have a terrible taste in men," he said.

343

"And I'd say you've never looked in a mirror," she replied.

"I look every day when I shave my ugly mug," he said.

"Then you've never truly looked," she said.

"I'm not arguing any more," he said. "You deserve someone younger. Someone who will put you first. I'm a sucker for duty. Always have been."

"I'm okay with that," she said.

Nick wanted to scream at her.

"Maybe it's too soon," he said.

"It's been more than two years," she replied, referring to the death of his wife Anne.

"I've made up my mind," Nick said. "If it's meant to be, it'll be. But for now, I've got to go. I've still got some command in me and you've still got time before you settle for an old codger like me."

"I understand," she said. "I honestly do understand."

Nick looked at her in awe. He thought of her father, killed by the cartel. And her brother, stabbed to death in a nasty street fight by a gang. Only thirteen years old. This remarkable woman, who'd gone from lawyer to cop to detective, she really did get him. And she really did scare the shit out of him.

"I'm sorry," he said.

"I'm not," she replied.

Nick walked out the room and didn't look back. He couldn't.

And he certainly couldn't stay for a single extra minute. Not even a final hug or kiss or even a goodbye. The thought of any of those things scared him too much. Do even one extra thing? With a woman like Isabella? And you'd look down and your heart would be gone.

Nick drove an hour away before he could drive no more. He bought enough liquor for a platoon and rented a room. And he drank and drank for two days, trying to flush the thought of Isabella and so many dead and shot-up men in S3. It was the death of Lizard that still hurt him the most. And it was that man's death more than any other that caused him to call Mr. Smith and Marcus on the third day, telling them he was coming back to S3.

Nick couldn't deny that he had a gift for war. Or perhaps

it was a curse. But he was good at it. And in a sick way, it was all he enjoyed. It was what he lived for. And it was damn sure easier understanding war than it was contemplating life with Isabella. Home ownership. Kids. Day jobs.

No, Nick could never return to that. At least not anytime soon.

Besides, he had a unit to rebuild and if he knew anything at all about his employer, he was betting they already had the next shithole lined up where they wanted to send the men of S3.

THE END

AUTHOR'S NOTE

I really hope you've enjoyed this book. I've certainly tried to make it as good a book as I possibly could, even if there were a ton of moving parts that all had to come together.

I need to acknowledge one pretty big mistake I made in this book. It involves the position of Mexico's president. I learned just weeks before my publishing deadline that Mexican presidents can't actually seek re-election.

They only serve one term.

Unfortunately, a pretty good chunk of the book's premise were the many political challenges President Rivera faced and how the people had re-elected him with the sole mission of taking down the cartels.

Remove the need to get re-elected and you cut down significantly much of the tension that he faces. And as an author, one of your key tasks is ramping up and increasing the tension.

Thus, after much deliberation and consideration on how to fix the book, I opted to leave it as it stood. Unfortunately, I just saw no easy way to correct the book and make it more accurate.

Certainly, there are probably more inaccuracies, but the cities and towns named all exist. As does the massive slum of Neza-Chalco-Itza.

There are a ton of people I need to thank and what follows is a very incomplete list.

But to each of them, and those I've overlooked, a big thanks.

To Mark Allen, a hell of an author, and a man with whom I've spent literally hundreds of hours discussing stories and scenes. And debating the merits of leg stabs versus disembowelments.

A big thanks to my good friend April, who made the book immeasurably better.

To Tim Dittmer, an Army vet who served in Vietnam, who stumbled across me on the internet and wrote some crucial emails that helped me when I was doubting myself and the whole author gig.

To USMC Cpl Michael Pressley 1/8, '79-'83. A fellow brother in arms and a huge supporter.

To Ashley R. Luna. And to all the big-time supporters that I've picked up along the way. Thanks a million for your words of encouragement and your assistance in spreading the news about my books.

A REQUEST FROM THE AUTHOR

If you enjoyed "Mexican Heat (Nick Woods, No. 2)," please consider dropping a short review of it on Amazon. Reviews go miles and miles toward helping readers discover new authors, such as Mitchell. Here is the link to leave a review, should you choose: "Mexican Heat (Nick Woods, No. 2)."

P.S. Want to talk to me directly? Email me at the following address: stan@stanrmitchell.com. I love hearing feedback, compliments, and even constructive criticism.

Other works by Stan R. Mitchell

Nick Woods series

- **Sold Out** *(Book 1)*.
- **Mexican Heat** *(Book 2)*.
- **Afghan Storm** *(Book 3)*.
- **Nigerian Terror** *(Book 4)*.

Detective Danny Acuff series

- **Take Down** *(Book 1)*.
- **Gravel Road** *(Book 2)*.

Other works

- **Hill 406**.
- **Hell in the Mountains**.
- **Little Man, and the Dixon County War**.
- **Soldier On**.

ABOUT THE AUTHOR

Stan R. Mitchell is an author and prior infantry Marine, who earned the Combat Action Ribbon. He's written eleven works and some of his favorite authors and influences are Tom Clancy, Vince Flynn, Robert B. Parker, and Stephen Hunter. If you enjoy them, then more than likely you'll enjoy his writing. He also hosts a podcast every Tuesday and Friday, where he discusses military and defense news, as well as some history, motivation, and wisdom. (All from a moderate perspective.) You can learn more about that here:https://stanrmitchell.substack.com. All books can be found at amzn.to/3yKtYNR.

Mitchell lives in Knoxville, Tennessee, and enjoys writing, lifting weights, and martial arts. You can learn more about the author at http://stanrmitchell.com.

Don't miss the next installment of the Nick Woods series: Afghan Storm.

CHAPTER 1

Present Day – Just inside Pakistan near the border of Afghanistan

Nick Woods took a knee and wiped the ample sweat from his forehead, adjusting his pack in the cool night air. He made a mental note to thank the gods of war that this was the middle of summer and not the freezing, bone-chilling winter that drove even the tough locals into their compounds and caves.

The three men accompanying him used the short break to adjust gear and sip water while Nick's brain worked in overdrive as he scanned his sector. He was definitely putting his men out on a limb this time – more so than when he had led the assault on the Mexican slum of Neza-Chalco-Itza just six months ago.

The unit's overall mission, this time, was as simple as it had been in Mexico: take down Rasool Deraz, a venerable elder who inspired hundreds of Taliban and al Qaeda fighters across the country and into Pakistan.

Over the years, Rasool Deraz had grown so powerful that most analysts and several computer simulations reported that under his leadership the Taliban would soon topple the Afghan government. And America felt that it had invested too much in the past fourteen years to allow the Taliban to once again assume control of Afghanistan.

Thus, Nick's company – Shield, Safeguard, and Shelter, or S3 – had been contracted by the Afghan government to ostensibly provide training for their police force and consult with the government at the highest levels to assist them in reducing the threat from the Taliban. Or, at least that's what it looked like on paper. S3, however, wasn't just some private security firm. In reality, S3 was an arm of the CIA. A private company that filed annual paperwork and paid its taxes, which helped create enough distance to allow the U.S. government complete deniability.

S3's job in Afghanistan had nothing to do with training the police. Although Nick and his band of headhunters had severely limited resources, the plan was simple: find Deraz, shoot Deraz, and hopefully set the Taliban back as much as they could.

However, actually executing the plan would prove to be no small challenge.

So far, they had made it past their first obstacle. The four men of S3 had snuck across the border of Afghanistan and into Pakistan nearly an hour ago with no problems. That, of course, was the easy part. But now, on this side of the border, they were completely on their own. Just four men with no chance of backup, air support, or extraction. In fact, the only guarantee they were given was that America would deny any ties to S3 if they were captured or killed.

You sure know how to dig a deep hole, Nick thought to himself.

But, at least he had brought three of his best men with him. He had Marcus, the tall, commanding Marine drill instructor, who served as his right-hand man. He had Truck, the merciless, insubordinate Special Forces trooper, who had seen as much combat as any man alive. And he had Red, the cocky, quick-tempered Marine, who carried a trainload of fight on his 5'5" frame. Red was also one of the best point men Nick had ever encountered.

Their objective on this raid was to infiltrate forty-plus miles into Pakistan (moving only in darkness). They would travel along a moderate mountain range, crossing the border 100 miles south of Khost, and stay at higher altitudes to avoid detection from the more populated valleys.

At the end of this forty-mile journey, they planned to raid a single compound and locate a man named Ahmud al-Habshi.

Ahmud al-Habshi was the primary communications man for the Taliban. Therefore, his private compound promised computers, probably several servers, and loads of files. Essentially, it was a smorgasbord, a tide-turning honey hole, of invaluable intelligence.

Then there was Ahmud al-Habshi himself, who knew the habits, movements, and possibly every hiding spot used by Rasool Deraz. Nick Woods and his three S3 shooters planned to wake him up late one night and take him on a one-way field trip to Afghanistan. If they failed, a drone strike would quickly silence al-Habshi, but it would in turn also destroy tons of evidence and any chance of taking down Rasool Deraz.

Thus, it was critical that Nick and S3 properly execute this raid. Failing to capture the intel from al-Habshi and eventually take down Deraz would certainly doom Afghanistan.

Deraz was seen as a respected leader and legend by the people in Afghanistan, most of whom supported him. Blessed with high esteem and a nation's loyalty, his power and reach were difficult to fathom.

With just a few words delivered by messenger, Deraz could call upon local fighters among the people, who would spring up and strike an Afghan compound before disappearing into the countryside.

And the strength of Deraz knew no bounds. He had supporters in the countryside. He had supporters in the farmlands. He had supporters in the cities.

Without question, Rasool Deraz was the spiritual leader for many of the Afghan people, and Nick and S3 had to find a way to take him down or Afghanistan was doomed.

CHAPTER 2

Only two hours later, and the fun and enthusiasm had definitely worn off.

Now it was just dirty, grueling work, pure and simple. Each man hauled an 80-pound pack, a 20-pound assault vest, and a 5-gallon water jug (another 40 pounds) that had to be carried by hand. Even their trusty rifles had become burdens no longer welcomed.

No amount of training could prepare you for continuous slogging across such rough terrain. Steep slopes covered in loose rock in the dark made for a very strenuous and slow pace. Plus, they had to halt at the slightest detection of any movement or sound.

So far, Nick and his S3 entourage had heard a lot more than they'd actually seen. The area was known for quite the array of wildlife, some of which were often large and catlike. So the sudden rustle or the cascading of rocks was a common occurrence. Luckily, almost every incident, after further inspection at the evidence (paw prints, a startled bird's cry, scat, and other fecal material) was agreed to have been animal-based. Apparently, four over-loaded and heavily armed men stumbling across a mountain top worked wonders when it came to deterring curious wildlife.

But then there had been a few close calls of the human variety.

There had been the occasional stray, unarmed villager, including a set of young boys, both no more than ten, playing a game that involved whacking each other with sticks. It would have been a pleasant moment if the damn kids, so enthusiastically lost in their play, hadn't chased one another all over the hill, and at one point gotten close enough that Nick and his men were forced to fall back and hold until the boys tired of their antics and left.

They had also spotted several goatherders, who thankfully seemed to prefer managing their flocks in the lower lying areas. Perhaps they were avoiding predators or working their goats back home.

However, there had been one very unique exception. After a good hour without seeing another human soul, they suddenly spotted a particularly hearty goatherder literally hopping up the daunting slopes with apparent ease all the while singing a peppy tune. Based on the numerous inserted "baa's," Nick guessed the song had been composed by the man himself and in dedication to his goats.

Nonetheless, all had been oblivious to the four heavily armed, English-speaking men who most certainly didn't belong in this part of Pakistan.

Still, from a distance and under the cover of darkness, they might have remained safe, if spotted. They had worked hard to make an effort to blend in as much as possible, carrying Communist Bloc weapons and wearing Afghan-style clothing: boots, loose pants, and turbans.

But even with distance and darkness to aid them, it was their packs that could easily give them away. Although theirs were foreign in make, packs, in general, were uncommon in this area. Sure, there was the occasional shoulder bag or belt pouch, but the closest thing to a pack one might see in this part of Pakistan was the random small child's backpack, maybe. Most families couldn't even afford those.

And it didn't help that these particular packs were massive. Any local transporting a load of this size would almost always use a mule, truck, or dirt bike. Even if all a witness could make out was a rough silhouette in the dark, the sheer size and odd shape of the packs could easily draw unwanted attention.

But Nick couldn't do anything about the packs. He, Marcus, Red, and Truck needed everything from food to water to ammo, and you didn't go wandering forty miles into a foreign country – uninvited – unless you brought along some toys in case you were discovered.

Nick's back was already screaming in pain, and he was

certain his men were hurting, too. Nick raised his fist, signaling a halt. The darkness allowed for hand and arm signals to be passed, as stars and a half-moon shone down unimpeded by clouds or fog.

The men of Shield, Safeguard, and Shelter passed the signal up and down the line, then stopped, spreading into a defensive circle on the side of the steep hill. Each man eased his pack to the ground and sprawled behind it, facing outboard behind their weapons. They reached for canteens and bits of chocolate or other energy snacks.

Nick's whole body protested loudly – several hours of hard rucking was tough for a man in his mid-forties – as he attempted to lay his pack down as quietly as he could. He wanted to rest a few minutes, like his men, but knew he needed to appear unfazed by the three miles they had covered tonight.

Three miles didn't seem like much, but the unforgiving terrain and need to keep every sense on high alert really took every ounce of energy out of you. Especially when you added in the adrenaline rushes that came from hearing a disturbance or seeing something in your night vision googles.

Despite wanting to rest, Nick heaved himself up and walked toward his point man. He knelt beside Red and put his hand on his shoulder, looking out to their front. The small man was breathing hard and sweating heavily.

"How you holding up?" Nick whispered.

"This ain't shit," Red said with a smile.

Nick imagined that the weight they were carrying had to be especially difficult for a man of Red's size. Being the smallest man on the team meant that proportionally, he was carrying much more than the rest of them.

"Good," Nick said. "Go ahead and relax a few minutes. Then you and I can check our maps and compare where we think we are."

"Roger that, boss."

Feeling his legs and back threaten to mutiny if he attempted to stand from a kneeled position again, Nick made a mental note to stay on his feet as he moved over to Truck. The big man was laid down behind an RPK machine gun. The gun's bipod legs supported its weight on the front while the rear of the gun lay on its seventy-five round box.

"Hey, Truck. How you holding up?"

"Good. I was wondering if you might give your pack up so I could make this more of a challenge?" the smartass managed to choke out between deep gulps of air.

Nick smiled, shaking his head.

"Yeah, yeah. Now shut your mouth," Nick said, "or you'll be carrying three of them."

"Shit, sir. I'm Special Forces. I could carry three packs plus little Red up there."

Nick patted Truck on the head and said, "I'm glad you're on our side. And you better pray that Red didn't hear that little comment. Because there is no way I'm carrying your big, dead, dumb ass through these mountains.

Lastly, Nick walked up to Marcus, who was leaning against a nearby rock to keep him from squatting and having to stand again.

"How you holding up, man?" Nick asked.

"I'm hurting," Marcus admitted. "Damn packs are heavy as hell, and I'm twice as big as Red and in way better shape than Truck. We'll need to keep an eye on them."

Nick nodded.

"I was thinking the same thing," Nick said. "I know my back's killing me, but I'm not some diesel, former linebacker. Tell you what, before we move out, let's make sure all of us take eight hundred milligrams of ibuprofen to kill the pain and help keep us focused. I know Truck's probably starting to feel that busted knee about now, too."

Truck had reinjured his knee five months earlier – an old football injury that had never fully healed – but it wasn't just Truck. All four men were nearly twice the age of most military men, and they'd all been banged up over the years in training or various scrapes.

In truth, all of them were a bit old to be doing this kind of work. They certainly lacked the qualities of younger fighters, but no amount of youthful vigor could make up for the decades' worth of experience among them.

And there was no question that Nick would always choose

seasoned, accomplished fighters over young bucks still trying to prove themselves. Besides it wasn't like his unit was into parachuting, diving, or any of the other crazy feats elite units had to be capable of doing.

Nick groaned as he pushed himself off the large rock and slipped back to Red's position. Red was breathing easier and sweating less, the break already doing its trick.

"Ready, Nick?" Red asked.

"Sure," Nick said.

Red pulled a poncho liner out of his pack and draped it over the two of them. Inside it, they both produced small flashlights, covered by red lenses.

They compared each other's pace count and azimuth, confirming their location on the map. In the day and age of the GPS, neither man used one. Both had learned that when you relied on GPS, you checked your azimuth and pace count less frequently. And in turn, you paid less attention to your land navigation.

GPSs were a serious crutch that were all too easy to become reliant on, but GPSs broke. Batteries died. Not to mention neither man wanted to tote an unnecessary device and its required batteries.

After determining their position, Red put the poncho liner up and Nick hunched over as he crept back to his pack to rest a few moments. His legs and back ached to the bone and he caught himself guzzling more water than he should.

Part of the thirst came from the fact he was anxious. Nick hated to admit it, but it was true. It was one thing for two scout snipers to sneak into a foreign country, as Nick had against the Soviets numerous times in the '80s, but quite another to take four heavily weighed down guys.

Two men could sneak and hide better, but four required larger hiding places. And larger hides were more obvious and limited. And more likely to be searched by the enemy if they ever detected your presence.

Even now, if the Taliban discovered them, just three miles inside Pakistan, they would be screwed. If one man got hit, it would be all they could do to fight their way back to the border while carrying a man. And even then they'd have to get by the

Pakistani army on the border, who would be more alert this time.

Shut up, Nick, he thought to himself. This is how missions fail. You start thinking about all the things that can go wrong, and then you lose your confidence. Before you know it, you lock up with fear. Get in character.

The sound of Marcus approaching broke him from his thoughts.

"Here are those pills," he said, before handing them to Nick and moving on to the next man.

Nick shook the pills in his hand, placed them in his mouth, and swallowed them with a large gulp of water. He braced himself for the next hour-long leg of the mission.

To purchase or read an extended sample, visit Amazon. Or, if you're on an electronic device, you can click this link: Afghan Storm.

Made in the USA
Middletown, DE
23 September 2023

39133327R10205